Strange Karma

Willow Healy

BookLocker
Saint Petersburg, Florida

ISBN: 978-1-64718-450-6

Published by BookLocker.com, Inc., St. Petersburg, Florida.

Printed on acid-free paper.

The characters and events in this book are fictitious. Any similarity to real persons, living or dead, is coincidental and not intended by the author.

BookLocker.com, Inc.
2020

First Edition

Library of Congress Cataloging in Publication Data
Healy, Willow
Strange Karma by Willow Healy
Library of Congress Control Number: 2020907041

To my husband, Devin, may the adventures continue.

Acknowledgements

Strange Karma is a mystery/thriller set in two eras: 1920s England and Tibet and the present-day Himalayan mountains. From my research, I've incorporated as many known facts as possible when writing about the ill-fated 1924 Mount Everest expedition. But to further the plot, I have altered some aspects of Andrew Irvine's life, events at the base camp, and speculation about his disappearance on Mount Everest. Irvine's fiancée Emma, the town of Little Brough and the monastery on Nameless Mountain exist only in my imagination. Any resemblance to actual persons, living or dead, other than the historical figures, or actual events, is purely coincidental. I'm appreciative of the Sherpas I've met who have inspired me by their feats of courage. They are the bravest of the brave.

I'd like to extend my thanks and gratitude to the following people, who have been so helpful with comments and constructive critiques. Members of the PAWS writing critique group: Tony Chairchairo, Yvonne Ruiz, Candy Avila, Cynthia Kumanchik, Barbara Robison, Gil Roscoe, Jay Brakensiek, Jeff Pollak, Darrell James, and Anna Bresnahan. Members of Book'Em writing critique group: Mark Hague, Lois Osborne, Sharon Nelson, Jessica Faraday, Jean Utley, Kaumudi Marathe, Stefani Rico, Carol Lewis, Catherine Schofield, Gay Kinman, Helen Angove, Kevin Gallivan, and Candice Pegram.

Gillian Bagwell and Pamela Knott also offered advice and suggestions.

Marc Sarvas, U.C.L.A. instructor extraordinaire, much appreciation for your mentoring.

I especially thank professional mountain climber Dan Mazur who generously answered all of my technical mountain-climbing questions.

Last, but not least, I want to thank three people for their time and energy: Ken Kuhlken for editing my first draft and suggesting the title of the novel, Patrick Lobrutto for an in-depth edit, and Devin Thor for a final edit.

Chapter One

Mount Everest Base Camp, 1924

Five miles above sea level, Mount Everest rose above the Tibetan plain like a monstrous stalagmite. Surrounding her were the cloud-piercing Himalayan peaks Lhotse, Nuptse, and Pumori, and at her base lay the frozen tongue of Rongbuk Glacier. Directly below the glacier, seeming like it had been birthed by the mountain itself, stood Rongbuk Monastery, stepping up the mountain in a series of stone buildings. The monastery served as a spiritual sentinel for Buddhist monks who lived, meditated and searched for enlightenment.

The British expedition camped in the great mountain's shadow. Their canvas tents sprouted over the moraine like a field of wild mushrooms. For weeks, the men had waited for a break in the weather, waited for the opportunity to be first to climb Mount Everest. Time was running out. The monsoon was coming.

Andrew (Sandy) Irvine, at age twenty-two, was the youngest expedition member. With the high peaks looming behind him, he sat perched on an outcrop repairing the bent strut of Bentley Beetham's camera. The new Vest Pocket Model B Kodak had just been introduced. Being lightweight made it perfect for mountain climbing. He brushed back a lock of straw-colored hair and blew on his reddened, wind-chaffed hands for warmth. Sandy understood that he was the expedition's go-to-man when mechanical things needed fixing, and he didn't mind it a bit. As he oiled and manipulated the bellow mechanism, in the distance came the welcome clank of yak bells. Bloody wonderful, he thought, supplies were here and along with the letters from Emma and his family. Emma. His beautiful, free-spirited fiancée. He'd reread each of her letters so often that they were practically in tatters. Just to see her words on the page brought back vivid memories of her love.

At the sound of boots crunching on ice, Sandy glanced up to see George Mallory approaching with his usual cat-like grace. His thick, dark hair, disheveled by the wind, stood straight up above a pair of robin's egg blue eyes. After all their months together, Sandy still felt a sense of awe in his presence. No one in England had a more dynamic style or a more intuitive understanding of rock climbing than George.

Sitting down next to Sandy, he brushed the dirt off his puttee leggings. "The supplies and mail are arriving. I'm expecting a letter from my sister, Mary, she's going to let me know the moment the monsoon hits Ceylon."

"Ceylon's thousands of miles away," Sandy exclaimed.

"True, but after leaving Ceylon, the monsoon barrels straight for us, so it'll give us some idea when to expect it here."

"If we don't summit by the end of May…" Sandy's voice trailed off with concern.

"Doesn't give us much time, does it? Probably two more weeks, maybe three, if we're lucky." Then George twisted around and studied Mount Everest as if he'd never seen it before. "Not a beautiful mountain, is it? Jagged, asymmetrical, and one deadly brute."

Sandy nodded his agreement. Deadly was right. During the 1922 Mount Everest expedition, seven porters were swept away by an avalanche and buried alive.

"I've come to tell you that Bruce and I will make the first summit push."

"Jolly good. When do you go?" Sandy asked.

"Very soon, probably in a couple of days."

"You can count on me for any support." Sandy held up the camera he'd been fixing. "These new cameras are fragile, you should bring two along, just in case one malfunctions."

"Excellent idea, I'll borrow Sommerville's."

The bell's clanking grew louder until the caravan, a long ribbon of men and animals came into sight, wending its way up the slope. Bataar, the leader, was out in front, followed by men and yaks. In the intense cold, vapor streaming from the animals' noses appeared like dragon smoke. Except for the eyes and nose, every inch of a yak was covered by an extraordinary amount of shaggy hair.

Picking up the camera, Sandy started snapping pictures. "Emma's a professional photographer and is always asking me for more photos."

George looked interested. "You seem keen on her."

Sandy smiled. "Very. We're to marry."

"Ahh, so it's serious. Then I look forward to meeting her one day."

"Dance at our wedding, but after I return, my expedition days are over. The danger frightens Emma too much."

"Ruth feels the same way." George took out his pipe, carefully cleaned out bits of charred tobacco, then packed in fresh. When he lit a match, the sharp smell of sulfur wafted up.

By now, Bataar and his men had set up a makeshift corral near the camp. Due to the steep terrain, the animals couldn't climb higher. Now it was up to the men to ferry goods to the upper camps.

"There's something mysterious about that man."

"Bataar? Why?" Sandy asked puzzled.

"Look at him. See how different he is from the others, much taller and with green eyes. Speaks Chinese, Tibetan, English, even a smattering of Latin, and who knows what else."

George gave a sigh and tamped the glowing embers of tobacco with a pipe tool. "He's leaving tomorrow, best get all our letters ready for the yak express."

After the mail was given out, Sandy rushed back to his tent, his face flush with excitement. He opened Emma's letter first and looked down at the one page in surprise. Usually, her letters consisted of at least four sheets of paper.

> *My Dear One,*
> *I think of you always and miss you in ways that you can't believe. Mother was beside herself in anger when I broke off my engagement with Freddie and told her I would marry you instead. But you mustn't worry. The situation at home became so intolerable that I am moving in with Christina Broom, my lovely, kind teacher, who sends you her regards. She offered me a room in her house and a position as her photography assistant. We are constantly busy photographing, so I am making a decent wage, and besides, I have a cottage in the Lake District, which was bequeathed to me some years ago. Please be safe*

and careful for my sake. I can't wait for the expedition to be over, and once again, you are in my arms. My new address in London is written on the back. I'll write more when things are calmer. All my love.

> *Your,*
> *Emma*

Sandy became crazed with worry. Emma's mother was beside herself in anger... living with Christina Broom. This hellish situation of Emma's was all due to him. From the very start, her mother had hated him. She insisted he wasn't suitable, for Sandy was neither rich nor was he titled, and Emma had offers from both. It was made clear to Sandy that he was in the way. Her family's fortunes suffered from bad investments, and their future rested on Emma marrying well.

Bubbling with agitation and helplessness, Sandy thrust the letter into his pocket and wandered over to the corral where Bataar was tending to a yak. He liked Bataar, liked his gentle dignity.

"Namaste. "

"Hello, English."

Sandy lifted the lid of a can of Dunhill My Mixture 965 tobacco with his penknife and offered him some. Bataar reached into his pocket and pulled out a narrow, foot-long pipe partially covered in silver filigree and embedded with turquoise and coral. Sandy filled his Meerschaum pipe. They fell into easy conversation.

"Nice taste, English. Like the smell of old leather."

"How was your trip?" Sandy asked.

"Travelling a big danger now, many bandits and warlords. New government very weak. I afraid Russia or Japan attack us. "

"Why do you believe that?"

"I see this before. It is the way of nature. We are like an injured animal." He made a gesture with his hand slitting his throat. "Other animals will see that and hunt us."

A man's shadow crossed Sandy's field of vision, and a porter with a scar traveling down his left cheek, like a puckered seam on a jacket sidled up. He opened his grimy hand and there, sparkling in the sun, were two blueberry-sized uncut red stones resting on his palm. Holding up one of the stones to give a better view, he began speaking in a wheedling tone.

Sandy couldn't understand a word of Tibetan, but clearly, the porter wanted to sell the stones. When Bataar shook his head, the porter turned to leave.

"Wait!" Sandy insisted. "Are you sure you don't want them?" he asked Bataar,

"No, English."

The porter was savvy enough to know when a man was interested. Smiling at Sandy like a brush salesman, he exposed a rotting front tooth. Sandy pushed down his revulsion for the man as the stench of decay wafted up, "How much does he want?"

"This man is evil, English. He picks the bones of the weak. Best not to have these stones. There is a bad story here. I feel it."

But Sandy visualized Emma wearing the stones and thought how beautiful they'd look against her red hair.

"What are they?"

The porter's answer was a shrug of the shoulders and a cold stare.

"Where are they from?"

"Ama Dablam. " But there was a reluctance to the porter's reply.

Sandy could tell the man wasn't going to add anything more.

He counted out the agreed-upon money, more than he had intended to pay. Now to take them to Noel Odell, the expedition geologist, for his opinion. Probably just garnets, but still, they were beautiful. "Thanks, Bataar."

Bataar's expression turned grave. "Don't keep them, English." With that as a goodbye, he stooped to pick up a wooden pack-saddle, and a wool saddle blanket decorated in an orange peony design set against an indigo blue background and went to join his men.

Not surprisingly, Sandy found Noel Odell in his tent, studying a rock with a magnifying hand lens. Next to him was a small table stacked with dozens of rock specimens.

"They all look the same gray-brown to me, how can you tell the difference?"

"And I could ask how you were able to improve our oxygen bottles so that they function so much better?"

With a laugh, Sandy handed him the small red stones. "Say, Noel, be a good egg, I just bought these. Can you tell me what they are? I hope I'm not a bloody fool for having done it."

Noel shifted the focus of his hand lens, smoothed his light brown beard and mustache, and examined each one carefully, then picked up the pocket knife that lay next to his notes. "Do you know the Mohs scale?"

"Never heard of it."

"It's a standardized scale of hardness to help identify minerals, developed a hundred years ago by the German geologist Fredrick Mohs. All minerals have a characteristic hardness. For example, very soft talc is rated a one, while a diamond is a ten on the other end of the scale." Noel tried to scratch his knife blade with one of the stones.

"Wait, Noel, what are you doing?"

"This little test just told us plenty, because forged steel is a 7.5 on the scale. This stone left a scratch mark on my knife, so we know the stone is harder than the knife blade."

A note of excitement crept into his voice. "Sandy, you may have something here. It certainly could be a topaz or ruby, but until we do further testing in England, we won't know. How exactly did you get them?"

Sandy proceeded to describe the porter, Bataar's help, and the sinister feeling Bataar had about the stones.

Back in his tent, Sandy wrote a letter to Emma. He included in the envelope a roll of film: photos of the expedition members, an itinerant monk, camp scenes, yaks, and Bataar with his men. He was about to seal the envelope when he paused. Why not put in one of the red stones as a surprise? He'd present Emma with the other on his return home. All of his letters had reached Emma, so he wouldn't worry about the stone going astray. He wouldn't tell her about the lama from Rongbuk Monastery, who warned them not to climb Mount Everest because of the demons who lived there. Just superstitious nonsense.

Chapter Two

Lake District, England, present day

Odds are, when you receive an inheritance, you know the person you inherit from, but that wasn't true for Cynthia Graham. Try as she might, she couldn't come up with any memories of Lydia Dunton. Cynthia had wrongly assumed that her grandmother was long dead. But now, this recently buried stranger filled her thoughts, and left her with the unanswerable question, how could she have not known about Lydia Dunton?

Double-checking the address on the business card, she stood motionless until a fierce blast of wind spurred her to action. Time to put a face to the voice and meet the solicitor, Mr. Jones.

Inside the old Victorian, she was greeted by a motherly woman with a short, gray bob. "Terrible weather we're having. You must be freezing, you poor lamb. I'll make tea." She then pointed to a corner, "Go ahead, miss, leave your suitcase over there by the printer. I'll tell Mr. Jones you're here."

Cynthia smiled ruefully to herself at the term "poor lamb." At 5'8", she towered over the motherly woman.

Cynthia then was shown into the solicitor's office.

After shaking hands, he got down to business. "May I see your documents?" His manner was dry, but not unkind.

Cynthia handed over her U.S. passport, birth certificate, and her mother's immigration papers and death certificate.

As he read her passport, he glanced up to examine her.

Assumedly he was going over passport details with a lawyer's thoroughness: hair color red, check; eyes blue, check; twenty-seven years old, check.

The gray-haired woman entered bearing a tray holding a teapot, two cups, and a plate of cookies. Carefully she set the teapot and porcelain cup ringed with a festive holly pattern in front of Cynthia. "This'll warm you up."

Cynthia smiled her thanks.

Having found her documents satisfactory, Mr. Jones' manner warmed. "What do you know about Lydia Dunton?"

"Unfortunately, absolutely nothing. You see, my mother died in a fire when I was eight." Just uttering those words brought back the horror.

Cynthia was on her way to her best friend's house when whispers of anger filtered into her bedroom. Not again. Hugging her *My Little Pony*, she collapsed on her bed in a cascade of tears. Her parent's whispered fights were far worse than the loud ones. What were they saying? Pressing her ear to the door, she tried to hear more.

"Gambler! Not enough money for rent this month. You promised! My part-time job can't pay the bills." Her mother's English accent thickened with each accusation.

She was also aware of how much the anger had intensified over the past several months to become daily fare.

"I'm taking our daughter and leaving you."

Her father's hiss rose to a roar. He pounded his fist on the kitchen table. "No, you're not! If you ever try…" The implied threat hung in the air.

Not wanting to hear more, Cynthia escaped by the back door and walked four blocks to Rita's house.

The hours ticked away quickly as they always did when she was with Rita, but finally, it was time to go.

"For you and your parents," Rita's mother said, wrapping up three éclairs to take back with her.

Cynthia had walked and skipped a block when the wail of fire engines shattered the quiet. The sirens decibel's climbed, and the neighborhood dogs howled in protest. Where was the fire? Black smoke billowed in the distance, but even though she jumped up, she was far too short to make out where it was coming from. By the time she'd covered two blocks, fear had swamped her and, she started running as fast as her legs allowed. Her street! The fire was on her street. Soon she smelled the acrid odor of smoke. She dropped the éclairs and raced on. When she reached her home, she was panting for breath and found it swarming with firemen and a milling group of neighbors. Hoses spurted water at the flames, but the house burned like a torch. In the background, a radio crackled out instructions.

"No," Cynthia screamed, racing past the firemen and onto the porch. Suddenly, strong arms swept her away and back to safety.

She kicked, squirmed, and struggled. "Mommy! Mommy!"

The fireman's sooty face turned grim. "Your mom's in there?"

"Yes!"

A fireman wielded his ax and smashed it against the front door. It splintered and flung open, but he leaped back as the impenetrable wall of fire roared out. The hoses continued gushing water, but within five minutes, her home had crumbled into a smoldering, blackened hulk.

Cynthia sobbed uncontrollably.

"Why didn't she come out?" The fireman named Doug asked. "It's daytime, so it's not like she was asleep. Why didn't she come out?"

Her mother's body had been found in the bedroom, but what had proved all too conclusive was that nightmare day had ripped a hole in Cynthia's heart that no amount of scar tissue could cover.

"Ms. Graham, are you alright? You look pale." Mr. Jones asked with a look of concern.

"Sorry. Just some stray thoughts. To the best of my knowledge, mom never mentioned my grandmother. I assumed she was dead. Dad knew nothing about her, either."

Mr. Jones pushed his glasses back onto the bridge of his long nose and ran his fingers through thinning hair. "As I explained on the phone, your grandmother, Lydia Dunton, died two months ago. She left her entire estate to her daughter, your mother. When we discovered your mother was deceased, we did further digging and discovered you. Mrs. Dunton's cottage in our Lake District, its contents, the surrounding land, and about 10,000 pounds are all yours."

"I'm overwhelmed. Of course, I have questions. What was she like?"

Mr. Jones coughed then looked intently at her. "As you want more information about your family…" The solicitor paused as if collecting his thoughts. "Mr. Hollander told me there was a scandal way back when, but that was during more conservative times."

"What was the scandal?"

"Your great-grandmother, was, well, in the family way and unmarried. Of course, these days, it means nothing, but back then…."

"Yes, I can imagine how awful it must have been."

Cynthia signed multiple pages then did the math in her head: 10,000 pounds amounted to about $16,000. Not a fortune, but certainly welcome.

"Where's the cottage located?"

He answered with a smile, "It's on my way home. As you're my last client today, I'd be happy to drop you off. Do you intend to stay long?"

"Just for the night."

"Pity you can't stay longer."

"I'm the marketing manager for my company so… well…it's difficult to take time off now. But I'll be back. Thanks for your offer to drive me."

He stood up to go. "Not at all. We'll pick up supplies for you."

After getting supplies, the solicitor asked. "What sort of marketing do you do?"

"For a software company. Plan events, make sure all sales information is up-to-date, approve advertising, that sort of thing."

"Sounds interesting."

"In this economy, it's a challenge. Don't get me wrong, I'm grateful for my job, but I used to have a staff of three, now there's just me."

"What do you do in your off-time?"

"Meet up with friends, write, and do some mountain climbing. Mostly peaks on the West Coast. Funny, I remembered mom saying that during her summer breaks, she loved running around exploring the hills and valleys. I suppose she meant here."

"You're in the right spot for mountain climbing. We've had a lot of famous climbers, including Sir Christopher Bonington, and much further back in time, in the 1920s, George Mallory and Andrew Irving."

After thirty minutes or so of polite conversation, the bulk being anecdotes about his three children, the solicitor turned off the main road and slowly drove down a muddy country lane. After a few moments, he pointed, "Over there."

Cynthia wiped the condensation off the window for a better look. A creeper-clad cottage composed of gray stone, with a slate roof, a curtained window near the front door, and a bay window on the side stood waiting for her.

"Excuse me," The solicitor reached over to open his glove compartment, pulled out a flashlight, and handed it to her. "You'll need this torch. I'm sure you'll find candles inside; everyone keeps a good stock out here in the countryside."

"There's no electricity?"

"After Mrs. Dunton's death, it was turned off."

She looked around and saw only one cottage in the distance. "Is it safe out here?"

"Very. I can't remember the last time a crime's been committed. You're fortunate. Most of the land surrounding your property is owned by the National Trust, so it's left as is."

He set her suitcase by the door, handed her the groceries, then the house key. Cynthia thanked him for the lift and for the assurance that he'd return the following morning to take her to her grandmother's grave and then to the train station.

After opening the door, she flung open the windows to let out the musty air. Fire, that's what she needed. The rolled-up paper and kindling caught right away and soon licked the coals into a roaring fire. For the first time that day, she felt warm. Everything in the cottage was orderly. Newspapers and magazines in neat stacks, no unwashed dishes in the sink. One thing she already knew about her grandmother, she was a tidy housekeeper. The cottage had only one bedroom, so it didn't take long to rummage through cabinets and drawers in the living room and dining room. There were some family silver, good dishes, and needlepoint projects mostly of flowers and leaves. She found more books of matches and put them on the kitchen counter. "Who were you, grandmother?" she said aloud. "Why didn't I know about you?"

When the wind picked up and whirled leaves into the house, she latched the windows shut. She found candles in the kitchen, lit them, and placed them around the cottage. In part, she felt like an interloper; here, she was going through a complete stranger's things. Wandering into the bedroom, she picked up a silver brush on the nightstand and pulled out a gray hair. Her unknown grandmother's DNA. She opened the night stand's top drawer. Next to several pill bottles lay a yellowed, creased letter, some photos, several hand-embroidered handkerchiefs, and various odds and ends. Curious, she picked up the photos first. One was of three generations of women, all looking so similar they had to be related. The youngest of the group was her mother looking about eighteen. Cynthia was struck by her carefree smile. She rifled through the other photos. But they were strangers to her. Next, she picked up the letter. By its condition, it looked decades old. It must have been important to her grandmother if she kept it next to the bed. A love letter?

Cynthia began skimming it.

Lydia, my dear girl,

We've rarely seen each other since you had moved to London so many years ago. In case something happens to me, I've left special letters, photos, and a locket, under the bird's wings. Before your father disappeared in Tibet, he sent me a gem with a strange history that he purchased under mysterious circumstances. It came from a mountain called Ama Dablam. He'd bought two off a Tibetan porter. Some years later, I took mine to a geologist, Cates-Smith, who spent one summer in the old Waterfield place. Gemology wasn't his expertise, but he suspected the red stone could possibly be a ruby, and worth a tidy sum. He considered it rare, and he suggested that I have it tested and appraised in London, but I never got around to it.

I wore it in the locket with your father's photo, so, my daughter, this is your heirloom. It was Sandy's last gift, and that meant much more to me than money.

Your loving mother,
Emma

Cynthia plopped down on the bed, still clenching the page. It was all so disorienting. Her grandmother was Lydia, so Emma must be her great-grandmother. Her great-grandfather, the man who disappeared. What was he doing in Tibet? A military campaigner, or an explorer? She wondered if Lydia read this last letter from her mother every night before she went to bed. Cynthia's pale blue eyes were devouring the letter a second time when the flashlight's bulb weakened into a watery pool of light. A ruby! She strained to capture the last sentences in the candlelight, as shadows flickered on the stone walls' irregular surface. Her disbelief turned to shock. Could the locket still be here? "…under the bird's wings." It had to mean somewhere inside the house.

She spun around. The chairs! They were covered in that flower and bird pattern. She picked up the cushions, checking carefully at the seams, but when she probed the lining, she saw that the stitching hadn't been tampered with. Back in the kitchen, she searched for more candles, then placed them in strategic spots. A warm glow like sunlight filtering through dense clouds filled the rooms.

Where else could the locket be? Her eyes rested on a watercolor of a raven hanging on the far wall. She immediately took it off its hook. Nothing on the back except an old, yellowed map of Tibet. She tapped the wall behind it. Solid stone. A chair sat beneath, and above was the beamed ceiling. She paced the cottage. No bird photos, no bird figurines, no duck decoys, no bird dishes. How hard could this be? This was a small cottage. The desk! Of course. But the ornate drawers only held bills and letters. Piece by piece, she examined everything: kitchen cupboards, under the bed, above the mantle, and then the furniture. She tossed thick sweaters, woolen shirts, and a rain slicker from a heavily fluted armoire then lugged several cardboard boxes onto the floor. She found nothing.

Where was it? Could her grandmother have lost or sold it? Was that it? Or could someone else have found the letter and got to the locket before her? She shook her head. Who'd ever take the time to read a dead woman's letters? Besides, she couldn't imagine the kind Mr. Jones doing anything unethical.

She'd covered everything; there was no other place else to look.

She fought the need to sleep for as long as she could, then with a yawn stepped back into the bedroom. Stripping the sheets off on her grandmother's bed, she replaced them with clean ones and slipped under the covers. Within minutes she'd drifted off.

The scratching woke her. She blinked her eyes open and stared around uncomprehendingly. Her eyes rested on the shadowy apple tree near the window, which was backlit by a full moon. A handful of withered apples, dangling like so many miniature jack-o-lanterns from twisted, skeletal branches, gave the tree a faintly sinister look. In the distance, she almost expected to see the Headless Horseman riding off on a black stallion.

Then, scratching again. For another minute, she listened, trying to get her bearings. It seemed to be coming from the front of the house. With a touch of fear, she grabbed the flashlight and made her way to the front door, pulled back the curtain at the window next to it, and looked out. A dog! Opening the door, she found a border collie looking up at her. Was it injured or lost? When she went out to check on him, he turned and melted away into the darkness.

For a moment, all she could do was stare. Why had he come?

All warmth had left the cottage hours ago. Cynthia shivered as her bare feet on the wooden plank floor, got colder and colder. With the curtain pulled aside, the moon washed the living/dining room, filling the area with strong light and dark contrasts, like those old black and white photos from the 1920s. With just the moonlight filtering in, everything looked so different, so shadowy. Her eyes darted over the room, then lazily half focused on the desk in front of her, and when she did, she saw it, the bird's wings.

Her heart thudded as she lightly touched a frieze of stylized bird's wings sculpted along the top portion of the desk. Funny she

24

hadn't noticed it earlier when she'd checked the desk drawers. Could there be a secret compartment? Hurriedly, with her hand shaking, she lit a candle. At the third attempt, she had a flame.

She ran her fingers lightly over the frieze until she felt a slight depression. She pressed firmly. With a click, a panel popped open, exposing a dark hole.

In the light of the wavering candlelight, her eyes centered on a cobwebby, black velvet jewelry box. By the amount of dust inside, she guessed the hole hadn't been disturbed for years. First checking for creepy crawlies, she gingerly pulled out the box then softly blew the cobwebs away. White strands of silk and a layer of fine dust floated in the air before settling onto the floor. Looking in again, she spotted something else. Letters tied in a faded blue ribbon; she pulled them out as well. She couldn't open the box quickly enough. Inside, set against the dark velvet, glittering up at her was a large, gold filigree locket, faintly Asian in design, suspended from a gold chain. Her throat constricted as she used her thumbnail to pry it open. Frustratingly, her nail was too short, and it stayed stubbornly closed. She rummaged through the desk drawers until she found what she needed: a letter opener. She finessed the locket and with a snap, it opened. Out spilled a red, uncut gem. The ruby! Holding up a slightly bigger than blueberry-sized stone, she gazed at the fire deep at its heart and thought, how utterly beautiful.

Then she examined the locket photo of her great-grandfather, looking circa the 1920s. A young man with blond, slick-backed hair, full sensuous lips, and air of self-confidence seemed to smile at someone behind her. She caught herself about to look over her shoulder to see who it was and laughed. But a sense of recognition settled over her. "I've seen him before," Cynthia whispered to herself. "Why can't I remember where?"

Chapter Three

Los Angeles, California, present day

Back home in L.A., Cynthia was driving her Jeep Wrangler, if you could call doing five miles per hour on the I-5 freeway driving. She took the first exit, deciding surface streets would be faster when her phone rang. The digital display read her dad. She pulled over on a side street and picked up the phone. While her father might not be "the dad of the year" material, she loved him.

"Hi pumpkin, I wanted to let you know we're boating to Catalina for the weekend."

"You don't own a boat."

"A loaner from a friend."

What was his current girlfriend's name again? Ginger? Jennifer? Pamela? They all ran together, those tall blondes who were around her age. This girlfriend probably wouldn't last any longer than the others had.

Her father said, "I was flabbergasted when you told me a law firm had contacted you. How in the world did they even know about you?"

"Through a detective agency. They were looking for mom. Found her immigration papers, her marriage and death certificates, and my birth certificate." Cynthia lowered her voice. "Dad, we never talk about family. But I need your help. What do you know about mom's background?"

"Next to nothing. Your mother and grandmother had a falling out before your mother immigrated to the States, and as far as I know, they never spoke again. My understanding was it was over a married man, your grandmother was seeing at the time. Your mother did tell me that her own father died in a car crash before she was born. I tried to find out more details, especially before we first married, but she completely clammed up. I just gave up trying."

Cynthia blinked back her tears and asked, "After mom died, weren't there papers? Letters? Photos?"

"Everything burned up with her in the house fire. God, if you'd been inside the house, well, it frightens me to even think about it."

Then her father coughed. A cough she recognized. Acid pumped into her stomach as she steeled herself. So that's what he wanted.

"I didn't want to bring it up tonight, Cynthia, because you've just got back, but finances have been a little rough lately. If you could loan me a bit to tide me over? If you sold the property, it would help me out. Naturally, I'm curious, did you inherit money at all?"

She took a deep breath. I can't believe this is happening again, she thought. Money continually was a source of tension. She recalled the terrible screaming matches her parents had. By the beginning of her senior year in high school, Cynthia realized that there wasn't going to be money for college. She was on her own. Her father was a well-paid accountant, but his gambling roiled them into an alternate reality of feast or famine. Back then, as their present shoddy two-bedroom apartment attested, it was famine.

"Cynthia, did you inherit any money?"

She touched the locket under her shirt. I can't tell him about the gem, she thought, he'll insist I sell it. How could this keep happening? He was a well-paid accountant. She'd rescued him from gambling debts before, and he always promised to stop. She wanted to distance herself, but like it or not, he was her sole relative, and she loved him.

"Dad, I gave you most of my savings. Please believe me. My salary isn't enough to pay off your gambling debts. And yes, I did get a bit. But only enough for property taxes and repairs. At one-time, grandmother's family had money, but with the wars, death duties, and bad investments, not much was leftover. She died a relatively poor woman."

He gave a nervous laugh, then changed the subject. "Paul Bellame told me he hadn't seen much of you recently. He's worried. Said you don't return his calls. Been trying to contact you ever since he returned from Hong Kong."

"I've told you before, Dad, I'm no longer interested. Paul knows that too. I know he's your boss, so I've tried being diplomatic."

She thought back on when she and Paul first met at her father's office. Paul, the company president, had come into the office wanting data. In the beginning, there was instant chemistry. She had been flattered by his interest, this powerful, older man with the mesmerizing gray eyes. They both enjoyed the arts, hiking, and mountain climbing. But on their first and only climb together on Mt Rainier, she discovered his darker side. It sickened her the way he treated the guides. Bullied and goaded them into taking risks that endangered her and the others. Then and there she decided to end it. The problem was, he wasn't taking no for an answer. Perversely, dumping him had only egged him on.

Her father broke into her thoughts. "Paul's a good man. And Baby, he's a billionaire. Do you have any concept of what that means? He's extremely fond of you. Be nice to him, Cynthia. For my sake."

"He's cruel, Dad. Hides it well, but it lurks there under the surface like an alligator in a swamp. I've tried being diplomatic for your sake. But these aren't the Middle Ages. I'll see whoever I want to see."

"What I don't understand is why you changed your mind. When I stopped dating him, you said, 'Good.' You shared stories of how he'd fire people on the verge of retirement, or those with medical problems, and single mothers. Only the bottom line, you said, interested him. So what's different now? Why keep dangling him in front of me like a shiny object?"

"I told you before, I just got to know him better and realized I'd misjudged him. Cynthia, with the downturn in the economy, and at my age and position, if he lets me go, well, I can't tell you how difficult it would be to replace my job. Do me a favor. Call him tonight. I said you would."

His fear was palpable. "You need to understand that I'm finished with Paul, and no, I have no intention of phoning him. Of course, I care about you, but you have a gambling addiction and need help. Giving you more money won't solve the problem. But if you choose rehab, I'll do whatever it takes to scrape together the money."

Her father hung up.

Back at the condo, and feeling unsettled, she poured herself a glass of zinfandel and walked out onto the balcony where a light breeze ruffled her hair. Glancing down at the street, she was suddenly taken aback. An Asian man with blond hair and a cigarette dangling from his mouth was focusing his binoculars on her. What the? After spotting her, he picked up his phone and texted someone.

Soon afterward, her cell phone rang. Cynthia automatically picked up.

"Cynthia. Wonderful to finally catch you. But why haven't you returned my calls?" Paul Bellame demanded in a slightly irritated tone."

"I've been busy catching up with work."

"Your father mentioned you were in the U.K. Something about an inheritance. Good for you." Then he jumped to himself. "Have I told you that I have a ghostwriter on staff writing my autobiography? I don't want it to be purely work-oriented, so she's covering my charities and outdoor adventures, but more of that later. We need to talk. I'll pick you up at your condo on Thursday for dinner at 7:00 p.m."

Cynthia took a deep breath. Ghostwriter? Who'd hire a ghostwriter? Why hadn't she appreciated before just how huge an ego he had? And talk. About what?

"I can't," she replied in an icy tone. "Deadlines to meet and lots to do. Goodnight." She quickly hung up.

Again the phone rang. Reluctantly, she picked up.

"Don't condescend, Cynthia. You have a week to finish your deadlines; then, we talk at dinner. I won't take no for an answer."

Chapter Four

Pasadena, California, present day

It wasn't your typical L.A. day. The drenched palm trees looked more Pacific Northwest than Southern California, and the steady rain wasn't giving way to sunshine anytime soon. It was 11:30 a.m., and the warehouses in L.A.'s flower district were closing for the day. The early closing was understandable when you realized the opening hour for the growers and sellers was 2:00 a.m.

Cynthia and Rita parked at a lot on Seventh Street. Strolling up Wall Street, they passed shops specializing in everything floral related: vases, floral foam, wire and picks, and artificial flowers. They turned right on Eighth Street and headed toward a circa 1930s, six-story brick building. Upon entering the building, they were met by an African American doorman who looked like an ex linebacker.

"Can I help you, ladies?" he asked, his voice surprisingly soft.

What was it about a New Orleans accent, Cynthia wondered, that just seemed to radiate warmth and friendliness?

"We're here to see Saul Blum, he's a gem dealer on the third floor," Rita answered.

He went over and pushed the button to call the elevator. It was an old fashioned metalwork cage elevator with ornate fretwork. He opened the door. "Have a good day, ladies."

Cynthia said, "I've meant to ask you if your uncle lives in Tel Aviv, why does he have an office here?"

"He's in the States often enough on business, so that's why he rents a small office here."

"Rita, I can't stay long. I know you're trying to help, but I'm drowning in work. And the marketing won't wait. Besides, I bet the stone's only a garnet."

"Having a break from work will be a new experience for you. It's how the rest of us live."

Cynthia laughed. "Sorry for being a jerk. I owe you one, and I know it."

"You should be kissing my Jimmy Choos. I did some real arm twisting to get Uncle Saul to see you. Luckily, he dotes on me. Says I'm his favorite niece. Of course, I'm his only niece."

When they reached the third floor. Rita teetered down the hall on four-inch stilettos then used her umbrella handle as a battering ram on a door marked Altas, Ltd.

"He's a bit deaf, the old sweetie," Rita announced.

"Why have an office here on the edge of the Flower District? Why not in the Jewelry District?" Cynthia asked.

"He likes the people better; he says diamond dealers spy on each other."

A few seconds later, an eye stared at them through the peephole.

After clicks of multiple locks, they entered a room decorated in Arts and Crafts style; Cynthia recognized the furniture as Stickley, and from its aged patina, it looked original. If the Stickley was original, she assumed the lamp on his desk had to be a real Tiffany. A glass vase of love-lies-bleeding mixed with orchids and ferns sat next to the lamp.

After giving Rita a kiss on the cheek, he turned and said in a heavy Dutch accent, "So this is Cynthia. Sit down. Right over here so I can see you better. Good." He switched on the overhead light.

"Would you like coffee? I have a special blend imported from the Indonesian island of Sumatra. Perhaps because I'm Dutch, and we'd traded there for centuries, I can smell a hint of spice in it. "

"Sure," Cynthia replied.

The coffee grinder whirred while Uncle Saul brought down three gold-rimmed blue cups from the cupboard. Antique and expensive-looking, they joined a matching coffee pot, sugar bowl, and creamer already set on a silver tray. He brought the tray over and poured. Immediately, the rich aroma of coffee permeated the air.

While Cynthia sipped at her coffee, Uncle Saul said, "Rita tells me you have a mystery stone."

She opened the locket. "It's inside. According to my great-grandmother's letter, it could be a ruby."

For a moment, he fingered the locket. "Very fragile chain, best wear it only occasionally."

He picked up the blueberry-sized stone. As he maneuvered his arthritic fingers around the jeweler's loupe, Cynthia wondered if it pained him to hold it. Uncle Saul examined the gem from every angle before setting it down. "*Ach, zeer mooi,*" his accent thickened with excitement. "Truly remarkable."

Lifting the loupe, he peered again at the stone. "Once I held the Moussaieff Red, but this one is larger and with a deeper scarlet coloration." His fingers drummed on the desk.

Cynthia's excitement ratcheted up as she watched him. "What's the Moussaieff Red?"

"Important stones are given names."

34

Uncle Saul brought out a tiny instrument. "Gems conduct heat in individual ways, so this will verify the findings of my loupe." He then focused a pin-point beam of light on the gem. Uncle Saul rubbed his eyes, then picked up his loupe again. His hands trembled when he set the stone down.

Cynthia and Rita leaned closer.

"Uncle, tell us! Don't keep us in suspense! What is it?" Rita insisted.

"A fancy."

"A what?" Both women replied.

"A colored diamond." He turned and looked searchingly at Cynthia. "Do you know where it came from? Or how it came into your family?"

"It came under mysterious circumstances."

A squall passed over, and other than rain pounding on the windows, quiet settled over the room. Even Rita, who knew the stone's background, waited expectantly to hear more.

"Please explain!" Uncle Saul exclaimed.

My great-grandfather was in Tibet. Doing what, I don't know. Supposedly, they came from the mountain, Ama Dablam."

"Where is that?"

"Nepal."

Uncle Saul looked thoughtful. "I've been in the business for more decades than you've been alive, but I've never heard of gems coming from that area. Are you sure about it?"

All I truly know is that it was a gift from my great-grandfather to my great-grandmother, Emma. Emma wrote about him having two red stones, and he carried the other gem with him when he disappeared in Tibet. I think I've seen his photo before, but have no idea where. " She pointed to the locket photo. "Does he look familiar to you?"

Uncle Saul shook his head no then gave a huge sigh. "Ach! Imagine. Two of them! What a shame one's lost."

"But Uncle, don't diamonds come from Africa."

"Schatje, have you forgotten all I've taught you? Diamonds come from everywhere. "And while we're on the subject of weighing. "He pulled a scale out from a drawer and dropped the diamond on it. "A bit over seven carats. When it's cut, it'll lose a carat or so. I work with a master cutter who would do justice to this beauty. Before you have it cut or sold, talk with me first."

"You mean it's actually worth something?" Cynthia asked.

He handed the stone back.

"It's so remarkable that I can hardly speak. What you've brought me is the rarest stone on earth, a red diamond. But not just any red diamond: a completely flawless stone and the deepest of reds. Only three of this quality and weight exist. The last red diamond whose price we know of was..." He stroked his beard and looked thoughtful. "Ach. That was in 1987. A 0.95 carat that sold for almost a million dollars. At the very least, your diamond is worth 2 million a carat but, I suspect, it could fetch more. The upper figure would be around 15 million."

The cup flew out of Cynthia's hand like a wild bird startled into flight, shattering into antique shards on Uncle Saul's desk. Coffee pooled onto his sketchbook, staining the top page, almost obliterating the drawings. "I'm so sorry, I'm so sorry," Cynthia cried out.

Uncle Saul rushed to the cupboard, returning with a handful of paper towels that they all used to dab up the liquid.

Cynthia picked up the fragile blue and gold pieces. "Please let me pay for the cup."

"No, Cynthia, accidents happen." He stared intently at her. "Of course, you're shocked with the diamond's value. Who wouldn't be?"

"But, but, but..." she managed to stutter out. "Don't you mean thousands of dollars?"

"No young lady, this gem is worth millions. If ever you want to sell it, I'll quietly find a buyer."

"How could something so small be worth so much?"

He nodded. "To answer your question, it's rarity, clarity, coloration, and the lack of inclusions that determine worth."

"But I don't know what to do with it!"

"If I may give some advice. Even my darling Rita doesn't know this, but I bought this building twenty years ago. I had heard rumors that it had once been a bank, so I had a construction crew go into the basement to do the renovation. They discovered a false wall. Behind it was an enormous safe, while I kept the safe, I had it rekeyed."

"Let's take the elevator down. I want to show it to you. Take your diamond with you."

Feeling confused, she and Rita accompanied him to the basement. He turned on a switch, and the basement was flooded with light. They followed the corridor until they reached a brick wall. Uncle Saul pulled out a brick; it slid open, then he pushed a button. Silently the wall slid back. The largest safe she'd ever seen stared back at her. After opening it, he explained. I keep my prized diamonds and those of some close friends here. Nobody but a hand full of us know about it. I am afraid of letting you out on the street with something of that great of value. I would be happy to keep yours here too. The diamond will be safe."

Cynthia looked carefully at Uncle Saul. Rita had always spoken highly and lovingly of him. If he had wanted to cheat her, he could have told her the gem was a garnet, and she would never have known the difference. She decided to trust him.

"Thank you, Uncle Saul."

She handed him the diamond, and he gave her a safe deposit box key. I'll write you up a receipt.

"What if I want to see it, and you're not here?"

"Clifford at Roosevelt Diamonds is the only other person who can open the safe. I'd trust him with my life."

"As I said, important diamonds are named, think about what you'll call it. Perhaps the Cynthia?"

She didn't hesitate, "The Emma, after my great-grandmother."

"Then the Emma it is," Uncle Saul replied.

"Uncle Saul, I have a small favor to ask. If you discuss this diamond with anyone, don't mention my name."

"Of course not, Cynthia. I wouldn't have lasted long as a diamond dealer if I'd been indiscreet."

The flower market had closed for the day, leaving the once-bustling streets almost deserted. Rita bubbled over with plans of what Cynthia could do with all that money. "Wow! You can quit work, go on around the world cruise, buy a nice home, and think of all the shoes you'll have!"

Cynthia couldn't wrap her head around it. It was as if she had eaten a popsicle, and her brain froze. She remained uncharacteristically quiet, her mind a slipstream of disjointed thoughts. Should she sell it now or keep it until she could figure out what to do with the money. There was a sense that it wasn't really hers, it was Emma's, and at least for now, she would keep it in the vault. Fifteen million dollars. After unlocking the jeep's door, Cynthia climbed into the driver's side, turned on the engine, and began to physically shake. "Rita, I don't think I can make it home, you'll have to drive."

Chapter Five

Mount Everest, present day

The Foreigner watched a snow plume fly off Mount Everest's summit with such a fierceness that it snaked across the sky like a dragon's tail. The Himalayas in winter was a brutal experience, but the timing was everything. The weather ensured that he and Tsai Zhi would be all alone on the lower flanks of the highest mountain on earth. Up in that icy graveyard, what was another body?

For the Foreigner, it'd been a year of frustration. Computers were beyond Tsai Zhi, so all correspondence was done by snail mail until money and date were agreed upon. Then the old Chinese bastard kept upping his price. In that flowery, careful English of his, he wrote about the enormous risk he was taking, and he needed to be paid accordingly. If the honorable Foreigner would kindly meet him in Tibet with the money, the object would be his. Admittedly, being called the honorable Foreigner amused him; gave him an aura of mystery.

Anxiety crept into the Foreigner's thoughts. Could the old man make their meeting at the 19,000 foot Interim Camp? Not technically challenging, more hiking than climbing, but still, with the rarified air, bloody arduous. And his memory? After all those years, could he really pinpoint the camera's location? Tsai Zhi was middle-aged when they'd met years ago on a mountain in China. That would now put him in his 70s. But the Chinese man struck him as a tough old bird: a survivor.

What a brilliant stroke of luck! That Tsai Zhi kept such an amazing secret. A secret he was now willing to sell; a camera hidden on Mount Everest from the 1924 expedition. The film in that camera was worth millions! To think that for almost a century, it'd been lost on the mountain. If it remained frozen, and up in that icy hell, why wouldn't it be? The film could be developed. Solving once and for all the great twentieth-century mystery of who climbed Mount Everest first: George Mallory and Andrew Irvine in 1924 or Edmund Hillary and Tenzing Norgay in 1953? The Foreigner knew just the man to sell it to. A man so obsessed with the ill-fated 1924 climb that he'd do anything to get his hands on George Mallory's camera.

He could get more money in an international bidding war, but that was a potential minefield. What if China or one of the descendants of the expedition members sued for ownership of the camera? He could be in court for years. Yes, this back doorway was best.

Roaring wind and stinging sleet forced the Foreigner to turn his thoughts on the here and now. Ignoring the frigid cold and the wind tugging at his clothes, he adjusted his backpack, heavy with gear for his overnight stay on the mountain, then cinched the straps tight until the weight felt evenly distributed. After the five hours, kidney-jarring, night ride from Shegar, it felt good to stretch his legs. He'd left his driver a half-mile back on the dusty road with instructions to pick him up in two days. He wanted no witnesses for his meeting with Tsai Zhi.

Sleet lessened then stopped altogether. In the eastern sky, the just risen sun cast a rosy glow on Rongbuk, the highest monastery in the world. At nearly 17,000 feet, the multi-level structure built of local stone blended seamlessly into the background of glacial moraine and seemed more fortress than a holy place. He pulled his wool hat far down on his face and kept to the shadows. The trail skirted the monastery and its guest house. Who knew if the odd tourist or Buddhist monk might be watching?

Why wondered the Foreigner, would anyone in their right mind choose to live in this bleak, plantless Asian plateau in a world of slate, granite, and limestone, where the only touch of bold color were prayer flags. But nuns and monks had lived in the nearby caves for centuries, spending their days meditating long before the monastery was built. Glancing around, he noted not much had changed, but then, he hadn't expected it to. Tethered close to the monastery stood two yaks covered in shaggy coats of thick hair, which almost swept to the ground. The piebald animal swished its horse-like tail and grunted as the Foreigner passed by, while the black yak stood motionless as his breath formed puffs of vapor. Probably belong to a trader bringing in supplies.

Before him lay the trail, a vast expanse of scree, rocks, and boulders, interspersed here and there with frozen ice melt. He estimated five hours to the Japanese Base Camp where he'd spend the night.

A strong gust whipped prayer flags near the domed Chorten housing Buddhist relics, and their flapping sounded like a deck of cards being furiously shuffled.

"You go alone?"

The Foreigner whirled to find a middle-aged monk wearing a ratty brown parka over his maroon robe staring at him.

Where in the hell had he come from? Tension bubbled as he stared into those deep-set eyes surrounded by fissure-like wrinkles.

Usually, it was easy for the Foreigner to read men, but the monk's quiet gaze was unfathomable. Was he a danger? No, how could he be? Yesterday Tsai Zhi preceded him up the mountain and had already spent a night at a lower camp. When or if they found his body, no one would connect the two of them.

"Just doing a science experiment up there," answered the Foreigner.

"No, go. Danger now. Bad storm come to Chomolungma, the monk cautioned, using the Tibetan word for Mount Everest. As if to underscore his words, the wind picked up and blew the dusting of snow off the monk's parka.

The Foreigner shook his head, "Must go."

The Monk threw him a long look then pointed to a row of brass prayer wheels embossed with Tibetan lettering, embedded in the thick wall. "Spin prayer wheels. Good karma."

The Foreigner had checked the weather report beforehand; the blizzard wouldn't arrive for two more days. Long before the storm broke, he'd be safely back down.

Striding over to the prayer wheels, he spun one after another, listening to them rattle and whir. Not that he believed this pagan nonsense, but why not appease the mountain gods? Good karma? His childhood hadn't any. A brutal father, and a frightened rabbit for a mother. Since then, he'd created his own karma, and it was stellar. George Mallory's Vest Pocket Kodak camera was about to become his, and that was the best karma.

"Namaste," said the monk, turning to leave. For a brief moment, the Foreigner watched him pick his way past the yaks and head over to the monastery.

Sucking in a lungful of air, the Foreigner worked his way up the moraine trail. In the quiet, he was left to his own thoughts, and unwanted childhood memories, long suppressed, came to the surface. He remembered that day like it was yesterday.

***

With balled fists the size of ham hocks, his old man had menaced toward him. "You're effing sixteen, Donnie," he shouted. "On weekends and after school, I want your butt out there working. Don't come back until you find a job. Pay for your own damn room and board!"

It was 4:00 p.m., and already five empty beer cans lay like cadavers on the coffee table next to a bowl of old peanuts. Glassy-eyed, Donnie's old man popped the tab of another beer can and grabbed a handful of pretzels. Jobless for close to six months, he'd now even given up the pretense of looking. Although his mother worked full time as a waitress, the pay wasn't great. They eked by, barely.

"Go!" His old man pointed to the door and threw a beer can. Freddie ducked as it flew past, spraying him with droplets.

He trudged into town to a single-story office building. Going inside, a woman manning the front desk, on the plump side, but with a twinkle in her eye. He could tell that she enjoyed bantering with the men.

"Yes," she said.

"I'd like to work here, and I'm willing to do anything," he answered, throwing her a warm smile.

Charm's in your DNA, you can't learn it, you can't fake it; either you have it, or you don't. His maternal grandfather had it in spades;

he was a raconteur and a friend to all. His mother, the mouse, hadn't a touch; it'd skipped a generation and came down and blessed him. People gravitated toward him, liked him, listened to him, wanted to help. But one man was utterly immune to it, his father.

"Arnie, she said to a rotund fiftyish man, this young man's looking for a job."

Arnie eyed him carefully. "Come back on Monday. I'll give you a chance, but if I don't like you, you're out of here like a bag of old garbage."

Donnie returned home to find more empty beer cans on the table, and his old man on the couch almost passed out. The house stunk of rage, stunk of hatred, stunk of failure.

***

A raven feeding on something caught his attention. Perched on the left side of the trail, when he saw the Foreigner, it flapped its wings and flew off with its prey in his beak.

All alone with his thoughts, he returned to his early memories.

The months rolled by, and one day, when a dusting of snow covered the hardened ground, Freddie was shifting gears on the forklift when Arnie approached, gesturing for him to stop. Surprised, he turned off the engine and jumped down. "Sir?"

Arnie put an arm around him. "Mike told me you're doing a good job out here. When you're done, come to the office."

One day while they were talking, Madge popped a blue M&M into her mouth and confided, "You know Arnie started with nothing, and he sees himself in you. He may not show it, but he likes you."

After he'd learned the ropes in the front office, Arnie brought him to the back room. "How are you with numbers?"

"Good."

"How good?"

"Very."

"We'll see." Arnie lowered his voice. "Know about double bookkeeping?"

Donnie slowly nodded.

"Boot up the computer. If you ever repeat what I tell you, I'll call you a liar, and you'll never work around here again. Understand?" Arnie stuck an unlit cigar back into his mouth. "I'm going to teach you a life lesson. Never fiddle your customers, especially the small ones, they'll soon know about it, but when it's the government, that's fair game. Just don't be greedy, it'll do you in for sure."

***

Shrugging away his memories, he stopped for a moment to rest. What with his tent, the liquid nitrogen gas container for keeping the camera frozen, a sleeping bag, food and water, the pack weighed heavy. At least he didn't need oxygen bottles; Tsai Zhi was adamant that they wouldn't climb above 22,000 feet.

The sun clouded over, and the temperature dropped another ten degrees. Climbing ever higher, his boots bit into the scree, sending loose mini avalanches of stones down the hillside. When the gravelly path transitioned to the glacier's tongue, he followed a yak trail hugging the east side for several hours.

Listening to the glacier creak and groan as gravity forced its slow slide down the mountain, he thought of the river of ice as almost a living thing, and, like the mountain itself, it had moods. For another three hours, he hiked on until he spotted the large yellow rock at roughly 18,000 feet: the Japanese Base Camp where he'd spend the night acclimatizing and where he'd leave most of his gear. In the morning, he faced another four to five-hour hike up the trail to meet Tsai Zhi at the next camp. Then what? The crafty bastard wouldn't tell him anything more.

***

Higher up on the mountain, a slender, forty-year-old Chinese man shivered in the breaking dawn on Mount Everest's north side. Still sleepy, Tsai Zhi's son rubbed his eyes while sunlight crept down from the mountain's snow-covered ridges towards his tent. The wind's constant howling frayed his nerves. A pounding headache and nausea had kept Tsai Zhi's son awake for most of the night. Mountain sickness, he was sure of it. Fear of dying filled him with dread. How much time did he have before his symptoms worsened? A few hours? Many hours? He berated himself. Why hadn't he spent an extra day acclimatizing at a lower altitude? The loneliness overwhelmed. Only the wind and his aching muscles kept him company.

Thrusting away dark thoughts, he huddled closer to his tent. With his back to Mount Everest, he let his eyes sweep the trail below. What did this foreigner look like? His father had died before he'd thought to ask. He grimaced and tried to relax. The tourist season had ended months ago. Who else but he and this man would be up here? He only knew that when he left this barren, bleak moonscape, he'd start life over as a wealthy man. He popped two aspirins, sipped cold tea, and waited. An hour ticked by, then another. His stomach churned. What if the Foreigner changed his mind? Didn't come? Then $500,000 and the promise of a new life would disappear like melted snow. He took out his father's gun and examined it. Stupid to bring it. But it made him feel safe. As he huddled to keep warm, he ignored the beauty of the snowcapped panorama. He couldn't understand men like his father, who loved them. Joy would light up his father's face when he'd pour over maps, or speak to climbing friends. That glow was never there when his father looked at him.

***

Fit as he was, the Foreigner's lungs fought for more air. Each breath taken at sea level needs an equivalent three on the mountain. He paced himself accordingly. Up and up, he climbed until he spotted it. A bright, rain-slicker yellow tent at the agreed-upon coordinates. What a miserable night the old man must have spent in this hellish place.

Scrambling up the remaining yards to the camp, for a heartbeat, he stared in disbelief. "Who the fuck are you?"

"Wen. Tsai Zhi's son."

The Foreigner gave the camp a quick scan. Good. No guide or porters just as he had instructed. "Where's Tsai Zhi?"

"He dead."

"Why are you here?"

In halting English, the man answered. "I know about camera. I have map. You have money?"

He assessed Wen. Was this some kind of double-cross? Wen looked harmless enough, like an office manager at some second-rate factory. "Where is it? Where's the camera?"

Wen's eyes glistened. "First, see money."

The Foreigner pulled out a bundle of hundred dollar bills from his pack and tossed it to Wen.

"All $500,000 is in the bag. When I get the camera, it's yours. Let's see the map."

Wen handed it over, then reached for the bag of money.

The Foreigner grabbed the man's gloved hand and twisted hard. Wen yelped.

"Didn't you hear me? No camera, no money."

The Foreigner leaned back against the rock face and peeled an orange. "If the camera is under snow and ice, the film will be frozen. If the camera's not frozen, the film's damaged and worthless to me."

"Frozen," Wen said, massaging his wrist. "Buried."

"That's the part I don't get. Since Tsai Zhi understood its value, why didn't he take it down with him?"

"Communist officials very strict then. Check everything. Everyone spy on everyone. Father no want to go to jail or have camera taken, so he bury it. He think someday he come back."

The Foreigner checked the map. "So it's near Advance Base Camp." He mentally groaned, 21,000 feet, another four or five-hour walk from here. Even as he assessed Wen, a new concern kicked in. "What about all those hikers, climbers, porters and yaks that have been up there? The bloody thing's probably been ground to a pulp by now."

"No. Away from camp. Easy to find. By rock outcropping look like face. Buried there."

"Easy to find," said the Foreigner. "This mountain's littered with rocks."

The Foreigner stared uneasily at the clouds amassing in the distance. "Wind's picking up. Time to go. You lead."

Snow pissed down hard. Wave after wave of dark clouds roiled overhead bringing mist, sleet, and snow. Damn, the Foreigner thought, watching the storm race towards them. It wasn't supposed to arrive for another day. "Give me the map," the Foreigner screamed at Wen. "Weather's closing in."

After a careful circling of camp, he saw it. A profile-like rock.

The Foreigner returned to Wen. "Get going. What else did Tsai Zhi tell you? This area is huge."

Then the Foreigner pushed him in the direction of the rock face. Wen stumbled but kept going.

"Is this it?"

"Maybe."

The Foreigner's arms swept the area underneath the rock profile. "I need more, or I'll never find it!"

Wen rubbed his eyes. "Here somewhere. Father say under a dog rock."

"What does that mean?"

"A rock like a dog."

The Foreigner eyeballed the slope; trolls, turtles, half faces, and maybe a dinosaur, but nothing resembling a dog. He took off his goggles. He moved eastward, changed his angle of view. He stared intently at all large rocks. Then he saw it. Dragging Wen over, he asked, "This it?"

Lightning zigzagged overhead. Wen looked terrified as he scanned the threatening sky. "Maybe? I go now. Bad weather come. Must go down. Give me money."

"Not until I find it." Pushing him away, the Foreigner untied the shovel secured to his pack. Ignoring his exhaustion, he began chipping away. The wind picked up, peppering his face with sleet. Pulling down his hat, he thrust the shovel into the ground. Concrete hard. A measly few inches. Tossing the shovel, he switched to his ax and swung. Shards of ice and rock splintered up like shrapnel. At least now, he was making headway. He paused, took a deep breath, swung. Little by little, the hole grew. Digging ever deeper, he realized that the spot hadn't been touched for years. If a camera lay buried, it was authentically old, and not a plant.

"You," he said, grabbing Wen, then forcing the ax into his hands. "Make yourself useful."

Light flurries intensified into heavy snowfall. The temperature dropped further. Even the Foreigner's bones felt cold. Within minutes, visibility diminished. The highest mountains on earth, completely disappeared as if they'd never existed. The granddaddy of all blizzards had arrived at the roof of the world.

Worthless, the Foreigner thought, watching the other man make a hash of it. How could Tsai Zhi have spawned such a son? Grabbing the ax out of the Chinese man's hands, he began digging again. It took a few more swings before he saw it: a piece of ratty blue cloth.

The wind increased, flailing their exposed skin. Staying much longer on the mountain in this weather was a death sentence, but the camera, damn it, the Foreigner couldn't leave without it.

Ignoring the storm as best as he could, the Foreigner squatted down by the blue cloth. Behind him, a boulder provided some protection from the wind. He pushed away the bigger stones, and with his knife, gently chipped at the surrounding rubble. Like an archeologist, he carefully removed bits of debris. It was the home stretch, and the last thing he needed was to cut into the camera. He rocked the cloth gently back and forth, then tugged. Out it came. With a grunt of satisfaction, he unwrapped it. Staring back at him was George Mallory's 1924 Kodak. Originally sold for under ten dollars, now it was worth millions. His millions.

As he brushed away the film of dirt, he savored the moment. Admittedly, he had doubts about its existence. But here it was. Now to protect it. He took the specialty container from his rucksack, leakproof, made of lightweight metal, and containing liquid nitrogen. With the greatest of care, he placed the camera into it, a perfect fit. Around the container, he then wrapped a blanket. Nothing could hurt it now.

Just one last detail to take care of: Wen.

Wheeling around, the Foreigner strode forward. For a couple of heartbeats, the Chinese man stood perplexed, as if wondering why a man was coming towards him brandishing an ax. When the Foreigner raised the ax above his head, Wen's wide-eyed bewilderment turned to terror. Stumbling backward, he fumbled for something in his pocket. Out came a gun. He fired. It was the Foreigner's turn to be surprised.

The bullet ricocheted off a rock, sending chips flying into the air. The Foreigner lunged. His ax bit into the side of the other man's upper arm. Wen's full-throated scream competed with the storm's howl. The Foreigner cursed in frustration. Wen's wound was bloody, but it didn't appear deep.

Vibrating with fear, Wen aimed again. A click, then another click. The gun refused to fire. Wen then began a mad scramble down the slope. Tripping, falling, and stumbling, he raced on. A thin trail of blood, like a snail's slime, stained the snow behind him. Even in the storm, the droplet trail would be easy to follow.

The Foreigner scooped up his pack and ax, then started his pursuit. Unlike the Chinese man, he picked his way carefully. Wen was fueled by an adrenaline rush. That wouldn't last.

The Foreigner narrowed the gap between them, then step by step, he forced the Chinese man onto the body of the glacier toward a deep crevasse.

Wen clenched his shoulder and whimpered. "Why? Why you do this?"

"Did you really think I was going to give you that money?"

"You keep money. Let me go."

Instead of answering, the Foreigner used the ice ax to prod Wen to the crevasse's edge. Had shock frozen Wen's brain? Sheep-like, he did little to stop the short march backward. At the very edge, when he could go no further, Wen unexpectedly lowered his head and charged. Grappling wildly over the ax, the two men tried to push the other into the crevasse. Finally, the Foreigner managed to kick the Chinese man's legs from under him then gave him a heave.

Wen clung onto the edge with his fingertips and struggled to pull himself up. Enough of this drama, the Foreigner thought and stomped down hard.

"No," Wen screamed as he was swallowed up by the crevasse.

The Foreigner peered down and found Wen sprawled far below on an ice ledge, clutching his arm. No way he'd be able to make it out. As an afterthought, he threw in the ice ax. Not likely anyone would find the man, but even if they did, so what? A tragic accident. Just another body on Mount Everest and the mountain was riddled with them. Turning away, he headed downhill to the Chinese man's camp, where he'd overnight.

Chapter Six

Nepal, present day

In his darkroom, the Foreigner smiled. Smuggling George Mallory's camera through Chinese immigration at Zhangmu took some doing, but now, back at home, the magic was about to begin. The nearly one hundred-year-old film would reveal secrets. Here was all the best equipment money could buy: lights, developer baths, chemicals, anti-foggers, and research books. He had read everything he could get his hands on about old cameras, and taken courses. Even practiced developing old rolls of 127 film. He was ready.

He opened the small metal box where inside lay, Mallory's camera. Now that the process was about to begin, he felt dizzy with concern. If the film had thawed, it was ruined, no salvaging the images. He gently touched the camera, and a sigh of relief escaped him. It was still frozen. If the camera were frozen, the film would be too.

As he put on latex gloves, he thought how primitive it seemed with its collapsible leather bellows and self-wind mechanism. To him, it was more beautiful than any woman. Giving it some time to warm up, he carefully extracted the fragile roll of film. For a minute, he paused before souping it in chemical baths. The final step was hanging the film up to dry.

He felt as exhausted as if he had summited a mountain, but now all he could do was wait. If he rushed it…Then, before his eyes, the film gradually developed. To his horror, each and every image was fogged. He grabbed the images, placing them on the table, examining each photo closely. All that preparation, all that planning, all for nothing. Just some writing on two pictures.

He pushed over the tray of chemicals. Liquid splashed over the floor and pooled onto the hardwood floor. Then he smashed his fist into the wall. The dream was gone; everything was thrown away on the gamble that the film was viable.

At least he had Mallory's camera. He could sell it. That's right, and he'd make money that way. A chill swept through him as he remembered, the only man who could verify the camera was Mallory's lay dead in a crevasse. The Foreigner picked up the camera again, and a faint rattle caught his attention. Funny, he hadn't noticed that before.

Although the room was dark, he could just make out that something was lodged in the empty spool section. With a gentle shake, it spilled onto the table. A stone? He turned on the light, and a pebble the color of a ruby glinted in his hand. A piece of paper was lodged inside as well. He took a pair of tweezers and, with great care, extracted it.

> *Noel,*
>
> *It's bloody cold up here, but we're giving it one last push! If something happens to me, make sure this stone goes to Emma Laughton at Fairy Glenn, Thistlebloom Lane in Little Brough, Cumbria, England. She already has the other one, so this will*

*make a matching pair. Depend on you to make sure it
gets mailed to Emma.*

    Sandy

The Foreigner stood mystified. Sandy? What was a note from Andrew Irvine doing in George Mallory's camera? And the pebble? Why was it lodged in there? Then he recalled an old story. No one knew for sure, but there'd been a rumor. When Mallory and Irvine disappeared, both men carried Vest Pocket cameras. As he surveyed the damage around him, he realized this wasn't Mallory's camera at all. It was Andrew Irvine's.

He went back to check the photos. Fogged. Still no images, now there never would be. Why would a dying man scratch on the paper backing of the film with a stylus and write Everest and Ama Dablam? Of course, Sandy was on Mount Everest; everyone knew that, but why had he written Ama Dablam? That mountain was located in Nepal.

Chapter Seven

Cape Town, South Africa Present day

The Foreigner strode into the lobby of the pink, colonial Mount Nelson hotel, passing by two elderly women enjoying afternoon tea. A stack of thin sandwiches along with an arrangement of desserts and scones that looked like it could feed six people were set before them. Botanical prints hung on the cream walls, and chairs were upholstered in soft pastels. Table Mountain loomed in the background, and clouds called the tablecloth spilled over it. Stopping by a potted palm, the Foreigner called the number he'd been given.

"Suite 205. Don't forget to dispose of the burner phone," ordered a voice as abrasive as forty grit sandpaper.

"Naturally," The Foreigner answered.

Inside the suite, two bodyguards frisked him, then stood on alert, just out of earshot and watched the meeting, At 6'7" Hansi Groblers dwarfed his guards, but his muscular body had softened, and his once flat stomach now rounded like a small pumpkin. A half-smoked Gauloise cigarette burned in a glass ashtray next to him. Obviously, Hansi enjoyed the perks of the good life. Although specializing in blood diamonds, he also dealt in armaments or anything else that offered a quick profit.

"Can't be too careful," Hansi said, half apologizing for the frisking. "Listen, if you're going to have skin in this Mali arms deal, come up with thirty million dollars. No money, no deal." Hansi poured out a glass of scotch and handed it to the Foreigner.

Thirty million. The Foreigner desperately wanted in, but thirty million. Where to get that much?

"Can you do it?"

The Foreigner nodded. "Give me three weeks."

"I'll give you two."

The Foreigner handed Hansi an envelope with the stone inside. "Since you're an expert, tell me what this is." Hansi was a crook and honored the code of honesty to brothers in crime so as not to burn bridges unless, of course, he didn't care.

Hansi picked it up. Rolling it between his thick, manicured fingers, he put the loop to his eye and stared. A low whistle, then his reply. "Looks like your down payment on the arms deal."

"What?"

"Where did you get this?"

"An inheritance," lied the Foreigner.

"Hell of an inheritance," Hansi quipped.

"What do you mean?"

"Didn't mean to keep you in suspense. It's a red diamond. When it comes to diamonds, I keep my ear to the ground. This one is so rare that until very recently there were only three of this size in existence, now with yours, almost overnight the number has jumped to five. I heard of a young woman who came into a red diamond inheritance too." Hansi gave a belly laugh. "Maybe you're related. Without a diamond tester, I can only give an approximate value. Let's say in U.S. dollars, between $11,000,000 and $15,000,000."

The Foreigner knocked back the rest of the scotch in one large gulp and held out his glass for more. It was as if the amount had seared his brain, and he couldn't think straight. So much for such a tiny gem. This diamond was worth a damn sight more than any film in Mallory or Irvine's cameras. "Are you sure about the number?"

"I was raised by the big hole in Kimberly. The family has mined gems for generations. No one knows diamonds as I do. You want me to give you a receipt and hold it as your down payment?"

The Foreigner placed the gem back into the envelope, then carefully buttoned his jacket pocket. "Not yet. Need to consider something first."

In the lobby, the two elderly ladies had consumed all of their sandwiches and were now attacking the desserts. Once outside, his thoughts went to Sandy's note in the camera. That was the key. It had to be the other red diamond Hansi talked about. Okay, the note was nearly a hundred years old, but it had the name and address of the woman who originally received the other diamond. Of course, she was long dead. Rotting bones in some graveyard. But she'd have had heirs. Yes, she'd have heirs. He'd start from the beginning. He'd find the heir and the other diamond.

Chapter Eight

Pasadena, California present day

It'd been a long workday. Just when Cynthia put her key in the car lock, her cell phone rang. She quickly checked the digital display, then heaved a sigh of relief. "Hi, Dad."

"Hi, Sunshine. Where are you?"

"About to drive home. Why?"

"Good, so you haven't eaten yet. Stop by Havanas on your way. My treat. I have a surprise for you."

"I'm tired, Dad. Can't it wait?"

His voice turned anxious. "No. I need you to come. It's important. It's not about money. I promise."

"All right, but it's been a long day, I'll only stay a few minutes."

His voice returned to normal. "Fine, honey."

Parking in Old Town Pasadena, even on a weekday, was a nightmare, so she parked at her condo and walked the nine blocks to the restaurant. As she entered Havanas, a wall of Cuban music flooded the room, washing over her, cleansing away the garbage of the day. A smiling hostess greeted her, "Are you, Cynthia?"

She nodded.

"Your party's waiting in the back."

She rounded the corner to find her father conversing with another man. Both turned as she approached. When she saw who it was, her red hair practically burst into flames. Sitting with her father was the last person she wanted to see. Paul Bellame! Her father stood up to greet her with a worried look, but Paul's smile radiated complete total confidence.

She glared at both of them. She'd been set up!

Cynthia's father's smile faltered when he saw anger tighten Cynthia's face. "Now, Sunshine. When I said I was meeting you, Paul overheard and asked if he could join us. Said he's missed you and wants...."

Paul interrupted. "Cynthia, I have a surprise for you. I've booked a first-class trip to Paris next month for us."

He was still talking when she marched out of the restaurant.

Chapter Nine

Los Angeles, California present day

Cynthia wiped a rivulet of sweat trickling down her forehead, grabbed an orange sloper, and scrambled up the climbing wall. From the sloper, she swung to a jug, the easiest and largest form to hang onto, then balanced on a foot chip. She went flying from jugs, pinchers, crimps, foot chips, and slopers. Her arms and legs ached. Faster, she told herself. For a moment, she balanced with one foot on a crimp no bigger than a thick bolt and stared up. Which way? To the left or right? She shook her cramping arms. Use your legs more, she chastised herself, grasped at a side pull and jumped for an incut. Slick with sweat, her fingers locked onto a hand pincher; when she felt herself slipping, she balanced on a foot chip, jumped for a hold to the right, and steadied herself. Just as she readied herself to go down, her hand froze on the rope: mountains, climbing, Tibet, 1920s. It was like looking through a microscope's lens where a blurred image sharpens into something completely recognizable. With a sense of shock, she now knew where she'd seen her great-grandfather's photo.

Cynthia gripped the rope and rappelled down so fast she touched the wall only once. Hitting the floor, she unhooked her rope like it was burning object and stepped out of the harness.

Jeff said, "Hey, you're looking a little pale. Are you okay?"

"I'm sorry, but I need to go home."

"Anything wrong?" Jeff asked.

"Just need to check something out." Cynthia gave Jeff a goodbye hug and left.

***

She sprinted up the condo stairs, then made a direct line to the bookcase, and rifled through it until she located, "Amazing Climbs." Her fingers flew over the pages until she found it: "The 1924 Disaster."

There was one black and white group photo. She examined each grainy face. In the back row, she found him wearing puttees, a heavy sweater, leather boots, and a wool muffler and hat. After a moment of just staring, her numbed mind wrapped itself around the fact that her great-grandfather had been involved in the most famous mountain mystery of all time: the ill-fated 1924 Mount Everest expedition. As she stared at the page, all she could think about was how young and happy he looked. The caption read *George Mallory and expedition members.*

She bit her lip in frustration, okay, but who was he?

She turned to her computer and surfed from hyperlink to hyperlink. Drilling down, she found her answer on **EverestNews.com.**

His name was Andrew (Sandy) Irvine. 'He died at twenty-two accompanying George Mallory on the final assault of Mount Everest in 1924. 'He and George Mallory were last seen approaching Mount Everest's third step.' Mallory's body was found in 1999, but my great-grandfather is still missing.

She glanced over at the cardboard boxes of her grandmother's things stacked and unopened in the corner. Perhaps, she thought, just maybe, there was something in there of Andrew Irvine's. She ripped off the tape and unfolded the cardboard flaps: books and more books. In the last box were documents, bills, and letters, most of which she fed into the shredder. At least her grandmother hadn't been a packrat. Then she came across those letters tied with a blue ribbon. She took the first one off the pile and began reading.

> *Dear Sweet Emma,*
>
> *Although I've been thinking of you all day today, this is the first opportunity I've had to sit down and write. Everyone's excited about the big push to scale to the top. It's now or never.*
>
> *Frostbite and dysentery have affected some of the men, but Mallory and I remain well. We have some interesting local characters here. Zatrul Rimpoche is the head lama at Rongbuk Monastery, which is quite near Mount Everest base camp. He's given us blessings and some supplies, but he's also told our porters that our expedition is doomed. Glad we don't believe in such nonsense.*
>
> *Finally, there's Bataar, nicknamed The Trader. Different looking from the rest. Features are Mongolian, but he has green eyes. Bit of an air of mystery surrounds him. He's from the Qilian Mountains, which are tied to the Old Silk Road. No one knows why or how he ended up here.*

I include a roll of film of the expedition members, the Trader, assorted monks, and porters. If you have time, would you mind having it developed, my sweet one.

Love,
Your Sandy

Cynthia rocked back in surprise. Sandy's letters? They were sitting in her condo for almost a week. Fascinated, she felt compelled to read them all. Greedily, she pored over one after the other. By the time she'd finished with the last one, night had transitioned into the early morning. Tears pricked at her eyelids when she placed them back into the box and closed the lid. This was one of the great, tragic romances of the 20th century, and only she knew about it. The world had to know too. Could she write a book about Sandy and Emma? Did she have it in her? And the red diamond? Dealing with selling it, handling her father, and the tax and legal ramifications were too much now. She'd wait until she finished the book and worry about the other things later.

Chapter Ten
The Lake District, England 1923

Sandy Irvine swallowed yet another yawn. Nothing, he thought, was more mind-numbingly dull than listening to middle-aged men prattle on about politics. Sandy was eager to motor away immediately after breakfast, but Dick, who'd brought him here, was insistent they stay for dinner so that he could reconnect with a late-arriving friend.

His host said, emphatically, "Why did King George pick that chap Baldwin as our Prime Minister? I bloody well don't understand it. Nice enough man, but not a leader. Definitely not a leader. I like that man Churchill; he's an up and comer. Heads screwed on straight comes from a good family. Walter, you remember, you met him at last year's derby, he had a devilish fine horse racing then, well, he heard a rumor that Churchill was about to rejoin the Conservatives. After that licking by Edmund Morel, I don't blame him. Should never have left the party in the first place."

"I have my doubts, Edward," said the retired Major General to his host. "Remember the Dardanelles fiasco when Churchill was First Lord of the Admiralty. The less said about that, the better."

The Major General lowered his voice and straightened his black tie. "This is confidential, but a chappie in the Home Office confided that Lenin is about to curl up his toes. A highly placed spy has let it be known that he's suffered a series of strokes, can't speak, and can't last much longer. Of course, no one in the Russian government admits to it."

Sandy waited for a pause in the conversation to make good his escape. Not only was the conversation deadly dull, but the manor itself was a dreary pile steeped in gloom.

Sandy glanced around the room for Dick and spotted him in a corner, standing next to an enormous potted plant, speaking to a young woman. Her back was to him, but Sandy noted a tall and slender figure. She hadn't been there earlier, because he would've absolutely remembered her. So this was Dick's childhood friend. When she turned, he caught a look at her profile. Lovely. Suddenly, he felt a twinge of jealousy toward Dick. He had to meet this woman.

When his host turned to a ruddy-faced man who just joined in on the conversation, Sandy excused himself and slipped away. Straightening his dinner jacket, he sipped at his gimlet and made his way over to Dick. A woman in a Grecian-styled dress, whom he'd spoken to earlier, made smiling eye contact long enough to let him know she was interested. Sandy merely nodded and strolled on.

"Dick," he said, joining them. "Rescue me from all these politically-minded men. I have no idea who they're talking about."

As the woman turned to face him, he stared into the most alluring eyes he'd ever seen. They reminded him of the glaciers of Spitsbergen, where, when the light was just right, the ice took on a greenish cast, and when you stared into the depths, it was as if emeralds sparkled deep inside, just out of reach.

"Emma, may I introduce Andrew Irvine. Sandy to his friends."

He shook her hand. "This is Emma Laughton. Emma and I grew up here in the summers. On our walks in the hills, she'd read the Lake poets to us."

She gave a throaty laugh. "Yes, but Dickie would plead for me not to."

"The Lake poets are my favorites," Sandy said, focusing all his attention on Emma. Thankfully Dick drifted away to converse with an older man sporting a salt and pepper trimmed beard and mustache that had been fashionable during Edward VII's reign.

While Sandy engaged her in conversation, what he really wanted to ask was: have you a boyfriend? Instead, he settled on a safe topic. "How do you know Dick?" Sandy then realized she had already answered that question and was embarrassed.

"Our families summered here for years, so I practically grew up with Dickie. Same with the Charleston's children."

"Then you live nearby?"

"In Little Brough. We would have arrived earlier but had two flat tires and became bogged down in the mud. Fortunately, a motor car stopped to help. Usually, we're back in London by now, but father had important business matters to attend to, so this year we arrived late."

Sandy blessed fate for the delay.

"And how do you know Dickie?"

"Met when we were boys at Shrewsbury School. I'm in my last year at Oxford. Dick and I are having a last hurrah. A bit of exploring a bit of mountain climbing."

"What are you studying?"

"Chemistry, engineering. I like to tinker to know how things work, then make them better."

A middle-aged woman with auburn hair shot with silver motioned to Emma to come over, so with a half-smile, she excused herself.

As the evening wore on, Sandy's eyes barely strayed from her. Her red hair was cut in the modern bob fashion, and when she neared the fireplace, the flames gave her hair an other-worldly glow. He'd like to push the hair behind her ears and caress her neck, then work his way down to her shoulders, then her breasts.

Dick stared at him in a perplexed way. "Say, what's wrong with you? You've been acting strange all evening. We've got a devil of a long trip ahead of us. I'll say goodbye to the Charlestons for us."

As Dick went over to thank their hosts, Sandy headed for Emma, who happened at that moment to be by herself.

"Say, I know this is a bit abrupt, but would you mind if I call on you? Sometimes I go up to London."

She peered up at him and said with an inviting smile, "Dickie has my address and phone number."

Both men buttoned their duster coats against the cold night air, for the temperature had dropped dramatically from the daytime highs. Fog settled in, obscuring the undulating hillside, which was now more sensed than seen. The dim headlights of the Vauxhall attempted to illuminate the way as Dick drove up and over a steep pass. At their slow speed, it would be midnight or later by the time they reached Dick's summer home, Swallows Nest. Dick was busy shifting gears when Sandy interrupted his concentration. "Tell me about Emma."

"Emma? What do you want to know?"

"Everything."

"Don't tell me you fancy her?"

"And you don't?"

"Oh, God, no. Devilish fine girl, but I like flaxen-haired girls with baby blue eyes and big breasts. But to answer your question. She comes from a good family. They used to have piles of money, but her father, according to mine, and he should know, is a terrible businessman. Doesn't have a head for it. So their finances of late have been in the cellar. She had a brother, but he was killed in the war. I liked him a lot. Don't get too interested in her because her mother wants her to marry well."

"Is she engaged or….?"

"Not that I know of."

Sandy leaned back with a sense of contentment. That was until his thoughts turned to Dick's stepmother, the lovely, and wantonly sensual Marjory. She'd been a former chorus girl who'd met and quickly married Dick's father, Harry, or as he was fondly known to friends and family, H.S. She was then nineteen and he, fifty-two. Marjory admitted H.S. was kind but unexciting. The business was everything; his hobby, his lifeblood, his obsession. She, on the other hand, wanted fun and good times.

Marjory exuded sex. When she pursued Sandy last year, he, flattered, became caught up into a vortex of her passion. He couldn't say no to those long nights of hot lovemaking. Was he Marjory's first affair? He thought not, but he did know that she would expect him to slip into her bedroom after everyone was asleep, then slip out before the servants started their day. After meeting Emma, the desire for Marjory evaporated like a puff of smoke. Time to break it off. Tonight he could feign tiredness, but what about the rest of their stay?

"Say, Dick. Would you mind us leaving tomorrow? If a miracle happens and I'm accepted on the Mount Everest expedition, I have to be in climbing fettle. Peaks in the East I'd like to try while the weather holds up."

Chapter Eleven

London, England 1923

Although it was October, it already felt as if winter had settled in. The constant wind carried an icy undertone hinting of sleet, and the sky was as dark and threatening. A few curled leaves, brown as old parchment, remained on the stand of plane trees growing near the station, and underneath them, the yellowed grass had a sodden, waterlogged quality, as if the earth were drowning.

Outside the train station, Sandy took his bearings and reached into his pocket to recheck Emma's address. Even in this weather, the sidewalks were busy: nannies with wind-reddened cheeks pushed prams towards the park, a delivery boy trotted ahead carrying a brown wrapped package, and several gentlemen, deep in conversation, strolled by without a glance.

In the street behind, Sandy heard a startled whinny and spun around to see an automobile race past, just inches away from a cart and horse. The cart driver's face strained with exertion in his attempt to control the bolting horse. When the frightened animal had settled down, the cart driver shouted at the automobile, "You bloody bull's pizzle."

Sandy was thankful that he had had the presence of mind to have his suit cleaned and pressed a few days before; that, along with his new tie, made him feel well-turned-out and ready to impress Emma.

His excellent sense of direction guided him unerringly, and after a half-hour walk, he quickly located the Laughton's residence. The all-over impression was of a Georgian home with good bones, but as he walked to the front door, it was apparent that minor repairs had been neglected; several steps were deeply chipped and cracked, the left-hand railing had pieces missing.

Were they economizing? Then he remembered Dick saying that the family's finances had taken a downturn.

With a firm knock, he rapped on the front door until a butler opened it and shepherded him in.

"Miss Laughton is expecting me."

"I'll see if she's at home, sir."

The butler escorted him to a large drawing room filled with a potpourri of different eras. Shadow boxes full of seashells, butterflies, and insects were displayed on several mother-of-pearl tables. Hanging near the windows was an 18th century Richard Bonington watercolor of fishing boats. A Grecian urn with a row of carved dancers stood next to the fireplace; large Art Nouveau vases inlaid with twisted vines and overblown flowers rested on the fireplace mantel; and here and there was Egyptian sculpture, which, to his untrained eye, appeared authentically ancient. A carved stone sarcophagus, leaning against the wall, seemed a bit over-the-top creepy for him, and he hoped there wasn't a mummy lurking inside. As his eyes took in the room, he wondered about all the Egyptian stuff.

As he wandered about, examining objects, a stuffed great horned owl seemed to follow his movements with its glassy orange eyes.

While inspecting a pharaoh's bust, he replayed the night he and Emma had met. Her lustrous flame-colored hair, emerald green eyes, and slim body had captivated him immediately, and although they had exchanged letters and phone calls, this was their first face-to-face meeting since then. Sandy liked to think of himself as brave, but his palms, moist with sweat just thinking about her, contradicted that assumption.

A slight creak alerted him. In she walked wearing an apricot dress with a scalloped hem. When she moved, it flowed with her body. He sucked in his breath in awe and was momentarily rendered speechless. But when she threw him her inviting smile, his nervousness evaporated. God, how he wanted this woman.

"You look lovely."

"Thank you. Were you admiring Ramses the II?"

"Is that who this fella is?"

"Lived to the grand old age of ninety-one. He ruled during the 19th dynasty and is considered by many to be the greatest of the pharaohs."

"So, you're interested in Egypt?"

"Lord Carnarvon was my godfather; he and father shared a passion for Egyptology. When I was a little girl, my favorite god was Khepri, the scarab, the god of creation, who pushes the sun to the underground at night then back every day."

She offered her arm so that he could get a better look at the gold bracelet studded with green and amber scarabs. "This was a present from Lord Carnarvon on my eighteenth birthday."

He held her hand and wrist feigning admiration for the bracelet, but all he could think about was how soft and smooth her skin felt.

"These statues all were gifts from him to my father."

"Lord Carnarvon, wasn't he the chappie who funded the King Tutankhamen expedition, then died from an infected mosquito bite? Lots of talk about ancient curses."

Emma's smile faded into a more somber look. "I was invited to join his next expedition to the Valley of the Kings, as the photographer. But then, of course, when the tragedy occurred..." Her sentence faded away, unfinished.

Sandy still held Emma's wrist when her mother swept into the parlor and glared at him. He gently let go of her hand and stammered out a hello.

"How do you do?" she said, then proceeded to ignore him. "Emma, it's time to get dressed for dinner. The Thompson's son, Jimmy, will be there tonight, and his mother said he's looking forward to becoming reacquainted with you. Smith," she said, turning to the butler, "Please show Mr. Irvine out."

Several days later, at Oxford, Sandy confided to Dick, "Mrs. Laughton doesn't like me. Made it quite apparent."

"Everyone likes you."

Sandy slipped a v-neck sweater over his head. "Apparently not."

"You understand that it's not about you, don't you? She's a tough old bird, probably sees you as a threat. You're not rich. Are you going to see Emma again?"

"Next week. I'll lodge with the Robinsons."

"Hey old man, slow down, don't rush your fences."

"I heard a fly boy's after her and some rich baron's son who looks like a strand of spaghetti. Mrs. Laughton likes them both."

***

October and November drifted by and, much to Mrs. Laughton's great displeasure, Sandy continued to call on Emma. Because of Mrs. Laughton's intense dislike, Sandy tried to meet Emma in alternative locations whenever possible. Christina Broom's photography studio and house on Munster Road became a favorite rendezvous point.

When he first met Mrs. Broom, Britain's first woman press photographer, he guessed she was in her sixties, and to Sandy's mind, her face held tremendous strength and appeal. It was a face which tragedy had visited, yet where humor lurked. Emma had told him that in addition to freelancing, she had a stall at the Royal Mews, where she sold her postcards.

"So this is the young man you've been telling me so much about. Feel free to wander and look about. I have to mix chemicals in the darkroom." Mrs. Broom told him.

While Emma cropped a picture, Sandy admired the photos on the walls and was pleasantly surprised to find Emma's photos included in the display. Her Thames series captured the river's moodiness with mists rising from the river and men hard at work on the boats. Two fishermen pulling up a net full of swirling silver fish caught his eye, and he felt inordinately proud of her.

"Nice. I like them."

"Tomorrow, I go on a shoot. Would you like to come?"

"Absolutely!" Sandy tried not to think of the chemistry class he'd once again be missing, but well, what else could a chap do?

They met early at the St Paul's station, and for a change, the weather was sunny.

"Where to now?" he asked after kissing her on the cheek. "Or are you going to blindfold me and keep me in suspense?"

She laughed. "St. Brides. Mrs. Broom has an assignment to photograph Christopher Wren designed churches. I'm assisting her with the smaller ones. Did you know that the first printing press was housed at St. Brides?"

"I didn't," he replied as he helped carry her supplies. And for the rest of the morning, he watched her take photos of the church from various angles, focusing mainly on the arched windows and the famous wedding cake steeple.

"Done," she said, as she packed up her camera.

Sandy was reluctant to let her go. "Lunch? Ye Olde Cheshire Cheese is nearby."

She nodded.

They walked off Fleet Street and down a narrow alley to the pub constructed around the same time as St. Brides. Once inside, they maneuvered a tiny passageway to a private nook upstairs. The room was so dark that the elderly waiter seemed to materialize out of nowhere to take their order. After finishing the meat pies, Sandy took Emma's hands into his and took a deep breath. What if she says no, he thought, then what would he do? "I appreciate this is sudden. But I have to tell you how I feel. I love you. I need to know how you feel about me."

She offered him a smile. "I care. Very much. But there's mother. She suspects I'm fond of you and wants you just to go away. She's accused me of being too independent, bohemian, and influenced by modern thinking. I told her I'd see who I want to see."

"I'll be up again next weekend," he said, kissing her hand.

***

"Up to London again? After all the lectures you've missed? Rather risky, old chap, the tutor won't be happy," Dick remarked, his tone worried, as he and Sandy prepared for crew practice.

"Dick, I'm pulled in all directions. With my studies, keeping fit, and Emma. And, well, between you and me, I'm proposing soon."

Dick let out a long, low whistle. "She's a lovely girl, but you're not even done with school yet."

"I've cadged an invitation to the Lovelet's party through Tommy Barnes. Emma said she'd be there."

"Does Emma know you've lobbied for a good part of the year to be part of the Mount Everest expedition?"

"Not yet. I'll tell her once the committee informs me if it's a yes or no."

Dick waved an envelope his way. "Marjory writes that she's back at Cornist Hall and invites us for a visit this weekend. She insists that I bring you along."

A blush spread over Sandy's cheeks. Marjory! He'd meant to contact her to tell her that their affair was over. Tomorrow, he'd call; it had to be done. "I'm afraid I can't go, old man."

***

Located three villages over from Marjory's, the two-hundred-year-old Blue Prince Pub offered the lovers cozy, intimate corners to ensure privacy, and privacy became all-important when conducting an illicit affair. With a twist of self-revulsion, Sandy felt like slug slime.

The dark oak beams overhead surely had witnessed centuries of love, hate, and if the rumors were right, even murder. Above the bar hung a replica of the original painting of an Ottoman prince, who, during a pitched battle, had saved the owner's life. The painter captured the prince's devil-may-care quality and aura of wealth with his gems scattered haphazardly about his azure silk robe. A tasseled fez, set rakishly on his head, completed the exotic-looking sultan's outfit.

Sitting there, waiting for Marjory, was the hardest thing Sandy ever had to do. He felt wretched. Miserable about having begun the affair, and wretched for knowing the hurt he was about to cause. The Blue Prince had been a frequent bolt hole for them. First, they'd devour a ploughman's lunch or a shepherd's pie full of minced lamb, topped with hot mash and served with a rich gravy, then on to hot, wanton sex, or sometimes, the food didn't matter, it was just about sex.

Marjory was usually late, and today proved no exception, so lost in thought, Sandy sipped at his beer and waited glum-faced. Across the table, seeming to mock him, sat Marjory's favorite drink, a gin, and tonic.

The scent of Chanel Number 5 floated in before Marjory.

She ruffled his hair, then kissed him lightly on the lips and teased, "Darling, it's been ages. You haven't been avoiding me, have you?"

Sandy reddened, stood up, and pulled out a chair for her.

Her blue eyes peeked out from under her saucy, rolled brim hat. A gray feather swooped across the upturned brim to offer contrast against the citron green felt.

"The ploughman's or the shepherd's pie?" she asked while adjusting her hat.

Sandy pushed his chair back until it touched the wall. "I say, Marjory," Sandy stuttered out, "first we need to talk."

As she waited for him to continue, some of Marjory's effervescence fizzled like old, uncorked champagne.

Sandy took a deep breath. "I take full responsibility. I've been a cad to have even started this affair, and, well, it, it must end."

"You can't mean that! Is there another woman?"

"No, Marjory, there isn't," lied Sandy. For the last thing he wanted was to drag Emma into this mess. "I'm so sorry."

Marjory shoved her chair away from the table with such violence that it wobbled precariously, then with a flick of her wrist, threw the gin and tonic into Sandy's face. The cold liquid dribbled down in rivulets, and the lime peel became caught in his shirt collar.

"We're not done yet!" she spat. With that, Marjory stalked away, but the ghost-like scent of her Chanel Number 5 lingered.

Chapter Twelve

Oxford, England 1923

Founded in 1264, Merton College was one of Oxford's oldest institutions. Sandy's rooms were high up in the Merton College attic and, fellow attic dweller, Alatan Tamchiboulac, an American, shouted out a hello as he was leaving. "Aren't you going to lectures, old sport?"

Sandy put down his pipe with its many chew marks on the stem and shook his head. "Too busy."

The American waved goodbye and raced down the stairs. For the time being, Sandy put his studies on hold, instead concentrating on improving the functionality of oxygen bottles. A disassembled oxygen unit lay in front of him in proper order, and after examining each piece, he was dead sure that he could make the unit lighter and better. Along with the oxygen bottles, his college room was choc-a-bloc full of crew equipment, climbing gear, textbooks, and the useful odds and ends that made living comfortable.

He rubbed his tired eyes then pulled back the crimson drapes covering the mullioned windows to allow in more light. Outside, the low hanging nimbus clouds echoed the gray tobacco smoke that layered the ceiling inside.

He was busy drawing a schematic when his scout, Owen Brown, coughed gently to get his attention. "You have a visitor, sir. She's waiting for you at reception."

"She? Who is she?" Sandy asked.

"I don't know, sir, she refused to give a name."

Sandy was intrigued. He couldn't imagine who would call on him unannounced. "Tell her I'll be down shortly."

Also, you have a special delivery letter," Brown said, handing it to him.

Sandy stared at the return address, the Mount Everest expedition. His shaking hands opened it, and his eyes raced through the letter, hardly taking in what he'd read. He forced himself to slow down and reread it, then whooped in sheer delight.

Brown raised a questioning eyebrow.

"I've been accepted! I'm a Mount Everest expedition member."

"Congratulations, sir."

Sandy changed into a fresh shirt, put on a tweed jacket, and a tie then went down to meet the mystery woman.

Her back was to him. He found her gazing out at the broad sweep of trees and grass that comprised Christchurch Meadow. She dressed well, but severely, in a coat with a matching wide-brimmed hat that was saved from solemn drabness by a magnificent spray of golden pheasant feathers. He hadn't a clue who she was.

"Hello. You wanted to see me?"

She turned around. Immediately Sandy's good mood evaporated.

"Mrs. Laughton!"

"Hello, Mr. Irvine. I thought it best to speak with you alone. I won't beat around the bush, I've come to warn you away from Emma."

For a moment, Sandy struggled for words. "But I don't understand; I have nothing but the highest regard for your daughter."

Her voice dripped acid. "If you have such high regard, you'll stay away. She has suitors who can make her happy, suitors that can provide for a good life. Your constant visits are becoming a distraction. You're not suitable. I want your assurances that you'll honor our wishes."

"Did Emma agree to this?"

There was a slight pause. "She's too young to know her own mind. That's why, as her parent, I speak for her. Will you do as I ask, Mr. Irvine?"

"I can't, Mrs. Laughton."

"Then, you will no longer be admitted to my home, nor will you meet with Emma again."

Her back was ramrod straight as she put on her kid gloves and stalked away.

***

The Lovelet's dinner party was in full swing while Sandy waited for Emma to arrive. She entered with two friends in a blue gown edged in maroon beads that clung to her slender frame. With her fiery red hair pulled back by diamante combs, she seemed exotic, untouchable.

Sandy couldn't have described what Emma's companions looked like or wore, if his life depended on it. For politeness's sake, he chatted briefly with her friends before swinging Emma onto the dance floor to foxtrot. He inhaled jasmine, rose, and sandalwood; by her smell alone, he'd locate her in a crowd. They slow danced to the faint sound of the band playing "April Showers." While he led her around the room, she stumbled a few times. It amused him to realize that he was the better dancer, and she wasn't so perfect after all. He liked that she had flaws. When the music ended, he pushed her hair behind her ear and whispered. "Come," he said, dragging her by her hand. "I desperately need to talk to you in private."

Sandy escorted Emma by a billiard room. A cigar-smoking man cracked a solid break, and a blue ball shot forward then paused teasingly at a hole before rolling in. That was followed by the soft sound of cue sticks being chalked. No privacy there. They next passed a conservatory where a group sipped champagne. "Another dead soldier," a male voice announced, then the sound of laughter as champagne corks popped.

Strolling toward them, assumedly to the ballroom, was a woman with wheat-colored hair piled atop her head, and sapphires dripping down a deep decollate. She clenched her companion's arm possessively as they passed, as her partner eyed Emma appreciatively.

"Bloody frustrating! Emma, there's no chance of having a private moment here. "

"Sandy, what about Christina Broom's studio? She's out of town taking suffragette photos for the *Tatler*."

"But how would we get in?" he asked.

"There's a key near the door; she leaves it there so that I can come and go at will."

He snatched a kiss. "Perfect."

"I'll pretend I have a headache and tell the others, you're taking me home."

The butler helped Emma into her dark blue velvet wrap, and after hurried goodbyes, they made for the street. Rain drizzled fitfully, and a cold wind had picked up. Three full taxis motored by before an empty Citroën stopped. "Evening, guvnor. What's yur pleasure?"

"Munster Street," Sandy directed, helping Emma over a puddle.

"Thanks for the tip, guvnor," said the driver, after letting them off.

Christina Broom's establishment was located in a middle-class neighborhood lined with similarly constructed brick row houses. Manicured boxwood hedges defined smallish lots, and the limited visibility from the streetlights indicated rain had given way to a heavy mist that hinted of an incoming fog.

Mrs. Broom's home consisted of two separate entrances; the front one to her house proper, and the side to her studio. Sandy bumped against a propped up rake when they rounded a corner, and it fell with a clatter. A light flicked on at the house next door.

Emma placed her forefinger to her mouth, picked up a brown ceramic pot, retrieved the key from under it, then opened the studio door.

Suddenly a window squeaked open, and a man's surly voice announced. "Margaret, stop your yammering, there's no one out there. It must have been a bloody cat."

After Emma turned on the light, Sandy went immediately to the heater. There was a whooshing sound as it caught flame. The acrid smell of chemicals hung heavy in the air, and cameras, equipment, and photos were neatly stacked and around them. The studio consisted of a large front room and a back one for souping and developing film. Against a wall was a gold crushed velvet couch that had seen better days, a table, and two oak chairs.

When the room warmed, Emma took off her wrap and shook it; then, they made their way to the couch.

Sandy picked up her hand. "I have wonderful news, sweetheart. A dream of mine came true. I'm accepted as a member of the Mount Everest expedition."

Instead of the excitement he had anticipated, her eyes filled with concern. "Isn't that dangerous?"

Sandy kissed Emma's neck and held her close. "I'll be fine. I'm the youngest member, so I don't imagine I'll have a whack at the mountain. I've been brought along more for backup, for brawn, and because I'm useful at fixing equipment. George Mallory, Noel Odell, and the others are the more experienced climbers. They'll lead the charge. It's quite an honor to be asked."

Although the room had warmed, he felt her shivering. "When? When are you going?"

"Very soon, my love."

"Oh, no."

The stark realization settled over them; they hadn't much time left together.

The atmosphere became suddenly charged as if the chemicals hanging in the air had combusted and had enflamed their internal chemistry. Heat and passion raged through Sandy. He gathered Emma into his arms, and she responded with a depth of ardor that surprised him. Running his hands all over her body, he pushed the straps of the gown off her shoulders, pulled off her chemise, cupped her buttocks, then positioned her on the couch. He practically ripped off his clothes. Soon they became intertwined legs and arms. Hungry mouths that sucked explored, tasted, nibbled.

Emma's nipples hardened, and she moaned as Sandy explored her wetness. When he felt her ready, he drove into her ever deeper until he shuddered in ecstasy at the pleasure of having her. Spent, they lay in each other's arms.

Sandy turned over and looked down at her."I have something to ask." He paused then took her hand. "Will you marry me when I return?"

Her eyes widened in surprise, and a flush crept up her cheek. "Yes," she answered without hesitation. "I will. What are we going to do about mother?"

Sandy visualized the gimlet-eyed Mrs. Laughton, her mouth pursed in anger, forbidding the marriage. But Emma had reached her majority and he'd do his best to get Mr. Laughton on their side. Granted, it would be an uphill battle, but they'd worry about it upon his return.

"Our secret until I get back and we tell family and friends."

Chapter Thirteen

Los Angeles, California present day

Cynthia's eyes blinked gritty from lack of sleep. As the night hours melted into one another, transitioning from 2:00 a.m., the time her mother had called the hour of the witch Morgan le Fay, the hour of betrayal, to 3:00 a.m., she couldn't stop reading Sandy's letters. Ignoring the go-to-bed signals emanating from her sleep-deprived body, she kept trying to push down her emotions. Don't cry, don't cry, she told herself. They're long dead. Their pain's over. But after finishing the last letter, the emotional dam broke, and a flood of tears flowed unchecked. Wiping them away, she asked herself, why do I care about these two people? Why do I feel their love so strongly? Was she experiencing genetic memory? Genetic inheritance was complicated; she knew that. She'd read that scientists had discovered that phobias and fears are sometimes passed down through generations. Could that be true of other emotions such as love? Could powerful love change DNA so profoundly that it became a genetic whisper in her cells, a generations-old echo?

Opening the door to the balcony, she felt a steady Santa Ana wind blow warm air across her face. Cynthia pictured the eternally young Sandy forever frozen on the mountainside, and Emma was living all those loveless years without him. Damn, it was heartbreaking. She grieved. Why she didn't know, but she mourned for them.

With a suddenness that made her jump, her iPhone pinged. At this hour? On a weekend? She thumbed through the message. *"The competition just bought our company. That's the bad news. The good news is that both of our jobs are safe. Ray."*

She slowly texted back. "Thanks. We'll talk tomorrow!"

Sitting there, breathing in the early morning air, she flipped through Sandy's photos, about thirty in all: yaks, Mount Everest, and monks lined up in front of a monastery. Was the middle one the abbot, she wondered? Then a jolly-looking monk standing by himself followed by George Mallory's handsome face, and with his perfect features, wasn't he considered the most beautiful man of his generation? Other expedition members, and a close up of a tall Asian man, (Bataar)? She wanted to dive into the sepia-colored sea within those photographs, to smell a yak, to see those mountains, to feel the bitter wind on her face, to meet the men, to experience it all.

Studying the photographs strengthened her resolve. By now, Sandy and Emma had become a searing passion. Even an obsession. All she could think about were the two of them. Sipping at her tea, she stared down into her cup, wondering what those tea leaves foretold. It was kind of Ray to let her know that her job was secure. But she hadn't the energy to both write the book and work her long hours. Lou Reed's *"Hey Babe, Take a Walk on The Wild Side,"* looped through her mind. Yeah, she decided, I'll walk on the wild side. Then and there she decided to quit. Sandy Irvine took life-threatening risks, and she would too.

She went to her computer to read articles about the 1924 climb. At the end of each article came the speculation. Had they made it to the top, or not?

In a blink moment, she realized there was nothing more she could learn here. How could she possibly write about Sandy and Emma without having a sense of place, culture, or knowing the local people? She mentally calculated how much she had left without selling the diamond. She could do it.

She googled climbs and treks in Nepal, pouring over available online mountain climbing information, and there was lots of it. Everest, she ruled out right away, far too costly and dangerous. Over two hundred people had died up there, and many of the bodies remained as grisly reminders of failure. And did she want to climb a mountain her great-grandfather had died on? If she thought Mount Everest was deadly, Annapurna had a forty percent death rate. She moved on. Then she found it, a peak that tugged at her like a magnet: Ama Dablam. She read on, "Arguably the most beautiful mountain in the world." The photos were stunning, the dates worked out for her, and though it would be the highest she'd ever climbed, and she'd have to stretch.

Chapter Fourteen
Oxford, England 1924

Sandy found Dickie down at the boathouse, putting away gear. "Old man, I need your help."

"What's wrong?" Dickie asked.

"Mrs. Laughton. Demanded that I never see Emma again."

"I warned you. She's not to be messed with. Wears the trousers in that family."

"Do you know a female who can slip Emma a message?"

"My cousin, Victoria. They're old friends. But Sandy, be realistic, there are many wonderful girls out there. Move on. Find someone else. You don't want to go up against Mrs. Laughton."

"There is only one Emma. Ask Victoria to tell Emma that I'll be in London next Thursday. I'll let her know where to meet me later." Sandy picked up a letter. "The Everest Committee sent me a supply list as long as my arm. They're financing most supplies, but not all. Let me read what I need to buy; Shackelton jacket, horse saddle, puttees, felt and hobnailed boots, a camp chair, a dinner jacket, and more."

Dickie whistled. "Where are you getting all that quid from?"

"From father. He's a game one, but we're not that well off, so I need to budget wherever I can."

Later that evening, Sandy phoned to make reservations at the Jules Hotel on Jermyn Street. Due to their frequent London visits, Marjory and her friends were on the hotel's V.I.P. list, allowing them special discounts. Sandy, to his self-disgust, was about to piggyback on that fact.

"Good evening. Jules Hotel."

"I'm a friend of Marjory Summers, and I'd like to make a reservation."

"Certainly, sir. Just checking. Yes, we have availability."

"Does that entitle me to her special discount rate?"

"Yes, sir, it does."

Adding to his sense of complete self-disgust were Marjory's letters. Her previous two had begged him to resume their affair. This unopened letter, smelling of Chanel Number 5, was assumedly more of the same. Feeling a stab of remorse, he tossed the unread letter into the wastebasket, but the scent of Chanel Number 5 clung to his hand like a bad habit. Honestly, he was sorry for the pain he'd caused, but the affair was over. Dead and buried. How had life become this complicated? He only had himself to blame; if he had thought with his head instead of his cock, he wouldn't be in this predicament. He'd deserved that thrown gin and tonic.

At least he didn't tell Marjory about Emma. A loose cannon if he'd ever met one. Who knew what she'd say or do? Eventually, she'd find out from Dick about Emma, but by then, she'd be on to someone new, and it wouldn't matter.

The week ground by and every minute seemed an hour and every hour a day until Sandy finally heard from Emma. Victoria had passed on Sandy's message to meet in the lobby of the Brown Hotel and dine afterward at the Savoy. Her mother, Emma, had assured, was visiting a cousin over the weekend, so no need to worry.

***

Checking in ahead of him in the Brown Hotel lobby was a tall, aristocratic woman accompanied by a manservant towering at over 6'6", two snowy white afghan hounds, and an uncountable number of trunks and suitcases. An army of bellboys surrounded her and positioned themselves near the bags like the Queen's Guards. When it was his turn, he joked with the clerk about his one, lone, sad-looking suitcase, then inquired as to who the woman was.

"A Russian Countess, sir. An émigré, and one of the lucky ones. Her former husband had the presence of mind to leave before the Bolshies took over. Whenever she's in London, she resides with us."

After Sandy unpacked, he mulled over the list and his finances. Yes, the money the expedition provided helped, but it wasn't nearly enough to cover everything, and his funds were rapidly disappearing. There still was the expense of specialty clothing, a pair of felt boots, and a saddle.

As he totted up the numbers, there came a knock. A bellboy? When Sandy opened the door, he stood there appalled. Marjory! Drunk and disheveled, she held a silver flask out to him.

"Surprise," she said, elbowing past him, her twin dimples dancing on each side of her mouth.

She tossed the flask and her coat onto the bed, then twirled around and did a shimmy. Without her coat, she was next to naked, wearing only a garter belt, stockings, and shoes.

Six months earlier, Sandy would have salivated with desire, but not now, not since knowing Emma. He stared at her in panic. I've got to get her out of the room immediately, he thought.

As she swayed to her own internal rhythm, she crooked her finger at him and began singing her favorite Irving Berlin song.

> *"You cannot make your shimmy shake on tea*
> *It simply can't be done*
> *You'll find your shaking ain't taking*
>
> *The shimmy, it is intricate*
> *And so you needs a little bit*
> *Of Scotch or rye to lubricate your knee*
>
> *A cup of Ceylon*
> *It may be strong or weak*
> *Won't help you spoil on*
> *Because it's much too meek*
>
> *Besides, a drink that's soft*
> *Will very often ruin your technique*
> *No, you cannot make your shimmy shake on tea."*

Finishing her wobbly shimmy, she collapsed onto the bed in a fit of giggles.

He tossed the coat over her. "I say. Put this back on. How did you know that…?"

She kicked the coat away. "That you'd be here, darling? Dick wrote that you were shopping for the expedition. The how doesn't matter. Have you missed me? It's been way too long since we've been together."

"Marjory, I'm truly sorry, but it's all over. I don't mean to hurt you, but you must leave."

"What!"

"Please, go! You have to realize…." His sentence was interrupted by yet another knock.

"It's room service. I ordered it for us, darling. I'm starving."

He sighed and went to the door and froze in shock. Instead of a waiter carrying a tray laden with food, there, smiling up at him, was Emma.

He blurted out. "Sweetheart, what a surprise. You're supposed to meet me in the lobby. Is anything wrong?"

She shook her head. "I just wanted to see you."

He put his arms around her and walked her down the corridor towards the lift. "Give me a few minutes to change, and I'll meet you downstairs."

"What's keeping you, darling? I'm hungry." Marjory peeked around the door and made eye contact.

Emma looked as though she were about to be sick. Pushing Sandy away, she ran towards the lift. He ran after her. "Sweetheart, I can explain, it's not what it seems."

Tears washed down her cheeks, while she frantically jabbed the down button. "Don't you ever speak to me again. Dickie's stepmother! Oh, God!"

***

Over the following days, Sandy sent flowers, and letters of apology, to no avail. He phoned, but Smith, the butler, in his cold, detached manner, would inform him that Miss was not at home. Despite his best attempts, he was confronted by an insurmountable wall of silence.

He paced up and down, thinking furiously. What could he do to make Emma listen to reason? Dick was out of the question. He couldn't possibly talk to him about what had happened without explaining his affair with Marjory.

As Sandy stood to leave for crew practice, Dick raced in holding up a newspaper. "Have you read the announcement section of the Times yet?"

Sandy shook his head.

"Read the second announcement down."

The words were blunt and to the point. Emma was marrying the baron's son.

Chapter Fifteen

Oxford, England 1924

Weeks rolled by, and the pain of losing Emma sunk Sandy into a place as dark and foreboding as Emma's description of the Egyptian underworld. He felt as if his soul and body resided in the realm of the dead, on that dark side of the moon, in that hell where blood drinkers lurked, and lakes of fire prevented his passage to paradise. Others noticed the change in Sandy, but he fobbed them off with excuses about the upcoming Everest expedition and concentrating on his studies. Dick watched helplessly. After asking a string of questions about Emma and getting no satisfactory answers, he stopped asking.

Sandy sat listlessly in his room reading the items in the for sale section of the *Times* when an ad caused him to sit bolt upright. ***For sale: topaz and jade Egyptian scarab bracelet of the god Khepri set in gold.*** He sucked in his breath and rocked back in his chair, clutching the newspaper as if it were a living thing about to escape. Who else in London owned a bracelet of that description? No one. The ad ended by providing a phone number: Emma's.

Why would she sell her favorite piece of jewelry given to her by her beloved, deceased godfather? He set the paper down and began thinking furiously. Dick said that the family was experiencing financial difficulties. Maybe it was worse than he'd imagined. She loved her photography class, said it gave her a sense of freedom.

Could the family no longer afford it? Was that the reason? Or something else? He had to help; he had to get hold of that bracelet.

First, Sandy hunted down Dick and found him at the boathouse, "Say, old man, can I borrow some folding stuff off you? It's terribly important."

With Dick's money firmly in his pocket, he rapped on the door of one of his oldest friends at Merton. "Geoffrey, be a good egg, I need a favor. Would you phone this number? Pretend to be interested in the bracelet, then set up an appointment for viewing. She'll want to meet you in London, so I'll owe you."

Although puzzled, Geoffrey nodded. "But I say, old man, why are you doing this? What's the secrecy? What's this all about?"

Sandy blushed, then hemmed and hawed. "I've had a bit of a facer with someone that I care deeply about, so I'm trying to make amends."

"What if she asks me why I'm buying it?"

"Say your mother's fascinated by Egypt, especially the god Khepri."

Geoffrey looked glassy-eyed. "Khepri?"

"A dung beetle god. Pushes the sun into the underworld at night or some such."

"Oh, Lord. A dung beetle."

After phoning Emma, Geoffrey returned to the room. "All set. She's to meet me at a tea shop. I have no idea what's going on, or what this is all about, but I can see from your expression that you're not going to tell me. How much am I supposed to offer for the bracelet?"

Sandy wrote a number down. "I can go up to this amount, but no more."

The meeting was arranged for Thursday, and by the time Geoffrey finally returned, Sandy had nearly chewed through the stem of his pipe. At the knock on his door, he bolted out of his chair and wrenched the door open. "Well, did you get it?"

"Yes, but I never want to go through that experience again. Dreadful."

"Emma was dreadful?"

"No, a charming girl. It was the tea shop."

Sandy was about to quiz him but thought better of it. You couldn't rush Geoffrey.

"The tea shop was littered with twee things. The curtains matched the table cloths, china shepherdess and milkmaid figurines were placed on every shelf, the cups were so dainty that I couldn't hold on to one properly. I spilled my tea, the food was finger-sized with not enough sustenance to keep an elf alive, let alone me, and then…." He gave a shudder. "There were all these old tabbies."

"Cats in the tea shop?"

"Not cats, women. As soon as I entered, all conversation stopped. I mean, they literally stopped in mid-sentence to stare at me. When I looked around, I found that I was the only male haunting the place. It was like entering a secret society without the proper password, and by the surprised looks they threw me, I might have been a zebra trotting through Hyde Park. Then, when Emma arrived, it got worse; they all tried to listen in on our conversation. It'll take me days to get over this experience!"

"I'll buy you a pint at the King's Arms. How did Emma seem?"

"Fine, but lost in thought."

"What was she wearing?"

"Wearing? I don't know, some blue thingy with a matching hat."

"Where is it? Where's the bracelet?"

Geoffrey handed it over.

The gold bracelet felt heavy in Sandy's hand, but it was as beautiful as he'd remembered. Half of the scarabs were a deep jade, the other half honey-yellow topaz. He pictured the first time he'd gone calling on Emma. She'd worn that bracelet and told him how much she cared for this last gift from her godfather, Lord Carnarvon. But now the tricky part; how was he going to return it?

***

Less than a week remained before the first leg of his journey to India on the *SS California*. The Mount Everest expedition had been wined, dined, and feted, and Sandy, along with the others, attended a series of parties in their honor. But while he feigned good humor, his sadness remained. As he readied for their party at the Savoy, he reflected on earlier in the day, when he had phoned Emma's home, but as usual, he got Smith, the butler. "Sorry, sir," he had said, "Miss Laughton is not at home."

Not at home for him was what the butler meant. As he finished dressing for his evening out, he slipped on his tuxedo coat, and as an afterthought slipped Emma's bracelet into his pocket. Might tempt the maid if he left it in the room. He then smiled grimly; it might be the closest he'd ever get to Emma again.

A cab dropped him in front of the Savoy, where the hotel's lights glinted and glowed like a mini-universe of stars. "Welcome, sir," said the doorman, sporting more brass buttons than a general. Sandy's shoes sunk into the plush rose and green carpet as he drifted by the trompe l'oeil murals of rural English countryside in summer, past elegant couples fizzy with gaiety and dressed to the nines for their night out. He felt an outsider, a shadow man who couldn't connect to other's happiness.

The bar area was packed and lively, but then, the Savoy always booked good bands. An eight-piece ensemble backed a platinum-blonde female with one of those new shingle cut hairstyles, swaying as she crooned, *"Ain't Nobody's Business if I do."* Sandy spotted his group in the back sipping cocktails. He wove his way through the crowd, and from his groups loud laughter, they'd been enjoying themselves for a while. Norton moved over to accommodate him, and behind him, a man let out a dirty laugh, "She can misbehave on my Charleston anytime she wants to."

Sipping his Manhattan, Sandy tapped a foot and listened to the band play that new American music called jazz. Idly, he glanced to his right and caught a glimpse of a tall red-headed woman wearing a metallic silver dress. Sandy stiffened. The shock was so overpowering he couldn't breathe. Emma! Excusing himself, he made straight for the dance floor, dodging twirling and swirling couples. He would give up anything, do anything, to have her back. He tapped the shoulder of her fiancé. "My turn to dance. Don't worry; I'm an old family friend."

The fiancé's amber eyes narrowed, and he shot Sandy an annoyed glance, but he reluctantly gave way and walked back to his table. For a moment, Emma stood stunned. "You," she said as he gathered her in his arms.

He spun her out through a doorway and foxtrotted to a deserted corner, where a trompe l'oeil wisteria vine climbed up the archway. "We need to talk, sweetheart." Then, leaning her against the wall, he implored, "Please, Emma! Hear me out. Oh lord, how I've missed you!"

Her eyes spit green fire at him. "Hear you out? You betrayer. What more is there?"

"I love you. I've been miserable without you, and I can't think of anyone but you."

She slapped him hard across the face, marched towards the dance floor, then turned around. "You bloody cad! And don't call me, sweetheart."

His voice cracked with emotion. "Emma, please stay for just one minute. I'm not proud of what I did, if I could change the past, I would. I was naïve, flattered and seduced by Marjory, but it wasn't love. You're love. The affair was over as soon as I met you. Since then, I've been faithful and will always be. But when I broke it off, Marjory pursued me, and wouldn't let it go. She came into my room uninvited that night. I was as shocked as you were. When you arrived, I was trying to escort her out."

"So you say." She looked over his shoulder to the bar. "By now, Freddie must be looking all over for me."

"Emma, think back. What was I wearing that night?"

She took a moment before answering. "A brown suit."

"If I were seducing Marjory, would I be wearing all those clothes, especially when you and I were about to go to dinner?"

Mixed emotions played across her face.

"Ask your closest childhood friend, Dickie. He'll tell you that I never went to see Marjory again, except for one time at a pub. I had to give her the courtesy of breaking it off in person. I owed that to her. God forbid that Dickie ever finds out about the affair, for I'll never tell him, but he does know that whenever I'm invited to Cornist Hall, I don't go. He innocently told Marjory I'd be in London buying supplies for the Everest expedition. That's how she knew I was there. Ask Dickie, he'll confirm it. That's all I ask."

"How can I trust you?"

"I made a mistake, a big one, but I didn't know you then. I do feel a cad for being involved with her. He looked at her meaningfully. "And I've paid for it."

He picked up her hand and placed it on his heart. "This will always belong to you. All I want is your happiness, so if you tell me that you don't love me, I'll go away. Forever."

She sighed and remained quiet.

Sandy continued. "I'm absolutely to blame. Just give me another chance to make it up to you. You'll never regret it."

She pushed back a lock of her hair. "When I saw Marjory peeking around the door, naked, I fell to pieces."

"I meant it when I said that all I want is to make you happy. I'll support your every endeavor, whether it's photography, Egyptology, or something else. Your goals are as important to me as my own. I've asked you before, and you said yes. Please marry me."

A slow smile played across her face, and she nodded. "Before I do, I will ask Dickie. And if I find out that you've lied to me about this…"

He wrapped his arms around her, and they held each other close until she finally said. "Freddie must be frantic. I have to go back."

"Freddie, be damned!" He reached into his pocket, pulled out the scarab bracelet, and wrapped it around her wrist.

Her eyes widened. She stroked the bracelet like it was a living thing. "How did you get this?"

"It doesn't matter; it belongs to you. The expedition's leaving in a couple of days, promise you'll wait for me until I get back."

She nodded. "I promise."

Chapter Sixteen

Nepal, present day

Dorje shifted uncomfortably in his wooden seat. He'd discovered, all luxury buses were booked, so reluctantly, he'd settled on this relic. Miserable, that's how he felt. With every pot-holed mile, his foul mood worsened. He paid little attention to the scenery of central Nepal; the water buffalos straining in their yokes, women with rolled up saris bending shin-deep in flooded paddies tending to young rice shoots, and vendors squatting by the side of the road selling wares.

Sweat trickled down the back of Dorje's neck. He yanked hard at the grimy window. Stuck. Sure it was. What else could he expect from this ancient junk heap as it traveled from Pokhara to Kathmandu, overloaded with passengers, crates of chickens, a piglet, and only held together by caked mud, rust, and bad karma?

Unzipping his black windbreaker, he pushed up the sleeves of his khaki t-shirt. Tall and muscular, his height and wide cheekbones reflected Kham Tibetan heritage. Hundreds of centuries ago, his ancestors migrated from the Tibetan plains into the high valleys of Nepal and were now called Sherpa or East People. Cursing his luck, Dorje swore by the multiple arms of Kali that never again would he take another bone-rattling bus ride.

When he wasn't thinking about his nephew, the purpose of his trip, he half-listened in on the conversation of a woman and her granddaughter sitting across the aisle, chatting about selling their produce in Kathmandu. They both wore identical dark shawls. The thin, wiry elderly woman was wrapped in a sari that might have been a vibrant yellow at one time but had faded to a washed-out cream. Her granddaughter's bright turquoise sari, though, looked new.

Many hours later, at twilight, Dorje was fuming, as the bus limped to a halt at the Kathmandu terminus. What was his oldest nephew up to? Dorje's sister was sick with worry and had insisted on Dorje visiting him before flying home to Namche Bazaar, the gateway to the Mount Everest region.

For the family, it had been a year of tragedy. His sister's husband had died, leaving her the owner of a trekking/climbing agency, which, although once profitable, now barely managed to make ends meet. At the age of twenty-two, his nephew was managing the company. Money was tight, but even so, his sister refused Dorje's offer of financial assistance. Stubborn woman. But then, he thought ruefully, that's what she accused him of being.

Dorje's career had been successful, but checkered. He'd been a British Gurkha soldier for five years, then a mountain guide, and now he was the proud owner of a lodge in the Mount Everest area. Up until a week ago, he'd been in Borneo and Malaysia for several months visiting friends who still were Gurkha soldiers with the British army. All he wanted was to be back home, but how could he say no to his sister?

After the bus stopped, he watched a young man in a red shirt shove the older woman in the faded yellow sari down the stairs. She stumbled, then sprawled in the dirt. A collective gasp rose from the passengers. Her granddaughter ran to help, but the red-shirted man ignored the commotion and left.

Dorje snapped. "You in the red shirt. Come back, and you were in such a hurry to get off the bus that you pushed that woman down the steps. Help her up."

The man shrugged his shoulders and continued walking.

"Dung eater. I'm talking to you." Dorje grabbed, lifted him up with one arm, and threw him into a nearby pile of garbage. Shock and fury tore across the man's face. He jumped up, brushed off the rotting refuse, and with fists balled headed for Dorje.

"I'm going to...."

"Going to what?" Dorje asked, with a wolfish grin and an open stance. For the first time that day, he was enjoying himself.

"Nothing," the man mumbled.

"I'll tell you what you're going to do. Tell that woman you're sorry."

Dorje frog-marched the man to where the old woman stood and listened until satisfied with the apology.

In the meantime, the driver had shimmied up to the roof, unlashed the luggage, and begun handing it down to waiting passengers. Dorje helped the woman and granddaughter with their woven baskets overflowing with cauliflower, eggplant, carrots, and root vegetables, into the back of a three-wheeled, exhaust-spewing *tuk-tuk* taxi.

"Danubad," the women said gratefully, before being swallowed up in traffic.

Kathmandu is a city of gods; their presence is felt everywhere. This is especially true in its heart, Durbar Square, an area so rich in cultural artifacts that it is a UNESCO World Heritage site, but the city still suffered from the disastrous aftermath of the 2015 earthquake. Repairs had been made, but there was much reconstruction ahead.

Strolling across the square, Dorje ignored the seventeenth-century brick palaces, the pagoda-styled temples, and the residence of the Living Goddess. He paid no attention to carvings of gods and goddesses locked in erotic embraces, the tourists, or the orange-robed Hindu holy men.

Dorje mulled over ways to help his sister and nephew. Only one solution came to mind, but would his nephew agree to it? Dorje turned up Freak Street, the decades-old destination for budget travelers. Bob Seger's hippy anthem *K-k-k-k-k-k*-Katmandu blared from a nearby momo restaurant. The 1960s Hippies long ago gave way to trekkers, climbers, and those seeking spiritual enlightenment, but the ghosts of hippies past remained in their music.

An hour later, Dorje reached Ring Road, the separator between Kathmandu and the suburb of Bansbari. After a fifteen-minute walk up the street, a Mercedes sedan passed slowed to a crawl, then stopped altogether, as if waiting for Dorje to catch up. Dorje's eyes narrowed, and his hand rested reassuringly for a brief moment on his Gurkha Khukuri knife. A tinted car window rolled down, and a man with hooded brown eyes and an aquiline nose leaned out. "Dorje. I thought I recognized your walk."

"Tommy."

Tommy certainly wasn't his Hindu name, but he dealt with so many ex-pats who couldn't pronounce it, he now just went by Tommy.

"What are you doing in Kathmandu?"

"Visiting my nephew," Dorje answered. "He just doesn't know it yet. What's the police commissioner doing slumming in Bansbari?"

"I'm on my way to Old Blue Throat."

"At this time of night? Why?"

"There's been a murder. The head priest is screaming for vengeance, so I thought I'd better go up myself. Say, you're just the man I need. Do you have to be anywhere right now?"

"Not really," Dorje answered.

"Talk about a coincidence, according to his papers, the dead man is from your neck of the woods. Maybe you know him."

A white-gloved driver jumped out and opened the car door, allowing Dorje to slide in. Soon they arrived at the empty Budhanilkantha Temple parking lot. The 1,500-year-old statue within (nicknamed Old Blue Throat) had been discovered in the 20th century by a farmer tilling his land. How such a stunningly crafted work of art ended up buried in the field in the first place remained a complete mystery.

At the edge of the parking lot, a harassed looking policeman waited next to an angry Hindu priest. When they came within earshot, the priest poured out a torrent of pent-up rage, and one-sentence galloped after the other. "A desecration. They must be punished! Lord Vishnu's shrine has been defiled. Such an abomination."

Dorje enjoyed watching Tommy in action, "Mr. Diplomacy," that's who he was. Tommy calmed the priest down with the usual assurances. It didn't hurt that Tommy's clan was a minor offshoot of Nepal's most powerful family, the Ranas. That, and being a distant cousin of the recently murdered king and queen. The priest would respect Tommy's caste and hear him out. Did Tommy know more about that Royal bloodbath then had been made public? Dorje suspected so; Tommy hadn't been Police Commissioner back then, but he'd have been privy to insider information.

Dorje refocused on the priest and Tommy's conversation. "Was anything taken from the shrine, or was Lord Vishnu vandalized?"

"No," The priest answered without hesitation, "but the desecration! A special *puja* ceremony has to be performed to drive away evil spirits."

"We won't take long, Dorje." Then the three men moved toward the shrine. Tommy was subtly reminding Dorje that non-Hindus were forbidden to enter Hindu shrines. That hardly mattered because from where he stood, Dorje could still listen in and observe. A wind rippled across the large pond, causing water to lap against the eighteen-foot, partially-submerged basalt statue of Lord Vishnu resting on a bed of coiled snakes.

The two men returned without the priest. The policeman looked curiously at Dorje, but when Tommy offered no introductions, he turned on his flashlight and led them to the murder site.

"The guard found him here, but I think he was stabbed over there." The flashlight played across the parking lot, and in the darkness, the pooled blood looked like one of the many oil slicks staining the lot. The body lay sprawled on the ground next to a thicket of bushes. The man had been short and stocky, and brutally beaten, and his shirt was bloody from stab wounds.

"Do you know him?" Tommy asked.

Dorje stared down at the swollen face. "Hard to tell with his face beaten like that."

"What do his papers say?"

"Nyi-ma Sherpa," the policeman answered.

Dorje looked thoughtful. "There's a thief by that name who steals from trekkers at restaurants and lodges."

Tommy turned to the policeman. "Was he dead when you found him?"

"Almost."

"Did he say anything useful?"

"Just that his fellow partners in crime were trying to steal his money, but they hadn't enough time to do a thorough search before the guard raised the alarm. Then he rambled about smuggling monster bones, and because of it, he was cursed. Probably wasn't in his right mind by then. I found his papers and money hidden in the lining of his jacket."

"Bones of monsters? You're sure he said monsters?"

The policeman nodded.

"What about the others?"

"Guard scared them away. When I arrived, the guard was trying to stop the bleeding, but it was like plugging up holes in a termite hill. The man said that he'd been betrayed. His last words were about a foreigner being in charge."

"A foreigner?"

"He died before I could ask him what he meant."

The wind picked up as he and Tommy walked back to the car. On the ride back, Dorje wondered if the Nyi-ma Sherpa lying in the parking lot was the petty thief known for lurking around and stealing from the lodges, and if so, how had he graduated into smuggling?

Tommy dropped Dorje off in Bansbari with an invitation. "Drop by, and we'll play poker."

Dorje walked by a crumbling wall on which a family of goats balanced, nibbling on the overhanging tree branches, then continued up a narrow lane to where it dead-ended at a brick-walled property. A sign read Salla Ghari Camp. He pounded on the gate.

A round-faced man with a thatch of thick black hair ran to open it. The compound itself contained three buildings, a stable, a vegetable garden, and about twenty lodgepole pine trees.

"Dorje!"

"Yes, Cook, it's me. Where's my nephew?"

"Out with friends."

"Is anyone rooming with you tonight?"

He shook his head.

"Then, I will. If you see my nephew, tell him I'm here."

Chapter Seventeen

Nepal, present day

The following morning Dorje found Cook warming tea and gruel on a camp stove. When he spotted Dorje, he ladled out the gruel and handed it to Dorje along with a cup of tea.

When Dorje finished, Cook handed him a plate with a piece of pie on it. "Try this dish. It's a new recipe."

Dorje took a bite then spat it out. "Are you trying to poison me? This can't be right."

"Maybe it needs more sugar," Cook answered.

"Where's Basu?"

Cook pointed to the other side of the house. "I told him you were here; he's cleaning and going over equipment."

Dorje found Basu along with a porter surrounded by ropes, ice axes, tents, and miscellaneous trekking and climbing equipment.

Basu dropped the ice ax he'd been polishing. "Uncle. It's good to see you."

"Don't 'uncle' me. No one tells me anything, and you're the worst. Your mother thinks you and your brother are up to something. And she's usually right. And what's the matter with that fat cook of yours. He tried to poison me with some strange foreign dish that looks like yellow pudding and tastes like vinegar."

"It's his lemon meringue pie. Cook's testing recipes on us before our climbing group comes. Foreigners like it."

Dorje motioned for the porter to leave. "Well, I don't. Give me tsampa or Sherpa stew any day. Let's go to the office. Your mother insisted I talk with you and go over the books. But you haven't answered my question. Why wasn't I told?"

"Told what, uncle?"

"Something's going on, your mother said. What is it?"

A look of desperation flashed across Basu's face, but he crossed his arms in defiance. "We've lost… lost a lot of money, but we'll make it up. We have a climbing group scheduled for Ama Dablam, and our treks to Mount Everest and around Annapurna are full. That'll help pay the bills. I can handle it. Turn the company around."

Dorje gentled his voice, "I never thought you couldn't handle it. But, Basu, be honest, I'm here to help, now tell me, just how bad is it?"

Basu choked up. His voice broke as he continued, "The family home is mortgaged, but worse still, Dawa is dead. He was our best high-altitude Sherpa. They think he was murdered by Maoists." Basu wiped his eyes. "He was my closest friend, and I still can't believe he was killed. I was prepared for my fathers' death because he was sick, but not for Dawa's."

"Was he political?"

"No. Dawa completely stayed away from politics. That's why I can't understand it."

Dorje gave Basu a big bear hug then rested his hand consolingly on his shoulder. "Sometimes, there are no good answers. Tell me about the climbs and trekking groups."

Basu went over to a shelf and pulled out a ledger. "First climb's Ama Dablam. I've interviewed three Sherpas to replace Dawa as sirdar. Right now, I'm deciding on which one to hire. But you know how expensive sirdars are."

Dorje plopped down in a chair with a sigh. "How will you pay him? Your father was a top mountain climber and guide, one of the best, but no businessman. Especially at the end when he was so sick. He's left you and the family with a pile of debt and a climbing company on the edge of ruin, but we will turn it around. You've just found your high altitude sirdar. Me."

Basu's eyes widened. "Uncle, you want to be the head guide? You haven't climbed in years, and you're old."

Dorje pulled up his shirt, exposing his chest. "Old? What are you talking about? I'm only forty-two and in great shape!"

He turned his body for Basu to view and preened. "I'll lose this fast," he said, patting his slight paunch, "I still have time to train before your group comes."

Basu frowned, not convinced. "What about your lodge at Namche Bazaar? Can you afford not to be there during the trekking season?"

"The lodge runs itself. When you have competent staff as I do, they do the work, and I get the credit." Dorje started coughing. "By the multiple arms of Kali, every year, Kathmandu's pollution gets worse and worse." Dorje opened a window to let a breeze blow through. "Smells as bad as a dog's fart out there."

Dorje took out his large Khukuri knife, issued to him while serving as a British Gurkha soldier, and his smaller Karda knife. Even though the blades were kept razor-sharp, it relaxed him to hone them, and more importantly, helped him to think.

They sat beneath a *Visit Nepal* poster, which was taped up on the wall since day one. The snow-crested Himalayan giants, Everest, Nuptse, and Lhotse, loomed over the Khumbu Glacier and were backlit by a full moon. Year by year, the poster had progressively aged until finally achieving the amber patina of an old painting. "Anything else?" Dorje asked. "Now's the time to tell me."

Basu's face became pinched with worry. "I didn't tell mother, but Ang stole from us. I tried getting the money back, but Ang insisted father had given him the money for an investment that failed. Father signed paperwork, so I couldn't prove Ang was lying. Then when father died, he quit."

"Your father's brain tumor affected his thinking. When I get hold of Ang, I'll stick my arm down his gullet until he coughs up the money or his lungs. That family has bad blood flowing through them. Where is he anyway?"

"In Tibet, on business. After he left us, he started up his own trekking and climbing agency. It's on Durbar Marg, the most expensive area in Kathmandu. They say he has a silent partner who's funding him. I think he took a list of our clients with him, and now he's trying to take away our business."

"How many on the Ama Dablam climb?"

Basu handed him a list.

"A woman's on it! All we need is some helpless woman to get frightened and freeze up on the mountain. We're Sherpas, not babysitters."

"She wrote that she was researching the 1924 Mount Everest climb."

Dorje sheathed his knife. "An ancestor of ours was on that expedition." He sat back deep in thought, then changed the subject. "Is your brother still happy studying in America?"

"As far as I know. His scholarship lasts for another year, but even so, he's been helping us."

"How can he help you from the States?" Dorje asked.

"With IT help."

Dorje and his nephew stared at each other.

Dorje tapped his fingers on the desk, "All right, do I have to drag it out of you? Who or what's an IT?"

"Information technology. Pasang built our web site, and when I need it updated, I e-mail him information for posting. It was my idea to market climbs in the Khumbu, but we couldn't have done it without Pasang's help."

"Is that it?"

"It's good to have you here, uncle."

"In the future, tell your mother what's going on. She has a sixth sense when something's not right. If you don't, she'll just worry more. See to it that Cook prepares something edible for tonight."

***

Later on, Dorje and Basu were repairing the outside wall surrounding the compound, which had incurred structural damage from the last earthquake.

Dorje slapped a dollop of mortar onto a brick, then smoothed it out and handed it to Basu. "Tomorrow night, I'm having dinner with Dr. Steve from the CONTAC Medical clinic, then, afterward, I might go to the Rum Doodle to see who's there."

Just don't drink too much," Basu replied with a shudder. "Remember, you're the lead on the climb. You have to be in good condition. I remember what happened the last time you went to the Rum Doodle."

"Why bring that up? I didn't start it. Arrogant bastards. Those men had belittled the reputation of Tensing Norgay, so what could I do? And I paid for the broken tables and chairs. Besides, both men were only in the hospital for a day."

Chapter Eighteen

London, England present day

The Foreigner's arms dipped deeply as he counted out his sit-ups; ninety-eight, ninety-nine, one hundred. At one hundred ten, his muscles spasmed. Then he dipped even deeper until his chest kissed the plush wall-to-wall carpeting. After five days of no exercise, he was paying the price.

After finishing his workout, he wiped down his sweat-soaked body and looked around the hotel room. Why was it that they all exuded the same transient feeling, even the high-end ones? His thoughts then traveled to the red diamond. Except for a twist of fate, that stone should have been his. If only Sandy Irvine had kept the two diamonds together when he died! The Foreigner twisted his towel and seethed. After weeks of obsessing about it, he knew he was right; the solution lay in Sandy's note.

After so many readings, the faded writing had become as familiar to him as his own. He knew the words by heart.

Noel,

It's bloody cold up here, but we're giving it one last push! If something happens to me, make sure this stone goes to Emma Laughton at Fairy Glenn, Thistlebloom Lane in Little Brough, Cumbria,

*England. She already has the other one, so this will
make a matching pair. Depend on you to make sure it
gets mailed to Emma.*
    Sandy

The Foreigner considered the era, the 1920s. Sandy Irvine hadn't much money, so Emma would naturally have thought the gem a garnet. It would be her last keepsake from him so she wouldn't have sold it. Too bad, Emma was a pile of moldy bones in some graveyard and couldn't be questioned. But who was she? A girlfriend? Sister or cousin? Friend? No, not a friend or a sister. Jewels were far too intimate. Emma had to have been a lover. She wouldn't have sold it; it would have been too precious to her, so her heir must have it. It made sense that the woman Hansi told him about must be Emma's descendant.

He checked the calendar on his iPhone. Only six days of vacation left. But that should be enough time to fly to the Lake District to see if the house in Little Brough still existed and then find out who lived there.

The flight was short and uneventful, and after deplaning, he proceeded to rentals. The bored glance of a customer service representative skipped over him as the Foreigner filled out the rental car paperwork. Outside, dark clouds thick as bog scum hung over the Newcastle countryside. Shivering, he turned the heat in the car to high. Though it was still fall, snow flurries coated the windshield.

The Foreigner ignored the picturesque towns that rolled by; he had no interest in local history or beauty. Instead, his thoughts swirled around Irvine's note, the diamond, and Emma. But what if too much time had gone by? After all, the trail was almost one hundred years old. What if no one had heard of Emma? What if she hadn't heirs? Then what? He gritted his teeth and refused to let negative thoughts intrude. That diamond would be his. He'd be able to get Hansi the thirty million.

Sleet turned to rain as he reached Little Brough. He left the A 66, which serviced the town and followed a rutted country road towards rounded hills. The rain lessened, and a sliver of weak sunshine peeked out from behind the clouds. Continuing on the way for several miles, he stopped when the road forked, then turned left up a narrow track. After ten minutes, the lane petered out into a field. A dead end. He reread his map and realized he should have taken the road before this one. He tried making a U-turn, but the tires spun impotently in the mud. Cursing, he got out. The rain intensified, and cold droplets trickled down the back of his neck like glacial melt. He assessed the damage. Stuck in the fucking mud. He rocked the car over and over, then gave a mighty heave. On the fourth heave, the vehicle moved.

He continued for another several miles, then turned left. Later, in the deepening shadows, he found a solitary stone cottage surrounded by an over-grown garden. The mailbox read Fairy Glen. As the car crept down the rutted lane, he searched for signs of life. Nothing. No lights, no smoke from the chimney, just the steady drumbeat of pelting rain.

When he reached the house, he noted that leaves had piled up on the right side of the door like a snowdrift of old newspapers. No one had been here for weeks, or even possibly months.

He rapped hard on the front door. Unsurprisingly, there was no answer. He tried the doorknob. Locked. Taking out a credit card, he finessed the lock until it opened. Could it be this easy? He turned on his flashlight and looked in. Deserted.

Spotting a light switch, he turned it on. Nothing, obviously the electricity had been turned off.

He switched his flashlight to high and followed the beam as it skipped around the cottage. Near the small kitchen stood a dining table and chairs of good quality but marred and scuffed from age and use. To the right of that was the bedroom. I'll start with the bedroom he decided, that's where most people keep valuables. Then room by room, he conducted his search.

In less than two hours, he had given the home a thorough sweep. He'd found the secret compartment in the desk, but it yawned emptily. The red diamond wasn't in the cottage; he was absolutely sure of that. So where in the hell was that damn diamond?

The neighbors, they would know who the owner was, yes, but they'd be far too curious. The Land Registry? Not enough time. Then he smiled, of course, someone in the neighboring town would know, and if he asked, there'd be no gossip.

Chapter Nineteen

The Lake District, England present day

By the time the Foreigner reached the closest village, his temper was under control. Losing his temper was something he couldn't afford to do. A stream divided the Victorian town full of picturesque shops. The freestanding market clock painted banker's green read 6:15 p.m. It didn't take him long to find the post office, but inside it was as dark as a black hole. Cruising around, he spotted lights still turned on at a greengrocer. Parking the car around the corner and out of sight, he went inside.

A plump woman in a floral frock that stretched tight around her bosom looked up and greeted him. "Just about to close. Can I help you? Are you lost? Don't have many visitors this time of year."

Picking up some tins of food, he put them on the counter and smiled. "I was thinking about buying a property in the area. I'm a writer and want a private place."

"Is that right, sir? Can't think of any property around here for sale or rent."

"When I was driving around, I saw a pretty cottage up by Brough Castle. On Twistlebloom Road. It appeared empty with no sign of anyone living there. "

"Oh, you'd be meaning Fairy Glenn. Mrs. Laughton recently passed on, and the cottage went to her granddaughter, an American girl."

"Is there a way of contacting her?"

The woman took his money, put the tins into a paper bag, and said. "An interesting story, sir. The solicitor's wife told me that the young American had never even met her grandmother before, can you imagine that? Didn't even know she was alive."

His mood lifted. She had information. "Has the same family owned it for a while?"

"Why, yes. For as long as I can remember."

The continuous ring of a phone shattered the quiet. "Excuse me, sir." She left him and went to the far counter, picked it up, and started chatting.

His mood shifted. *She's forgotten that I'm even here.* He purposely dropped the bag and watched the tins spill out on the floor. The clatter caused her to turn around and stare at him in surprise. "Sorry, Muriel, but I've got to go now. I've got a customer. We'll talk later."

The Foreigner picked up the tins, keeping his smile plastered on his face. "Sorry for being so clumsy."

"No harm was done, sir. Let me help you with that."

"You mentioned that the same family had owned the cottage."

"Oh yes, the Laughton's have owned Fairy Glenn since before World War 1. But that family certainly had their share of tragedies. Before the Great War, my gran said they had a home in London, plenty of money, and used Fairy Glenn as a summer cottage. But the head of the family hadn't a knack for finance. Then, when his son died in the battle of, now, what did my gran tell me?" She paused for a moment to think.

"Oh yes, it was the Battle of the Somme. The father died shortly after from a broken heart, they say. He left his only daughter, Emma, with a little bit of money, and the cottage was left to her by a cousin or maybe an uncle. Emma was pregnant too. Bless her soul, with no husband. Raised her daughter, Lydia, here. But the daughter was a wild one and moved to London as soon as she was eighteen. Had several bad marriages, I hear. Finally, she came back to live here when her mum died. She's the one who passed away. The daughter that is."

"Do you know the name of the American girl? The one who inherited?"

She pursed her lips and stared ahead. "Seem to recollect the last name was a type of American biscuit. What was it now?"

"Oh yes, Graham, her name was Cynthia Graham. Comes all the way from California. A place called Pasadena, next to Los Angeles, it is. I always wanted to visit Los Angeles and see the stars. My wouldn't that be fun? The solicitor will be in his office tomorrow if you want him to contact her."

"I may do that," he said, picking up the bag and strolling out the door.

All the troubles he'd had today were worth it. He wouldn't need the solicitor. He had her name and knew where she lived.

***

Back in Newcastle, the mist and fog obscured the city's industrial edges and softened its gritty character. Driving into the heart of town, he got a hotel room for the night. Booting up his laptop, he first created an e-mail account under a fictitious name, then he Googled the online White Pages and read down the list. No Cynthia Graham listed. But there was a C.L. Graham on Palmetto Drive.

He tried that number first. A voice mail message switched on to explain that she was out of the country. Was it the right woman? If so, she might have a family in the area. The White Pages showed forty Grahams. He began phoning the list and was at the J's when his luck held.

"John Graham?"

"Yes," he answered with a tinge of irritation as if anticipating a telemarketer.

The Foreigner's voice dripped honey. "Don't know if I have the right person, but I'm looking for Cynthia Graham, and I was wondering if you might be a relative."

The voice registered concern. "Why, yes, I'm her father. Is something wrong with Cynthia?"

The Foreigner answered in a calm, soothing voice. "I certainly didn't mean to alarm you. As far as I know, she's perfectly fine. I had learned she owns a cottage in England's Lake District. And I'm interested in buying it."

The voice warmed up. "What sort of numbers are we talking about? As I mentioned, I'm her father."

"How can I reach her?"

"She's in Nepal, mountain climbing. I'd be happy to consider your offer and advise her."

The Foreigner's grip on the phone tightened. Had he heard, right? Nepal. That was his next stop. "What a coincidence, I'm a mountain climber too, which mountain is she climbing?"

There was a pause then the rustle of papers. "I don't know how to say it, but I'll spell it out for you, AMA DABLAM."

"I know that mountain. What hotel is she staying at?" The Foreigner asked.

There was a slight pause and a definite cooling in the voice. "I can't give you that information, because the sale will go through me."

"Of course, of course, I'll be happy to work with you, but I need to crunch some numbers first."

"Call me back when you're ready to talk then. You can move in right away if you'd like."

"Thanks." Perfect, he thought, clicking off the phone, just perfect. She's in Nepal; now, all I just have to find her. But of all the mountains in Nepal to climb, why Ama Dablam? It was the name etched on that old photo from Sandy Irvine's camera. A coincidence? Or did she have information that he hadn't?

He popped a lemon drop into his mouth. As it melted away, he considered. What they say about killing is true. It does become easier. He hadn't expected to like it, but he had. The power he felt when he shoved the Chinese man into the crevasse. But he knew better than to get complaisant or sloppy. That's how you get caught. He was smart, much smarter than most. And once he found Cynthia, he'd question her thoroughly, very thoroughly, and if she didn't cooperate, well, whatever he had to do to get the diamond, he would.

Chapter Twenty

Kathmandu, Nepal present day

Laughter and music floated up from a cocktail party hosted on the British Embassy grounds as Dorje strode by. Fear of terrorist attacks prompted the embassy to install new gates and add additional guards, and the days of lax security and friendly smiles were long gone. Dorje had attended embassy functions in the past, and could readily picture the ambassador entertaining his guests with his collection of bad jokes and old puns. At least the drinks flowed freely. He remembered the hot sex he had with a woman he'd met there one night. Always had a soft spot for New Zealanders, and there she was with her dark eyes and even darker wit. What a month of passion it'd been.

Under the watchful eyes of two Gurkha soldiers, he turned down a narrow lane and followed it until it dead-ended at a walled compound, the oldest in the neighborhood.

Dorje yelled out, "Open up."

An older man shuffled from the shadows and wordlessly tugged the sagging gate open then wrestled it shut. Dorje continued up a winding gravel path around a giant banyan tree with aerial roots raking the soil like an eagle's talons. Overhead, in the lush, overgrown garden, birds flitted from branch to branch hunting for insects. After rounding a curve, the path ended at a three-story white stucco building, built in the early 1900s.

Although loosely defined as a palace, the structure ahead was more mansion-sized, and in an apparent state of disrepair. The cream stucco exterior was chipped and broken, and vines as thick as an elephant's leg twisted up the front and wrapped around the Victorian building like huge boa constrictors. Dorje knocked on Dr. Steve Kaiser's door, and moments later, it opened.

"Glad you could come. It's been a while," said the tall American doctor, extending his hand in greeting. Dorje shook it, noting that the doctor's skin was smooth and well cared for.

Years ago, a Sherpa with a fractured leg had been the cause of their initial meeting. Dorje had half carried the man to a clinic which Steve Kaiser had operated in the Khumbu. Later on, when Steve transferred down to Kathmandu, occasionally, they'd run into each other and go out for a beer.

Dorje noted the dark circles under the doctor's eyes and his burnt-out demeanor and wondered why the invitation to dinner. Steve seemed more in need of sleep than company.

"My cook's gone for the day, but the food's warming in the kitchen. Make yourself comfortable while I pour you a drink."

The dining room was a welcome surprise. While the exterior of the house appeared to be barely holding itself together, the interior gleamed with fresh paint and recent re-stuccoing. An oil painting of a Rana nobleman replete with a military uniform dripping with medals hung above the fireplace. He went over to take a closer look.

"Jung Bahadur," Dorje said, as Steve offered him a drink.

"You recognize him? I found the painting in the attic covered with mice droppings and cobwebs. I liked it, so hung it in a place of honor. Who was he?"

"The founder of the Rana dynasty here. His family stayed in power for over a hundred years, intermarried with the Shahs, and one of his descendants was the murdered queen Aishwarya."

"2001, what a bloodbath," Steve replied. "And still all of these conspiracy theories swirl around, everyone blamed from the CIA, the Chinese, the Indians, the Russians, to even the prince's uncle."

Dorje glanced around. "Not many Westerners live in a Rana palace."

"True. Aren't many left, but I love it. The owner calls it a drafty old ruin. Luckily for me, his taste runs to modern architecture. Part of the rental agreement was that I would spend my own money fixing up the interior. I'll get dinner out before it cools."

Steve brought out dishes of momos, spicy lamb vindaloo with achaar, rice, palak paneer, and for dessert, lemon meringue pie; the pie Dorje eyed with distaste.

Both men were hungry, so they ate their meal in relative silence.

A slight tremor rattled the building, followed by a more definite shudder. The living room chandelier swung back and forth like an out-of-control trapeze.

Steve's face turned as white as the plaster covering the walls. "Second time this week."

"Monks predict a big quake soon. There've been small shakes up in the Khumbu too," Dorje said.

Steve exhaled slowly. "Do they? Then this building will collapse into a pile of rubble with me buried beneath."

"Get yourself a dragon painting or amulet."

"Why so?"

"Protects against earthquakes and fire." Dorje glanced over to a large cabinet filled with skulls, bones, and eggs. How's your fossil collection coming along?"

Steve enthusiastically opened the ornately carved cabinet and passed Dorje a recent purchase. "Bought this from a supplier specializing in Gobi Desert fossils. My larger ones are back home in the States, but I keep some smaller ones here to study. Dinosaur eggs of the Cretaceous period are my passion. The creatures laid their eggs in nests, just like birds."

"How do you study them?"

"Several different ways. Sometimes I take thin slices and view them under a microscope, or I'll use the clinic's CAT scan to penetrate an egg's exterior. It allows me to focus on microstructures."

A massive skull with fifteen-inch teeth caught Dorje's eye, and he tried to imagine what the saber-toothed tiger must have looked like when alive. "How much, say, for this one?"

Steve sighed. "Mine is an expensive hobby. Some collectors spend hundreds of thousands of dollars. At home, I have a … Well, never mind. It's the jewel in my collection. I've heard that extremely rare fossils are being smuggled into Nepal. A contact showed me photos of several specimens, so unique, they're worth a fortune."

Steve's eyes slid away from Dorje's. "My contact said there's a new player in the business. Smuggles the illegal stuff through your area."

"Who is he?"

"That's the million-dollar question. No one knows. He's being very careful, and uses intermediaries."

Smuggling was a way of life, but why would anyone spend good money on old bones, Dorje wondered. Then a thought crossed his mind. Where was Steve getting that kind of money? Western doctors in Nepal don't earn much, and he had been talking hundreds of thousands of dollars.

Steve interrupted his thoughts by lovingly stroking a Troodon egg. "A real beauty, isn't it? My collection grows by fits and starts. Heard they discovered a new oviraptor from the Gobi, a bigger and stranger specimen than they've found so far."

Dorje cocked an eyebrow and waited. "What's an oviraptor?"

"A birdlike dinosaur. Had feathers but couldn't fly."

Steve threw him an intent look. "What are you doing in Kathmandu?"

"Helping out the family business, by leading a climb."

Dorje fished a moth from his drink. "Be careful with your old bones, Steve. If you're doing anything illegal, it could be a dangerous hobby. I heard that Chinese soldiers gunned down fossil hunters just last month. The Chinese play for keeps."

Steve's tone hardened. "I don't buy illegal fossils." Changing the subject, he said. "Remember how beautiful, green, and quiet it used to be outside of Kathmandu? With water buffalo pulling plows, fields of crops. During the season you could see the mountains. Now the farmland has been eroded, and we're left with traffic jams, pollution, and overcrowding, like any big city.

"If we're not wise," Dorje added, "We'll destroy ourselves. Pollution and ugliness won't attract tourists."

Steve nodded. "So you're leading a climb. Lucky you, I'd love to go myself. One of the doctors up at Pheriche is going on holiday next month, so I'll cover him and be in the area for a month. The clinic's not far from Ama Dablam. Wouldn't have enough time for a climb but would for a visit."

"Come then. We'll be there for weeks."

A shudder, more intense than the first, shook the Palace. Plaster cracked and fell from the walls onto the hand-woven Tibetan rugs. Lights flickered. The cabinet storing the fossils crashed to the ground spilling out fossils.

Dorje and Steve braced themselves under a door frame. For long seconds the shaking continued, then the roiling stopped.

"My fossils!"

"Careful!" Dorje cautioned, picking his way over broken glass.

They struggled to raise the heavy cabinet and finally managed it. Right afterward, Steve made a beeline to a medium-sized box on the floor. Steve opened the box but blocked Dorje's view. Intentional or not? Dorje wondered. Steve shut the box and clicked the lock.

What was Steve hiding from him? Fossils? Or something else?

"It could have been worse," Steve said, his face tight with tension. "The rug acted like a cushion. Only one skull is damaged beyond repair."

"Might be a good time to move," Dorje commented.

Steve's voice steadied. "I probably should."

Striding over to the French doors at the rear of the house, he flung them open, and the scent of jasmine wafted in. Moonlight bathed a large veranda and the garden beyond where flamboyant cannas grew in showy yellow and red spikes along with an ancient bougainvillea, so dense with purple bracts and so towering that it screened the rest of the garden from view. "This is why I stay. I fell in love with old Nepal, and this is a rare link to the past."

Steve left the doors ajar but closed the screens. He ran his fingers through his thinning hair as a bat fluttered by and winged its way into the inky darkness. "Nasty flying rats. Get the chills just looking at them. They roost by the hundreds at the Royal Palace then come here to feed."

Dorje answered with a twinkle in his eye. "Steve, bats could help you."

"How's that?"

"My grandmother was a healer; she said bat oil grows hair on bald men."

Steve chuckled and once again changed the subject. "Did you know that Nova, National Geographic, or one of those large groups, is funding an expedition to find Mallory's camera and Irvine's body."

"I did. The group has hired Khumbu men to carry in supplies," Dorje answered.

"From Nepal? Wouldn't it be easier to bring supplies in from Tibet?"

"With the Chinese crackdown, it's difficult. The group needed special supplies to be brought in quickly if you call yak caravans quick."

"Which route?"

"Nang-La. Sherpas have used the pass for generations. Not easy but doable. What I don't understand is why can't they leave Irvine's body alone. He's long dead."

Steve tapped his pipe. "Too fascinating a mystery. As you know, they located Mallory's body but not Irvine's. That leaves the world's greatest climbing mystery still unsolved; did Mallory and Irvine summit Mount Everest first or not? This expedition thinks they've pinpointed where Irvine died on the mountain. A Chinese climber, Xu Jing, viewed the body of an Englishman dressed in old-fashioned climbing gear on Mount Everest in 1975 at about 27,000 feet. He said that 'The body was lying in a concave hollow or gully running down from the ridge crest.'

Steve continued. "New rumors are circulating about that Mallory climb. Gossip has it that a Chinese climber has found Mallory's camera. Not the Chinese man who discovered the body but someone else. Kept quiet about it until he could sell it. Probably a tall tale."

Dorje brushed plaster dust from his pants. "If it's true, he'd have a fortune in his hands."

Steve lit his pipe. "But you have to ask yourself, if the camera were already bought, why hasn't it emerged?"

Dorje shrugged. "Maybe the photos were no good. After all these years, the film would be bad."

Steve looked thoughtful. "There have been articles written on the subject of film preservation. According to the Kodak Company, if the film stays frozen until it's developed, it could be salvaged. Those pictures would be worth millions. Speaking of rumors, interestingly enough, there's a new theory going around."

"What's the theory?" Dorje asked.

"That there was more than one camera. Some say two and others three."

Steve walked over to his floor to ceiling bookshelves, which, slightly askew, had managed to stay upright during the quake. He pulled out a black box the size of a small paperback book. "Another hobby of mine. I confess to being completely intrigued by the whole mystery." Opening the box, he extracted a camera and handed it to Dorje.

"Same year and model as Mallory's, a Vest Pocket Model B made in 1924. Mine has no film inside, but you can buy film from specialty stores, I just haven't gotten around to ordering any yet."

Dorje stared through the viewfinder then snapped the shutter. A sharp click filled the room. "Who told you the story about the Chinese man? The man selling the camera?"

"Someone you know, your nephew's sirdar, Dawa. He came in for Diamox pills for altitude sickness. I was sorry to hear that he was killed a few days later by the Maoists. Seemed very excited, mentioned he was coming into a lot of money soon."

"Did he?" Dorje replied thoughtfully as he stood up to go. Did that money have anything to do with his death, he wondered.

Just then, the guard came to the door speaking in rapid Nepali to Steve. "An emergency at the clinic. There's a car waiting out front for you."

Dorje hurriedly said his goodbyes, then followed the lane towards Kantipath, where a swarm of bats swooped overhead like a plume of black smoke and disappeared into the trees. As he walked up Bans Bari, he wondered about the big money Dawa was referring to. He came from a poor family. Would Basu know? They'd been close friends.

***

"Nephew, wake up. We need to talk."

Basu turned in his cot and blinked groggily at his uncle. "What? What's wrong?"

"Dr. Kaiser brought up Dawa tonight. Did Dawa mention coming into money?"

Basu rubbed his eyes and sat up. "Dawa? Not to me. The only money Dawa had was his salary from us."

"That's what I thought," Dorje said. He walked towards his shared room, thinking hard. Who was paying Dawa? And for what?

Chapter Twenty-One

Kathmandu, Nepal present day

The eighteen lodgepole pines growing tall and spear-like on the Salla Ghari Camp compound was a well-known landmark for international pilots, who, on a clear day, used them as a visual guide. Turn left at the pines, then prepare for the descent into the Kathmandu airport.

Dorje glanced up at a pair of bearded vultures resting on one of the pines. No one knew why one particular pine, situated halfway between the house and stable, attracted the pair, but year after year, it was their tree of choice.

One flapped its massive wings, then quieted down as Dorje passed on his way to the stable, while the other remained still as a temple guardian. Cook was particularly fond of the big birds and threw out the occasional chicken carcass or handfuls of offal their way. They soon recognized Cook and were particularly watchful when he was outside. Not that long ago, tens of thousands of the magnificent birds soared on the Himalayan thermals, but now, due to the chemical Diclofenac, vultures teetered on the verge of extinction. Those birds would wait patiently on a hillside, then swoop down to Tibetan sky burials where a human corpse, chopped up according to Buddhist custom, would be laid out for them to feed on, and in so doing would continue the cycle of life.

From vultures, Dorje's thoughts steered to last night's conversation with Dr. Steve Kaiser. Dorje was a village elder, and anger pumped through him, knowing that in the two months he'd been away, a new smuggling ring had reached its tentacles into the Khumbu. Who the hell was the mastermind?

Smuggling was a fact of life, but not all smuggling was equal. For centuries, the high passes provided trade between Tibet, Nepal, and India; some legal, some not so, but the last thing he wanted was for the area to be overrun by Kathmandu police. He grimaced at the thought of the drug ring of thirty men who had been caught up in a sting, but the ring leader managed to escape the police net. No one wanted a repeat of that. After the Ama Dablam climb, he'd sniff around to get answers.

Then there was Dawa. Murdered and with a baby on the way. He expected to receive a lot of money. For what? From whom? After the Ama Dablam climb, he'd sniff around to get answers about that too.

The sound of footsteps brought him back to the present. He pivoted to find a concerned-looking Basu. "Uncle, this is the third night in a row you've been sleeping in the stable. Is something wrong?"

"I don't like sharing a room with Cook. Snores so damn loud that I'd rather sleep next to a garbage-rooting pig."

"Use my room; I'll sleep with him."

Dorje glanced back at the small brick house with its elaborately carved peacock window and the adjoining shed housing climbing supplies. Clapping Basu on the shoulder, he said, "I feel cooped up and need to think. The stable is good enough for the likes of me. Besides, your elephant is a lot better looking, than some of the women around here."

Recognizing his voice, the small elephant called Laksmi lumbered up to the divider and touched Dorje with her trunk. Currently, she was the sole occupant of the stable, and the stall was widened to accommodate her size. A barrel of drinking water was on the north side, and a few wisps of hay from her dinner lay on the floor. Dorje patted her thick, leathery chest. "Tonight, we're roommates, old girl." He eyed his nephew. "Remember, when you're ready to settle down, Namche Bazaar is the place to get a good looking wife."

He threw his sleeping bag on a pile of hay and grasses at the far end of the stable. Basu returned to the house, Laksmi settled down in her stall, and Dorje drifted off to sleep.

It was late when Dorje was jolted awake. He listened intently to the faint sound of muffled conversation, followed by approaching footsteps. Basu or Cook? Why would they be out this time of night? Two figures crept stealthily into the stable. A flashlight beam skipped here and there before settling at Laksmi's stall.

"Over here. Give it to me."

The taller figure rummaged through his pack.

"Hurry!"

The taller figure pulled out something from a bag and carefully handed it over. "Why does he want to kill it?"

"It doesn't matter why. He just does." He dropped a brown ball of food about the size of three fists into the stall, they both watched the elephant lumber over and then examine it.

"Okay. We're done. Let's go."

"No. We have to make sure it eats it. He'll ask."

Dorje had heard enough. He slipped out of his sleeping bag as quietly as only an ex-Gurkha soldier could, unsheathed his Karda knife and tiptoed toward them. Crouching low, he moved silently forward, skirting the beam of moonlight from the open stable door, and staying within the shadows. So intently were the men watching Laksmi, that they didn't spot him until Dorje spun the taller one around and kneed him in the groin. Doubling over in pain, the man fell writhing to the ground. The shorter, stockier man's reflexes were unexpectedly lightning fast. Pivoting on his right foot, the shorter man karate chopped Dorje's wrist. Dorje dropped his knife and watched it skid across the hard-packed floor and land out of sight. Mentally Dorje cursed himself. He was too cocky, too sure of himself. He knew better than that.

The shorter man grabbed the shovel leaning against the wall and came at him swinging. Dorje ducked, but one blow landed on his shoulder with a sickening thud. When it came down again, Dorje grabbed the handle, wrenching it away. The man he'd kneed in the groin recovered enough to grab Dorje's arms from behind. As the tall man locked his arms around him in a tight embrace, the shorter man pulled out a gun. Dorje kicked up, and it flew out of his hand. All three men dove for it.

The shorter man reached the gun first and fired. A searing pain shot up Dorje's left shoulder, but ignoring the pain, he tossed the taller figure to the ground then scrambled to get clear. He felt a bullet whizz by him. Running deep into the shadows, he frantically searched for his knife. In a beam of moonlight, he saw a glint of metal flash near his sleeping bag. Picking it up, he aimed, and let it fly.

"Ayyee," screamed the tall man, clenching his leg,

Behind them, house lights flickered on.

"Let's get out of here." The shorter man half carried the other to the gate and melted into the darkness.

Dorje stood torn. Should he follow them or not? No, Laksmi came first; he needed to figure out what the bastards had been up to. In the near distance, Dorje heard the sound of a car racing away.

Basu and Cook rushed into the stable. Basu was bare-chested but dressed in a pair of jeans. Cook just wore his underpants. They both looked at Dorje.

"I heard gunshots. What's wrong? " his nephew cried out.

Dorje glanced down, then gingerly touched his shoulder to assess the damage. Blood streamed down his arm, and he was beginning to feel woozy. There was no exit hole, so the bullet had to be still inside. He picked up his gray t-shirt from the floor and tied it around his arm to staunch the blood.

Basu was instantly at Dorje's side. "Uncle, you're bleeding!"

"The hell with me. Check on Laksmi! They were trying to kill her."

Dorje, Basu, and Cook raced to her stall. Laksmi's mouth yawned open, exposing a pink tongue and huge molars, she picked up the ball of food with her trunk and was about to eat it.

"Laksmi. No! Drop it!"

She stared balefully at Dorje with her wise eyes, as if thinking it over, but then slowly, reluctantly, dropped it.

He stepped inside and patted her wrinkled hide. "Good girl."

Outside of the stall, he kicked the brown ball open, and shards of glass sparkled and glinted in the moonlight.

Dorje, Basu, and Cook stared at each other, wordlessly. If Laksmi had eaten it, she'd be slowly dying in excruciating pain.

"Uncle, you're bleeding, you need a doctor."

"Clean up this glass, then call Dr. Steve. Have him bring medical supplies here. Tell him to keep quiet about the shooting. Damn," he added, "that tall bastard has one of my best knives in his leg, I want it back."

"You're lucky," Dr. Steve said, suturing the wound. "The bullet missed your arteries, bones and hit the muscle mass instead. The next time you get shot, remember that. I'll let you know if anyone comes to the clinic with a knife wound, but I doubt he'd use a foreign doctor. Probably find a local." He handed Dorje a bottle of pills. "I know you're tough, but in case of need, this is for pain. Rest until the wound heals. Try to stay out of trouble."

"We'll see," Dorje replied with a faint smile.

Steve added, "What you've told me is fantastic. Why would someone try to kill your elephant, then shoot you?"

"They weren't after me. I just got in the way. "

"Is the elephant vicious?"

"Laksmi? She's very gentle. Goes to children's parties and gives them rides, and she's the only elephant allowed at the airport to greet people. Never hurt anyone. Her handler, Raju, looks after her well."

"Is he here?"

"No. He's in Chitwan. Visiting family. Comes back tomorrow, though."

Dr. Kaiser snapped his bag closed. "You've got me curious. Why are elephants no longer allowed at the airport?"

"They're considered nuisances because they create traffic jams and aren't as efficient as trucks. In the old days, there wasn't as much traffic, so it wasn't as dangerous for the animals, but now...."

"So, what's so special about Laksmi?"

"It's a strange story. After King Birendra was murdered, a special ceremony was performed to free his spirit from the valley. A Brahmin priest wore the dead king's clothing and rode an elephant across the river, accompanying the king's soul out of the Kathmandu Valley. That priest can never return."

"Why is that?"

"If he does, the king's spirit would return with him to haunt the valley. The king's elephant is Laksmi's brother, so, because of that connection, Raju got her a special license. Expats pay a lot to have an elephant wearing a banner to greet their family and friends at the airport. During the season, she's a good money maker for the company."

Just before leaving, Steve whispered to Basu. "Make sure he rests."

Basu nodded and escorted the doctor to the door. Basu came back looking crestfallen. "Uncle, The climb's in three weeks. I'll look for a new sirdar tomorrow. But at this late date…"

"What are you talking about? I'm the sirdar."

"You've been shot. The doctor said…"

"I don't care what Steve said. Tomorrow go to that Tibetan healer behind the Boudhanath Stupa. Tell him what's happened and that I need herbs for blood loss and energy. And be careful."

"Careful?"

Dorje ticked off on his fingers. "Dawa was murdered. Ang stole the company's money and knows you're trying to get it back. And someone was trying to kill Laksmi. Too many dangerous things are happening. This just isn't a run of bad luck; something else is going on."

Chapter Twenty-Two

Kathmandu, Nepal present day

Kathmandu's airport offered all the charm of a warehouse. There was little signage. No one knew where to go, so the custom's lines were pure chaos, then, at the exit, Cynthia was confronted by a swarming wall of bodies.

"Miss, Miss, I take your bags. Only five hundred rupees to the city."

"No, come with me. I give you a good price to town."

Her eyes skipped desperately over signs and placards. Then she spotted it: Salla Ghari Camp. Holding it was a young man of medium height, with shaggy black hair, dressed in jeans and a faded blue flannel shirt and appearing about five or six years younger than herself.

"Hi, I'm Cynthia Graham."

He reached over to take her bag. "Welcome to Nepal. I'm Basu."

"Am I it?"

"Uncle Dorje already took the others to their hotels."

"Your e-mail said that I'd be staying at the Kathmandu Guest House?"

"You wrote you wanted inexpensive."

"Inexpensive is great."

Basu's voice deepened in awe. "One man on the climb has two suites at the Dwarika Hotel, the most expensive hotel in town. Two suites for just one man."

She grinned. "Two suites I don't need. So we leave for the climb on Thursday?"

"Yes, but until then, you are on your own. My uncle Dorje will lead the group when we reach the Khumbu."

"Wow. You'd never see this at LAX," exclaimed Cynthia.

Beyond the taxi line, stood an elephant with a wizened man sitting on top and a banner draped over her side which read, *Welcome Salla Ghari Camp Climbers*. The elephant swished her tail.

Laksmi made a low rumbling noise of greeting to Basu. The man on top said something in Nepali, and she shifted her body, touched Cynthia with her trunk gently messing up her hair as she did so. Cynthia giggled, and Laksmi seemed to smile back.

"Your uncle Dorje was the man I was in last e-mail contact with."

Basu nodded. "When uncle was younger, he climbed a lot and was also a Gurkha with the British Army. Here we are."

He loaded her bag into the back of a taxi. What she could see so far of Kathmandu surprised her. It was a vast amoeba of a city sprawling across the valley. A haze of yellow smog filtered the sky, and black exhaust spewed from passing trucks and buses. She had assumed it would be more pristine, more Shangri-La like. The taxi driver slammed on his brakes as three monkeys of the hear no evil, speak no evil, see no evil variety scampered across the road, then disappeared into a stand of trees.

"What's that over there?" Cynthia pointed to an immense white dome crowned with a golden spire and festooned with fluttering prayer flags.

"Boudhanath Stupa and those painted eyes near the top are the all-seeing eyes of the Buddha."

Behind the stupa rose the jagged peaks of the Himalayas, their spines thick with snow.

"Which one's Everest?"

"You can't see it until we fly into the Khumbu," Basu answered.

A short while later, they ended up in Thamel, a popular tourist destination within Kathmandu, dotted with budget hotels, souvenir shops, and inexpensive eateries. Basu accompanied her into the hotel and gave her his card. "In case you need anything, here's our number. We'll pick you up Thursday at 7:00 a.m. The plane to Lukla's small, so bring only one duffel bag."

Basu chatted with the hotel clerk in Nepali then turned to her. "Another of our climbers is staying here too; he's in room 210. His name's Professor White." Then, with a wave, Basu said, "See you on Thursday."

The Kathmandu Guest House, an old Rana palace with a modern wing, had a funky charm, an informal, easygoing atmosphere. Many guests were either mountain climbers or trekkers, and they lounged in the flower-filled gardens, reading, writing postcards, or journals. Deeper into the garden smells of ginger, coconut, cumin, and coriander wafted from the courtyard's restaurant. Her stomach growled, so she picked up a menu and ordered a vegetable curry and a mango lassi. The lassi, thick with yogurt and mango pulp, was better than any milkshake she'd ever had. After paying her bill, she strolled back into the hotel.

***

The Foreigner was beyond bored. There was absolutely nothing here to distract him. His iPhone's battery was stone cold dead, and how many times can you reread a menu. From the restaurant booth, he watched an eddy swirl up Thamel's main road, catching bits of leaves and scraps of debris in its vortex. It spun among the tourists on the street like a whirling dervish, then disappeared down a lane populated with souvenir shops, restaurants, and trekking agencies.

The restaurant booth was a perfect choice. He could easily watch the comings and goings of the Kathmandu Guest House. Yesterday, he'd researched Ama Dablam mountain climbs and found only one scheduled for that date, the Salla Ghari Camp agency. From then on, it was a tedious but straightforward job to locate Cynthia Graham. He phoned all the major hotels and finally found where she'd registered. Check-in was for today. In most countries, providing that sort of personal information wouldn't be allowed by hotel staff, but hey, this was Nepal, and they were a trusting bunch. So for over two monotonous hours, he had watched the hotel entrance waiting for her. For two hours his eyes had been glued to the front gate. But no redheaded woman had appeared. He knew what she looked like by going on Facebook.

The hovering waiter jacked the Foreigner's irritability level into the red zone. Hanging around for his tip, and was as subtle about it as a broker trying to unload high-risk derivatives. The Foreigner ignored him and toyed with his rosti potatoes. The cheese on top was now cold and congealed and looked like melted plastic. God, he had to pee badly.

"More coffee?" The waiter asked.

"If I want something, I'll ask for it."

The waiter slunk away. The Foreigner tapped a rhythmless tattoo on the table with his spoon, trying not to think about his bladder. When he couldn't hold it any longer, a battered taxi crept into the hotel's compound and disgorged a Nepali man and a woman with lush red hair.

Finally, she's here. The next step was to get her alone. He'd get that diamond.

Chapter Twenty-Three

Kathmandu, Nepal present day

The security guard dropped his inch-long cigarette butt then ground it under his well-polished black shoes. After unlocking the compound gate, the guard allowed Cynthia to slip from the green, serene oasis of the guesthouse garden.

The street was a chaotic stream of honking cars, motorcyclists, bike riders, and vehicle-dodging pedestrians. Her stomach clenched, watching a grandmotherly woman with a gray, waist-length plait, totter across carrying a canvas bag brimming with vegetables. The cabbage on top tipped over then rolled into the street like a leafy soccer ball. Grandmother tottered back to retrieve it, barely missing an oncoming taxi.

A family of four whizzed by on a motorcycle, and following them was a trishaw carrying two women in plain saris. Peddling the ancient trishaw was a man with bodybuilder's legs and a face rigid with concentration. Tassels swung from the handlebars, and the revolving back spokes spun a cheerful red, yellow and blue. Motorbikes and cars surged past the trishaw; nineteenth-century clashing with the twenty-first.

The further Cynthia explored, the more medieval-looking the city became. Before she even saw it, the pungent rot of garbage assailed her nostrils. Sacred cows rummaged through piles, searching for food. The dogs slunk away if you approached, but the cows, perhaps knowing they were gods, stayed put.

Back at the guesthouse, she decided that what she needed was company, so she went down to the lobby, picked up the in-house phone, and asked to be connected to Professor White. It rang three times before he answered.

"Hello."

"Professor White?"

"Yes."

"Umm. We haven't met yet, but I'm Cynthia Graham, and I'm on your climb. How about sharing a get-to-know-you meal?"

"Call me, Jon. Do you like momos? There's a restaurant close by specializing in them."

"What's a momo?"

"Easier to show than to tell. Shall we meet down in the lobby in, say, fifteen minutes?"

"Sounds good to me. Ahh, what do you look like?"

"Five foot ten, slim, and am wearing a brown sweater."

Back in the lobby, she watched a thin, ascetic man in his late forties or early fifties drift down the stairs wearing a brown sweater. After shaking hands, they walked down Freak Street toward the restaurant and grabbed an empty table in the back. The restaurant was bare-bones basic; tables were covered with the local woven Dhaka fabric in an abstract pattern in red, white, and black.

"What are you a professor of?"

"Oriental studies at Oxford. For the past two weeks, I've been on a fact-finding mission in Kathmandu. Thought I'd embark on some research before the climb."

Their waiter brought plates of fist-sized, white steamed and fried dumplings to their table then left to get Jon a beer.

She forked one, dipped it, and took a bite. A burst of coriander, garlic, cilantro, and chilies flooded her mouth. "They're fabulous."

"A man I know haunts this place, so they've nicknamed him Momo Joe. If you don't watch out, they'll become an addiction. Say, we have a free day here tomorrow, why don't you join me? I'd be happy to show you some interesting sights."

"Great," she answered with a big smile.

***

After a morning of temple hopping with Jon, she spent the rest of the day on her own, loading up on souvenirs for her father and friends. It took just a few minutes to arrive at her room. She fished around for the key in her pocket, then unlocked the door. She flicked on the room light. Nothing. Power outage? After tossing her packages onto the bed, she tried turning on the bedside lamp. Nothing. Fumbling around, she discovered the cord was pulled from the wall. When she plugged it back in, the thirty-watt bulb flickered to life, and she spotted a piece of paper under the door.

> *Cynthia,*
> *Dorje phoned and wants a short meeting around*
> *7:00 p.m. to discuss the climb. The phones are out, so*
> *we'll knock on your door.*
> *Cheers,*
> *Jon*

It was 6:45 p.m. If she hurried, she'd have just enough time for a quick shower. She was unbuttoning her shirt when a hiss like a leaky valve caused her to pause. Odd, she thought, that thick rope hadn't been there earlier. What was it doing next to the bathroom door? In the bulb's dim light, the shadowy line uncurled as if maneuvered by an invisible hand. Cynthia's mouth went cottony. In a heart-pounding moment, reality shifted, and a dark presence rose from the floor. The room filled with a palpable menace. All she could do was stare at a flickering tongue, and a body slithering toward her.

Run, screamed her brain, but the unblinking reptilian eyes held hers, and her feet felt stapled to the floor.

The cobra's flickering tongue tasted the air as if memorizing her scent. Watching her, its mottled brown and yellow hood flared open like a pharaoh's headdress. Escape? But where to? The bed. She leaped up.

The snake paused, then unbelievably, reared up to the height of a man. How could it do that? Grabbing souvenirs she'd bought as ammunition, she lobbed them. A demon mask and copper bowl hit the snake squarely, forcing a retreat by the door. The hissing became angrier.

Her eyes swept the bed. Nothing left but beaded necklaces. She tossed an aqua one, it tangled in the snake's hood, giving the cobra a jaunty, pirate-like look. The cobra's furious hiss now sounded like a steam locomotive.

Then, shockingly, it flew right at her. She ducked. With a dull thud, it landed on the opposite side of the bed. Now what? Her eyes fixed on the desk chair. She jumped off the bed, picked the chair up, and turned it upside down. Chair in hand, she advanced towards the wriggling heap. Only one of them would leave this room alive.

Fighting back a wave of nausea, she maneuvered the squirming, writhing, hissing mass against the wall. It wriggled free. Again, she pushed it back, making sure the darting head couldn't reach her. A stalemate, but for how much longer? "Help! Snake!" She screamed.

The door burst open behind her. A voice commanded. "Don't move."

"As if I'm going to!"

"Lean to the right, but keep the head pinned."

A rush of motion, then a knife-wielding man charged the snake. Grabbing it by the throat, he stabbed, but like a giant kraken, the snake coiled its tentacle-like body around his arm and squeezed. The undulating mass now totally obscured the man's arm and inched toward his neck. The man stabbed and stabbed until blood pooled on the floor, and with a shudder, the snake stopped struggling.

The man wiped his knife on the orange and yellow bedspread like a smear of strawberry jam. "Were you bitten?"

Too drained to talk, she only shook her head.

"Good. Bad enough, this was a king cobra, but consider yourself lucky it wasn't a spitting cobra if it'd hit your eyes with its venom…. Anyway, let's get out of here."

She didn't need a second invitation. Along with Basu, and Jon, a crowd of mostly Nepalese staff, had gathered around the door.

The tall Nepali man motioned to one of the staff. "Don't just stand there, clean it up. Basu, tell the manager she needs a new room."

A concerned-looking man quickly returned with a garbage can muttering, "*Naga.*"

There was a sick satisfaction as Cynthia watched the snake's body drop with a plop into the can.

She took a deep breath. "I want to thank you for all you did in there. How'd it get in?"

"Even large snakes can squeeze into tight places. Could've entered while the maid was cleaning, and hid under the bed," Dorje said. "You did a good job pinning it down."

Cynthia stared at his slab of granite cheekbones, basalt black eyes, eyes that had seen a lot of life, and didn't look like they missed much. "Who are you?"

"I'm Dorje."

Chapter Twenty-Four
Kathmandu, Nepal present day

Reoccurring nightmares drenched Cynthia in a film of sweat, so, finally accepting defeat, she got up and squinted at the clock; 6:00 a.m. If the restaurant was open, she might as well have breakfast. By the time she'd taken a shower, packed, and walked down to the restaurant, it was pushing 7:00 a.m. She nodded to the waitress and ordered.

Finished with breakfast, she stepped out of the restaurant, and half-way back to her room, her cell phone rang.

"Hello."

"Sweetheart. How are you? Enjoying yourself?"

"It's fascinating, Dad, only wish I had more time to explore Kathmandu, but I'm taking a flight to Lukla this morning, then it's a five or six-day hike to Ama Dablam base camp. Is anything wrong?"

"Why no, honey. I've some good news. A man called wanting to buy your grandmother's cottage. We exchanged e-mail addresses. Wants to contact you ASAP."

She clenched the phone. "Dad, it's out of the question. I won't sell Fairy Glenn."

"Sweetheart. Reconsider, he's anxious to buy. Says he wants peace and quiet. I told him I'd talk to you."

She lowered her voice as she passed a German couple in their twenties, who, oblivious to her, leaned into one another and began making out.

"No! It's been on Mom's side of the family for over a hundred years. It's my legacy; I felt a connection as soon as I walked in."

A sudden spasm of coughing interrupted the conversation. "Air quality's terrible today. Fires in the San Bernardinos."

A slight pause on the line before he continued. "Didn't want to worry you, but, ahh, I have an urgent debt."

She leaned against a wall. "Dad, not again! You promised."

"No more betting for me. Ever. Swear."

"Dad, you always say that. You know I haven't the money, just a few months' savings to tide me over when I return to the States. Besides, I gave you most of my savings already. We discussed all this before I left."

"I know. I know. But please, if you sell that cottage, it'll be enough to cover me."

"I won't. I'll take out a loan for a rehab clinic for you, but that's all. Dad, you need major help, and giving you more money isn't a cure. The plane's leaving soon. I've got to go now. Bye."

As she continued leaning against the wall, she felt guilty and emotionally spent. It didn't help to know that tough love was the right approach. Her father was her only living relative, and it tugged at her heart to say no, but without counseling, he'd continue accumulating more gambling debt. There'd always be excuses, and when she ran out of all her assets, what then? You can't fix your father's problems, she told herself, only he can, but even as she told herself that, her emotions bubbled inside like a pit of molten lava.

Chapter Twenty-Five

Kathmandu, Nepal present day

A wave of excitement swept through Salla Ghari camp, but then it always did for the first climb of the season. All the equipment had been loaded into the van. Yak Herder and his men and animals were all at the ready up in Lukla waiting for the climbers. Lentils, pasta, flour, chicken, and fresh vegetables had been purchased at the market and boxed for the flight.

While Dorje mulled over the extended weather forecast, Cook walked beaming into the all- purpose dining, living, and recreational room.

"Food's ready."

Dorje grunted. "Where's Basu?"

"On the internet, e-mailing your other nephew."

Dorje was halfway through breakfast when Basu plopped down beside him. "Uncle, should I make two round trips in the van to take the climbers to the airport?"

"Best to take two different vehicles. I'll pick up Cynthia and Jon and meet you there."

Basu reached for a piece of bread. "The American woman. She's pretty. I think you like her."

"Don't be ridiculous. She's got courage. Not many women could coolly fight off a king cobra. She'll do well on the climb."

"Whatever you say, Uncle," Basu answered, with a suspiciously innocent look on his face.

Dorje loved his sister's children, Basu, best of all. But when he thought of babysitting a bunch of amateur Western climbers on Ama Dablam, that made him cranky. In the short term, there would be rocky times ahead for Salla Ghari trekking. In a few years, Basu would have a deeper understanding of the intricacies of the business, more experience on the mountains, but until that day, Dorje needed to take him under his wing.

Dorje wandered outside and eyed the climbing equipment with approval. Then his eyes drifted to the oxygen bottles stacked up against the shed sitting under the shadow of two lodgepole pines, and approval turned to concern. "Basu, are those the new Poisk oxygen bottles?"

"Yes, there for next months' Cho Oyu climb. Chodak's our head guide on that one."

"Bring three bottles over here."

"What is it?" Basu asked, his voice rising in urgency.

"Just bring the bottles over."

Basu lugged then deposited the three seven-pound bottles at Dorje's feet.

Picking one up, Dorje scrutinized it carefully, turning on the regulator, which controlled oxygen flow. He tested one four-liter bottle after another, all malfunctioned.

"Get me three more!" Dorje instructed.

Basu did, but as with the others, none worked.

Basu looked shocked. "I don't believe this."

"Bring over the rest while I bring out the scale."

Dorje placed each one on the scale, weighed them, then separated them into separate piles.

"Why the scale?"

"If the weight's different from what's written on the bottle, it's been refilled. Who bought these?"

"Ang did, just before he left."

"Bastard," Dorje said, throwing the bad ones out in the garbage area. "Each brand new canister costs over $400.00, so Ang must have bought them for cheap and charged the company full price. There's a crook in the south end of town who buys used bottles, sends them to India where they're refilled with crap air. Sells them as the real thing."

"I know that that's why we only buy from the official agent."

"Well, Ang didn't. If your watch is counterfeit, it doesn't matter, but with oxygen bottles, that's a death trap. Climbers have died because of fake air."

"How did you know?"

"The plastic packaging. Poisk would never let bottles leave a Russian factory looking like that.

It's time to go. I'll see you at the airport."

Dorje then mentally calculated how much money he had with him. "Send Cook and a porter to buy bottles from the agent. I'll pay."

Dorje handed Basu an envelope. "Here, I've changed your ticket."

"What?"

"Because of Laksmi. I want you to take the elephant and Raju to the jungle. Raju has family there. I contacted the head of Tata trucks in Kathmandu. He said he'll help. He owes me a big favor."

Basu's eyes widened. "You want me to drive the elephant to the jungle?"

"Haven't you been listening? I found out from a porter who I'd helped once that Ang was involved in the attack. He wants to run you out of business and may try again. I might not be there to stop them. You know how old Raju is, so we can't leave Raju and Laksmi alone at night."

After securing a taxi, on the drive to the Kathmandu Guest House, the more Dorje thought about Ang, the angrier he became, but it would be next to impossible to prove that he had stolen the company's money. Ang possessed signed documents from Basu's father, instructing him to make certain investments. Those investments with Ang's friends had soured. No one understood until it was too late that a brain tumor had affected Basu's father's judgment. Now Ang had money, contacts, and their client list. Where was that son-of-a-bitch spawn anyway? When he found him, there would be hell to pay.

Having arrived at the Guest House lobby, Dorje looked approvingly at Jon and Cynthia. Not only were they on time, but they had followed instructions to bring one duffel bag each. The Twin Otter was a small plane, and every ounce mattered.

Dorje watched Cynthia pick up her bag. Basu was right, she was very pretty, but she also looked pale and tired. Little wonder after last night's adventure.

"Over here," he instructed, escorting them to the taxi. Hanging from the taxi's mirror was a garland of sunshine yellow marigolds and a protective amulet of Ganesha, the elephant god. Dorje winced as he picked up both duffle bags and tossed them into the back. The

Tibetan medicine helped, but the bullet wound in his shoulder still hadn't completely healed.

***

The domestic terminal was undergoing a frenzy of construction upgrades. Piles of bricks, smells of asphalt, sounds of machinery, and workers carrying and stacking supplies all added to the overall chaos.

They were dropped off near the entrance, and the three strode into the airport, where hundreds of trekkers and locals mingled. Hindu women in saris floated along in groups or were accompanied by men with form-fitting *topi* hats.

"Where are the other climbers?" Cynthia asked.

"Nephew's picking them up. They'll be here soon." He untied a folder stuffed with tickets. "Let's check you in. Gate's over there. Don't drink out of the water fountains."

"Why not?" Cynthia asked.

"Most of the time, they forget to turn on the water purifiers, so that you could catch dysentery, giardia, or something just as bad. We want you healthy up in the mountains."

As the two made their way to the gate, passing luggage handlers, Sherpas, monks, climbers, and trekkers lugging backpacks and duffle bags, Dorje stared out at the road. A long line of taxis, cars, and buses was jostling for position near the terminal entrance. Where the hell was Basu? He and his group should be here by now.

A hand clapped Dorje on his left shoulder, the one healing from the bullet wound. Dorje winced.

Alden Droiter, second in command of the airport extension project, stood grinning. "Steve said you were in town, but I never thought I'd run into you."

Brushing off the hand, Dorje attempted to return the grin.

"Waiting for the rest of my group."

"Steve said you were down helping your nephew with his trekking company. Which climb are you on?"

"Ama Dablam."

"Then this should interest you. Read this morning's extended weather report for the Everest area. Big storm's moving in. Pretty unbelievable weather for this time of year. But there it is, must be global warming."

"Saw that too. We'll have to wait and see how bad it is." Dorje gestured. "It's been months since I was last here, I barely recognize the airport. You've made real changes."

"Not nearly enough, though. Behind schedule as usual." Droiter's round, normally smiling face looked drawn.

"Had to travel to Canada and the States for meetings. That's the problem with these large consortiums, too many chiefs. I've worked for some good contractors in my life, but this bloody well isn't one of them and Hank," he complained of his Canadian boss, "is a worthless bugger, but what can you expect from an architect? More interested in finding the right aesthetic than being on schedule. Last week I found him sifting through a pile of bricks. Asked him what he was doing. Do you know what he said? Picking out bricks with character. Bloody unbelievable. Head of a multi-million dollar project, and he's picking out bricks with character. Took one to his office and set it on the desk for inspiration."

"Bricks? Why?"

"The bloke's in a la la world of his own. The airport's outside facade is going to be brick, and Hank wants to make sure the bricks near the entrance are the most beautiful."

Before Dorje could reply, Droiter changed the subject. "Have you heard the newest Ambassador Dickenson story?"

Dorje chuckled in anticipation, "The Russian wrestler?"

Droiter shook his head. "This one's even better. I tell you it makes me embarrassed to be a Brit."

"What's he done now?"

"Remember the garden in the back of the British Embassy? He's always puttering out there with his gardener. The story goes that he especially likes to grow eggplant. But every time an eggplant's ready to be picked, a monkey climbs the wall and raids the garden. The ambassador tried everything to get rid of it; yelling, throwing things, putting up a scarecrow, the works. But the monkey always came back. So he got the idea to shoot it. Took out his rifle, lined the monkey in his sights and pulled the trigger, but he forgot to open the window. Bam! Glass flew everywhere. He tried again. He lined the monkey up in his sights, and pulled the trigger, but shot the chair under the window instead. Forgot to allow for his scope, aimed too low. By this time, Gurkha soldiers tore into his office with guns drawn. Thought it was an assassination attempt. The ambassador ranted about the monkey, commanded them to fire at will, but by this time, there was no monkey in sight; he'd eaten the eggplant and jumped the wall. So now the Gurkhas think the ambassador is crazy."

Dorje roared with laughter "Might not have been a regular monkey at all, but Hanuman the Monkey God. He's smarter than most ambassadors."

"Anyone or anything is bloody smarter than Dickenson! I take that back; he's tied neck and neck with Hank."

Changing the subject yet again, Droiter ran his fingers through his thatch of light brown hair then pointed to the departure lounge.

"Over there! Look at the cock-up the contractor made with that column, not even straight. They're going to have to tear it down and rebuild it."

"By the way, I'm going up to the Everest region to work on the airstrip. Your mountain isn't that far away, so depending on how complex the project is, you may have a bored Brit visit. Doc said he'll be up there too," Droiter added, referring to Steve. Dorje spotted Cook herding the remaining group through the front entrance and toward check-in.

"Climbers are here," he said to Droiter. "If you're bored, come to camp. But beware, Cook's trying out different recipes. Say no to his lemon pie."

Droiter then focused on three men working near the end terminal. "Look at the way they're laying those tiles!" he said in disgust as he walked briskly away.

Dorje cocked a questioning eyebrow at Cook then quickly distributed airline tickets to the group. "You need to hurry. The flight's about to take off. We'll take care of your bags. Just go to the gate."

After they left, Dorje turned to Cook. "Where the hell's Basu?"

"Waiting for that rich man. He said he had e-mails to send."

"If he doesn't get here soon, he'll miss the flight."

Ten minutes later, Basu hurried in with the final climber, an American man with cold blue eyes. Glancing at his Rolex, the man said, "I have one more e-mail to send. There must be a Wi-Fi area here somewhere."

Dorje held his gaze. "You haven't time. The flight won't wait for you."

The American barely contained his annoyance. "You don't appreciate how important this is. Not being in touch can cost me millions."

"Your choice. You can either stay down here or climb with us. Namche Bazaar is a two-day trek from Lukla; there'll be internet cafes with Wi-Fi that you can use there on our rest day."

Shooting Dorje a look of intense dislike, the man strode to the gate.

Dorje passed duffel bags to Basu, who, in turn, gave them to airport personnel for weighing. "What kept you? Being late is no way to start a climb."

"That American wouldn't leave, said he had business to conduct, an important phone call to make, so I had to wait around for him. These three bags are his."

Dorje growled, "I don't care how rich he is. He'd best understand I'm in charge. Everyone knew they were to bring just one bag. I'm tempted to leave two of his behind. He's trouble. I smell it. Worse than a musk deer downwind."

Chapter Twenty-Six

Kathmandu, Nepal present day

Near the departure gates, Cynthia and Jon waited with about sixty other people for flights to Pokhara and Lukla. Out the bank of windows, she spotted a water buffalo loping down the asphalt runway trailed by three harried airline personnel trying to shoo him off. Having had enough of shooing, the bull turned on his persecutors and, with fire practically snorting out of his nostrils, shot right toward them. The chasers soon became the chasees and in panic raced behind a Twin Otter plane.

The bull pawed the ground then charged the piled-up luggage sitting next to the cargo hold. He hooked a bag and tossed it. Up it flew. It came crashing down, and clothes and a laptop computer scattered across the tarmac.

"Not your luggage, I hope?" Jon said.

Cynthia squinted. "Not mine."

"Someone's not going to be happy. That laptop's cracked."

"Who'd bring a computer on a climb?"

Jon left the question unanswered as they watched the bull snatch a tuft of grass, then trot toward Ring Road. A baggage handler ran out to gather the strewn contents, stuffing them back into the ripped bag. Another man duct-taped the bag shut.

"Water buffalo usually are fairly docile, but when I was staying in a village in the Himalayan foothills, I had to go through a corral to use the outhouse, and a female with a calf took an instant dislike to me and chased me both ways. I seem to have a negative effect on some females."

"Was this when you were doing research?"

Jon nodded. "Ethnobiology, etymology, the history of myths, and legends."

"What sort of legends?"

"Oh, there are so many strange ones. Shape-shifting monks; the Tibetan hero, Gesar Khan and his flying horse, rather like our Pegasus; Mongolian death worms; and the fungi of immortality." He stopped, as if deep in thought, then said, "Still so much we don't know about this part of the world, even now; new mammal, plant, and insect species are continually discovered. That's what makes it all so fascinating."

"Tell me about the fungus of immortality."

"The tale begins, as most do, in the mists of time. In either ancient China or Mongolia, a lone hunter followed a deer who led him to the fungus. Since then, it's believed that only a special deer can locate the plant. Scribes wrote that the neon orange and purple plant is uniquely colored and can't be confused with other fungi. Throughout the ages, as you can well imagine, emperors lusted after it. In their desperation, they offered princely rewards to any man bringing them the fungus. To have immortality, power, and great wealth, that would have made an emperor unstoppable."

Jon chuckled. "Imagine if Kublai Khan, ruler of the greatest empire the world has ever known, had obtained the fungus. This very day we might be living under his rule."

Cynthia's eyes sparkled with curiosity. "Think it's true? Not immortality, but a fungus extending life?"

"There's certainly no proof, but there are tantalizing hints about a particular family originating from Mongolia. Centuries ago, a male member from this family found and ate the fungus, ensuring an extraordinarily long life for himself and his descendants. When you think about it," Jon said, something like penicillin could be seen as miraculous, right?"

"Yes."

"Our ancestors might have considered pharmaceuticals to be potions of long life. Remember in the 19th century, which wasn't that long ago, life expectancy was in the 40s, and now, we've practically doubled that."

He offered Cynthia a lemon drop, then popped one into his mouth. "Nepal has its own set of myths. Traveling lamas transmogrifying into snow leopards, magical ravens. Kipling was right when he wrote, 'The wildest dreams of Kew are the facts of Kathmandu.'"

"Do you believe any of those tales?" she asked.

"I'm a rationalist. What I believe is what's shown in the real world. I separate fact from myth."

Suddenly, Jon slapped his forehead. "I'm the stereotypical absentminded professor. This envelope should have been mailed days ago. Maybe Dorje knows someone who will take it to the post office for me." And with that, he left.

The baggage handlers had finished loading, and an announcement blared over the loudspeaker, "Now boarding for the Tenzing-Hillary airport." Cynthia turned and headed outside.

A Twin Otter has nineteen passenger seats, and a small cargo hold, it wasn't a plane for the claustrophobic. Cynthia bypassed the two empty front seats and squeezed her way down the toothpick-narrow aisle to a back row. As she did, she glanced at the other faces and wondered who else was on the Ama Dablam climb. Scrunching up in her seat, with her day pack resting on her lap, she felt cramped and uncomfortable. Jon entered and nodded her way before taking a back seat.

The curtain separating the cockpit from the cabin was drawn open, and they all watched the pilot and co-pilot check the controls, then start up the engines. Suddenly, the whir of the plane's propellers intensified into the drone of a million bees. Anxiously, she looked out the window for Dorje. He and another man entered the cabin. Recognizing Dorje, the pilot took off his headphones, and for a couple of minutes, good-naturedly bantered back and forth. Cynthia strained to see the man standing behind him, but couldn't quite make him out, but when Dorje sat down, she got a look, a real good one. Her fingers dug into her daypack like talons clawing to get inside. Locking his laser blue eyes onto hers, he was the very last man she'd ever expected or wanted to see. Her stalker. Paul Bellame.

Eddies of conversation ebbed and flowed around her, and there she sat frozen with shock, trying to make sense of it. Why this insane pursuit? Paul could have multitudes of women. So why her? Desperate for advice, she'd asked her friend Dan that very question. His answer was, "You don't understand psychopaths because their brains work differently, and I promise you, from what you've told me, this guy is a certifiable one. It boils down to this. His ego can't handle it. Trust me; he didn't make it to the top of the heap by being Mr. Nice Guy. He's an asshole who has to have his way. Either hope he tires of trying or report him to the police. Yeah, I appreciate your dad works for him but, still, it's your life."

One by one, Cynthia weighed her options. What choice had she? Turn around and go home? That would mean complete failure. Then she recalled Basu mentioning that the waitlist out of Lukla was so tight that without a reservation, it'd take a week or two for a return flight. If she took that route, Paul would probably give up the climb just to harass her. Damn it, why should *she* have to leave? Besides, Paul would track her down eventually, no matter where she went. Never let a bully win, she told herself, you have research to do, a book to write, and a mountain to climb. What she would do, though, was inform Dorje.

As her thoughts swirled, the plane gained altitude and headed towards the looming green foothills and faraway glaciated peaks. Terraced hills and gray smog of Kathmandu Valley faded away. Terrain steepened, became more rugged, and halfway into the forty-minute flight clear blue skies gave way to a thick blanket of clouds.

A boyish-looking man, in his mid-thirties with chestnut brown hair and a smattering of freckles sat across from her. During a break in the clouds, he focused his camera out the window, then turned to her. "Are you on the Ama Dablam Climb?"

She nodded.

"Trevor Paddock," he said, extending his hand.

She shook it.

"Looking forward to being back in the Khumbu region again."

"My first time."

"Then prepare yourself for Lukla's runway. I keep forgetting it's called Tenzing-Hillary airport now. It's considered the world's most dangerous; a sheer drop of two thousand feet on one end and a solid wall of mountain at the other. No room for pilot error. There have been multiple crashes with fatalities."

Thanks for sharing, she thought.

When the clouds lifted, she saw spectacular views of craggy mountains sliced through by deep valleys. Here and there waterfalls cascaded in long vertical ribbons of white and foamed into watery pools half-hidden by giant boulders.

Trevor focused his camera back on the window, "I want to be sure to catch the landing."

The plane veered left, then seemed to drop endlessly. With a bounce, they hit the ground and raced up the runway toward the mountain, skidding to a stop with a scant few yards to spare. A round of clapping erupted.

Half in jest, she leaned over to Trevor, "Think I'll hike out on our return to Kathmandu."

Dorje was first off the plane and pointed to a fence. "Your bags have red decals on them. You'll get them over there."

After deplaning, Cynthia headed immediately for Paul, who stood off the runway near a yellowing bush. His smirk spoke volumes. "How did you find me?" she demanded.

"Cynthia, how could I possibly know your plans? This is just a wonderful coincidence. You know I'm a climber. An adventurer. How could you forget our climb on Mount Rainier?"

"Coincidence? Oh Right. What you are is a liar, and yes I do remember Mount Rainier, not only were you abusive to the guides, you put all of our lives in jeopardy by going off trail and demanding that the guides take the most dangerous route. Then you complained to management when they didn't. I'm warning you. Stay away from me. Or else. "

Amusement played at his lips. "Or else what, Cynthia? We'll be sharing some quality time; then you'll get to know me better. We share a lot in common, and I want to show you how much I care for you. I…"

Cynthia stormed off and beelined straight for Dorje, standing by himself near the long chain-link fence which separated the airport from the town. Paul quickly followed.

Her face flushed red as she held her temper in check. "Dorje, I know you don't know me, and I understand how this must sound, but this man is stalking me. I ask that you throw him off the climb."

"That's ridiculous!" Paul answered. "I barely know this woman. Just a coincidence that we're both on the same climb."

Dorje focused on Cynthia. "What do you mean by stalking?"

"I dated Paul for a few months then realized it wasn't working out, and I told him so. Since then, he's made my life hell. Constantly phoning and showing up unexpectedly. He refuses to leave me alone."

"Absolute nonsense!" Paul replied.

Dorje put on his poker face, the face Tommy, the Police Commissioner, knew so well and studied them both. Cynthia crackled with anger; Paul looked smug. Where did the truth lie? Dorje didn't like Paul, not one bit, but he couldn't kick him off the climb on an unsubstantiated claim. Cynthia had proved herself brave, and he thought she had an aura of sweetness about her, but he was a much better judge of men than women. What if Cynthia was paranoid, crazy, or an exaggerator? He knew nothing about either one of them.

He took out his Gurkha knife and started honing it. There was a hypnotic snick, snick as the honing tool met the razor-sharp steel blade. Then Dorje paused, "Rule number one. I don't want any trouble on this climb."

Dorje turned to Paul. "If you only know Cynthia slightly, and she wants no part of you, stay away from her. Understood?"

"Of course," Paul answered.

Dorje put his knife away. "Go over to the baggage and identify yours so we can send them on their way."

Cynthia joined the rest of the group gathered by the duffle bags. As she stood in front of hers, she noted that including her, there were five of them, and she was the only woman. Jon, Paul, and Trevor she'd met already but the not the last man who looked like a skeletal figure from *Día de Muertos,* but as thin as he was, he looked sinewy and healthy.

Cook trotted over from the plane and announced, "All bags are out."

Behind her, Paul's voice rose in a fury. "What the fuck happened to mine? It's all wrapped up in duct tape."

Cynthia allowed herself a slight smile, finding a sudden fondness for water buffalo.

Then she dropkicked Paul into that dark pit in her mind where she deposited all life's garbage, the stuff she had no control over, the bad memories she didn't want to revisit, and clamped it down tight. Paul wasn't going to get under her skin.

The air was fresh and tangy with the heady, resinous scent of conifers. As Cynthia gazed out at the surrounding mountains, excitement rippled through her like a current of electricity. Here she was up at nine thousand feet, and in a couple of days, she was to view the tallest peaks in the world; her adventure had begun.

***

The climbers followed Dorje into a restaurant called "Yeti's Den."

Photos of Mount Everest, Lhotse, and other Khumbu peaks decorated the homey interior. Picnic-style tables encouraged conversation and brought strangers together to swap trekking tales.

An attractive Nepali waitress wearing a striped red and black t-shirt and a long brown skirt squealed with delight. "Dorje! You're back! I'll tell cousin you're here." Disappearing into the kitchen, she returned with a stocky man wearing a white apron over faded jeans.

After exchanging greetings, Dorje scanned the dining room full of trekkers. "You're busy, my friend, but can you take care of my group? I need to meet with Yak Herder."

"Don't worry; I'll find them a table. That group over there is about to leave."

On the wall, a large chalkboard detailed the menu options, and someone with artistic talent had drawn a Yeti scaling Mount Everest. As she scanned the options, Cynthia decided on lentils and rice with curried vegetables.

With his face tight with irritation, Paul gestured to the simple picnic tables dotting the restaurant. "I expect to eat at a more upscale restaurant than this."

"Food's good here."

"How long will we be? I don't want to spend the day lolling around."

Dorje's eyes locked onto Paul's. "We leave when I'm ready."

Paul blinked first, then glanced away.

Dorje strode over to the group. "You all haven't had a chance to meet. Introduce yourself and order what you want. You'll be taken care of."

"Paul," Dorje said, pausing to light his once a week cigarette, "try some Sherpa stew, our people say it gives a man a good temper."

Cynthia's laughter followed as Dorje headed toward the trailhead.

Paul Bellame was an irritant, and Dorje suspected it would only get worse. There was only one leader on this climb, and that was him. At least the others seemed fine. And the woman, well, was more than fine.

Chapter Twenty-Seven

Lukla, Nepal present day

A brisk, fifteen-minute walk from "The Yeti's Den" brought Dorje to the edge of town to where the dilapidated, two-story Himalayan Sunset hostel stood. Behind the hostel three, rangy men clothed in fleece-lined, sheepskin chubas, the traditional knee-length robe of Tibetan nomads, waited. Nearby, their yaks, dzos, and zhoms, which are yak-cow hybrids, lipped at the sparse grass.

Dorje greeted the men, then clapped the leader, Yak Herder, on the shoulder. "Gear's over by the plane tagged with red decals. By the way, you lice-ridden-old thief, you'd better not overcharge us, or I'll feed you to the vultures."

Yak Herder's grin exposed two gold front teeth. "You hard-nosed yeti, I've yet to make a profit from you or Basu. As it is, I barely make enough to feed the yaks."

"Tell that one to the tax collector, and if you give him enough beer, maybe he'll even believe you. What's the local news?"

Before answering, Yak Herder doled out instructions to his two men. "Time to round up the animals."

Yak Herder scratched at a flea bite. "You've been away for a while, haven't you? The biggest news is that Pemba's brother, Choden died on Makalu. Fell into a crevasse and broke his neck. Another tragedy for that family."

"A real shame," answered Dorje.

Yak Herder broke into the silence to bring up a new subject. "The Chinese have cracked down on trade between Nepal and Tibet. Soldiers even shot at a caravan last week."

"What about smugglers, are they getting across?"

"If the right amount of money changes hands. Talk's going around about someone new in the smuggling business."

"Someone new," Dorje repeated thoughtfully. "I heard that down in Kathmandu too. I think Nyi-ma was involved. He was murdered at Old Blue Throat, stabbed to death. His dying words were that he was cursed for smuggling monsters."

A surprised look flickered across Yak Herder's face. "Smuggling monsters. What did he mean by that?"

Dorje shook his head. "Who knows what a man sees at the time of death. He was probably hallucinating and not in his right mind."

"Murdered! Not a man to like, but still. A rumor's going around that he and some others are involved with a man who calls himself the Foreigner."

"Who's this Foreigner?" Dorje asked.

"No one knows. Either he covers his tracks well, or it could be a made-up story to throw the police off. Rumors are like brush fires; they burn both the guilty and innocent alike."

Yak Herder took out a sliver of wood from his pocket and picked at his teeth. "You missed last week's remembrance ceremony at Tengboche Monastery for Hillary and Norgay. It was something. Monks, elders, and climbers from all over the world attended, even two men who worked that climb."

"They must be ancient."

"They are, but both are surprisingly active. Old Trader was one."

"Still alive?" Dorje said.

"Unless I spoke to a spirit."

"It's been years since I've heard his name mentioned. He was a friend of my grandfather's. As a child, I remember his home was filled with foreign treasures, or it seemed so to me."

Finished with his teeth, Yak Herder tossed away the sliver of wood. "He's not exactly a hermit but doesn't travel as he used to on those long caravan trips. All those strange tales about him! I asked about one, but he just laughed it off. Said it was all nonsense. "

So you saw Old Trader, how's his memory?" Dorje asked.

"Mind's still good. Filled with pride recalling how his men brought in supplies for that 1953 climb. He was at base camp the very day Hillary and Norgay reached the top of Mount Everest."

"You've heard the news about Dawa's murder by the Maoists," Dorje asked.

Yak Herder, nodded.

Dorje looked at him intently, knowing that his son was high-up in that organization.

"He wasn't killed by Maoists. They weren't in that area." Yak Herder replied.

In the far end of the field, a white yak suddenly raised his shaggy head, sniffed the air, then stared long and hard in Dorje's direction. Letting loose a loud bellow, he trotted toward the stone wall on which they sat. At the rapid clanking of a bell and the thudding of hooves, Dorje twisted around in surprise. He watched a massive yak lengthen his stride, and then, with the effortlessness grace of a show-jumper, the sixteen hundred pound animal with his red ear tassels swinging, cleared the wall with inches to spare. Trotting over to Dorje, he proceeded to lick his face with a tongue rough as a pumice stone. Dorje wiped his face, which now felt like it had a bad case of razor burn, and stayed out of the way of the curved horns while he patted the animal.

"Nice to see you too, White Ghost."

Dorje scratched under the yak's chin, and the yak grunted in pleasure, shifted its weight, and leaned against Dorje. Dorje's knees groaned in protest.

"I've never seen him act like that before. The White Ghost certainly remembers you."

"I've known him since he was a calf. You remember your friends," Dorje replied, slapping the yak on the rump. Dorje whistled. "Frisky today, isn't he?"

Dorje instructed. "Tonight's camp will be at the usual place, and at dawn, we head for Namche."

***

At the Yeti's Den, not surprisingly, Paul turned on the charm in his attempt to impress everyone. She blocked out much of what he was saying and concentrated on demolishing the last of a lentil dish called dal bhat. Mopping up the last of the lentils with roti bread, she watched Dorje dodge a boisterous Australian group as he advanced to the table. Catching the waitress's eye, he nodded, and soon, a steaming bowl of stew was set in front of him.

"Is it far to our camp?" Cynthia asked.

"Three hours or so. The camp's at a lower elevation, it's a good place to sleep to get acclimatized."

Focus, she told herself and turned back to Dorje. This was the perfect opportunity to tell him why she was here. "I hope you can give me advice. I'd e-mailed Basu earlier, explaining that one of my reasons for being here is to research the 1924 Mount Everest British expedition. The odds aren't in my favor, I know that, but I'd still like to try. I'm looking for descendants of porters who worked on the expedition to interview, if they're willing."

The waitress presented Dorje with the tab, and for a minute, they chatted back and forth. Dorje handed her some bills, and the waitress went giggling back into the kitchen. Dorje turned again to Cynthia. "Basu did tell me about it. What's your purpose for doing it?"

"There's a family connection that I want to write about it. It'd be great to have oral histories to see if there are stories about the climb which haven't been told."

"At this late date? There are so many books out there about that expedition. That climb has been so mined over. I doubt you'll find anything new. Besides, you're in the wrong country. Tibet is where it all happened."

"That I know, but the border's closed, so I have no choice but to see what I can discover on this side. Tell me if I'm wrong, but back then, weren't the borders fluid and porters came from all over to support that expedition?"

"True enough. A relative of mine, Lak-pa, was on that climb, but I know no stories about it." A thoughtful look crossed Dorje's face. "I have an idea. Oddly enough, I was just speaking to Yak Herder about two old porters who were on the 1953 Hillary climb. Possibly they know stories from the earlier days. I can't promise you anything, but since we have some rest days, we could try. "

Cynthia threw him a warm smile of thanks. "That 1924 expedition was a generation before theirs, but, as you say, they may remember stories about the people and events." She put the cap back on her bottled water. "I hope I'm not being too nosey, but where did you learn such fluent English?"

"From a teacher at the Hillary School up at Namche Bazaar, that, along with childhood friends from New Zealand. Back then, the Mount Everest park rangers came from New Zealand. I lived close by and became friends with the sons of one of the rangers. I taught them Sherpa; they taught me English. Later on, I became a Gurkha with the British Army." He winked at her. "My slang and swear word vocabulary rose to new heights."

She laughed. "They're often the easiest words to remember. I take it that a Gurkha is a soldier."

"A Nepalese fighter. Most are Hindu, but I was an exception. Spent time in Brunei and other places."

He stood up to go. "Time to move on."

Outside the snowcapped mountains were more dramatic than the travel posters had led her to believe. While men loaded up yaks, Cynthia wandered over and was about to stroke one.

"Careful," Dorje cautioned, "they're not tame. They can gore or kick. If one comes towards you when you're trekking, pass on the inside of the trail, that way, they won't push you off a cliff."

Great, Cynthia thought, as she threaded her ponytail through the back of her baseball cap, killer yaks.

"Are they intelligent?" She asked.

"Very," Jon answered from behind them. "On the level of a cat or dog. That white yak over there is extremely rare; in the olden days, they were presented as gifts to high lamas."

"You know about our culture. The White Ghost here is more intelligent than most." Dorje said.

"Can you ride them?" Cynthia asked.

"In an emergency, but they're a pack animal. The White Ghost once led a lost and hungry trekker to safety during a blizzard in the high country. It was as if he sensed the man was in trouble and stayed with the trekker for several days, he even led him to a hut that had food. When the blizzard died down, the trekker followed him to Yak Herder's camp. The Englishman swore the White Ghost had saved his life."

Dorje then announced to the group, "Today will be an easy day, just a short trek to our camp. It's important to sleep at a lower altitude tonight to acclimatize, if you don't feel well, tell me. Altitude sickness kills."

Chapter Twenty-Eight
Khumbu Region, Nepal present day

They left Lukla through an arched gateway lined inside with brass prayer wheels. Cynthia followed Dorje's lead and spun them one by one, sending her prayers to the gods, a prayer of protection for the climbers, a prayer to discover more about Sandy, and a prayer to rid herself of the detestable Paul Bellame.

They followed the stone and dirt trail connecting Lukla at 9,000 feet to Phakding at 8,400 feet. On the following morning, there would be a more rigorous hike up to Namche Bazaar, situated at 11,000 feet. From Namche Bazaar, the trail then snaked into feeder tracks up to the smaller villages, to the monasteries, to the lakes, and finally dead-ending at the highest mountains on Earth.

At times the trail paralleled the frothing, fast-flowing Dudh Koshi River. Glacial melt from the uppermost regions of the Mount Everest area trickled down to feed this, the highest river in the world. Dorje had said that, in Sherpa language, the name of the white, foaming river meant mother's milk.

Glimpses of village life caught her eye as she walked on; women pounding clothes on the river bank or tending to their vegetable gardens, young monks with shaven heads on their way to monasteries. There were flapping prayer flags and spiritual blessings painted or carved into boulders called mani stones, and the ever-looming peaks.

After several hours on the trail, Dorje called for a rest stop, and while the group had tea at a nearby lodge, Dorje and Yak Herder conversed away from the others.

"You haven't led a mountain climbing group in years, why now?" Yak Herder asked.

"Family needs me. My sister is worried about Basu. He's trying to make a go of the family business. He's smart, but young, and needs guidance."

"That woman with you," Yak Herder said, looking toward the lodge, "is good looking."

"But unhappy."

Yak herder winked. "Maybe you can comfort her."

"Not me. Foreign women are nothing but trouble," Dorje answered.

A flicker of interest gleamed in Yak Herder's eyes. "Why's that?"

Dorje gave a rueful laugh. "For one foreign woman, my sleeping with her was just part of her cultural experience, like trekking in Nepal."

Yak Herder yelled to one of his men, "Check the load on the pied dzo; it's shifted." Then he said to Dorje, "I heard monks don't want tourists around Ama Dablam anymore."

Dorje passed him a cigarette. "Why should they care? It's frequently climbed." Then Dorje stood up. "Time to move on."

Towards evening they arrived at their destination, Phakding. The campsite was on the west bank of the village and separated from it by a steel suspension bridge. Crossing it, Cynthia felt a queasiness as the bridge swayed beneath her feet. A yak came from the opposite direction, and she hugged the cables as it passed her. Looking back, she watched the others cross. Paul fell against the steel cables, cursed, then dropped his camera into the chasm. Cynthia smiled. The porters set up canvas tents in a flat meadow thick with yellowing grass. Cynthia, Paul, and Jon had their tents while Trevor and Tim shared.

Cook performed his dinner magic, and Cynthia and the others hungrily dug into his chicken curry, spinach saag paneer, and apple pie. In the high Himalayas, night fell quickly. First, a couple of stars appeared, then dozens, hundreds, and finally, in a burst of brightness, the Milky Way transformed the sky into a dark pool dusted with millions of white dots.

It had been a long day, and eventually, everyone headed for their tents.

After a hurried breakfast the following morning, the group strapped on their day packs and started trekking.

"What do you think of them?" Yak Herder asked Dorje.

"Well, Paul, he's the tall, lean one in his early 40's, he seems in good shape. Trevor, though, who is ahead of him, is probably the fittest."

"That skinny man, think he'll make it?" Yak Herder commented.

"If he loses any weight, he'd just disappear."

As Dorje continued to assess the group, he wondered about the professor. He had a few years on the others and didn't look particularly strong, and there was that odd habit of thrusting his head forward like a turtle when he walked. But you never knew, sometimes people surprised you. Take Cook, for example, as chubby as he is, he has excellent stamina. And Cynthia, well, he enjoyed looking at her tight, firm hips. He'd get a better sense of their fitness when they began the long climb up to Namche Bazaar.

Onward they walked passing by a rhododendron forest, cairns, and carved stones inscribed with the sacred mantra, om mani padme hum. Prayer flags, atop tall bamboo poles, fluttered near the path and sent prayers to the gods, and beneath the poles, a spillage of scarlet barberries softened the gray hardscape.

After a few hours, they arrived at the official entrance to Sagarmatha, formerly known as Mount Everest National Park.

Set in a knife-like valley of cliffs, a forest of blue Himalayan pines clung tenaciously to the rock face. Cynthia thought that they, just like the Sherpa people inhabiting the land, thrived under adverse conditions.

Dorje presented the required permits while the climbers relaxed outside at a restaurant.

In such a small group, there was no avoiding Paul. Each time she looked at him, her muscles stiffened with tension, and just sitting at the same table with him made her skin crawl. Stop thinking about him, she told herself and turned her attention to Jon and Trevor, who were trading reminiscences of previous visits.

Trevor blew on his cup of hot milky tea. "Geology around here is fascinating; not many are aware that ocean fossils are on these mountains, or that the Himalayas continue to grow." He pointed. "Most of those peaks are granitic at the bottom and limestone on top."

"You seem to know a lot about these mountains," Cynthia said.

"Studied geology."

With her red diamond in mind, Cynthia asked, "Are there mines around here?"

"There's placer gold in some of Nepal's rivers, but as far as I'm aware, no gold or gem mining."

Jon coughed. "Speaking of mining and gems. When I was a grad student, I did six months of research in Beijing. After a few months, the guards became bored watching me pore over old, dusty chronicles, so they left me to my own devices. Some unusual documents surfaced. One, in particular, originated about eight hundred years ago during the rule of Kublai Khan. A scribe had written down a list of gifts the emperor had received that year. According to the log, he was given two important stones from a Himalayan prince. The in-depth description indicated that they came from where the highest mountains inhabit the clouds. They created quite a stir."

"Why was that?" Cynthia asked.

"Because they were red diamonds."

Her skin tingled. Of all topics to bring up! She hadn't even known of red diamonds until a few months ago, now the subject seemed to pop up at unexpected moments, and like hearing a new word, or an unfamiliar place, suddenly it's on everyone's lips. She touched the safe deposit key that hung around her neck for reassurance, then leaned towards him.

Jon added. "An unexpected source verified the gems' existence. A Jesuit priest, of all people. When I returned to Europe, a friend high up in the Catholic Church allowed me to research old archives. I dug deeper and discovered that centuries after Marco Polo's adventures, a pope sent Jesuits to China during the rule of the Wan-li Emperor. That was in the 1500s. The pope was intelligent enough to send the best and brightest. And Matteo Ricci was the best of the best, a true Renaissance man who spent three decades living in

China. In a letter home to Italy, he mentioned viewing those gems in the Forbidden City."

"Where are they now?" Trevor asked.

"Lost. Probably during a time of political upheaval. Not long after the end of Wan-li's reign came the fall of the Ming Dynasty."

"That reminds me of something else," he said, "about the Knights Templar...."

At that moment, Dorje arrived. "Time to move on."

Cynthia rose reluctantly. She fully intended to question Jon later about the diamonds.

Namche Hill separated the fit from the not so. Steep switchbacks zigzagged upwards as far as the eye could see, and as they inched uphill, Cynthia saw, except for birds flying overhead, no wildlife.

Porters streamed effortlessly by, carrying enormous loads, but the faces of tourists were scrunched up with exertion and the effects of high altitude.

Rounding a switchback, she stopped dead in her tracks. There it was. Mount Everest. A misshapen, brutal-looking pyramid. Mixed feelings bubbled up. Her great-grandfather, Sandy Irvine, and his partner, George Mallory, died on that mountain. On its slopes, still undiscovered, hidden perhaps forever in an icy crevasse, lay Sandy's body. But as she continued to stare, the mountain's power, grandeur, and allure became undeniable. What must it have been like to experience all that hellish danger and hardship back in 1924?

Chapter Twenty-Nine
Mount Everest, Tibet 1924

Camp VI sat in the death zone, where the body begins shutting down in the oxygen-thin air.

Sandy, George, and Lhakpa, the Tibetan porter, fought to breathe. Outside, the wind howled and bayed, threatening to pull up wooden stakes and rip the two-person canvas tent away.

Their bodies ached from ferrying supplies to 26,000 feet above sea level, but even so, a bubbling of exhilaration filled the tent. The months of travel and hardship honed their muscles and deepened their sense of purpose. The next day, mountaineering history would be made. Tomorrow, they'd be the first to conquer Mount Everest.

"Storm's letting up. Time for Lhakpa to leave," George said.

Sandy ignored his altitude-induced headache, concentrating instead on the piece of paper on his lap. "A minute to finish this letter to Emma."

Of the porters who accompanied them up, only Lhakpa remained.

With Sandy's and George's letters under his shirt, Lhakpa gave them a long, mournful look. "May the gods protect you," he said, then steepled his hands in goodbye. As Lhakpa opened the flap to go, Sandy noticed an eagle riding the thermals thousands of feet below in the mid-afternoon sun. How unnatural to be above the eagles, he thought. It was if the order of things had changed.

About an hour after Lhaka left, Sandy exclaimed, "Oh no!"

"What's wrong?" George asked, his blue eyes locking into Sandy's.

Sandy lifted his Vest Pocket Kodak camera. "By Jove, must be the altitude. What a fool I am. Completely forgot to send Emma the gem."

George's eyebrows shot up in surprise. "What gem?"

"I had two," Sandy replied, his big hands gently opening up the camera.

From out of the empty spool section of his camera, an uncut stone, somewhat larger than a blueberry, spilled out. "With all the excitement, I'd forgotten I'd hid it there. Now it's too late to send it down."

Sandy shook his head as if to clear his thoughts. "Bataar warned me about the stones. Thinks them cursed. Of course, I don't believe in curses."

George opened his palm, and Sandy obligingly dropped the gem onto it. In the lantern's light, a flame of deep scarlet glowed from the stone's heart.

George let out a low whistle. "What a beauty. A ruby?"

"Our geologist thinks maybe a ruby or even a diamond," Sandy replied.

"Red diamonds? Haven't heard of them before," George said, returning the gem. "I have to ask. Why is it inside your camera?"

"For safekeeping. I hadn't had a chance to tell you the story, but Vulture, the porter who sold them to me, tried stealing them back. The bastard came at me with a knife. Saved only by a whisker's breath," Sandy answered.

Then Sandy thought. What if the worst did happen? What if he didn't make it back? On a piece of notepaper, he scribbled a short message with Emma's name, address, and an explanation that the gem belonged to her. At least, he thought, it'd be hers. He put the note along with the other gem into his pocket, then placed a new roll of film into the camera.

They sat long in companionable silence until hunger prompted Sandy to fire up the stove and begin cooking dinner while George continued strategizing over the routing.

A crack like a snapping branch startled them from their chores, and Sandy stuck his head outside in concern. An avalanche shooting up a rooster tail of white ice and snow cascaded down the slope. That was the frightening thing about avalanches; a seemingly harmless patch of snow could turn deadly. Back inside, Sandy blew on his hands. "That was close! I'll be glad to see the backside of this camp!"

Sandy handed George a plate of macaroni and meat. "Only us now."

George nodded and picked at his food.

"I say, old man, is something bothering you?" Sandy asked.

George hesitated before answering. "That avalanche, and today's date, June 7th."

Sandy's forehead furrowed in puzzlement. What was George talking about?

"You weren't on the 1922 expedition, but you're bound to have heard about it. Occurred exactly two years ago today."

"The dead porters?" Sandy asked.

George nodded. "Slopes were treacherous. I knew better than to take a chance on that snow but decided to press forward anyway. An avalanche swept seven porters into a crevasse. I survived. They didn't."

"Mountaineering's a dangerous game. We all know the risks."

Regret etched George's face. "There's a fine line between a calculated risk and being reckless. I was reckless. If I could take back one day in my life and relive it, that would be the day."

As Sandy searched for words of comfort, George quickly shifted topics. "Tomorrow, we must rise to the challenge. A rumor is cycling around the Royal Geographic Society that the Americans and Germans intend to mount an expedition next year. For England, we must, we will be first to conquer Mount Everest!"

While listening to those stirring words and watching George's face fill with passion, an appalling thought entered Sandy's mind. Had George decided to risk everything tomorrow? His unquenchable ambition had killed before. Would George willingly cross that line again? No, Sandy reassured himself, George wouldn't. He'd learned his lesson with the death of the porters. The porters had been a once-off tragic mistake. George was England's finest mountaineer, he'd trust his judgment.

"Best, get ready for bed," George said.

Nodding, Sandy unlaced his hobnail boots, took off cashmere puttees, and crawled into his sleeping bag.

Exhaustion, worry, and the bone-chilling cold lulled Sandy into a fitful sleep, a sleep more hallucinatory than dreamlike, and filled with nightmarish images. A grim scene played over and over, which featured the scar-faced Vulture, now transformed into a half-bird man fighting a faceless monk to the death. Instead of hands, Vulture sported foot-long talons dripping with the monk's blood. As the men circled each other, Sandy knew the ending would be the same. The monk stumbled, Vulture made his final attack, and the monk writhed in agony as his life's blood pumped onto the snow in a spreading red stain. Sandy woke from the nightmares then drifted back to sleep.

It was sunshine beating down on the tent that woke him with a start. He squinted at his watch; 7:30 a.m. How could it be so unbelievably late! He crawled out of his sleeping bag with a speed that even surprised him then prodded George. "Hurry up! We've overslept."

An early departure was of the essence, and here another hour was wasted fixing a faulty oxygen bottle. But Sandy had little choice; without it functioning properly, the assault could be doomed. His fingers ached from the cold as he twisted valves and screws. George passed him a breakfast of cold tongue and biscuits, which they ate in silence. Sandy found eating excruciating. Despite all precautions, the fierce sun had burnt Sandy's fair skin red, and no matter how he had positioned his hat, there was little relief from the sun's rays.

Sandy put his camera into his Shackleton jacket.

"I'll check once more to make sure we haven't forgotten anything," George said, entering the canvas tent.

George reached across his sleeping bag to pick up his camera. "Somervell expects photos from the top. If I forget his camera, he'll have my head."

George was more like his old self, Sandy thought, amiable, and full of optimism.

"I wrote Noel that we'd head for the skyline. Think that's the best route," George declared.

Outside, a frigid wind blew, but the day was clear. Perfect summit weather. Both men took photos, then Sandy picked up a harness with two oxygen bottles and placed it on George's back.

George did the same for Sandy. With a fur-lined helmet placed firmly on his head, George smoothed out his gloves, donned goggles, and broke out into a wracking cough, a cough which he'd had for days.

When George was able to catch his breath, he said, "You lead." He tied the rope, their umbilical cord, between them. "I'll take over when we rest."

Far below, tiny black specks rode the thermals above the treeless, frozen landscape where massive slabs of ice rose in eerie, contorted shapes above the glacier floor.

Sandy pointed to the birds and thought back on the day spent at Rongbuk Monastery, the last human settlement before Mount Everest. Buddhist monks had lived and meditated in the mountain caves for hundreds of years, even though the monastery itself was newly built.

"A good day to be a raven," Sandy said. "Our translator said monks from Rongbuk Monastery transform into ravens when they have long distances to travel. Remember that old monk's warning before we left the monastery? 'The demons of the snow will defeat you utterly.'"

"Superstitious nonsense," George replied, "meant to scare us off."

Sandy winced in pain. His cracked lips bled from putting in his oxygen mouthpiece. Twisting the flow meter to maximum, he began the ascent toward the ridge.

Up ahead was a wild, desolate no man's land of snow and ice, with rocks strewn about in every shape and size. Recent fresh snow raised concern. Underneath were unseen loose stones that could send them free-falling thousands of feet onto the rocks below. They picked their way up the slope with great care, and after three hours, reached the first rock step.

Sandy took off his glacier goggles to brush away tiny icicles. In the short time that it took to put the goggles back on, his lashes had frozen to his upper lids.

George checked his altimeter. "Weather's deteriorating fast."

In front loomed their first real obstacle, the formidable second rock step. A stripe of light gray bisected the vertical monster of gray limestone, giving it a strange beauty. Mallory paced the upper headwall nervously, examining it.

"Sandy, you can't make it. Too technical for you. Want to stand on your shoulders."

George removed his boots and tied them around his neck.

"Frostbite?"

"Won't have my boots off for that long."

Disappointment ripped at Sandy's gut. There was no way he was going to stay here and just wait for George. He pointed to a section of rock. "Belay me up. I'll make it."

George considered, then slowly nodded his agreement.

Sandy felt like a circus performer as he balanced George on his shoulders; then came the welcome relief when George found hand and toe holds and began free climbing. Finally, after an hour and a half, a rope snaked its way down. Sandy grabbed it and inched his way up the limestone cliff face. As he neared the top, his stomach clenched. Now they were above the highest altitude any man had climbed.

As he topped the step, clouds closed in fast and furious. Thunder crackled. A flash of lightning splintered the sky. Even more worrisome, the temperature continued to plummet. Sandy glanced at his watch: 1:00 p.m.

The wind picked up. Above them, the summit was draped in a cloud plume like a dragon's tail. Looks like a real howler on top, Sandy thought.

"George. Must pick up the pace, or we won't make it."

Twenty minutes later, the first of Sandy's two oxygen bottles emptied. With a sinking feeling, he tossed it away. It should have lasted longer. Had he enough oxygen to take him to the top?

Casting a wary eye upwards, Sandy noted with increasing concern that the route was pitted with rotting ice.

Sandy slipped and smashed his hand against an outcrop. Wincing, he took off a glove to examine the damage. The skin was red and abraded. He also found a spot about the size of a farthing that was paler than the rest of his skin, frostbite. Memories of a porter screaming in pain as both hands and feet were amputated overwhelmed him. Was losing his hand, or worse, worth it? Was reaching the summit worth the risk? But as these thoughts swirled around in his mind, the mountain pulled him upwards.

More lightning strikes flashed to the west, and much closer this time.

The higher he climbed, the fuzzier his thinking became. With an ever-increasing weariness, they plodded on. One step, two steps, three steps. Rest. Then Sandy looked, really looked at the summit. He yelled at George.

"Need to turn back. It's too far."

"No," George yelled over the wind's roar. "We can do it. Moon will lead the way. Trust to luck." He pointed to the summit. "Look how close."

"Too risky. No lighting equipment. We forgot the lever torches."

George fumbled to untie the rope. "Go back. I'm going on."

George sucked on his oxygen before gasping out, "My last attempt. Give it a sporting try."

With a shock of insight, Sandy realized George hadn't learned his lesson. He'd crossed that line again and was willing to gamble both their lives for the glory. As Sandy looked down at the glacier beckoning him home, he realized all choice had been snatched away. Leave George up here all alone? If he did, how could he face the others? He'd be shunned, considered a coward. No man would climb with him again. With a cheerless heart, Sandy resigned himself to carry on.

The weather turned ugly with a surprising swiftness. Gale force winds clawed with unrelenting fury. It was sheer misery as they bent their heads into the wind and placed one hobnailed boot in front of the other.

The ridge narrowed significantly, and Sandy felt unnerved passing by wind-swept cornices, which cantilevered spectacularly over the abyss. Don't look down, he told himself.

Then an unseen ice patch.

He slipped, landed on his back, slid, burst through a cornice like a tobogganer, and careened over the edge. He dangled like a condemned man on the gallows, but instead of his neck, his noose encircled his waist. Fear pumped through him as his eyes became riveted on the vertical eight or nine thousand foot drop below. The plummet would be unsurvivable. He dangled helplessly. If he could just swing over to the rock ledge, he'd have a fighting chance. But Sandy dared not move. It would throw George off balance and bring them both crashing down to their deaths.

"Hold tight," George yelled.

The rope bit deeper into his waist as George pulled him up. Sandy twisted to face the rock, and as George pulled, he managed to find toe holds and climb. When Sandy finally reached solid ground, he collapsed and vomited. The rope around his waist had tightened uncomfortably, and when Sandy loosened it to breathe better, he noted with a sense of alarm that friction from being rubbed against the rock edge had frayed it. Not a good omen, Sandy thought.

After three intense hours of slogging from the second step, George crested the summit with Sandy trailing behind. They had done it! Whooping for joy, they hugged.

For a brief moment, the storm lessened. The clouds parted. Sandy stared in awe at the surrounding monster peaks, then at the sky above. He felt immortal. He was a mountain god.

"Must take photos. Must document this," Sandy insisted.

He pointed his camera, first snapping a photo of George against the backdrop of the neighboring mountains, then at the altimeter registering their height. George did the same with his camera.

Kneeling, George scooped a shallow hole in the snow and placed a photo of his wife, Ruth, into it.

"I promised her," he said.

Feeling dizzy, Sandy unbuckled the harness holding his last oxygen bottle and tossed it. "Hard to breathe. Oxygen all gone."

Sandy's initial euphoria vanished. With a sense of growing apprehension, he realized daylight was fast fading. They were atop the highest mountain on Earth, in the numbing cold without lights, and had hours of climbing in the dark ahead of them before reaching the camp's safety.

Once again, the clouds rolled in and obscured the surrounding mountains. It's like a shroud was thrown over the roof of the world, Sandy thought.

George erupted into a spasm of coughing. When he turned, Sandy saw to his horror that George's mouth had frothy bubbles of blood.

Sandy yanked hard at George's jacket. "We have to go. Now!"

Chapter Thirty
Mount Everest, Tibet 1924

Sandy leaned against a boulder in dazed exhaustion. At least it provided a temporary refuge from the battering wind.

Dusk had settled over the landscape. As the minutes ticked by, it proved increasingly difficult to orient themselves. By the time they had completed the terrifying scramble down the second step's headwall, night had indeed fallen.

Sandy scanned the undulating gullies, rock ridges, and deep crevasses for the way back.

"Which gully did we come up?" Sandy asked, his breath coming in labored rasps.

George's face turned bleak with worry. "Not sure. Maybe there."

For a half an hour, they struggled down the shallow gulley until George announced in defeat, "Wrong way. Turn back."

Then George stepped onto a rotting ledge. With a sharp crack, it shattered under his weight, and he dropped like a stone. The rope that tied them together wrenched at Sandy's waist, almost yanking him over. His legs groaned from exertion as he spread them and began hauling George up. "Just a few more tugs," Sandy shouted reassuringly.

His hand stretched out to George, who nearly caught it when the rope snapped. In an eerie silence, George disappeared like a phantom into the void.

Sandy stared in shock at the frayed rope end, where George had hung.

"No!" He screamed at the top of his lungs. "No! Not George!"

Tears froze on his face. For many long heartbeats, Sandy refused to accept George was truly gone. Crushing grief settled over him, but along with that came the bleak understanding that he couldn't wait any longer. Survival depended on finding Camp VI.

Sandy's eyes skimmed over the boulders and rocks, hunting for a landmark with a feeling of desperation. Nightfall had changed everything. Nothing was recognizable. He knew roughly where he was, but that wasn't good enough. As he trudged on, a fear consumed him, what if he couldn't find his way back? What if he were forever lost on Mount Everest?

He had to get back for George's and Emma's sakes. To tell the others to let them know they had conquered the mountain. Sandy choked up at the thought of telling George's wife, Ruth. Telling her would be the hardest thing he would ever do. He could picture the horror in her trusting eyes.

Death, he felt, stalked him in this shadow world of rock and ice. A misstep or a slip... Concentrate he told himself, concentrate on surviving.

At least there was enough moonlight casting light on the slopes and on the glacier below.

As he stumbled on, he willed himself to move forward. Then he slipped, fell, and began a dizzying descent down a steep incline. Gloved fingers raked at the frozen scree like claws. Sandy frantically thrust boots into the frozen rock surface, but the hobnails glanced off, and he couldn't get traction. On he tumbled. When he felt himself slipping over the ledge, he covered his face for protection, and for what seemed like minutes became airborne before smashing onto the stone-studded terrace below.

Pain radiated from every inch of his body. A pounding, wrenching pain threatened to overwhelm him; even so, Sandy made himself take inventory. His left leg splayed at a ninety-degree angle, right leg was also broken, but his arms worked. He could crawl. And he did. Bit by bit, using his hands and elbows, he pulled himself onward until confronted by a massive wall of boulders. The only way forward was to climb over, but with his broken legs, it was impossible. With a thud of fear, he understood the enormity of his situation. The bloody mountain had won.

His fear then turned into an all-consuming rage. His death, without a doubt, was to be on this frozen piece of landscape. The mountain laughed at him. She knew he was helpless.

He watched a shooting star streak across the heavens and wondered where its final resting place would be.

As the cold intensified, his pain lessened, and he drifted into a hallucinatory jumble of remembrances and visions. His thoughts floated to the expedition members. They wouldn't know that against all the odds, he and George had accomplished greatness. Dead men don't talk. Then a surge of hope. Perhaps dead men do. The camera! Their photos! Those photos would document their journey. What if, he thought, what if someday his camera were found? The glory would be theirs. Then all this would have been worth it. The camera caused him to remember the gem, his last gift to Emma.

Increasingly it became more difficult for Sandy to flex his swollen hands. Gritting his teeth, he forced himself to reach into his pocket and take out the camera. Two pictures left. He clumsily wrote with the camera's stylus on the back of the film the word "Everest." His clue to the others that they had made it. Then he advanced the film to the last photo and wrote "Ama Dablam." His code to Emma where the gem originated. When he wound the film, it left one film chamber empty. Opening up the camera, he inserted the gem and wadded the note to Emma into the now empty spool chamber.

His body began shivering uncontrollably. Never before had he experienced such cold. It was if his blood were freezing. As his body shut down, thoughts of his love for Emma welled up. Emma. Her name echoed in his mind like a mantra. To once again see that slow smile that lit up her face and transformed her into someone otherworldly. To hold her, to kiss her once more, and to tell her how much he loved her. This was Sandy's lone and last regret.

Chapter Thirty-One

Khumbu Region, Nepal present day

"Hey, I need to get by."

"Oh, sorry." Cynthia stepped back, allowing the exasperated trekker to pass her. How long had she stood there, staring at Mount Everest, wondering about Sandy, wondering about his final thoughts, wondering where on that vast expanse of rock and ice his mangled body lay? All were unanswerable questions, and how very strange, even remarkable, that both she and Sandy were drawn to climb mountains. It was as if on a profound level, whispers of genetic memory tied her to Sandy, and the closer they approached the mountain, the tighter those strands of DNA twisted around her heart.

Then, mentally shaking herself, she concentrated on hiking the harsh, rocky trail. As they trudged on, all she could see were never-ending switchbacks. Although Cynthia was fit, the altitude began affecting her breathing, and as she looked at the faces of other Westerners trudging ever upward, she realized she wasn't alone. Only the Sherpas seemed unaffected.

The roar of the Dudh Koshi River faded away as her group climbed higher. An alpine forest thick with fir and pines surrounded the stone and boulder-strewn trail, and the scent from those trees clung heavy in the still air. Cynthia could almost taste pine resin. Hidden by the forest's cover, birds flitted and chirped, but only the occasional raven flew overhead in plain view. She passed a caravan of yaks loaded with bags of dry goods resting by the side of the trail, their tongues lolling out from exertion.

Cynthia pushed herself to speed up, and after rounding a switchback, caught up with her group. Dorje continued to lead, followed by Trevor, Tim, Paul, and Jon. Yak Herder and his men brought up the rear. After another hour of steep trekking, they crested the top of the hill, and there it was. Before them lay the legendary village of Namche Bazaar, the heart of the Sherpa Kingdom. An abundance of white and gray stone buildings topped with bright blue and green galvanized roofs staggered higgledy-piggledy up the steep, terraced amphitheater. Unimpeded by the forest, the views became more dramatic, and the iconic, fluted Himalayan peaks were in the near distance. Was this the type of setting, she wondered, James Hilton had imagined when he wrote *Lost Horizon*?

After making sure everyone was accounted for, Dorje and Yak Herder left the group for a short chat. Dorje said, "The climbers need to become acclimatized, so we won't need you for a couple of days, but if you hear anything new about smuggling or the Foreigner, let me know. Oh, and that porter you told me about, the one on the 1953 Hillary expedition…"

"The Old Trader?"

"No. The other one."

"Lhak-pa Gyal-tshen? He lives with his niece in Khumjung."

"I have a favor to ask. After you unload the yaks, go there and ask him if he'll talk to the redheaded woman about the old days."

"What old days?"

"The days before Hillary climbed Mount Everest. She wants information about the 1924 expedition."

Yak Herder shook his head. "But that was long before Lhak-pa Gyal-tshen's time, and everyone who worked that expedition is dead."

Dorje shrugged his shoulders. "She wants to write a book and thinks the old man may know stories from back then."

"I'll bring him a bottle of chang and see what I can do."

When Dorje returned to the group, an angry-looking Paul confronted him. "Where the hell have you been? You've kept us waiting out in the middle of nowhere."

"You're in no hurry, Paul," Dorje replied in a measured tone. "You'll be acclimatizing here for a day before going on. Tomorrow we'll have a hike and…"

Paul barked. "Are we going to stand here all day? Where's the damn hotel?"

A grin flickered over Dorje's face; then, he directed their eyes to the top of the amphitheater. "You still have some more climbing to do, Paul. It's up there, about another thousand feet, it's called Dorje's Roof of the World."

Cynthia grinned at Paul's expression. Dorje's lodge was aptly named.

There was no straight way to the top of the horseshoe. The windy path followed the topography, and when a section became too step, rock steps had been inserted. They passed a dry goods store, next to it was a store renting trekking and climbing gear. Souvenir shops were intermingled with lots of lodges. By the time they reached Dorje's Roof of the World, everyone was out of breath. Already, the rarified air was taking a toll.

Cynthia found Dorje's lodge to be clean and rustic charming. She guessed the lodge offered about a dozen rooms. The walls were decorated with folk art; yetis scaling mountains, snow leopards stalking prey, and gods and demons locked in the never-ending battle between good and evil. Along with folk art hung photos of Gurkha soldiers and mountain climbers.

Dorje yelled something out in Sherpa. Once he did, two women, one middle-aged with black hair streaked with white wearing the typical long Sherpa apron, and a young woman wearing jeans and a thick pink woolen sweater, maybe late teens, rushed out to greet him. After a flurry of conversation, Dorje turned to the group, "My cousin and her daughter will take you to your rooms and make sure you're comfortable."

Chapter Thirty-Two

Namche Bazaar, Nepal present day

Wandering downstairs for breakfast, Cynthia felt rested, as she gazed out of an aqua-rimmed window to see the weekly market in full swing. Mothers with children who hid behind their mother's skirts bartered with vendors and all manner of goods, foreign and local, were displayed. Foodstuffs, cookware, and Chinese-made clothing and shoes vied for space with handwoven Tibetan carpets.

Lounging close by, men with red yarn tied in their braids spun prayer wheels. With their high cheekbones and deep copper skin, they could well have been Cherokee or Navajos.

She continued downstairs to the small breakfast room where Dorje sat alone. Returning his smile, she asked, "Am I the only one up?"

"Everyone's up but Paul. Trevor and the others are outside taking photos of market day." Dorje called out to the maid, "Bring cereal, eggs, and pancakes."

Oh, I have good news for you. The two porters who are still alive from the Hillary expedition, well, Yak Herder visited one of them yesterday, and he's agreed to talk to you. Although he's over a hundred, his mind's still good, and he does remember stories from earlier expeditions. It's about a three-hour trek, so we'll leave for Khumjung right after breakfast."

Cynthia's spirits soared, and she gave herself a mental high five. Surely the old man would know details about the 1924 expedition. There had to have been Sherpas who had worked on that climb who shared recollections around campfires. Maybe, just maybe, he knew untold stories about Sandy Irvine.

A moment later, Jon pulled up a chair. "I couldn't help but overhear your conversation. Dorje, you've planned for us to view the holy mountain, Khumbila, with a guide, but there's a yeti scalp at the Khumjung Monastery that I'd rather see. May I tag along?"

Dorje looked inquiringly at Cynthia, who nodded her okay.

"A holy mountain?" she asked.

"The god of the Sherpas lives there. Climbing it is strictly forbidden," Dorje answered.

Cynthia liked the idea of a peak off-limits to humans, one that belonged strictly to a god. It seemed right and just. She pictured the god with his hair braided with red yarn and dressed in a long Tibetan robe, staring sternly down at the goings-on of mortals from his frozen Everest-like perch.

"And Mount Everest's god?" She asked.

"She's a goddess, Chomolungma, one of the sisters of long life. She rides a red tiger."

Cynthia turned to Jon. "And the yeti scalp?"

Jon was about to reply when Paul approached. Dorje didn't bother to look up, but took out his Gurkha knife and concentrated on sharpening it. Jon took one look at Paul's angry face and got up to leave. "I'll be back in fifteen minutes."

The billionaire loomed over Dorje and spat out a litany of complaints, ending with, "And your solar shower is piss poor. It barely drips out warm water. Fix it, so it's up to acceptable standards."

Dorje's eyes narrowed. He continued honing his knife to a hair-splitting sharpness before answering. "You're at 11,000 feet in the Himalayas. What'd you expect?"

The sarcasm escaped Paul. "I'm too busy to hike today. I can't go. I've rented an internet café computer for the day. I need to connect to my businesses."

Dorje rammed his blade deep into the table, "Ahh, your businesses. Fine, then. But if I don't find you fit and in good condition, you won't be climbing Ama Dablam."

Paul stormed off.

Dorje gave Cynthia a slow wink and a grin.

Is he flirting with me? She wondered. She took in his high cheekbones, toned legs, and yes, she was a sucker for great legs and winked back. So now, who was doing the flirting?

Dorje considered her. Nice. Very nice. But he knew from experience two people from different cultures equaled heartbreak, but still, she had a slim body.

***

A short time later, Cynthia, Dorje, and Jon worked their way up a narrow track. As they progressed higher, she caught her first unobstructed glimpse of Ama Dablam, the mountain she had come to climb. Sun sparkled off the hanging glacier, and the mountain's two side ridges seemed to reach out to her in a lover's embrace. It was the most beautiful mountain she'd ever seen.

The steady pace of trekking became hypnotic, and her thoughts reverted to Sandy's red diamonds. Trevor was adamant that there were no mines in this area, and her internet research concurred. Had that porter lied when he told Sandy that they came from Ama Dablam? Had he protected his real source?

At the Khumjung Monastery, the rancid smell of burning yak butter candles drifted their way. Around them, were statues of Buddhas, gods, and goddesses set in deep niches. Scattered here, and there were furniture pieces painted in deep reds, yellows, and oranges, the vivid colors of Buddhist decoration.

A bald-headed monk joined them. Dorje draped the monk with a white kata scarf, while they talked in Sherpa.

The monk unlocked the glass cabinet housing the yeti scalp, and they took turns looking at the domed, auburn-haired relic. Jon pursed his lips and brought out a magnifying glass to carefully examine it. After the inspection, they thanked the monk with a donation and left.

"Now, to see the old man." Dorje asked Jon, "Do you want to wait here or come with us?"

"Do you mind if I come along?" Jon asked

"Not at all," Cynthia replied.

Khumjung was a small village, and after getting directions from a boy of about ten wearing a Jonas Brothers t-shirt under his parka, it wasn't long before they located the right house. Built with the same gray stone as the others, it had weathered teal paint flaking off the window frames. As they approached the house, Cynthia felt an uneasiness. She knew nothing of Nepalese culture, but whatever was happening wasn't right. Outside, a small crowd had gathered, and inside came the startling sound of women wailing. Cynthia stood stock still as the wails echoed around her.

"What's going on?"

Instead of answering her, Dorje pushed his way inside and spoke to an elderly woman. After a few minutes, he returned. "We're too late. He died this morning right after breakfast."

***

They trekked back in silence, each enveloped in their thoughts when Cynthia recalled something Dorje had mentioned earlier. She picked up her pace until she caught up with him. "I just had a thought. You said that two men from the Hillary expedition were still alive. What about the other one? Would he talk with me?"

"The Old Trader," Dorje answered slowly as if savoring the name. "He's a strange one."

"How so?" she countered.

"Years ago he settled in our valley with his yaks, but not much was known about his past. Once in a while, he'd drop a few hints, but all we knew for certain was that he made a living by leading caravans across Tibet and into China, sometimes disappearing for months or even years. Then he'd return with treasures and tales. He and my grandfather were friends, but that was a long time ago. Once when I was a boy, he sat me on his knee and told me a story of a caravan trip he'd taken to Mongolia. A monstrous snake had attacked the caravan, grabbed a camel, then disappeared into the dunes."

"A monster snake?"

"He probably made it up to entertain me, but that story gave me nightmares for months."

"I take it your grandfather isn't alive?"

"Dead for thirty years."

"Does the Old Trader live around here? Can we visit him?"

"Doesn't live too far away, and he may remember me. But I hear he's not so social anymore. The exception was last week's ceremony for Burra Sahib."

"Who?"

"Our name for Edmund Hillary. I'll see what I can do. But don't get your hopes up."

"It'd mean a lot."

***

"Where are we off to for dinner?" Trevor asked Dorje.

"To the Everest View Hotel. It's a short trek."

Cynthia had worked up an enormous appetite by the time they reached the hotel. Camouflaged by stands of Himalayan fir, scrub brush, and boulders, the stunning stone and glass building seemed to materialize from out of the hidden ridge like some magic trick. A more cathedral-like setting for a hotel Cynthia had never seen, and they stood in silence, paying homage to Chomolungma, the highest mountain on earth.

The hotel itself teemed with climbers and trekkers spilling into the lobby and patio area, waiting to be seated for dinner. Somehow, despite the crowds, Dorje secured a table next to the windows. The highest peaks in the world were framed by the floor-to-ceiling glass. Jaw-dropping didn't begin to describe the panorama. Shifting clouds scudded near the mountains' tops, and rapidly changing light played against the folds, crevasses, and snowbanks. It almost gave Cynthia a feeling of claustrophobia the way the scene seemed to fill the room and demand homage.

As they made themselves comfortable, Paul regaled them with stories. Tim, the shy one, appeared especially enthralled.

Dorje stood up. "Try our local dishes; momos, Sherpa stew, dal bhat or....

"Hey! Gurkha!" A sandy-haired man yelled out to Dorje.

Dorje countered, "Alden, what are you and Steve doing up here so soon? I thought I left you two back in Kathmandu."

"Everyone, this is Alden Droiter and Dr. Steve Kaiser," Dorje said, introducing the pair. Alden works on the airport expansion project in Kathmandu, and some of you already had met him when we were flying to Lukla, and Steve here takes care of the sick and wounded." Dorje then absentmindedly touched his healed shoulder, the one Steve had extracted the bullet from.

Taking off a frayed Seattle Mariners baseball cap, Dr. Steve pointed it at Alden.

"Had I known Droiter was working up here at the same time as me, I'd have volunteered for another posting." Steve's bushy eyebrows seemed to have a life of their own, dancing upwards like two caterpillars.

Alden Droiter punched him playfully on the arm, then thumped Dorje on the back, pulled up a chair, and winked at Cynthia. "Not a table left to be had. We'll be joining you."

Alden's cherub-like face beamed goodwill. "To answer your question, Dorje, V.I.P.s demanded my early presence up here. Some government ministers, along with the British Ambassador, are flying up ASAP for a quick visit, some bloody photo op. So all of a sudden, the Syangboche airstrip improvements project rises like cream to the top. It's a short walk to the airstrip, so I'll be staying here during the work. And speaking of the British Ambassador, have you heard the latest?"

"The six million pound accounting error?" Dorje asked.

"Old news. When the ambassador ran last week's hash, he was our hash horn."

"What's a hash?" Trevor asked.

"The official name is Hash Hound Harriers; it's an international organization. We are 'a drinking club with a running problem.'"

Then Alden continued, "That week, the Ambassador's job was to blow the horn to keep us together. So we were trotting along a stream when the Ambassador does his ta-ta-ta thing on the horn. All of a sudden, a water buffalo bellows back. Gave us all a start. She crosses the stream and trails the Ambassador. I mean, she won't let him out of her sight. He speeds up; she speeds up. Every time he blows his horn, she bellows at him. I swear at the end she was batting her eyelashes at him. Let me tell you he's never run a faster hash in his life. Or had a female show him so much attention."

Laughter rounded the table.

Alden pointed to Steve. "And Kaiser's up here from Kathmandu being a real doctor for a change. Aren't you off to the Health Post?"

Steve nodded. "Leaving after dinner. A doctor broke his arm, so I'm pinch-hitting. I'll room tonight at some lodge along the way; then tomorrow it's off to the clinic."

Paul Bellame slammed down his menu. "Do you mean to say that instead of wasting time hiking, I could have flown in here? Saved me all the effort?"

Dorje allowed the loquacious Alden to answer. "Only specially sanctioned flights are allowed in. If there's a medical emergency, or if government muckety-mucks need to be here for a short time. Helicopters with guests for this hotel are allowed, and when he was older, Sir Edmund Hillary would fly in. Steve and I flew in instead of trekking because we're still acclimatized."

Steve interrupted Alden's flow. "Besides, if you flew in, you'd probably be suffering from mountain sickness by now. Even with a preventative like Diamox, you need time to acclimatize at lower altitudes. People die of altitude sickness. Dorje, when are you heading for your mountain?"

"Tomorrow."

Cynthia's attention was distracted from the conversation by the intoxicating smells of spices, which drifted to the table moments before the waiters did. Cynthia helped herself to a heaping scoop of bharta, an eggplant curry, and kung pao chicken. She was sopping up the bharta with garlic nan when Alden, mischievously asked, "Seen any yetis yet?"

"I saw the yeti scalp at Khumjung," Cynthia replied.

In a tone dripping with condescension, Paul interjected, "Let me guess, Dorje, you believe in them."

Dorje ignored the sarcasm. "A few ancients in outer villages say they have seen them at a distance. But no, I've never seen one, so I can't say."

Jon drank the remainder of his beer and ordered another. "I consider them a myth, but there's a faction called Cryptozoologists who not only believe in them but insist there's more than one type."

"I was served a 'yeti' once in Kathmandu," Alden replied. "A drink mixed by an excellent bartender at the Rum Doodle. He called it the 'yeti's footprint.' It tasted like it too."

Laughter erupted.

After Jon ordered another beer, Cynthia remembered an earlier conversation she'd meant to ask him about, and said, "A couple of days ago you spoke about red diamonds and the Knights Templar. I'm curious, what exactly was the connection?"

Jon had been gulping down his beer, and his words were becoming increasingly slurred. "Jacques de Molay, the head of the order, through his intervention, had Marco Polo released from prison in Genoa. In gratitude, Polo presented de Molay with part of the treasure he collected during his many years of traveling in the East, a red diamond."

"But the Templars didn't enjoy it for long. In 1307, the stone disappeared during the great massacre of his order. If the stone existed, it's lost in some long-forgotten hiding place. Here's an interesting coincidence. Kublai Khan reportedly befriended the Polos, and Marco Polo's travels and the Himalayan Prince's gift to Kublai Khan occurred around the same time. It was certainly an era of strange events."

Tim stuttered out, "Kublai Khan! How would he know the Polos?"

"The Khan was a remarkable man, very open to foreigners and new ideas. At that time, he pretty much ruled the world. His kingdom stretched as far west as Eastern Poland."

Paul jumped back into the conversation. "Can any of this be proven?"

"Yes and no. In the 1700s, a document surfaced from the Vatican archives referencing a second Matteo Ricci letter, which went into more detail about the diamonds. Shortly afterward, the priest who discovered the document was murdered. The document disappeared."

"How convenient. So there's absolutely no proof. All hearsay. Along with Bigfoot and the aliens among us, it's complete and utter nonsense," Paul replied with a snort.

The professor coughed apologetically, then gave a quick smile. "Sorry to keep rambling on. I'd forgotten what alcohol can do to you at altitude. I'm used to giving lectures, and out of the classroom, I don't know when to stop."

Cynthia ignored the plate of food. "Are you saying that diamonds could come from here?"

"Possibly."

Her heart thudded. Maybe there was a connection with Ama Dablam.

Trevor countered. "Not to argue with you, Jon, but to have diamonds, you need kimberlite pipes. There's no history of pipes up here."

"Kimberlite pipes?" Alden asked.

"Nature's mechanism for creating diamonds. No pipes, no diamonds." Trevor explained.

"For all, we know, there could be ancient pipes up here," Jon replied.

"Jon, be realistic. The red diamonds were probably mined in India or Sri Lanka. Perhaps even Burma then reached China by way of Tibet or Nepal."

"Maybe, Trevor, maybe, but I'd happened upon a Cambridge geologist whose mentor thought precious stones came from here." Then Jon dropped the discussion.

As Cynthia glanced around the table, it seemed that the mood had shifted. The initial laughter and light-hearted banter dried up like so much dew on a hot day. But it was more than that; she couldn't pinpoint it accurately, but something dark lurked beneath the surface of the conversation.

In a change of subject, Alden asked Steve, "Any news about the expedition hunting for Mallory's camera?"

"Big money's funding it, so they have the best of everything, including high tech camera equipment. As far as I know, the expedition is still up on Everest looking for it. If the camera has photos that can be developed, it will pay for the expedition tenfold."

If Cynthia had felt shocked at the mention of a third red diamond, she was blown away to learn that an expedition was searching for Mallory's camera. If they found it, surely her great-grandfather's body would be nearby.

Dorje motioned to the waiter to bring the bill. "They'll be down soon. No one stays long in the death zone."

Chapter Thirty-Three

Namche Bazaar, Nepal present day

The Foreigner sat back with a smile plastered on his face. There was an element of amusement in all of this. Here he was, in plain sight, the proverbial wolf dressed in sheep's clothing, and no one knew. He didn't have to feign interest. The professor's information riveted. And sitting at the table was Cynthia. Where, oh, where, Little Red Riding Hood, is your diamond? He thought he knew the answer. When he'd broken into her condo in Pasadena, and then her cottage in the Lake District, there was no diamond hidden in either property, and he was thorough. He examined every possible nook and cranny. What he'd found, though, was her great-grandmother's will and a receipt for a safe deposit box, but no key. Could she have brought the key with her? He thought so. You don't know it yet, Cynthia, but it won't be yours for long.

Stay in the background; he cautioned himself. Don't act too interested. There was a tense moment when the professor referred to a Cambridge geologist, then stopped in mid-sentence. What was he keeping back? Then it suddenly hit him. Shit. Jon all but implied there were more red diamonds here. But the source? Where was it? The Foreigner clenched his hands in frustration. The professor must know more. His smile widened when Cynthia asked for a little time to explore the area, and Dorje agreed. He knew his next step, a heart-to-heart with the professor.

Watching Jon chat with the others; he felt like a volcano ready to explode. How to get Jon off by himself? As daylight fast faded into twilight, his stress level heightened. It wouldn't be long before the group left.

The professor apologized. "Need to clear my head."

Then he made a beeline toward a far stand of trees.

The Foreigner grabbed his parka and a balaclava and tailed, careful to put some distance between them. The pine's scent hung heavy in the cold wind, and unseen creatures skittered in the sparse undergrowth. Jon stopped at a small dell surrounded by scrub brush. Good, the Foreigner thought, as he approached.

"Hi, Jon," he called out, "wanted to ask you some questions."

The professor stumbled forward in his turtle-like way and blinked. "Glad you're not a yeti." He then tried to pass.

The Foreigner stepped forward, blocking his way.

Jon cocked his head and threw a confused glance. "Getting dark, need to get back."

"In a minute. Just a couple of questions. I was listening to you at the restaurant, and that geologist you referred to, you were about to add more but stopped. Why?"

"Huh? Why are you interested? Need to get back." Jon hiccupped.

"No problem. Finish your story, and you can go. Those red diamonds, I'd like to know about them."

Uneasiness flickered across the professor's face, and it looked as though he would push on past. Instead, he remained motionless, as if resigned to telling his story.

"When I returned from China, I continued searching for additional information, not expecting to discover anything. I asked geologists I knew if they had heard of diamonds mined in this part of the Himalayas. All but one laughed at me. An old geology professor from Cambridge recalled a long-ago conversation with another geologist who had been a member of an Everest expedition."

"That information was?"

The wind whipped up, and a hawk dipped and caught something in the brush and flew skyward with a rush of wings.

The Foreigner was now so close he saw vapor rise from the professor's breath and fear flame in his eyes. Suddenly, Jon strong-armed the Foreigner and tried to run. The Foreigner grabbed him.

"What are you doing? "Jon panted.

"Go back to the diamonds."

"Alright, alright. On that expedition, a porter sold two red stones to a climber. The geologist on that climb who examined them considered them rubies or even diamonds, but before rudimentary testing took place, the climber died on the mountain. The stones disappeared with him."

"Those stones, were they Kublai Khan's?"

"No, how could they be?"

The Foreigner's voice rose in excitement. "Then there are more red diamonds out there. Was this during the 1924 climb?"

"How could you possibly know that?"

"It doesn't matter. Where's the source? Where'd they come from?"

"I have no idea. I assume the dead climber knew, but…"

"One more time, Jon. Where's the source?"

"This conversation's over." Jon kicked out, then staggered up the incline, in his panic, his turtle-like gait became more pronounced, and his breathing came in gasps. The Foreigner caught up with him and slammed Jon hard against a rock face. Jon threw up his hands to protect himself as dirt and stones cascaded around them like a mini avalanche.

"Listen, you fucking ivory tower asshole, I want answers."

The professor managed to rasp out, "Noel Odell was the geologist who examined them. But I swear, I have no idea where they came from."

The Foreigner's anger bubbled into something colder, darker. He stood there thinking about Sandy Irvine's camera from that 1924 expedition. When he'd opened it, along with a roll of film was a note and a red diamond. The camera had a slit in the back to write on with a metal stylus. On one photo, Sandy had "Everest" scratched on another, "Ama Dablam." Those words had to have significant meaning to Sandy. Mount Everest he understood, but Ama Dablam?

"You're hunting for the source, too, aren't you, Jon?"

Wiping his bloody lip, Jon responded, "I don't know what you're talking about. I'm not after diamonds. Don't you understand? I study and write about this part of the world. Noel Odell probably thought they came from the Everest region because, well, why else would a local porter have them?"

"Are there mines up there?"

"I have no idea."

"What existed back then?"

"Only real human habitation on the Tibet side was Rongbuk Monastery. On the Nepal side, there was Namche Bazaar and assorted monasteries and villages."

The Foreigner stood and pulled Jon up with him. "Tell me about Rongbuk Monastery."

Jon sobbed. "This is crazy! What do you want to know?"

"Give me some history."

Jon's voice quivered. "Ahh, it was founded in the early 1900s by Dzatrul Rinpoche, who also founded Tengboche Monastery near Ama Dablam. The 1924 expedition had visited Rongbuk Monastery and received the abbot's blessings and warnings."

"So, one man founded both monasteries."

"Yes, but before Rongbuk Monastery existed, monks lived in caves around there for centuries." The professor massaged his arm, but fear still filmed his eyes. "Now, get away from me."

Questions and more questions thought the Foreigner, but no answers. Was there a tie-in with the monasteries? If so, why, over the past, almost one hundred years hadn't more diamonds surfaced? Mined out? But where was the original mine? How could it have been kept a secret for all these years?

The Foreigner placed his hand over Jon's mouth and began pounding Jon's head into the rock outcrop.

The Foreigner pulled his hand away from Jon's mouth. "Speak to me, Jon. The source!"

The professor moaned, "I swear, I don't know."

The thirty million dollar stake couldn't be jeopardized. Jon, he realized, had to die, so that information would die with him. Grabbing him by the throat, he battered the professor into the rock face. Jon's struggles weakened. Jon slumped, and his breathing stopped. The Foreigner let him fall.

Anger gave way to an icy coldness. He was always cool under pressure. It had to look like an accident.

The setup had to be believable. That Sherpa, Dorje, was way too smart and observant. Using a fireman's lift, he carried the dead man to the top of the hill then rolled him down. He scrambled after Jon, lay the body in a natural position, then placed a large rock under his head. Now those back of the head lacerations would be easily explained.

Chapter Thirty-Four

Namche Bazaar, Nepal present day

Cynthia was growing concerned. Where was Jon? Why hadn't he returned from his walk? Was he lost? It wasn't as if there were bears or wolves up here, but the terrain was steep and rugged.

Cynthia called over to Trevor and Tim. "Seen, Jon?"

They shook their heads.

Grabbing the flashlight from her pack, she started down the narrow track where she had last seen him. Stands of silver fir and juniper shadowed the ridges. A scurry of movement; then an Impeyan pheasant raced for concealment under bushes. She looked down for footprints, but the barren, stony soil offered nothing.

Turning the next corner, she caught sight of something that filled her with dread. A motionless shape lay at the base of the hill. She raced down the trail and knelt by the figure. "Jon, can you hear me? Can you speak?"

Gently, she went over his body, searching for a wound or a break. Lifting his head, she felt a sticky substance on her hand. Blood!

"Over here! I need help!" Cynthia yelled.

Dorje and Basu appeared a few minutes later.

"The back of his head. It's bleeding."

Dorje bent down next to her, unzipped Jon's parka, and put his ear next to Jon's heart. "Shallow breathing, but still, breathing. Basu, we'll carry him back to the hotel."

"Jon must have tumbled down the hill and hit his head after drinking all those beers," Basu replied, as he bent down to assist Dorje.

After moving him, Dorje picked up the rock Jon had been lying on. "This shouldn't be here."

"Why?" Cynthia asked.

Before he could answer, Jon moaned, and all their attention focused on making him comfortable.

While Dorje and Basu carried Jon, Cynthia sprinted ahead. He can't die, she implored. He can't die. Her breath came in gasps as she entered the hotel. She found Dr. Steve and the gregarious Alden sitting at the hotel bar drinking and chatting up a trekker.

Alden pulled over an empty stool and pretended to dust it off for her. "Cynthia, you don't look happy."

"Dorje and Basu are carrying Jon back. He's badly hurt."

She turned to Steve. "He's got a cracked skull, and is unconscious."

Alden looked flabbergasted. "Bloody hell."

***

When Jon arrived, they placed him in an unoccupied room. A maid carried in a pan of hot water and extra towels. While Steve examined him, the others milled around outside, waiting for news. The wait wasn't long. Steve returned with a worried face.

"Done all I can. Alden, we need medevac. Contact the military, have them fly a helicopter up. He has to be flown to Kathmandu tonight."

"In the darkness? At this elevation! We're at 12,500 feet. Too bloody dangerous for the pilot."

"It's a traumatic brain injury. If he isn't taken down..."

"All right. Enough said. I'll contact Lukla, it's the closest airstrip to us. They often have helicopters there," Alden said, pulling out his cell phone then dialing a number.

In the lobby, Dorje pulled a Sherpa friend aside. "Can you take my climbers back to my lodge?"

The man nodded, and Dorje introduced him to the group.

"I'll stay too," Paul insisted.

"No," Dorje replied, "Jon knows Cynthia better than any of us, so she can stay if she wants."

"You couldn't pull me away, I would have insisted on staying with Jon until the helicopter arrives."

A makeshift stretcher was cobbled together with broom handles and rope; then, blankets were piled on top of Jon to keep him warm. Dorje and Basu carried him as fast as they dared to the airstrip, while the others led the way with their flashlights. Cynthia found the airfield about as basic as you could get: unpaved, dirt-packed, and topped with a gravel dust. Adjacent to it was an office, and close to that was a warehouse undergoing construction. Tarps covered the half-finished roof, and as they approached, a sleepy-looking guard stumbled out from the building and smiled when he recognized Alden.

"Put him inside the airstrip warehouse," Alden directed. "It's closer to the landing path, I'll tell the pilot to take off immediately."

Cynthia, Dorje, Basu, Alden, and Steve, along with Jon, entered the stark, cinderblock building. Along one side of a wall, tools, equipment, and boxes were stacked in neat piles. Shivering, it seemed to Cynthia, colder inside than out.

"Over here," Cynthia said, pointing to a corner. "It'll protect Jon from the wind." She held Jon's hand and whispered, "Hang on. We're getting you help."

Steve took the unconscious man's pulse and blood pressure. "I hope that pilot gets here soon."

Alden faced the airstrip office. "Damn it. The generator's still broken. Guard, bring out all the lanterns we have, we'll light the strip with them."

Cynthia stayed with Jon while the others ran back and forth, carrying lanterns.

"Line them up, so the 'copter can see to land," Alden insisted. "It's as black as the devil's soul up here."

An hour later, Cynthia heard the thunderous whoop, whoop of rotor blades slicing through the thin air.

Dorje yelled, "Hurry, guard. Bring more matches."

The last lantern was set in place and glowing brightly when the chopper materialized out of the darkness like a prehistoric pterodactyl. The rotors' backwash stirred up loose dirt, snow, and ice as it landed. Squinting to keep dust and debris out of their eyes, they rushed Jon into the waiting helicopter. The pilot mimed that he had to leave immediately.

Steve cupped his hands and yelled over the engine's roar, "I can't go with him. I have to be at the clinic tomorrow. No other doctor there to take my place."

Dorje shouted to Basu, "You go. After the hospital, contact his embassy. Then trek back up."

Cynthia's throat constricted watching Basu jump in. The helicopter tilted forward, skimmed down the runway before lifting off vertically. It dipped to the right, then sped down the rugged valley and into the dark void. They stood there, motionless, staring into space until the engine's whine faded away, and the valley became quiet again.

Alden was about to say something when a phone rang.

"Damn," he said, sprinting towards the office. "Be right back. Think it's the big boss from Toronto. He tends to forget time differences."

Steve cinched his pack. "Got to go. Won't get anywhere tonight if I don't put down some shoe leather. See you in a week or two." With a wave, he headed upwards toward the silhouette of the high mountains.

A gust of wind blew through the warehouse, whipping a tarp off of the containers. It soared upwards, finally settling near an oil drum. Dorje carried it back to a stack of wooden crates. Odd, he thought, as he was about to secure the tarp over the crates. The boxes had Chinese labels. Dorje had a firm recollection of Alden complaining that, contractually, the consortium could only use Canadian and American materials, and that was causing the project to go over budget. So why the Chinese labels?

One crate had a loosened panel, so, taking out his knife, he pried at it, which caused it to snap open with a sharp crack.

Cynthia threw Dorje a quizzical look. "What?"

"Checking on something."

In the faint light, there wasn't much to see, so Dorje wrenched-off another board, but instead of the expected construction supplies, there, staring sightless at them, was a dinosaur skull its mouth frozen open from its death struggle.

"What in hell has Alden gotten himself involved in?" Dorje muttered.

Chapter Thirty-Five

Namche Bazaar, Nepal present day

The warehouse door swung open and, Alden strode in, along with an icy breeze. "Damn weather's deteriorating, so tomorrow's work will have to wait. It'll sure bugger up the schedule. And the phone call, Toronto! From the big boss. He's flying out here next month to check on things. Silly twit. Hey, where's Steve?"

"Gone. He's on his way to the clinic."

Alden's eyes darted to the open crate. "What's up?"

Dorje slipped his knife back into its sheath. "The tarp blew off. I was about to put it back on when I noticed the crate." Dorje's tone was flinty. "Alden, what are dinosaur bones doing here?"

"Huh?" In a flash, Alden stood next to Cynthia and Dorje.

The wood splintered in Dorje's hands as he ripped off another board to give Alden a better view. "I'll stake a bottle of chang that these bones were looted in the dead of night, then smuggled out of Mongolia or China, and the rest of the boxes contain pieces of him, or her, or other dinosaurs."

Cynthia's eyes traveled over the skull's bony ridges, over its rows of teeth with still embedded debris, over the enormous eye sockets, and curved snout. Was it a new species or something already known? In the lantern's light, the dirt-covered skull took on an eerie,

Jurassic Park-like quality, as if the creature were ready to spring back to life to terrorize the world.

Dorje wrenched open two more crates. "Another head. This one has horns. And here's a foot with claws as long as an ice ax." He put the boards back and swung the tarp over the crates.

Alden remained stunned. "I was warehousing the boxes as a favor, going to cargo them out on the next helicopter that emptied its load."

"A favor? For who?"

Alden's ordinarily cheerful face became drawn. "Dr. Steve Kaiser. He told me they were expired medical supplies, just old equipment he wanted to be destroyed back in Kathmandu."

"How did these boxes get here?" Dorje demanded.

"By yak." Alden blew on his hands to warm them. "Steve's obsession with dinosaurs seems to have got the better of him. Still, it's hard to believe he'd do anything illegal. I'll send word to the clinic, and insist, no *demand* that he take them away."

They made for the office, where once inside, the kerosene heater cranked out a welcome blast of heat. Cynthia noticed a whiteboard on the back wall with a flow chart of completed and pending projects written in a precise, steady hand. Next to the whiteboard stood a file cabinet piled high with what appeared to be invoices, and behind Alden's office was a small room filled with electronics.

The cramped office provided only two chairs, so Dorje perched on Alden's desk. Dorje's face was taut with tension as he leaned over to Alden. "I can't tell you how important it is to get rid of these fossils."

"But, Dorje, come on. I mean, they're only fossils. Okay, Steve's obsessed, but they're not contraband like drugs or guns."

"You're wrong. The Gobi desert is one of the richest fossil fields in the world, and because of that, there's a deadly multi-million dollar black market business. Just recently, Chinese soldiers shot two Nepali smugglers. Fossils are so valuable that the Chinese have a shoot to kill policy, no questions asked. Just a couple of weeks ago, a smuggler from Namche Bazaar, was murdered in Kathmandu."

"You mean to say if I'd been caught with this stuff, even though I knew nothing about it, I could have been charged."

"Charged and thrown into jail for a long time," Dorje answered.

"Why that cold-blooded asshole," Alden said. "My life and career were on the line!"

"We've got to do something with them," Cynthia said.

Dorje added, "As the murdered man lay dying, he confessed to smuggling monsters. If you'd never seen a dinosaur before, what would these look like to you?"

"Monsters," Cynthia whispered, remembering running her fingers over the row of teeth, dulled from being in the ground for a hundred million years. "Definitely monsters."

Dorje added. "There must be a tie-in with that murder and what's in these boxes. Dinosaurs are big money. It's easy to kill when millions are involved. You know as well as I do, Alden, if a situation involves China or India, we're the minnow between two whales. China will clamp down hard and, as punishment, impose all sorts of sanctions. If our government suspects that we're at the heart of dinosaur looting, this area will be swarming with police."

"Were the crates brought over Nangpa-La?" Alden asked.

"Had to have been. These are smaller dinosaurs; the big ones are too heavy for yaks to carry. Probably truck them to a port and ship them out, my guess is Shanghai. So they have at least two supply lines. If one shuts down, the other is up and running."

Cynthia recalled reading an article that the Gobi Desert, had some of the most extensive dinosaur finds in the world, and it was the first place where they uncovered dinosaur eggs. But why transport the bones through Tibet and Nepal? It didn't make sense. "Dorje, why take this long way around? There must be faster routes, and what's Nangpa-La?"

"A pass, part of an ancient trading route between Tibet and Nepal. There was an incident a few years back when Chinese border guards shot at unarmed Tibetans and killed several. Very dangerous to cross it in the winter. Last time I went, I found two dead yaks on the trail. I think the reason for this route is because it's easier to avoid detection. Chinese soldiers aren't going to open those crates."

Alden opened the office cooler. "Beer?"

Cynthia and Dorje shook their heads, no.

Alden took a deep sip then licked the foam off his top lip. "Nothing like Newcastle Brown Ale to calm the nerves. You're not going to tell the authorities about this, are you? I'll lose my job."

"Not if we handle this ourselves. I don't know how deep the smuggling ring goes, and I can't do anything about it now, but after the climb, Steve and I are having a not so friendly talk. Yak Herder said a rumor's going around that a man they call the Foreigner heads the smuggling ring, and who knows, this might be just the tip of the iceberg."

"Who is this Foreigner?" Cynthia asked.

"For all I know, it's Steve," Dorje answered. "Damn it, he's put the health clinic in jeopardy, and it's one of only a few up here. We need it to remain operational."

Alden's shock turned to anger. "Fucking Steve's set me up as the fall guy. If the authorities had discovered those bones, I'd be frog-marched straight to prison. What a dumb ass I've been. I should have checked the boxes myself. Dorje, you've got to help me."

"How, Alden?"

"You've scared me, shitless. If I'm caught with this stuff...."

"Do you still use that old cave for storage?" Dorje asked.

"No. That's why we're building the warehouse. Oh." Understanding filled Alden's eyes. "I see what you're getting at. Good idea."

They secured the entrance with chains after two hours of schlepping boxes and hiding them in the back of the cave.

Cynthia sucked at a sliver stuck in her finger from that last box she'd carried.

They said their goodbyes, and when Cynthia and Dorje shifted down the trail, the moon remained bright, but the cold had intensified. This whole night, she thought, had been surreal; Jon's accident, stories of Kublai Khan, Marco Polo, and the three red diamonds originating from where the highest mountains inhabit the clouds, and then dinosaur fossil smuggling. The coincidence of Jon talking about red diamonds was astounding. Could she be in danger? Could someone know about her red fancy, as Uncle Saul had called it? She hadn't the gem on her, but she did wear the safe deposit key.

By the time they reached the lodge, it was pushing midnight, and she stumbled in from exhaustion. Light filtered in from the side room indicating someone was up, and they walked in to find May-la, the young maid, dozing in the kitchen, with a cup of cold tea in front of her.

She yawned, then rubbed her eyes.

"Go to bed," Dorje demanded. "Tomorrow will be a busy day."

After May-la left, Dorje went over to a cabinet and took out two glasses and a bottle of clear liquid. "Drink?"

"I could use one. Vodka?"

"Raksi." A ghost of a smile played across his face.

She accepted the glass. "What an awful day!" First, that old porter died, then Jon suffers his horrible accident, and now it's dinosaur fossil smuggling."

The drink was clear and had a kick. After she downed it, came the welcome heat of the alcohol. Something Dorje had said earlier had gnawed at her, and now was as good a time to ask. "When you picked the rock from under Jon's head, you said it shouldn't be there. What did you mean?"

"There was no indentation under the rock."

"So?"

"The rock." He went across the room to pour himself another drink.

"Yes?"

"Was just placed there."

"What?" She blinked in disbelief. "You're saying it wasn't an accident?"

"Somebody smashed his head with a rock, then set up the scene to make it seem accidental. Although it was too dark to see clearly, I noticed branches of several bushes were newly broken off, and they weren't near the fall. The way I see it, Jon fought with someone and was rolled down the hill, then the rock placed under him to explain his head wound. Did you meet anyone else on the trail?"

"No."

Dorje threw her a hard glance. "You should have."

She gave him a blank stare. "Who?"

"You should have passed whoever did this to Jon when he returned to the hotel."

His look further hardened, like an interrogating cop.

Did he suspect her? The doubt in his voice hurt, she wanted him to like and believe her. Feeling drained, she stood up to go to her room. "If you think I had anything to do with Jon."

His look softened. "I never said you did. As soon as he heard you or saw your flashlight, Jon's attacker could have hidden in the bushes until you passed by."

"What about contacting the police?"

"Nothing to tell them. Just a rock in the wrong place."

"Have you ever contacted the police about anything?"

He ran his fingers through his salt and pepper hair. "Up here, we take care of our problems our way."

His voice became husky. "Best get to bed."

"When you get news about Jon, let me know."

He nodded.

Chapter Thirty-Six

Namche Bazaar, Nepal present day

Cynthia woke to the swish of a broom, and as it progressed down the hall, the previous day's events flooded her mind like so much bilge water. Mentally she counted down that day's events. First, the old porter's death, then Jon's accident or, if Dorje were right, not an accident but an attack, then there was the corrupt or even murderous doctor who possibly headed a fossil smuggling ring. It was all so fantastical. If she could, Cynthia wished she could thoroughly sweep yesterday into oblivion.

She hadn't known Jon for long, but in the short time she'd been with the group, she'd developed a real fondness for him. Sweet, kind, and brimming with arcane information, it was impossible to believe that anyone would intentionally harm him. Had a robbery attempt gone bad? But that didn't make sense; his wallet was in his parka. She thought about last night's dinner conversation. They spoke of yetis, the trek, and yes, red diamonds. Was there a connection?

Scrambling out of bed, she jumped into her clothes and ran down the stairs to find Dorje.

The longer she was in his company, the more she liked him. Those deep, dark eyes were hinting of danger, his mental strength was making him seem as solid as Ama Dablam herself. Outside the lodge, Dorje and Cook were tinkering with the solar shower. He glanced up at her. "Needs new panels."

"Any news about Jon?" Cynthia asked.

Dorje shook his head.

"Can I speak to you someplace private?" she asked.

Nodding, he put down his screwdriver. They climbed for about a half-mile on a switch-back path overlooking the horseshoe-shaped valley, finally resting on a flat boulder that offered a degree of shelter from the steady wind. Namche Bazaar, the capital of the Sherpa people, was an unlikely place for a village. A steep, stony, terraced land dotted with buildings and prayer flags. You had to be physically fit to survive here.

Cynthia tore her gaze from the valley and turned to Dorje. "I need a friend. I believe I know why Jon was attacked. You see, I think it has to do with red diamonds."

Dorje's eyes narrowed. "Diamonds? What diamonds?"

Her pale blue eyes darkened with emotion. Dorje had saved her life during the cobra attack; if she could trust anyone on the climb, it was him. "After you hear my story, it'll make more sense. You see, I recently inherited the estate of my grandmother, a woman I'd never met. Among her stuff were love letters and a red diamond. The diamond is incredibly rare, and only a few of its size exists. That's why I need your help." Cynthia fingered the safe deposit key under her shirt.

"How can I help?" Dorje asked, puzzled.

"Jon spoke of Kublai Khan, Marco Polo and red diamonds before he was attacked. There has to be a connection. His money wasn't taken, so it's the only thing that makes sense," Cynthia insisted.

"A connection, how?"

"I was inches away from death from a spitting cobra. And there's Jon's assault, and Paul is on the climb. Am I the reason? I feel hunted. Something sinister is happening."

"Who else knows about this diamond?"

"No one on this climb, or so I thought. I'm wearing the key for the safe deposit box it's stored in."

Dorje waited for her to continue.

Cynthia picked at a long piece of wild grass, pulling off the ripening seed pods and shredding them. "Paul Bellame was the worst mistake of my life. I met him at my father's office, although we dated some, we were never intimate. The more I saw, the less I liked. When I refused to see him again, he became obsessed with me."

"His eyes follow you when he thinks you're not looking," Dorje said.

"Do they? The situation is, well, complex. Dad works for Paul, and somehow Paul found out that I was on this climb. He may have bugged my phone, that's why he may know about the diamond."

Dorje took out his knife and began honing it.

"I detest him," she said.

"Don't like him much myself. But why would someone attack Jon? He didn't have the diamond." Dorje said.

"Okay, that's the flaw in my logic. I don't have an answer, just a gut feeling that the gem is somehow involved. Possibly someone thought Jon knew more than he did." She took a deep breath. "And maybe, just maybe, I'm next."

Dorje's face became guarded, and she wondered if he thought he had an unstable, crazy woman on his hands.

"Sounds pretty far-fetched, Cynthia."

"And that book I'm going to write."

He waited.

"What I haven't told you was that my great-grandfather is Andrew Irvine. Before he and Mallory made that final push to the summit on the 1924 Mount Everest climb, he sent the diamond to my great-grandmother and wrote in his letter that it came from here."

"From Tibet?"

"No. From Nepal. And he had two of them."

She swung around and pointed to Ama Dablam. "From there. That's what the porter who sold them to Sandy claimed."

"What happened to the other one?"

"Probably disappeared with him on the mountain."

Dorje put his knife away. "I grew up here, Cynthia, and I'm an elder. If there were diamonds, I'd know about them."

"But Dorje, Jon discovered historical proof that they existed. They came from the Himalayas. He saw the documentation himself. And he was so knowledgeable and now…"

"Jon's documentation was fuzzy. The highest peaks in the world include multiple countries. Let's say for argument's sake, it's true that the diamonds came from here. If you found any, do you think my government would allow you to keep even one?"

"Of course not, but that's not the point. I want to determine if they exist as a backdrop for my book to have a better understanding of my great-grandfather's world."

"Are you sure yours is real?"

"Verified by a jeweler."

She flicked a beetle off of her knee. "Truly, it's not about becoming rich; I'm leaning toward donating much of the money. I totally understand that I can't just come and hunt for gems. Sandy's story haunts me. It's the mystery. If diamonds are from here, where's the mine? And there's that other mystery. Did Mallory and Irvine reach the top of Everest? If so, what happened to the camera?"

"That 1924 expedition?" Dorje said.

"Yes."

"I told you my ancestor was a high-altitude porter on the support team. He had to have known Sandy. He blamed snow demons for their deaths. Now here you and I are, almost a hundred years later. Strange karma."

He was about to say more, but Cook headed toward them, waving his arms. Although he had hit the trail at a fast pace, the overweight Cook had barely worked up a sweat by the time he reached them. "Basu's back."

"How's Jon?" Cynthia asked anxiously.

"Flown to Bangkok," Cook answered.

Dorje threw her a grim look. "They fly the bad cases to Thailand."

Chapter Thirty-Seven

Ama Dablam, Nepal present day

"Oh no," Cynthia muttered, realizing she was the last to use Dorje's solar shower. Why hadn't she got up twenty minutes earlier? It'd be a miracle if there was hot water left. There was no miracle, and as a spray of cold droplets covered her body, she danced a jig to keep warm. It was the shortest shower of her life.

Going upstairs toward her room, she stifled a groan. Down the hall, with that stiff-legged gait of his, came Paul. She tensed and moved to the left. He did the same. She moved to the right, he followed. Damn it; she was blocked.

"We need to talk," Paul demanded.

"Get out of my way. Not interested. Get out of my life!"

"You'd better be interested. Without my protection, your father has one bleak future ahead of him."

"My father works for you. Big deal! If you fire him, he'll get a job somewhere else."

"The somewhere else will be scrubbing toilets in the pen," Paul answered.

"What are you talking about? What are you threatening me with?"

"I'm not kidding, Cynthia. Loosen up, or your old dad goes to prison. I brought evidence along to show you."

"You're a liar. Dad's done nothing wrong."

He smashed his fist against the wall and tilted his head towards her. He was so close that she could see razor nicks on his skin. Tim chose that moment to exit his room with his day pack. Shyly, he uttered a quiet hello.

Cynthia watched with sick fascination as Paul put Mr. Hyde back in the box and pulled out Dr. Jekyll. With a tone oozing charm, he said. "Ready for the trek, Tim?"

Tim nodded wordlessly.

Cynthia linked her arm with Tim's. "I'll go downstairs with you because I haven't had breakfast either."

They left Paul stewing in the hallway.

***

Soon afterward, they left for Tengboche, where they'd overnight. The steady uphill pace was hypnotic, and Cynthia let her mind float while she struggled to make sense of Paul's rantings. In the heat of the moment, she'd denied that her father could do anything illegal. But Cynthia couldn't shake the feeling that maybe, just maybe, he had. She bit down on her lip, trying to figure out how to access Paul's so-called evidence if indeed he had any. Then she considered the stunning coincidence of her great-grandfather and Dorje's relative having been on the 1924 expedition, and there were thoughts of red diamonds and the mysterious Foreigner.

According to Trevor, this area had been thoroughly explored for decades by both geologists and miners. Dorje, who lived here, insisted there were no mines. So they couldn't exist. But if they didn't exist, why had that porter told Sandy the gems came from Ama Dablam? Then there were Kubla Khan and Marco Polo's diamonds, which supposedly came from the roof of the world. Granted the roof of the world could be elsewhere, but still.

After an hour of watery sunshine, a cold fog settled in, obscuring all but a few feet of trail. When the wind blew away the thick mist, Cynthia saw teasing hints of the great Himalayan giants. The further they climbed, the more Cynthia had difficulty breathing, and her lungs pumped harder in the thin air.

***

The group walked along in comfortable silence, broken occasionally by short conversations. By midmorning, the fog had lifted entirely, and when the final wisps evaporated like so much smoke, there spread out before them, was the Shangri-La-like monastery and surroundings of Tengboche. Fir trees and rhododendrons ringed the grounds, and the great monoliths of Everest, Nuptse, and Lhotse provided a backdrop of drama like no other. Crowning the monastery was a towering white and gilded salmon spire that glinted like gold in the sunlight. A spiritual gravitas permeated the site.

"We'll spend the night here at a lodge. The rest of the day is free to do what you want," Dorje announced.

Dorje knew he had to confront Steve. To wait would invite disaster. Who knew if the army or police had a whiff of the smuggling. Even though they'd hidden the dinosaur bones in a nearby cave, it was still too risky to keep them. Now that he knew of them, he would be implicated if the police found out. No, Steve had to tell him what was going on.

Taking Basu aside, Dorje explained, "I'm an expedition leader, not a babysitter. The group's your responsibility until we reach the mountain. I should be back to base camp by tomorrow."

"Why, Uncle? Where are you going?"

He pointed to the Mount Everest trail. "To Pheriche, to find a man and confront a doctor. I'll tell you more later."

He left a puzzled Basu playing tour guide. Basu's a born teacher, like his father, Dorje thought, listening in for a few minutes before going.

Basu explained to the group, "In 1989 Tengboche Monastery was destroyed by fire, then rebuilt, but it's not the only monastery up here. After we arrive at base camp, we'll take you to a much smaller one at the base of Nameless Mountain, where you'll be blessed in a special ceremony before our climb."

Trevor thumbed through his guidebook. "Odd. No mention of another monastery up here."

"Probably because it's so small. It only has about ten monks, and it isn't a tourist destination. It's the oldest monastery here and a strange place. The head abbot is a reincarnated lama, and if we're lucky, he'll perform the blessing."

"Strange? In what way?"

There was a slight hesitation before Basu answered Trevor. "Just strange. Monks there keep to themselves."

***

Dorje headed for the village of Pheriche, the last inhabitable outpost before Mount Everest. He followed the trail through a glacier-carved valley. From the valley, the trail wound up a steep set of hills, and he passed a series of *mani* stones embedded in walls,

248

carved with the sacred mantra, *Om mani padme hum,* Hail to the Jewel of the Lotus. The smell of snow hung in the air, but if he were lucky, there'd only be flurries. As he gained altitude, the trees of the alpine zone transitioned to scrub brush, then finally to sparse grassland.

He saw a group of Sherpas reinforcing a cliff wall with stone blocks, a backbreaking ordeal. One man recognized Dorje and waved; Dorje returned the gesture. A bit before dinner time, he reached Pheriche and entered a lodge asking for directions to the Old Trader's place. He ignored his gurgling stomach, and the thoughts of his favorite Sherpa stew, and promised himself a heaping bowl when he'd finished his tasks.

The Old Trader's property proved easy to find. Three yaks grazed in a walled field, and beside it stood a large stone hut nestled into a hillside.

His knock brought a young Sherpa of about fifteen to the door.

"Looking for the Old Trader."

"He's away."

"Who are you?"

"Da-nu. I feed the yaks and watch his house while he's gone."

"Gone to?"

"He went to Tibet."

"Over Nangpa-La?" Dorje's eyebrows shot up in surprise. The Old Trader must be pushing ninety or so. Far too old to be leading a caravan over that pass. "A dangerous route."

"He took most of his yaks, and two men. The first time he's crossed Nangpa-la in years."

"What's he trading?"

The young man shrugged his shoulders.

"When will he return?"

Another shrug.

Dorje had more questions, but anticipating yet another shrug, said his goodbyes.

He wondered what could be so important that a man of his aged years would risk his life on that pass? He let out a sigh. Cynthia had her heart set on talking to him, but the Old Trader's return could be in days, weeks, or even months.

The low hanging sun caused him to pick up his pace. There was still time to confront Steve at the clinic. In part, he felt conflicted. On the one hand, he liked the guy, and not many men would give up their vacations to volunteer at the Himalaya Rescue Association Clinic, but how could he ignore the smuggling? Would Steve argue? Deny it? It didn't matter what he said; the proof rested in those wooden boxes at the airstrip. Steve had to leave Nepal for good, but before he did, Dorje wanted the names of those who helped him. An earlier concern crossed his mind. What if there was more to it, what if dinosaur bones were just part of the smuggling operation? And that murder in Kathmandu, was Steve involved?

Dorje strode by a memorial sculpture of stainless steel that commemorated Mount Everest's dead. He thought of men he knew who had died on that mountain. Shaking off his memories, Dorje proceeded to the clinic.

A sign in English read, "9:00 a.m. to 12 noon. Altitude talk at 3:00 p.m. daily. Emergencies are seen at any time." As far as Dorje was concerned, this was an emergency. He strode in.

The clinic was deserted. Two rows of windows above a window seat allowed the sun's last rays in. On the floor, several portable hyperbaric chambers were stacked against the wall; at 14,600 feet, acute mountain sickness was taken seriously. For those in the throes of mountain sickness, other than immediate descent, the portable chamber was the last line of defense to keep death at bay.

A lone woman with black-rimmed glasses and short honey-colored hair glanced up from her paperwork, stood and greeted him in halting Nepali.

Dorje thought her quite the tiniest foreign woman he'd ever seen. A tad under five feet, he guessed, and, about ninety pounds.

"Is Dr. Kaiser around?"

She looked relieved when he asked in English.

"He's delivering a baby in another village. There were complications."

"Any idea when he's coming back?"

She paused and considered. "Maybe tomorrow night, but that's a guess. I just arrived yesterday, and he'd already left."

Inwardly, Dorje groaned. That made it two out of two. This trip had been a complete waste of time. "Would you tell him Dorje stopped by? Are you a doctor?"

She nodded. "Dr. McDonald. Florence McDonald."

He left the clinic and made his way to a lodge well known for its Sherpa stew. It was a peasant dish, but the cabbage, potatoes, and yak meat suited him just fine.

"Dorje. What are you doing here?"

He turned to find a porter he knew.

"On an errand. Was looking for the Old Trader but found out he's gone."

"A friend saw him in Tibet. He'll be home next week."

Dorje clapped him on the shoulder. "That's the best news I've heard all day."

Chapter Thirty-Eight

Ama Dablam, Nepal present day

Ama Dablam towered above the boulder-strewn terrain. The mountain left Cynthia feeling awestruck. Atmospheric pressure had pushed a cloud mass to the mountain's upper reaches, and a recent, heavy snowfall obscured vast amounts of the Southwest Ridge, their treacherous route to the summit. Where Cynthia stood at base camp, a smattering of multi-colored tents mushroomed across the fan-shaped moraine like so many brightly colored M&M candies.

***

After dinner, when Cook had finished cleaning his pots and pans and chopping vegetables for the following day's meals, an inky darkness settled in, and the temperature plummeted even further. The propane heater pumped out enough warmth to remove the worst sting of chill from the air in the mess tent, but even so, a chill remained.

After the others had retired to their tents, Cynthia, Basu, and Cook relaxed in cushioned plastic chairs and huddled near the heater, playing poker. Solar-powered light bulbs offered enough light to read or play cards. In the corner, sitting by himself, Yak Herder kept them company by whittling a miniature snow leopard. "Four fives," Basu declared, with a big grin. Cook threw down his cards in disgust.

"You win again," said Cynthia, pushing the small pot of rupees toward Basu.

A rustle of noise, then the tent flap opened and in walked Dorje. Cynthia smiled her welcome.

"Everything all right here?" he asked.

"We have a morning hike to the monastery, so I suggest some sleep," Dorje announced. With that advice, he left and headed for his tent, and Cynthia, yawning, realized how tired she was and followed suit.

Cynthia slept well and woke hungry at sunrise and headed to the mess tent, where she heard the sound of sizzling bacon. Up at altitude, you burn more calories, so she didn't hesitate to stack her plate high with pancakes and smothered them with glorious, gooey, golden honey, then she added scoops of country-fried potatoes, bacon, and hash. Nepalese honey hunters occupied a death-defying class of their own, taking incredible risks when scaling sheer cliffs with flimsy bamboo ladders to reach the beehives. She'd never tasted honey with more depth and complexity in her life, slightly vanilla flavored with hints of citrus.

After breakfast, in the shadow of Ama Dablam, she grouped with the rest of them for their journey to the Nameless Mountain monastery.

"Tell me again, why we are going to this monastery?" A bored-looking Paul asked.

"To receive blessings from the lama. At the puja ceremony, the lama asks our gods for protection during our climb."

Cook remained behind.

***

When the group arrived at the monastery's entrance, a thick wooden door studded with rusting iron bolts swung open, allowing the group entry. Dorje led the way.

Greeting them was a young monk, thickset with an enormous breadth of shoulders.

"Tashi delek, Dorje."

"Tashi delek," Dorje replied.

Inside, yak butter candles licked the ceiling with their smoky tongues and filled the room with a musky, animal odor. When Cynthia's eyes adjusted to the darkness, she observed a handful of monks kneeling on prayer rugs, chanting. After all the gray uniformity outside, the monastery's interior shocked her senses; inside, it was all about color and pattern. Nothing was plain; the prayer rugs, walls, furniture, and the highly detailed religious paintings of deities called thangkas, were a riot of orange, crimson, green, and blues that added to the sensory confusion.

After the monks knelt in the altar room, a young monk brought in a wide-mouthed singing bowl and a portable container that held juniper branches and incense and placed it before the altar. He lit a fire, and soon, there were sweet smells.

A nod, then the chanting started. The monk's voices were so deep in tone, and so hypnotic, that they didn't seem human, it was as if the chanting began at their feet. When the chanting ended, the group rose to leave; the lama motioned to Dorje to stay behind.

The lama sipped at his tea. "Last night, a vision disturbed my peace."

A candle sputtered, flickered, then guttered out. The room darkened.

"About what?" Dorje asked.

"I will relate it to you. I transformed into a raven with great, black wings and soared above Chomolungma; then, I skimmed over the barren plains on my way to Eastern Tibet, where centuries before, I was a head lama. Like a silent ghost, I bore witness to my previous death in a battle against our great enemy. When I flew back to Nameless Mountain, a flood of tar enveloped the valley, blighting all it touched." He paused and stared intently at Dorje. "Much of what I saw, I cannot share, but this I can. You were in my vision."

"Me?" A pause that seemed to stretch for an eternity settled over the room, but Dorje remained silent, for he knew from experience that there was no hurrying a monk.

"You fought for your life against a deadly enemy within a mountain," The lama finally said.

"On a mountain?"

"No. Within."

"Fought who? Which mountain?"

The lama shook his head in sorrow. "Evil has gripped our valley. More than that, I don't know. Meanings in visions are not crystal clear."

Dorje slowly answered, "I think this evil is caused by a man called the Foreigner. He leads a smuggling group. One of his men was stabbed like a gutted fish in Kathmandu. I believe he ordered the killing."

Dorje said through clenched teeth, "I have a strong suspicion who this Foreigner is. But I must have proof."

The lama gave a deep sigh. "Find your proof then. This Foreigner must leave our valley and take this evil with him."

Dorje nodded and said in a hushed tone, "I need advice on another matter. The woman I brought for your blessing believes red diamonds come from Ama Dablam, and she wants to know if it's true."

A startled looked passed across the lama's face. "Red diamonds! She said that?"

"Yes."

"How can that be?" The lama asked.

Dorje shrugged his shoulders and replied, "A porter working on the 1924 climb sold diamonds to her ancestor, claiming they came from Ama Dablam. Holy One, the woman wants to know if there were any local mines."

The lama closed his eyes and sighed, seemingly lost in thought. The silence became so lengthy that Dorje wondered if he had gone into a trance. Just as Dorje stood up to go, the lama's eyes snapped open.

The monk visibly relaxed and said, "These are dark times. Be careful, my son. Trust to the ravens."

Ravens? Dorje left the chamber mulling over the cryptic message. What did ravens have to do with anything? As he walked away, he thought, what a strange conversation. He couldn't make heads nor tails of it.

"You seem grim," Cynthia said to Dorje on their way back to base camp.

He pushed back his dark thoughts and gave her a half-smile. "Just thinking of my stomach. If we don't return soon, Cook'll give us rocks to eat for dinner."

"Hey, Dorje," Trevor shouted from behind. "Up there. Above the monastery. What is it?"

Trevor hunted for his binoculars while Dorje scanned the mountain. He caught a flash of movement high up on Nameless Mountain.

By the time Trevor brought out his binoculars, the figure had disappeared. "Missed it. What was it?"

"Too high for a snow lion or bear. Probably a tahr. But it may not be an animal at all, could be a hermit."

Paul voiced surprise. "A hermit, in this environment? There's nothing to eat."

Dorje scanned the peak before answering. Villagers bring food for the hermits, although they tell me one hermit hasn't eaten or drunk in years."

"Impossible!" Paul said.

"Anything's possible. An old wandering monk told my grandfather that a Beyul exists in the valley," Dorje responded.

"A Beyul?" Cynthia queried.

"A Shangri-La," Dorje explained.

Cynthia was taken aback. "Oh, like in Hilton's book, '*Lost Horizon*.' Are you saying Shangri-Las exist?"

Dorje continued, "A Buddhist saint told of hidden places in the world which are protected, one hundred and eight exist, but if a Beyul is here, no one has ever seen or heard of it."

"But that monk?" Cynthia said.

"He was old; maybe his mind wasn't right."

Paul seemed especially interested. "These Beyuls, what's in them?"

"Knowledge, peace, protection, and treasure."

"Treasure!"

"Not the kind you seek, Paul. Come."

Chapter Thirty-Nine

Ama Dablam, Nepal present day

The trail followed a deep ravine that lifted to the foothills, then snaked along the mountain's contours and crossed a small stream fed by glacial melt. When the path turned east, the monastery dipped from sight.

After an hour of trekking, Cynthia's thoughts drifted to Dorje.

She couldn't deny the growing sexual chemistry between them. Last night she thought he was going to kiss her. Then she wondered what if would feel like to have Dorje's hands stroke her body. His lips, how would they taste? Tall with sharp cheekbones, he had an undeniable presence, a steel-like toughness. Turning aside lustful thoughts, she quickened her pace until she caught up to the object of her lust. "Dorje, what did the lama say about diamond mines?"

Before he could answer, the ground roiled and shook. Stumbling forward, Cynthia just managed to stay upright. A six-or even a seven-point earthquake? When the roiling subsided, she glanced up at the mountain above them. A puff of snowy smoke burst near the top.

"Dorje!" she cried out, pointing upwards.

A piece of cornice broke away from the upper ridge, picked up speed, and swept down the slope. From then on, the whole mountain seemed to explode. Cynthia watched uncomprehendingly as the familiar, natural world around her ceased to exist.

"Run!" Dorje yelled. "Avalanche!"

Fear etched their faces as they sprinted forward. She shouldn't look back, she knew that, but like Lot's wife, she couldn't resist. To her horror, the avalanche had quadrupled in size: snow, ice, and boulders rushed down the slope with speed and power that took her breath away.

A spray of snow coated them, and all white, they became almost all indistinguishable from their surroundings. From the corner of her eye, she saw Tim stumble and fall. Running back, Dorje, dragged him to his feet, and half carried him along. The tsunami of snow and debris became even more deafening; gaining momentum, it engulfed everything in its path. Her boots had never felt so leaden, so heavy. Willing herself to run faster, Cynthia panted with exertion and fear. With a last spurt of speed, she and the others rounded the mountain's base. Safety! She pressed hard against the mountainside. A shard of rock pushed deep into her shoulder, but she didn't dare move. Chunks of ice as large as cars hurtled past her as if launched by an enraged giant. Before her eyes, the avalanche completely buried the back trail under tons of debris.

While the river of snow flooded by, Dorje swung around to do a quick headcount, then yelled out, "Basu's missing!"

Chapter Forty
Ama Dablam, Nepal present day

The avalanche shuddered into an eerie silence; all the more surreal because of the surrounding devastation. Even the wind became hushed and muted as if nature were catching her breath. Snow, ice, boulders, and slices of the mountain mounded up into a panorama of destruction.

Death had lightly caressed Cynthia's cheek, toyed with her, and then, playfully, allowed an escape. That she and the others weren't a pile of broken corpses entombed under tons of debris, she attributed to sheer, dumb luck. If they'd been five minutes sooner…. Terror left Cynthia, shaking uncontrollably, and she wrapped her arms around her torso for comfort until her shaking subsided.

For a few heartbeats more, they stood stunned, snow-encrusted, and as rigid as ice sculptures. Then Dorje shattered the quiet with his heartfelt entreaty, "Spread out. Find Basu!"

Snow flew off Dorje's parka as he raced back to where the trail had been. Cynthia ran after him, but quickly, once she reached the debris field, her run turned into a wild scramble. Avoiding boulders, and the ice seracs they scattered, all eyes were intent on some sign, any sign of life. He was somewhere under the wreckage, but where? As the minutes ticked away, their search became more frantic. If he were alive, how long before his oxygen supply gave out? It all seemed so hopeless.

Then Cynthia spotted it. "Over here. It's his knapsack."

Laying on her right side, she pressed her ear into the snow and felt an icy tingle. Cupping her hands, she yelled, "Basu. Basu, are you there?"

Underneath, a muffled cry of distress. Like a dog digging up a bone, she furiously scooped with gloved hands. Snow spray flew into her eyes, temporarily blinding her. Ignoring it, she kept on digging. The others sped over.

"Hurry," Cynthia urged, wiping her eyes. "The snow's hardening."

Dorje used a pan he had in his pack as a shovel and made far faster progress. About a foot down, they found him; his face abraded with cuts.

"Thank God you're alive!" Cynthia said.

Dorje and Pemba, one of the Sherpas, gently pulled him out, then took off their parkas and wrapped them around him until the blue tinge in his face had faded.

"Anything broken?" Dorje asked.

Basu shook his head.

Cynthia picked up Basu's pack while Dorje and Pemba steadied him.

"Looks like you've got a touch of frostbite. Let's get you back to camp."

***

On the following morning, Cynthia woke up sneezing and sniffling and heavy-eyed. After dressing, she headed for the mess tent where she found Basu chowing down on a stack of pancakes, looking like he'd been in a barroom fight. Purple bruises blotted his swollen face, and he favored his left arm, but the injuries certainly didn't seem to affect his appetite. Next to him sat Tim, polishing off an omelet, and beside him was Paul, who was charming Tim with one of his many stories. From Tim's expression, Paul continued to mesmerize him; Cynthia had to admit that Paul was a first-class raconteur.

She gave Cook a wave and got a big, friendly grin in return. Cook wore a faded gray knit hat pulled low on his forehead, which barely hid a pair of bushy eyebrows.

"How are you feeling?" Cynthia asked Basu.

He gave her a thumbs-up sign and continued chewing his pancakes.

Cynthia gently patted him on the back, then walked over to the buffet table. Inspecting the buffet offerings, she appreciated that Cook had prepared his usual five-star breakfast on the basic portable camp stove. Fluffy omelets, and fluffier pancakes.

***

As the days marched on, the group acclimatized to the altitude: initially with low ascents on the mountain, then with overnights at ever-higher camps. It wouldn't be long now, Dorje thought, before the summit attempt.

At a rush of wings, Dorje focused on ebony birds swooping and wheeling across the sky on their way to the mountains. The birds' flight triggered memories of the lama's warning, disturbing and unsettling because Dorje couldn't make heads nor tails of it. 'You will fight a deadly enemy within a mountain' and 'trust to the ravens.' How could he fight within a mountain? Fight who? What about the ravens? Was the lama's vision real or just a vivid nightmare?

Dorje watched the ravens' dance on the thermals for a moment more, before dragging his eyes back to watching Basu climb the ice face. Dorje noticed that Basu still favored his left arm, but Basu swore that he was fine and up for the climb. He'd wait and see.

"Basu," cautioned Dorje protectively, pointing to the left of the slope. "Not there. Too dangerous. Fix the ropes below the spur. Paul, stay by the tent until the others come down. Double-check that the tents are secured. Especially the far one. Trevor, help Basu fix the rope. That's right. Now tighten it. To the right, up there. That's the route to the ice couloirs, then to the gray tower."

Trevor scrambled down. "And the rest of the gear?"

"We'll worry about it tomorrow," Dorje answered. "Just one more load of propane cartridges and food to ferry up. Careful of the ice face. That's right. Slowly. We're in no hurry."

Back at base camp, the smell of cooking wafted from the mess tent. Helping himself to a bowl of thukpa, a hearty soup of vegetables, noodles, and yak meat, flavored with chiles, turmeric, and cumin, Dorje dragged a plastic chair from out of the mess tent and opted to eat outside, Cook joined him. Untying his dark green apron, embroidered with a rooster crowing at the sun, he said, "Tomorrow Yak Herder returns with fresh supplies, he wants to know how much longer we'll be here."

"We'll summit soon. The groups had overnights at advanced base camp, camp 1 and camp II. Trevor is by far the strongest, Cynthia and Paul are somewhere in the middle, and Tim's the weakest. By the multiple arms of Chenrezig, how does Tim stay so thin? When he's not in the mess tent inhaling food, twice as much as anyone else, he's constantly snacking on energy bars."

"Maybe he has a demon inside, and he eats for both."

"Demon? More likely, a tapeworm." Dorje then wolfed down the last of the thukpa. "The men will summit soon, but Cynthia has a cough and fever. I've given her antibiotics, but she's in no shape to climb now."

"She likes you."

"What are you going on about?"

"The American. She likes you. I see it in her eyes." Cook blew on his steaming potatoes to cool them. "Basu and I have been talking about it. We think you like her too."

"You've been drinking too much chang!"

***

Earlier sniffles and a cough had settled into something more serious. Bronchitis, Cynthia suspected, and her frame of mind wavered between cranky and depressed. Her tonsils felt like they'd been scoured raw with a bristle brush. That, combined with plugged sinuses and achy lungs, completed her misery. The sobering thought crossed her mind. What if she couldn't climb? Not climbing would be devastating. The mountain itself was her link to her great-grandfather, Sandy Irvine, and she was challenged to climb it like she'd never been challenged before. When Sandy gifted that red diamond to Emma, he had written that it had come from Ama Dablam. Did the lama know about red diamonds or ancient mines? Because of the avalanche, she'd forgotten to ask Dorje.

Rolling out of her sleeping bag, she searched for her journal and wrote: Damn it, I will summit Ama Dablam. I haven't come all this way to give up.

Placing the journal aside, she pulled out her great-grandfather's 1924 sepia photos, the ones he'd sent to Emma, then shuffled them like a deck of cards. Twenty-three pictures and she'd practically memorized every one of them. On the back of each, in looping handwriting, her great-grandfather wrote descriptions, some amusing, some informative, and on others, just a name was scrawled. There was a photo of a tall man called Bataar, one of an itinerant monk, a woman porter carrying as much as the men, and some unposed camp scenes, all detailing the daily life of an expedition back then. Her favorite was of Sandy Irvine with his arm around George Mallory, mugging for the camera. She noted the date on the back. Two days later, Sandy and George would be dead.

What Sandy's life would have been like if he'd lived past twenty-two? Would he have been an engineer? An inventor? One thing she did know for sure from his letters: his love for Emma was deep and profound.

At the rustle of material, her head shot up, and she hurriedly put the photos back into a plastic bag.

"Cynthia?" Then Paul crawled inside. "Heard you weren't feeling well. Anything I can do?" His thick, manicured hair seemed to be missing those thousand-dollar haircuts.

"Yes," she said, scooting as far back as she could, "you can leave me alone."

Instead, he sat down beside her and unzipped his red parka. Dark circles rimmed his eyes, and he looked like he needed sleep. "I've come to apologize. I want to start over with you. What can I do to make it up to you? Jewelry? A car?"

With Paul just inches away from her face, the tent closed in on her, and like a trapped animal, she felt desperate to claw her way out. "Are you in complete denial? You've stalked me for months, and insinuated my dad has done something illegal. Now please, just leave me alone!"

"Your father wants us to be together. How else do you think I found out that you'd be in Nepal? From your dear old dad, that's how."

"My father? No way. Get out!"

Paul's face turned foreboding. "I'm tired of playing games with you. You have no idea how much you'll regret this."

After he left, Cynthia lay racked with doubt. Paul must be lying. He must. Her father wouldn't intentionally betray her, but how did Paul know about the climb? Basu had a phone. Would he let her use it?

She undid the tent's vents to refresh the air, to rid it of Paul's stench, then crawled out. She found Basu sitting next to a big boulder.

After a greeting, she asked, "Can I use your phone? I'll pay for the international charges."

With a smile, he handed it over.

In the privacy of her tent, her fingers dialed her father's number so quickly that it misdialed. Quieting herself, she carefully redialed.

"Hello," the familiar voice answered.

"Dad. It's me."

"Where are you, sunshine?"

"Ama Dablam base camp, 15,000 feet above sea level."

"You be careful. What's wrong with your voice?"

"Respiratory infection." She collected her thoughts. "Dad, I need to ask you some questions. It's important, and I haven't much time to talk."

"Sure. What's this about?"

"I need complete honesty from you."

"Of course, Baby. Always am. What's the question?"

"Did you tell Paul I'd be here? He said you did."

A long pause, then a sigh. "Guilty as charged."

"But why? Why break your promise to me?" Cynthia demanded.

"Because I love you. I want the two of you to be together. He's absolutely right for you."

"Then you don't know me. And Dad?"

"Yes."

Ginning up her courage, yet dreading his answer, she asked, "Have you done something illegal?"

A nervous laugh echoed down the line. "Me? Of course not. But I'm glad you called, Baby. Something I need to get off my chest. We touched on it the last time we talked. Honey, I've been unlucky again with the cards. I'm in trouble. If you sold that cottage, it would erase my debts. Then I can start over. I promise never to gamble again."

Her knuckles were white from clenching the phone. Listening to him go on about his promise to reform sickened her. From his hesitation and inappropriate laughter, the needle of her internal radar quivered into the red zone. What in God's name had he done?

"Dad, you can tell me."

"Truly, nothing to tell you, sunshine. About that money?"

"No more money, Dad. You've taken my savings, even my 401 k."

"Baby, you've got the cottage. That's worth a bit."

"Goodbye, Dad."

After returning the phone back to Basu, she went to the womb-like sanctuary of her tent. Now that she was by herself, her emotional dam broke. Tears rolled down her cheeks. The betrayal was a kick in the stomach. How many times had her dad promised to stop gambling, only to break that promise? As a child, she remembered her parents' arguments, the recriminations, her mother's threats to leave. Long ago, she'd taken over her mother's role as the adult in the relationship. Her dad was weak, but he was her father and her only living relative. What was Paul holding over his head?

"Miss Cynthia," Cook announced from outside, "I've brought you soup."

Wiping away her tears, she opened the flap. Smiling, Cook stood there, holding a steaming bowl of lentil soup and freshly baked bread.

"Thank you, Cook, it looks delicious."

Her taste buds were shot, but as she spooned the hot lentil broth down, it soothed her throat and filled a hole.

She'd fought it for as long as she could, but nature called, and she really had to pee. Men had it so easy. They used empty water bottles, so they didn't have to stumble out of their tents, especially when it was dark and cold. She picked up her flashlight and sauntered out.

The stars blinked brightly, and the moon was rising as she approached the toilet tent. A raven perched on the boulder Basu had been sitting by earlier, and seeing her, cawed before flapping its wings and soaring northwards. In the far distance, the White Ghost lifted his head, as if to acknowledge her, then continued eating.

After doing her business, she thought. Paul's tent! Why not investigate the so-called evidence against her father. What better opportunity than now? Other expeditions had climbed and left, and the members of her own team were still eating dinner in the mess tent.

After casting a furtive glance around, she quickly covered the rocky ground to his tent. But where to start? After focusing her flashlight, her shaking hands rifled through his duffle bag, digging to the very bottom. Nothing of interest. Next, she booted up his laptop. When the blue screen flickered, she typed in her dad's name. Password, the computer demanded. Damn! Biting her lip in frustration, she thought hard. Exactly what was she looking for? A piece of paper? A photo? Something else incriminating? Hurry up, she told herself, they'll finish with dinner soon. She opened a second bag.

Outside, quick footfalls sounded, then the tent flap opened.

"What the hell are you doing in my tent?" Paul demanded.

She swiveled in panic. "I…"

"Dorje," Paul yelled. "Over here."

Paul couldn't control the tight smirk that popped up on his face when Dorje joined them, trailed by Tim and Trevor. All looked curiously at her.

"As you can see, I found Cynthia rummaging through my tent, uninvited. I hadn't mentioned this before, but I'm missing over $2,000. I wanted to keep it quiet until I figured out who did it. No one's been in my tent but her. She's a thief just like her father."

Chapter Forty-One

Ama Dablam, Nepal present day

Cynthia's voice cracked. "Theft? Me!"

Paul's smirk deepened. "That's right, Cynthia. That's exactly what I'm accusing you of."

Some stuff in the bag had spilled onto the floor: socks, an expensive-looking sweater in multiple shades of blue, and a wallet.

Paul picked up the wallet and opened it. "This is what she was after."

Cynthia couldn't have felt guiltier if a detective had cornered her, leaving a store carrying a bag full of unpaid-for dresses. Her clenched stomach informed her how much in the wrong she was, and just how serious Paul's charges were. She had absolutely no right to be in his tent. While her thoughts churned and tumbled, four sets of eyes lasered into her. Trevor and Tim looked bewildered, while Dorje stood stony-faced.

"That's a bald-faced lie," she protested.

"Really? Then why are you in my tent?"

"You accused my father of committing a felony. I wanted the so-called evidence you're using against him."

"What you wanted was to help yourself to more money," Paul insisted, waving his wallet.

Dorje turned to the others. "Anyone else missing money?"

Both Tim and Trevor shook their heads.

"Dorje," Cynthia said, "I insist you go through my belongings. I'll wait in the mess tent while you do it. I have nowhere near $2,000. Perhaps, Paul, you've misplaced your imaginary money, or maybe you turned them into bitcoins."

"Basu, come with me. Everyone else waits in the mess tent," Dorje ordered.

Twenty minutes later, Dorje and Basu rejoined the others in the mess tent. Cook placed hot cups of yak butter tea in front of them as all eyes watched Dorje.

"We went through Cynthia's tent and checked everything. Like she said, there are no two thousand dollars hidden there, so Paul, you're mistaken." His eye's held the others. "We have to trust each other on this climb, our lives depend on it. Cynthia took no money."

Cynthia turned to the group. "I apologize for having you all involved in something that's just between Paul and me. I should have handled it differently."

***

The next morning's breakfast proved embarrassing, and Cynthia's cheeks burned as she greeted everyone. Not that she'd been given the cold shoulder, quite the contrary, everyone was exquisitely polite to her, but she imagined Trevor and Tim had made sure their money was now well hidden, just in case she, a.k.a. Ms. Sticky Fingers, came unexpectedly calling.

Cynthia and Dorje now sat alone in the mess tent. She needed an extra jolt of caffeine after a restless night's sleep. She spooned more instant Nescafe into her mug, stirred, sipped, then grimaced. Big mistake, she should have stopped at one tablespoon.

Dorje got right to the point. "Paul's made a grave accusation against you."

Cynthia fingered a small chip on the rim of her blue-ringed, ceramic mug, and steeled herself for what was coming next. Was Dorje kicking her off the climb?

"Dorje," she said, "Paul's full of it. Like I told you yesterday, I've never touched a penny of his money. He made that up to get back at me. Besides, you checked my tent, you saw that I didn't have $2,000 in cash."

"I get that you've had a bad history with Paul, but you shouldn't have been in his tent," he lectured. "Paul thinks you hid his money outside somewhere, but he's agreed not to press charges."

Cynthia's tone dripped sarcasm, "Isn't that nice! Especially since I didn't steal anything."

Dorje's face remained unreadable. Did he believe her?

Dorje changed the subject. "You seem better."

The tension lifted, and the room became less frosty. "Thanks to your medication, I'm almost human again, but I forgot to ask you, did the lama know anything about mining and red diamonds?"

"The lama seemed confused by your questions, so I gather he knows nothing."

Cynthia looked down, staring intently into her cup, not wanting Dorje to see her disappointment, which was as bitter as the coffee she was drinking. "It was a long shot anyway. I guess the mystery will always remain so. "

Dorje stood up. "Not all mysteries are solvable, Cynthia. As I told you before, there are no mines up here, and there never have been." Swiftly he changed the subject. "Weather's clear, the wind's died down. Tomorrow I'm taking the group, including Cook, along on the summit attempt. We'll be gone for four days, five at the most. You'll stay here, but I'll leave Phemba to cook for you."

She gripped the sides of the table so hard her knuckles turned bone-white. "I've traveled all this way and spent most of my savings. I can't begin to tell you how much I want to climb this mountain. I'm going up. Even if I have to do it alone."

He stared long and hard at her, sighed, then said, "Okay, I'll compromise. After we come down, if the weather holds up, you'll have your chance, but I'll only take you if you're strong and healthy. The last thing I want is an accident."

"Today, I'll practice on fixed ropes," she promised. "Build back my strength."

Hopefully, she thought, she was no longer infectious, as she leaned over and lightly kissed Dorje's cheek. The multiple-day stubble tickled in a sensuous, sexy way, and she could feel the heat radiating from his body.

"Thank you," Cynthia rasped out, stepping away.

She saw a flash of smolder in Dorje's eyes. A desire for her?

After Cynthia left, Cook set a cup of yak butter tea before Dorje and made no attempt to hide his grin. "See, I told you she likes you."

"If you're not careful, I'll have you work off all those extra pounds by carrying gear up the mountain."

Cook adjusted his gray woolen hat and started laughing. "Then, who will fix your Sherpa stew?"

***

Later, during dinner, an unexpected voice yelled from outside, "Hello, the camp." The tent flap opened, and Alden Droiter's cheerful face appeared. "Hey, Gurkha. Any leftovers for a hungry engineer?"

"Cook," Dorje turned and said, "bring Alden some food."

"Aren't you a bit far from the airstrip?" Dorje asked.

"My job's done. But I have to wait for my boss and the British Ambassador's arrival next week. I've little to do, so thought I'd come by and visit, and speaking of the ambassador, have you heard the latest?"

"Which ambassador?" Cynthia asked.

"When it comes to stories, there's only one ambassador, and he's a fellow Brit," Alden answered.

Dorje moved his camp chair back to accommodate Alden. "Go on," he said with an amused look of anticipation. "The golf story?"

"No. This happened the other day. It seems that the ambassador was at a party at the Chinese Ambassador's residence with all the other VIPs. Had some godawful drink called *baijiu* that's about 60 percent alcohol, and has a bloody kick. The story goes that the Ambassador was innocently knocking them back after being told it was Chinese wine, and by the time he was ready to leave, he could barely stand. When he staggered down the stairs, he slipped and grabbed onto the sari of the Indian Ambassador's wife. He all but ripped it off her. She had to go back inside and borrow a dress from the Chinese Ambassador's wife, who's about half her size. Looked like a stuffed sausage, and barely could waddle in it. Once she got into the limo, the dress gave way. It was the rip heard around Kathmandu. Now there's a diplomatic shit storm, and the Indian Ambassador refuses to take our ambassador's calls. "

Alden then regaled them with further accounts of the ambassador's adventures, all of which Dorje had heard before. He waited until the engineer had finished eating and storytelling and said, "Let's go outside."

The night was windless, but a cold chill had settled in the valley, and the overhead stars brought to mind millions of ice chips floating on the dark currents of the Milky Way. Surrounding them, the massive mountains loomed mysteriously and vaguely threatening. Both men zipped up their parkas.

"When are you starting your summit bid? Alden asked.

"Tomorrow. The weather's fine, and everyone's acclimatized. Cook will stay at Advance Base Camp while Basu and I go higher with the others. Then I'll climb again with Cynthia."

"Cynthia? Why isn't she going up with the rest of you?" Alden asked.

"Sick."

"Gurkha, you're an old softie. You wouldn't have done that for any of the men I bet. I'll be on my way in the morning then."

"No, I probably wouldn't have." Dorje's face turned tense with concern. "Alden, I've got to ask you. Are Steve's fossils still with you?"

"No." Alden countered by asking, "Have you seen Steve since Jon was helicoptered out?"

"Tried to," Dorje replied, "but he was away from the clinic delivering a baby the day I came looking."

"Then I'll update you. Our good friend, the doctor, and I hope you caught my irony, has flown back to Kathmandu."

"Does he know that we know what's inside the crates?"

"I point-blank warned him that I wasn't accepting any more. Said that he'd placed me in a real bind with his smuggled contraband. He tossed me a half-hearted apology, the kind people do when they're caught, and don't really care. What a real cold-blooded son of a bitch he is."

"And the fossils?"

"He sent men to pick them up. So I have no idea where they are now. At least they're away from the airstrip. Can you imagine if the police had caught wind of them while the British Ambassador was visiting? Talk about a diplomatic shit storm!"

Alden picked up a stone, threw back his arm, and flung the rock as far as he could. It whistled through the air and pinged as it bounced off of a faraway boulder. Stooping again, he picked up another stone, threw it, then, with a face pinched with worry, turned back to Dorje. "We touched on this before, but I need to be certain, are you going to the authorities about this? If you do, I'll lose my job."

"You did nothing wrong."

"Define wrong. Company regulations forbid flying supplies without proper papers. So, having done a favor for Steve, I'm in a bad way. What's that saying? No good deed goes unpunished. My bosses won't be forgiving," Alden said.

"I'm a village elder, not the police. As long as the smuggling stops and Steve leaves Nepal, I'm willing to keep everything quiet. The question remains, is he the Foreigner?"

Chapter Forty-Two

Ama Dablam, Nepal present day

For the climbers, it was an early morning full of promise heading to Camp I. For Dorje, however, it was bitter fruit: tart and raw-tasting. After the climb, if he could, he had to save Basu's trekking company from going under. Damn Ang! That mongrel had to be working with someone else, someone cunning and powerful. Ang, he suspected, had hired men to kill their elephant, Laksmi. Fortunately, fate had stepped in, and Dorje charged into the stall in time to prevent Laksmi from eating a food ball filled with glass shards. Those shards would have lacerated her stomach, and death would have been agonizing. Hiding deep in the jungles of Chitwan, Laksmi, with her handler Raju, was safe. Then there was Dawa's murder. Supposedly killed by Maoist guerrillas, but Yak Herder, whose son was high up in the Maoist hierarchy, said they weren't even in the area where Dawa's murder took place. Who killed Dawa? Was Ang involved in that too? Dorje balled his fists. That dung-eater would pay for all he'd done, and then some, but where the hell was he? He was as elusive as a snow leopard in winter. And as crucial as Ang was, who was this Foreigner?

There's a monks' saying, 'If your inner mind isn't deceived, your outer actions won't be wrong.' Dorje wasn't deceived. Ang clearly wanted to drive Basu out of business and, in doing so, completely crush him. That, promised Dorje to himself, wouldn't happen on his watch.

While Dorje stood in the early morning air, after an overnight at Camp I, the gravity of heading the expedition weighed heavily on his broad shoulders. Dorje examined the mountain, mentally traveling the route up to the summit. With last week's quake, how dangerous were the hanging glaciers now? Today was the push to Camp III. The camp was an eerie place, which spooked Dorje every time he stayed.

He wondered, do the dead whisper? Do they cry out in fear? Do some refuse to leave this world for the next stage in the cycle? Sometimes, Dorje thought they did. After death, there was Bardo, the transitional period before the next reincarnation, but maybe there was more to it than that. Could a violent, tragic, unexpected death create a barrier between the world of the living and Bardo, causing the dead to linger? And did the dead, in their anguish, call to the living to join them? Dorje didn't know the answer, but in 2006, when the hanging glacier calved, six men died in a sweeping avalanche at Ama Dablam's Camp III, their bodies buried. Afterward, there were stories about how, even on a clear day, the light was different-hazy with a grayish cast-and along with the strange light effect, there were the faint whispers as if the men were murmuring.

***

In the 2:00 a.m. darkness of Camp III, the climbers' helmet lights streaked the night sky like strobes, and with just those lights providing illumination, they appeared a congregation of one-eyed Cyclopes. As the tired and grim-faced men milled around, drinking hot coffee to keep warm, Basu sliced up spam and potatoes for breakfast. The spam spat and sizzled in the pan until the salmon color turned into a medium rawhide hue. Dorje ladled up heaping servings of the makeshift hash and handed them out. From everyone's expressions, it was abundantly clear that Cook's culinary skills were sorely missed.

Dorje squatted next to Basu to provide last-minute instructions. "We've been lucky on the mountain so far. Only a few minor snags. I'll take Trevor and Tim, you get Paul. Keep an eye on him. His technical skills aren't as good as he thinks they are."

"Let's concentrate on getting this bunch safely up and down." Dorje tightened his helmet then heaved himself up. "Careful of the hanging glacier."

"Uncle."

"Yes."

"For a forty-year-old, you're doing all right."

Dorje affectionately cuffed Basu, then joined Trevor and Tim, warning them, "Keep drinking water. Remember, your bodies need a gallon a day. Time to get going."

Little by little, the sky lightened. Dark blue inkiness transitioned into violet, which in turn, as the sun broke through the horizon line, marbled into oranges, reds, and pinks. With the clarity of sunrise, the mountain and the dangerous path upward now were fully revealed. The seven-hundred-foot drops on either side demanded extreme caution. Struggling on the narrow Southwest Ridge route, Trevor was challenged by an exposed pitch, and Tim needed frequent rest stops.

"So cold." Tim then stomped his feet and clapped his hands to keep warm. Sheer, jagged rock faces gave way to snow and ice, and even in the sunshine, the cold deepened. As they gained in altitude, there was only the harshness of belabored breathing, as lungs gasped for air, and the squishing sound of boots sinking into the snow.

"Soon we'll be at the summit," Dorje advised.

They worked their way up the fixed lines. Finally, they were able to unclip the carabineers off the ropes. Now, all depended on stamina. As their lungs screamed for air, and as the snow seemed to suck at their boots like quicksand, it was rest, move, rest, move, and a mental game ensued of placing one foot in front of the other.

Suddenly, Tim collapsed to the ground. "I can't go any farther."

"Tim, you're almost there. Look! There's the top. Don't give up. You can do this," Trevor encouraged.

They plodded on.

At the summit came that awesome "we made it" moment. Fluttering prayer flags and the incomparable surrounding panorama greeted them. Row after row of jagged peaks pierced the sky. It was as if the world consisted only of high mountains and deep valleys.

Dorje pointed. "There's Mount Everest, Lhotse, Nuptse, Changabang, and Makalu."

Tim wiped tears from his eyes. "I've never felt such joy."

"Unbelievable view," Trevor said, snapping photos. He thrust one arm upwards. "I feel I can touch the sun."

Tim then became quiet and then gnawed at an energy bar, which Dorje guessed was his sixth since breakfast.

What was taking Basu and Paul so long? They should be here by now. The snow squeaked under Dorje's crampons as he strode to the summit's edge to peer down, then he turned away. A scream filled the air, and Dorje swiveled in time to witness a free-falling body. "Bloody hell."

"What's happened?" Trevor asked, running to his side.

Dorje's voice cracked, "Accident. Can you make it back to Camp III on your own?"

"Of course, Dorje. But let us help," Trevor answered.

Dorje shook his head. "I move faster alone." With a swift desperation, Dorje slipped over the edge. Basu or Paul? Which one? Memories of cousins and friends who died on the mountains poured into his mind. The broken bodies, the contorted limbs, the loved ones left behind. Think about the here and, now, Dorje demanded of himself. This was no time for memories.

The acrid stench of gloves burning from the speed of his slide down the rope filled his nostrils. He had to risk it, had to take chances he usually wouldn't. When he confronted Paul, he found him uncharacteristically frozen with indecision, and his glance shifted away. "God, I'm not sure what happened. I tried to pass Basu and accidentally bumped into him."

Dorje narrowed his eyes. Basu was too good of a climber for this type of accident. Something stunk, it didn't feel right. Paul was holding something back, Dorje was sure of it. But now was not the time to confront Paul.

Fear laced Dorje's voice, as he demanded, "Show me. Where is he?"

Paul pointed down to an outcrop.

"Return to Camp III now," Dorje ordered.

Dorje scrambled on the unforgiving ice and rock at a breakneck pace, slipped, caught himself, but continued at that same speed until he reached the point above where Basu had fallen. His heart thumped and hammered while he dug in his ice ax and hung over the rock face. Basu was like a son, and to see him lying there unmoving was too much to bear. An ice pick stuck into his heart would have hurt less. If he were alive, Dorje detected no sign of it, and his despair deepened as cracks crisscrossed the ledge where Basu lay slumped. The shelf was shattering! "Basu, Basu, can you hear me?" The slumped figure remained silent and motionless. Dorje threw his pack aside, grabbed a length of rope, and chopped handholds downward.

At a brief glance at Basu, to Dorje's horror, a chunk of rock gave way under Basu's splayed right leg, which now dangled precariously off the ledge. Could he make it in time? Could he make it before it ultimately gave way?

At the moment Dorje's boots touched it, the ledge groaned. The maze of cracks widened into fractures that sped across the shelf like mini fault lines. Stumbling forward, his foot twisted, and his boot became lodged in a narrow crevasse. The ledge creaked threateningly. Frantically, he pulled and pushed, but the boot remained stubbornly stuck.

More of the ledge crumbled, and more ominous sounds echoed around. Only minutes or even seconds before the whole rotting thing collapsed. Sweat trickled down Dorje's forehead like a trail of tears, as death breathed down his neck.

Then he spotted it. A rock large enough to do some damage. After grabbing it, he started pounding at the area around the crevasse's edge. Chips flew. He pounded harder. Bigger chunks crumbled beneath the hammering rock. Pain radiated from his ankle when a strike went astray. Then, with a slurp, the boot was freed. With a quickness of a seasoned mountaineer, Dorje tied the rope around Basu and began the steep ascent. Halfway up, he slipped, and more by luck than skill managed to right himself. A sharp snap pierced the quiet, but Dorje didn't even bother to look. The ledge had given way.

Don't be dead, Dorje silently implored, don't be dead, as he pulled Basu up. How could he bring such terrible news to his sister? He could never forgive himself.

A slight movement, then a groan. Alive, but how badly was he hurt? On a piece of flat ground, he gave Basu a cursory check over. A broken leg for sure, but for the rest, he'd have to wait until he reached Camp III. He knew he was causing Basu more pain, but there was no other option but to carry him. Several hours later, by the time he reached Camp III, his back ached from carrying Basu, and the gnawing uncertainty remained, just how bad was it?

Trevor, Tim, and Paul waited, their faces full of concern. They lifted Basu from Dorje's back and laid the semi-conscious man on the ground. Dorje gently examined him and grimaced. "At the minimum, he has a broken left leg and maybe some broken ribs. Let's take him down fast."

"But… Can we do this in one day?" Tim asked.

"A day from hell, but if we don't…" Dorje replied.

Trevor stepped forward. "What do you want us to do?"

"Take a tent apart, we'll carry him in it. Bring the poles and rope over, I'll bind his leg and use them as a brace."

It was an arduous all-day slog. On one rock face, it was touch and go getting the makeshift carrier down the steep slope, but by nightfall, exhausted and famished, they reached the welcome sight of mushroomed-shaped tents at base camp.

***

Cynthia poked her head out of the tent to investigate the unexpected clatter of boots on stone, and upraised voices. Cook, with his gray wool hat pulled low over his ears, she recognized immediately, then the familiar figures of Trevor, Paul, and Tim. Bending down over something on the ground was Dorje. What, she asked herself, were they doing back so soon? And where was Basu? Out of the corner of her eye, she watched Pemba run toward the group. Grabbing her parka, Cynthia bolted from her tent to join in. When she reached them, her hand flew to her mouth. Basu. In an orange shroud. No, not a shroud, how could it be a shroud? A tent. When she'd last seen him, Basu's face had been bruised and swollen from the avalanche burial, but his purple bruises had now faded into the yellow-green of pea soup. Why had he been carried off the mountain? Looking down, she felt absolutely gutted and, with a deep concern, swiftly knelt next to Dorje. Was Basu even alive? A groan from him answered that question. "What," she entreated, "happened?"

Trevor briefly filled her in as fatigue filled their faces. Only Dorje and Cook, she noted, seemed to have the energy to spare.

Dorje glanced at the tents, then spoke a few hurried words to Pemba, "Where are Yak Herder and the porters?"

"Gone to Namche. They'll be back in a couple of days," Pemba replied.

Dorje grimaced. That wasn't the news he wanted to hear. "We can't wait."

Cook was practically hopping with agitation. "An army helicopter?"

"Not up here, Cook, not at night."

Dorje scanned the area where two yaks grazed. "Finally. Some luck." He whistled. The White Ghost raised his head and, with a grunt trotted toward Dorje until the rope in his nose ring pulled taut.

"Pemba, bring a pack saddle. Hurry."

Along with the saddle, Pemba carried a saddle blanket. Old, ratty, and riddled with holes, it had a woven dragon design that had faded into a dingy pink.

Avoiding the yak's curved horns, Dorje patted the White Ghost's back before slipping on the blanket, on top of which he placed the saddle. He parted the thick, silky hair and cinched the girth strap tight. "It's going to be a long night for both of us."

Pemba and Cook rushed to position Basu onto the saddle. The large yak kicked out in protest.

Dorje held out his open palm to stop Phemba and Cook from coming closer. He draped his arm over the great yak's neck, gave him a half hug, breathed in the pungent scent of the animal, and whispered into his ear, "Old friend, I know you've never had a man on your back before, and he's heavier than your normal loads, but I need your help. Please do this."

Whether it was due to Dorje's tone of voice or merely the sheer intelligence of the animal, but the yak looked at Dorje with his liquid eyes, quieted, and allowed Basu to be placed onto his back. Gently, Dorje adjusted Basu's broken leg into a comfortable position then secured him with a rope wound around the saddle. "The White Ghost will take care of you."

Basu nodded and mumbled something incoherent.

Then Dorje turned to the group. "Cook, you're in charge. Phemba, stay behind to help."

"Where are you going?" Cynthia asked.

"To the Health Clinic in Pheriche."

"You can't go alone. I'll come with you," she insisted.

He shook his head. "I'll be back tomorrow or the next day." Lowering his voice, he said, "This changes my promise to you about climbing Ama Dablam together. It all depends on Basu."

"Don't worry about me. The most important thing is Basu."

Overhearing the conversation, Paul vehemently protested, "I was cheated. I could have reached the summit if your damn nephew hadn't screwed up. If she's going up, so am I."

Dorje's face tightened in anger. Cynthia watched him ball up his fists and stride purposefully toward Paul.

Seeing the wrathful Dorje coming for him, Paul scuttled away, almost tripping over loose stones, but Dorje kept coming. Dorje growled out, "I don't know what you did up there, but I think you're the reason Basu fell."

"That's a lie!"

Only inches now separated them, and Dorje whispered, "I've wanted to do this ever since the day I met you." Dorje's fist flew into Paul's gut like a striking cobra. Clenching his stomach, Paul doubled over, gasping for breath, then spit out, "You. Will. Pay. For. This."

While everyone else stood stock still with shock, Cynthia smiled to herself, karma's a bitch. Cook broke the spell by disappearing into the mess tent and reappearing a few minutes later, clenching a cloth bag. His forehead crinkled with worry as he handed it over to Dorje. "Sandwiches and water."

Dorje nodded his thanks, put them in his daypack, and started off. The wind picked up and whistled down the valley as Dorje coaxed the yak onto the rough dirt trail. It soon forked, and Dorje followed the boney finger of the left path.

Dorje was grateful that night kept away curious eyes, avoiding the questions that certainly would be asked. By now, trekkers were in the lodges and the villagers in their homes. As Dorje moved up the well-trodden trail, he encountered just one lone porter, unknown to him, walking fast in the direction of Namche Bazaar. As they journeyed on, Basu cried out in pain. "Uncle, I must get off."

With more than a little concern, Dorje laid Basu on the ground and checked on his leg. Just how bad was he? "Nephew, I'm sorry for your pain, but there's no other way, we must go on."

Basu let out an involuntary moan, then gritted his teeth while Dorje strapped him back on the yak. At one point on the switchback, about two-thirds of the way up, Dorje rested the yak, whose heaving sides caused him to feel guilty about their fast pace. Dorje poured water into a bowl that Cook had provided, allowed the yak to drink his fill, and urged him on. The White Ghost had heart, and the animal continued on without protest, but the only thing fueling Dorje was adrenaline.

While Basu drifted in and out of consciousness, all Dorje could think about was getting to the bottom of the accident. What had happened up there? Trekking ever higher, they crested a ridge where cairns and prayer flags announced the high point of the journey. Distant lights informed Dorje that they were nearing Pheriche. Twisting downwards, the trail continued on to the frothing river where a primitive, wooden bridge spanned the water. The White Ghost's hooves clattered over the slats as they made their way over to the other side. An hour and a half later, they entered the small village.

At the health clinic, a long stone building with traditional wood-framed windows, he tethered the played out yak to a boulder outside. Thank Buddha, he thought, the lights were on; someone was still there.

He banged on the door.

A surprised Dr. McDonald opened it. "What is it?"

"A climbing accident!"

Dr. McDonald held the door wide open while Dorje carried Basu in.

"I'm fine," Basu mumbled.

"No, you're not." Dorje turned to Doctor McDonald. "Is Steve still in Kathmandu?" Once again, as he looked down at her, he thought how tiny she was for a Western woman.

"Yes," she answered, pushing a sweep of hair behind her ears. "It's just me here." Pulling a curtain aside, she ordered, "Put him on the table."

The two gently lifted Basu onto the examination table, and while Dorje covered the details of the accident, the doctor took Basu's vitals. "Give me a few minutes alone to examine him."

Spent and exhausted as Dorje was, he searched for and found an empty container, went to the sink, poured water into it, and brought it out to the White Ghost. Back inside, he plopped down, and within minutes fell asleep.

Forty-five minutes later, a female voice said, "Dorje, wake up."

His eyes snapped open.

The doctor slipped off her surgical gloves. "Basu has one broken leg, two broken ribs, and a possible concussion. I want him to stay overnight. I've given him pain medication and set his leg. He'll sleep well tonight."

Dorje gave a deep sigh of relief. "No internal damage?"

"None I could detect. But that's another reason he needs to stay overnight. Just in case."

"I'll see you in the morning," Dorje said as a goodbye.

Chapter Forty-Three

Pheriche, Nepal present day

After making the rounds at the hostels and being reluctantly turned away. Dorje mulled over his options. It was high season for trekkers and climbers, so unsurprisingly, all the lodges were packed. More importantly, there was no place in the village for the White Ghost to graze, and the animal needed food. As he absentmindedly patted the yak, he thought, why not stay at the Old Traders. The old man was in Tibet, and he couldn't imagine that the teenager who guarded his home would have any problem with Dorje sleeping near the house or the White Ghost staying in the corral with the other animals.

The moon was as good a flashlight, and the way forward was relatively flat, so it was easy to find his way. Before long, Dorje entered a field where the Old Trader's yaks stood sleeping. The gate creaked when he led the White Ghost in to join them. Needs new hinges, and oiling, he thought after shutting it. Then Dorje rapped softly on the front door. The door opened, but instead of the teenager, there stood the Old Trader himself.

"Namaste," Dorje said.

The old man looked inquiringly.

"I'm Jangbu's grandson. The lodges are full. I'd hoped my yak could stay in your field, and I could sleep next to your house till morning."

There was a glint of recognition in the old man's eyes. "Ahh, you must be Dorje. When you were a boy, Jangbu brought you by now and then for a visit. A good man and a good friend. I owed him much. Don't be shy. Come in. No grandson of Jangbu's sleeps outside."

The hut reflected the old man's exotic travels. Intricately designed carpets from Baotou, in Inner Mongolia, littered the floor. A gilded altar painted with auspicious symbols showcased rare objects, and in a place of honor, contemplating the room, and providing serenity, sat a beautiful gold, Buddha.

Wizened with age, the man stirred the glowing embers before throwing on more wood. A sheepskin robe exposed his right shoulder, and his feet were clad in intricately embroidered black and red felt boots.

"You look beyond weary, Dorje. Sit. I'll fix you an herbal remedy to chase your weariness away." From out of a carved wooden box, the Old Trader took pinches of herbs, added them to a cup, took the kettle off the hob, and poured boiling water into it. There was a mint-like smell mingled with citrus. Even just breathing, Dorje felt invigorated.

The Old Trader glanced out the window at the yaks.

"Ah, so you've brought the White Ghost. That's a deep sign of trust."

"I'm afraid Yak Herder doesn't know about it," Dorje replied. Then, he shared the events of the past two weeks, touching on Jon's attack and Basu's accident.

The Old Trader poured more hot water into Dorje's mug.

"The gods were merciful to spare your nephew." The old man then made his way to another intricately carved chest. He brought back a tobacco pouch, a narrow, foot-long pipe partially decorated in silver filigree and embedded with turquoise and coral for himself, and a small silver pipe for Dorje's use.

After loosely packing tobacco into the small pipe's bowl, Dorje took an ember from the fire and lit it, and after a couple of deep puffs, said, "So you've returned from Nangpa-La pass?"

"Each trip becomes harder. I foresee one more crossing for me, then no more."

Dorje's hand swept over the room. "Why do you do it? You're surrounded by wonderful things."

"In part, it's the excitement, although I go only to Tibet now. But I remember the days of wandering the vast ocean of sand and mountains on the Silk Road from China to Arabia. Once I even went as far as Rome. So many strange things. Ghost towns half-buried by the shifting sands, guarded by mummified soldiers who wore a type of armor I hadn't seen before. At night, it was terrifying. Eerie cries echoed from those towns. We never traveled at night, for fear of the dead."

A sweet smile spread over his face. "And there were some real beauties. Yes, some real beauties."

"Is it true that you saved a Chinese princess's life?" Dorje asked.

"Rarely do I tell that tale, but I knew at once that she was someone special. That one had porcelain skin and dignity, which surrounded her like a silken cloak. Those were the days of great uncertainty. Warlords had massed and were fighting for power. The old system was rotting and crumbling. We banded together in large caravans of hundreds of camels for safety, but there was still the constant undercurrent of dread. Fear of both warlords and marauding bandits."

"And the princess?"

"A Manchu lady. I'd eyed her earlier on, but because of her retinue, of course, and her high status, I kept my distance. Weeks passed without incident until we reached the foothills when bandits attacked. The fighting was fierce and bloody. I was shooting from behind a dead camel when I saw a man grab the princess. She fought back, but I knew it wouldn't be long before she was taken. I raced over with my sword and killed him. We fled. She was one of the few upper-class women in those days whose feet weren't bound. If they had been, she wouldn't have been able to run, and we'd both have died. I still think of her."

"What happened then?"

A sad look settled over the Old Trader's face. "An arranged marriage to a warlord. By now, she's long dead, and the Silk Road has changed forever. While I no longer travel far, I do take grain and other things to Tibet and return with bags of salt."

"Only salt?" Dorje asked, with a laugh.

The Old Trader's twinkle deepened. "Sometimes more than salt."

Dorje changed the subject. "Did you hear of Dawa's murder?" Dorje referred to the sirdar and best friend of Basu.

The old man sighed. "After the monsoon, I ran into Dawa and Ang on the trail."

Dorje voiced his surprise. "Together?"

"By their guilty reactions, I could tell they were smuggling something. Dawa seemed frightened, and out of his depth."

"So, it seems that he got in over his head."

The Old Trader lowered his voice. "A simple man. Not stupid or bad. I think he made the wrong man angry."

"And the wrong man was?"

"Maybe Ang or perhaps someone higher up. Yesterday Ang came by to hire my yaks. I flat turned him down. He abuses the animals, and I hate to see animals mistreated. Can't think of anyone who'd rent yaks to him anymore. He'll have to buy his own. Evil blood flows in that family's veins."

Dorje's face flushed with anger. "That piece of yak turd skimmed money from my nephew's trekking agency. Can't prove it, though. Basu's father was dying at the time. Ang claims he was given the money to invest by Basu's father, and the investment didn't work out. All lies, but…"

Dorje narrowed his gaze, then continued slowly. "So Ang's in town, and I just missed him. When we finally meet, I'll…"

The Old Trader looked at him understandingly.

While the intense heat from the fire might warm an old man's bones, Dorje felt stifled, and, it soon became difficult to focus on the conversation. Sweat trickled down his forehead as the effects of the herbal tea, which had earlier revived him, wore off. He began to nod.

"Time for sleep," the old man said, handing Dorje some blankets.

"Before I do, an American woman is climbing with us who seeks stories about the early expeditions, especially 1924. I told her you might have information."

"Yes, I know stories."

"Will you speak to her about that time?"

"Before I decide, I first must meet her."

Dorje made himself comfortable in the corner, and the Old Trader shook out his blanket and lay down on his cot. As he extinguished the last candle, the Old Trader asked, "Have you seen the ravens today? They're massing by Gorak Shep. Hundreds of them. Always a bad omen."

Before drifting off, a thought filtered into Dorje's mind, Gorak Shep meant dead raven, did Gorak Shep have anything to do with the lama's prediction, 'trust to the ravens'?

Chapter Forty-Four

Pheriche, Nepal present day

The squeak of the gate and grunts from distressed yaks startled Dorje and the Old Trader into wakefulness. Something terrible was happening in the corral. Throwing on his boots, Dorje charged outside. Following him with a spryness that defied his age, trailed the Old Trader.

Overhead stars cast a wash of silver light on the unfolding scene. A man struggled to lead the balking White Ghost onto the trail. He jerked at the nose rope, and when that didn't work, kicked the animal in his side. The White Ghost refused to budge. In a fit of anger, the man picked up a thick stick and smashed it hard across the yak's backside. Grunting in agitation, the other animals milled around.

Then, all hell broke loose. Rearing up, the white yak hooked the man with his right horn. A scream of pain filled the air as the man wrenched his arm away, then sprinted down the trail. But the enraged yak wasn't finished. A thud of hooves echoed down the path as the yak gave chase. Puffs of dirt kicked up as the animal lengthened his stride. Dorje watched the running man snap a backward look, his eyes widened in terror as the yak closed in. The man's foot caught on something, and down he sprawled. Crab-like, he crawled forward on hands and knees, trying to get up, trying to maneuver away, trying to distance himself from those deadly horns. Too late. The White Ghost loomed over him like an avenging angel, and in his fury, gored, stomped, and gored again. Full-throated screams shattered the quiet.

Dorje felt glacially slow as he raced to the scene. By the time he'd reached him, the man had laid motionless on the ground. Dead? He couldn't tell, but first of all, to prevent further bloodshed, Dorje had to take the wild-eyed yak away. Gore dripped off one horn, and blood spots flecked his white hair like a smattering of red freckles. Dorje grabbed the rope, and stroked the animal's heaving side, then coaxed him toward the corral. At the gate, the White Ghost looked back at the prone figure, and to Dorje's mind, seemed to give a snort of satisfaction.

Dorje rejoined the Old Trader, who had by now knelt next to the figure. When they turned him over, rivulets of blood streamed from the shredded gaps in his savaged face. With a wave of revulsion, Dorje noted that the nose was all but gone, and one eyebrow looked like a black worm split in half. Who the hell was he? Gurgles came out as the man tried to speak.

"Towels, Old Trader, or something else to bind his wounds," Dorje said.

The Old Trader quickly returned carrying towels and string. "This will have to do." Then he peered closer at the figure. "It's Ang."

"Ang! You're sure? Not even a mother would recognize this one."

"His jacket, I remember its odd pattern."

"Strange," Dorje said, wrapping him in the towels as best he could. "Ang shows up tonight, just after we were talking about him. Help me lift him. I'm taking him to the clinic before he bleeds out."

"I'll go with you."

Dorje patted the old man's back. "Not necessary. It's close by. Settle your herd. I'll put him on that black yak."

Thirty minutes later, Dorje was back at the clinic, pounding on the door. A sleepy guard opened up.

"What is it?" the guard asked. "The doctor's asleep."

"Wake her. I have a seriously wounded man."

After that command, Dorje carried Ang into the clinic's office, and a few minutes later, Dr. McDonald appeared, looking like a tired pixie. "You're bringing me a lot of business today. What have we here? Oh my gosh!"

Stepping over to a cupboard, she brought back two fresh sets of scrubs, then pointed to the sink. "Wash up. You'll have to help."

Dorje quickly lathered up, taking special care to soap his arms up to the elbows. Tiny bubbles popped as he dried off and put on sterile gloves. "I did this once when I was in the army when a man's guts were hanging out."

She put on a surgical mask. "What happened to this guy? I've never seen wounds like these before."

"Gored by a yak."

"First, we'll put him under. There. Give it a minute."

Dorje handed her an IV drip.

"I'm not a plastic surgeon, so there's not a lot I can do with his face except stitching it up. Unless he gets a first-rate plastic surgeon, he's going to look like Frankenstein. But it's his neck, and back I'm more worried about."

"Why?"

"Paralysis. Turn him on his side. See, I'm putting pressure on his right side, but he isn't responding. Hand me the scalpel."

Two hours later, the doctor took off her mask. "We've stabilized him. That's all I can do. Tomorrow he'll have to be helicoptered out to Kathmandu. Go ahead and look in on your nephew if you want."

After checking on a snoring Basu, Dorje returned to find Dr. McDonald at the refrigerator hunting for something behind the urine specimens. Finding what she wanted, she pulled out two bottles.

She handed him the locally made Khukuri Beer. "Unfortunately, this is all I can repay you with."

"Fine with me," Dorje replied, taking a sip.

"Exactly what happened?"

"He tried to steal a yak. The yak didn't like it."

"What am I suppose to do? Notify the police? Quarantine the yak? What?"

"You do nothing. That yak is special. Police won't want to get involved. The animal was only protecting himself."

Dorje finished the beer and stood to go. "I'll come back in the morning to check on Basu and Ang."

She nodded and stretched. "No more patients. You've reached your quota for the day."

He laughed, then his eyes fell on Ang's jacket. Instinctively he picked it up and went through the pockets.

Money, identification, and a cell phone. He pocketed the phone, intending to check it out later.

"Is there someone who can notify his family? From what I've seen, I'm afraid he'll be paralyzed from the neck down," Dr. McDonald said.

"He has a family. This will give him time to think about all the harm he's done."

Back at the hut, the Old Trader was up and waiting. Dorje longed for sleep, but that apparently wasn't going to happen. Dawn was breaking, and the old man wanted to talk.

"Why do you think Ang rustled the yak?"

"Last night you answered that question yourself, Old Trader. You wouldn't hire out a yak to him, nor would anyone else, so he resorted to stealing. He just picked the wrong yak to rustle."

"How bad is Ang?"

"Bad. He's paralyzed, and his vocal cords were ripped. So he can't name names."

***

The next morning Basu complained to Dorje, "I want out of here."

"Not yet. Your cousins can take you home when the doctor gives her okay."

Dorje pulled up a chair and brought it closer to the bed. "Basu, what happened on the mountain? What went wrong?"

"It was Paul. We were both using the same fixed-line. I was right below him and got tangled up in the rope, and it started pulling at him. Guess he got scared because he cut the rope."

"He cut the rope!" A haze red and hot filmed Dorje's eyes. That bloody bastard could have killed Basu.

After checking on Ang, Dorje returned to Basu. "I have to go back to the mountain. Stay out of trouble." Dorje said as he got up to go.

Chapter Forty-Five
Ama Dablam, Nepal present day

Cynthia took Cook aside, noticing when she did, his gray wool hat had a smear of chocolate across it, and his hands were peppered with recent grease splatter burns. She knew her question was unanswerable, but she hoped for a crumb of comfort from him. "Will Basu be okay?"

"He a Sherpa, Cynthia. No worry. We strong people."

She nodded. "Cook, it's too nice to stay inside in the mess tent, I'll eat my sandwich up in the valley."

She watched as Cook whipped up a tuna sandwich and sprinkled in chili flakes, then he topped it with an onion slice and wrapped it in wax paper. He added several still warm chocolate chip cookies and a thermos of tea.

"Cook, how do you do it? Bake cookies at 15,000 feet on your small stove?"

"Easy for me. My father a cook. He teach me."

With her lunch in her day pack, she brought a small sketchbook. Up here was alpine tundra, harsh, inhospitable, where only the hardiest plants flourished, until they hit the impenetrable wall of stone and ice. Beyond that, nothing but ice crystals grew.

Walking north, Cynthia climbed up a trail through the boulder-strewn valley to where a secluded stream of glacial melt flowed. Half hidden by boulders, she found an outcrop, so she sketched the panorama with a pencil after making herself comfortable.

As she sketched, she wondered. What was going on with her father? What had he gotten himself involved in? When she'd phoned and asked if he'd done anything wrong, there was that telling hesitation followed by nervous laughter. Something was clearly wrong, but what? Then there was Paul's threat that if she didn't play ball with him, her father was going to prison. Every time she saw him, her stomach flip-flopped. And the thought of sleeping with him....

After finishing three postcard-sized sketches of Ama Dablam, she realized she was ravenous. She bit into the tuna sandwich, finishing it hungrily. One thing about mountain climbing, you had a hearty appetite. After downing her last cookie, lazily, she turned her face to the sun, closed her eyes and let her thoughts drift to Jon, and Basu. The expedition seemed cursed. The unwarranted attack on Jon, leaving him on the brink of death, and then Basu's burial by an avalanche and the horrific fall on the mountain. Then thoughts of her father naturally shifted back. Could she ever wean him off of depending on her financially? Would he ever stop gambling? Those young girls of her own age that he dated, would he ever grow up? Did he really think he could stop the aging process by dating them? And then there was Paul's allegation. How true was that?

Hearing footsteps, Cynthia's eyes blinked open. Cook with news of Basu? Disgust mingled with fear when it was the very last person she wanted to see. Paul. All pleasure evaporated.

"Wanted to see what you're up to," Paul said, popping a hard candy into his mouth.

"You're a lousier bastard than I thought. To have told the others that I stole your money!"

He grabbed for her. His fingers bruised her shoulders as they dug in, then he pulled her to him and kissed her hard. The sticky candy-sweetness on his lips revolted her. "Get the fuck out of here." She shoved him away then wiped her mouth with the back of her hand.

But that seemed to only egg him on. Grasping her by the ponytail, he pulled her to him until he stood behind her with one arm tightly crossing her chest and the other fumbling at her jeans. The metal button gouged into Cynthia's skin as he unbuttoned it to push the jeans down. She broke away running, but before she could get far, he caught up and threw her violently against a rock face. With a gasp of pain, Cynthia felt the sharp edges dig into her back. Paul blocked her escape. While her lungs whooped for air, he attacked the buttons on Cynthia's blouse.

She swung hard, and her right fist connected with his jaw.

Shock filled his eyes. "You bitch!" He slapped her cheek hard with on open palm.

The hit stung, and her eyes watered. She kicked at Paul's groin, but missed, but landed a kick on his kneecap.

He winced. "I'll get both you and your father."

She stooped for her walking stick, using it as a weapon to force Paul backward.

"You have nothing on my dad."

"Your father is a thief. A smart thief, but a thief. When I bought the company two years ago, my team of auditors poured over the books. Guess what they found?"

"Nothing that has to do with dad."

"He'd been siphoning money from the accounts for years."

Cynthia backed away. "You're lying."

"He owes the company half a million dollars. I've cut him a break, at least so far."

Cynthia brushed the hair away from her face. She hated Paul, absolutely loathed him, but even so, weirdly, it all made sense. The way her father had been pushing Paul down her throat. He had given Paul her itinerary, and then that dinner when he sprang Paul on her in an ambush. The fear in his voice when she had asked if he had done anything wrong. It all made horrible sense.

Paul crept closer. "When he was caught with his hand in the cookie jar, he confessed to a gambling problem. So you see Cynthia, your father's future is in your hands." While she was absorbing what he'd said, she let down her guard a bit.

Lunging for the stick, he tore it away from her, then kicked her feet under her. When she hit the ground, sharp pain radiated from her already lacerated back. She kicked upwards and punched. Now he was on top of her. She screamed. He hit her, splitting open her lip. Blood trickled down as he put his hand over her mouth and nose. She pounded on his back. His fingers pulled at her shirt, and she heard buttons pop.

Suddenly, miraculously, his weight was lifted off. Cynthia sat up to find Paul sprawled on the ground with Dorje standing over him and Trevor right behind.

"You coward," Dorje sneered.

With the anger of an enraged bull, Paul rose up and lunged. Dorje stepped back and gut-punched him twice. With an oof, Paul bent over in pain, then he charged. Dorje caught him with an uppercut that left him reeling. Paul charged again. Dorje sidestepped, blocking his fists.

Paul was taller, wiry and slender, but with his broad shoulders, Dorje was slightly shorter and definitely more muscular. As they circled each other, spittle formed a ring around Paul's mouth. Boxer-like, Dorje danced over, and with a right smashed him in the face. She could see a bruise swell beneath his eye.

A rock hard punch here, a kick there, Dorje fists methodically punished Paul. It seemed to Cynthia that Dorje toyed with him.

After one last uppercut, Paul crumpled to the ground and refused to get up. Dorje grabbed him by his collar and frog-marched him over to the glacial melt. He tossed him in, and they watched the icy water swallow him up. Splashing and flailing, Paul staggered out, screaming a string of curses.

Dorje threatened him, "If you ever go near her again, you'll have me to deal with. We overheard what you said about her father. If you do anything to him, I'll tell the world you tried to rape her, and you cut the rope. You could have killed Basu."

"I'll back Dorje up on that. I might not be as famous as you, but I am well known. I'll shred your reputation," Trevor added.

"Pack your things, Paul," Dorje commanded. "You're done with the climb. A Sherpa will take you to Lukla."

"You haven't heard the last of me," Paul yelled, dripping from head to toe, as he headed toward his tent. Trevor trailed about fifty yards behind him.

"Are you all right?" Dorje asked.

"Shaken but not stirred," she quipped, with a slight tremor in her voice. "How's Basu?"

"A few broken bones. He'll be alright." Dorje's arm went around her, and she snuggled into his chest.

"I'll be right back," he said, getting up. He returned shirtless, wringing out the now wet material in his hand. First, he dabbled away the blood from her lip. "Any other place hurt?"

She partially lifted her shirt and bent down. "My back."

Tenderly he wiped her skin down. The cool water tingled and helped numb the pain. "You'll have some cuts and colorful bruises, but it's not bad. I'll give you a painkiller when we get back."

Turning her face up to his, she smiled. "Thanks for everything."

"Glad we were nearby."

Awhile walking back to camp, Trevor said, "Cook's meals are better than some high-end restaurants in London. I'll miss them."

"You're leaving today?" Cynthia asked.

"Tim and I finished the climb, so our party's over."

He stood up to go. "As soon as Yak Herder loads up our stuff, we're off, but I hear you're to make an attempt."

"Along with that engineer friend of Dorje's."

"Quite the character, isn't he? Best of luck to you."

Giving him a hug, she felt overcome by sadness. Sharing weeks with the others had bonded them, made them feel like family. Now, of the original expedition, only she was left.

Chapter Forty-Six

Ama Dablam, Nepal, present day

In the distance, a solitary figure strolling toward camp caught his attention. As the figure neared, he recognized the perennially cheerful face of Alden Droiter. Smiling to himself, Dorje wondered if he had a new British Ambassador story to entertain them with.

After a few minutes of light conversation, Dorje admitted, "I'm troubled. There's a significant change in the weather, I can smell it, that along with the earthquake. The sooner we finish with this mountain, the better."

"I get a hard-on just looking at her," Alden said. "Which route?"

"The Southwest Ridge. It's safest."

"Whatever the costs, I'm good for it," Alden added.

"Just pay for fees, food, and equipment. We'll make money off you on another climb. So you're serious about going up?"

"Only chance I'll have for adventure. After the VIP's visit, it's back to Kathmandu to finish the extension project." Alden clenched his jaw. "Steve and I planned on climbing, but after his betrayal... Those smuggled dinosaur fossils, and the fact he set me up, could have sent me to jail! It still gives me nightmares." Then he changed the subject. "That was some quake. Toronto sent an e-mail indicating that more shakes, rattles, and rolls could be in the forecast."

"I was afraid of that."

"I read snakes can predict quakes."

"Birds too," Dorje replied. "Lately, they've been acting strange. Never seen so many ravens together at one time. It's as if they are congregating for a purpose."

Dorje then told Alden about his encounter with Ang.

"I need a drink. Where's your beer?"

Dorje slapped him on the back.

"No beer for you. You're on the mountain tomorrow."

"Killjoy. What about the others?"

"All gone, but Cynthia."

Alden bent down, picked up a pebble, and threw it. The wind whipped it to the right. "You said that this guy, Ang, was involved with the fossil smuggling. Did he implicate Steve?"

"Couldn't implicate anyone. His vocal cords were ripped out. He's paralyzed."

Alden stopped in mid-throw. "Paralyzed? How'd that happen?"

"Attacked by a yak. I suspect Ang's the one who delivered the crates to you at the airstrip." Then Dorje went on to describe him.

"Sure sounds like the guy. I forgot to ask, how did the climb go? Successful summit?"

"For Trevor, Tim and me, but not for Paul. I roughed him up and sent him packing."

"You roughed up a billionaire? Have you a death wish?"

"He tried to rape Cynthia. Threatened me on his way down, with the Prime Minister, the U.S. Ambassador, and everyone else he could think of."

"Bastard. But aren't you worried? You've made a powerful enemy."

Dorje shrugged. "A bully on my turf."

"But a bully with fangs."

***

"What's a nice girl like you doing in a joint like this?" Below, Alden's pleasant face beamed up.

"Pretty good Bogie interpretation, Alden. So you're back."

"The VIP's visit has been postponed for a week, so here I am."

She stooped and undid her crampons.

"Your timing couldn't be better. Tomorrow's the climb," Cynthia said.

"That's me, Mr. Good Timing. Why did you decide on the climb?"

"I'm here researching my great-grandfather."

"Up here?"

"There's a connection."

"Anyone I'd know?"

"Andrew Irvine. He died along with Mallory on the 1924 expedition."

Alden stooped down, picked up a stone then tossed it away from the wind. It soared and made a faint crack as it hit the ground.

"They've never found his body," Alden said.

"To be honest, I hope they never do. RIP. The Chinese closed the border to tourists, so this is as close as I get."

"Have you heard about the expedition searching for Mallory's camera?"

She nodded.

"My memory's fuzzy, but wasn't Irvine unmarried?" Alden asked.

"There was a secret engagement, but before he could marry, he died on the mountain. My great-grandmother had his child and remained unmarried."

"That's quite a story," Alden said.

Chapter Forty-Seven

Ama Dablam, Nepal present day

They were standing at the imposing foot of Ama Dablam cinching packs, adjusting straps, and making ready when Cook ran toward them waving his arms. For once, he wasn't wearing his gray hat, and his thick, thatched hair mimicked the surrounding clumps of grass.

"What is it?" Dorje asked.

"A monk from Nameless Mountain monastery just arrived and insists on seeing you."

"Did he say why?"

Cook shrugged his shoulders.

Dorje removed his backpack and strode toward camp.

A lean monk, wearing a traditional crimson and yellow robe, waited patiently by the tents. A string of beads slipped through his fingers as he silently prayed. Upon Dorje's approach, he looked up.

"You wanted to see me?"

The monk steepled his hands in greeting. "I carry a message from the lama."

"A message?"

"You are to wear this during your climb." He placed a metal amulet painted black along with a chain into Dorje's palm. The image, he recognized, was of the powerful, tantric goddess, Tara.

With her voluptuous body and beautiful face, she embodied female perfection. The color of Tara bestowed unique qualities and attributes. Dorje ran his finger over the raised amulet. Worn by age, it was about the size of a large coin. In this, her black form, Tara personified righteous wrath and power.

"It's very ancient," the monk said, "Older than our monastery itself. Legend says that it was made over a thousand years ago and is blessed."

Dorje remained puzzled, "Why give this to me?"

"Last night, our lama had a disturbing vision, and he asks that you wear it on the mountain for protection. If Tara believes you walk on the right path, she may help."

A chill, having nothing to do with the weather, settled over Dorje. This was the abbot's second vision about him. What did he see to warrant loaning such a priceless gift?

Feeling unsettled, Dorje leaned closer to the monk. "Did he say why?"

The monk shrugged his shoulders. "Only that you needed to have this."

After putting it around his neck, Dorje steepled his hands in thanks. He rejoined the others, and they began their ascent.

***

Cynthia felt exhilarated finally climbing the mountain. Her skills had been tested on rock and ice, and her confidence soared. She was better on the vertical walls than she had expected, and Dorje's compliments on her technique meant more to her than she could have imagined. When his gaze lingered on her, her desire returned. She suspected he felt the same.

Alden proved a surprise. Gone was the quipping manner. In its place was a seriousness she hadn't seen before. He tackled the mountain with studied precision, not with the reckless abandon she had expected. But then, she considered, he was an engineer. Precision, attention to detail, and extreme care would be part of the job.

As she worked her way up the fixed rope, she felt free and alive, and could almost sense Sandy Irvine at her side, guiding her as she ascended. She'd brought a photo of Emma and Sandy in her backpack. I'm climbing for all of us, she whispered to the wind.

"Careful with the ropes," Dorje cautioned. "Some have been around for years and are completely rotten. Use only the ones I use."

As they climbed ever higher, Dorje scanned the landscape, focusing on a dark section of ice-glazed rock.

"I noticed it on the last climb," Dorje said. "The earthquake's changed the mountain." Then he pointed. "See over there. Those crevasses have deepened, and those openings are new. But it's the hanging glaciers that worry me most. We'll have a better sense of them tomorrow."

Dorje set a fast and they made Camp II on the first day. Cynthia woke up the next morning groggy and dehydrated, but after eating and drinking melted snow, she felt revived.

Leaving Camp II, they pushed onward. Dorje led, then Alden, then her. Stopping frequently in the rarified atmosphere, she forced herself to continue upwards. The slopes were steep, the rocks treacherous, but eventually, they reached the two glaciers at Camp III, which had concerned Dorje. With the razor-thin air at 20,000 feet and all the physical effort it took to climb, the struggle upward for Cynthia seemed interminable. At least, unlike Sandy and George, she wouldn't be above 26,000 feet in the death zone, where the body begins to cannibalize itself.

Luck was with them, by late afternoon they climbed without incident to the summit. Euphoria fought with exhaustion as she gazed out at the vast vista of folded and corrugated peaks. In the center of the panorama, commanding her utmost attention, was Mount Everest. Lost in her thoughts, she filtered out Dorje and Alden's comments and placed Sandy and Emma's photo into the snow looking out onto Mount Everest, then to keep the wind from blowing it away, set a rock on top. She willed their spirits to see what she saw. To feel what she felt. To witness the raw beauty of Mount Everest looming before her; that fateful mountain, which had separated her great-grandparents in life. Now, almost a century later, was it a blessing or curse that it continued to haunt her family?

Her moment of reflection was brief. Within minutes the weather started to deteriorate, the wind picked up, and an ominous bank of black clouds swarmed toward them like horizontal tornados. The storm had arrived earlier than predicted, and it looked nasty.

"We need to get down now to Camp III to take shelter. There's still a two-man tent there. I'm glad I had you bring your sleeping bags," Dorje said with urgency.

Dorje turned on his headlamp and clipped a carabiner to a rope. "Let's go. Alden, you're after me."

Shortly after leaving the summit, visibility worsened, and the storm lashed over them in a swirling fury. On an exposed pitch, gusts vibrated her body like a prayer flag, then swung her hard into a rock face. Pain shot up her already bruised back. With a rising feeling of nausea, she realized any misstep could result in death.

Death.

Don't think about it, she warned herself, it'll jinx you, eat you up alive, become a self-fulfilling prophecy. Sandy's spirit seemed to guide her; that's it, one foot in front of the other.

Down the steep slopes, they went, snow swirling around them in a white wrath. Cynthia's feet tingled. Early stages of frostbite?

Dorje didn't like it, but they'd have to bivouac at Camp III. Dorje thought of the dead still buried there, the avalanche concerns, the strange light effects, and the moans and murmurs he'd heard before. It was a cursed camp.

They reached the camp in a virtual whiteout but found the one remaining tent. Inside she collapsed weak with fatigue, fear, and the effects of high altitude; she had a headache and difficulty in breathing. The wind persistently blasted them with ever-stronger gusts.

After a meager dinner of biscuits, canned meat, and chocolate, they huddled in their bags and fell into a restless sleep. Three people crammed into a two-man tent didn't make for excellent sleeping arrangements; the snoring, the constant shifting, the oppressiveness of the humid air, and the smell of unwashed bodies.

In the morning the storm had lessened. Dorje went outside, filled a pot to the brim with snow for drinking water, and placed it on the burner, then went outside again. Alden sat next to it, giving it an occasional stir. A loud bout of sneezing and coughing caused him to reach into his pocket to pull out a handkerchief. Out tumbled his passport. Cynthia opened her mouth to tell him, but as she looked, her thoughts spun into free-fall. Alden was a Brit. Brits have burgundy red E.U. passports. The passport on the floor was blue. Dual citizenship? She inched closer to Alden. She recognized a gash on its upper corner. Right before she'd left her grandmother's cottage, she was cutting into a block of cheese on the kitchen counter when the knife slipped and sliced into the cover. That passport was hers. What the hell was going on?

Alden turned to her, "Water's boiling. Tea coming right up." Then he stopped stirring the pot. "You don't look well."

Cynthia felt cold and clammy and sick with dread. Just as she was about to demand an explanation, Dorje returned.

"Wind's still strong, but at least the snow's lightened up. Just think," Dorje said, passing around biscuits and chocolate, "Cook will be expecting us tonight, so there'll be a hot dinner waiting for us at Base Camp."

"Dorje!"

Both men looked in surprise at Cynthia's tone.

She snatched the passport lying next to Alden then flipped it open. It was hers. "What's Alden doing with my passport?"

Chapter Forty-Eight
Ama Dablam, Nepal present day

"You won't be going down," Alden said. He reached into his pack and pulled out a gun. The furrow between Dorje's brows deepened. "What the hell are you playing at?"

With sickening clarity, Dorje then realized that he stared into the unblinking eyes of The Foreigner.

"So, Steve had nothing to do with the dinosaur smuggling. It was always you. That's why you asked me if I'd talked to him yet. You could say whatever you wanted to about him because we hadn't been in contact."

"Clever, clever, Gurkha. Steve, that bumbler, he hasn't the intelligence to pull off half of what I've done."

"The man murdered at Old Blue Throat in Kathmandu?" Dorje said. "That was your doing?"

Alden nodded his head. "When someone tries to double-cross me..."

"And Dawa?" Dorje asked.

"His conscience bothered him a little too much. He worried about being disloyal to Basu. Ang overheard him confessing to a young monk, so he contacted me in a panic. I ordered him to kill them both. Loose ends will always trip you up."

"Why destroy Basu's climbing company? He's nothing to you."

"Dinosaurs are only a part of my businesses. I intend to have the biggest trekking and climbing company in Nepal, and I have to break some eggs to make an omelet. Basu was one of the eggs."

As Alden continued talking, Cynthia stared at him like she'd never stared at anyone before in her life. It was like seeing a Chihuahua transform into a werewolf.

Pointing the gun at Cynthia, "Let's get this over with. I know about the red diamond, I went through your cottage, and your condo, It wasn't there. I did notice a receipt for a safe deposit box and a missing key. Now what, I asked myself, would a twenty-something need a safe deposit box for? The answer was, ta-da, for a special diamond. You have the key with you."

She suppressed the urge to touch it around her neck, and it felt as if it burned against her flesh. "How did you...?"

"Fate was kind." He said, in his Bogie impersonation, "'Of all the gin joints, in all the towns, in all the world, you came to mine.' To Nepal, where I work. Now, where's the key?"

"In my condo."

"I just told you, I broke into your condo and checked out every square inch. The key," he demanded, dropping Bogie.

"No."

"I'll make you tell."

She clutched her hands. "Uncle Saul called and told me that another red diamond had just surfaced. You're the man who has it, aren't you? How did you know about mine?"

"Long story. It has to do with Sandy Irvine's camera. I found a red diamond and note inside."

"Impossible! His body hasn't been found."

"As I said, fate was kind."

"You're a monster," Cynthia screamed.

With a suddenness that shocked them both, Dorje kicked over the pot of boiling water. Alden screeched in pain and clenched his right arm as the scalding water soaked in.

"Run!" Dorje yelled.

Grabbing her helmet and ice ax, Cynthia fled, Dorje followed right behind.

A bullet whined then ricocheted off the boulder to their left.

"There." Dorje pointed down to an indentation. "I'll go first. Hurry. He's catching up."

Another whine of a bullet. Dorje gritted his teeth in shock, as a bullet struck the fleshy part of his calf. Ignoring the pain, he gripped the rope and descended. Cynthia followed on the adjacent one.

Halfway down, Cynthia's rope snapped. With a shriek, she slid down the incline. Yawning ahead was a thousand-foot drop, and nothing stood between her and the precipice.

Dorje's ice ax bit deep into the snow, and with a superhuman effort, he swung over and grabbed Cynthia as she tumbled by. She jerked to a stop, but Dorje's injured leg threatened to collapse from under him, and he groaned from exertion.

"Use your ax! You're slipping away."

Cynthia twisted around, surprised to discover she still clung on to it. Digging into the snow, she gasped out, "I'm okay!"

Dorje let go. As she inched herself over to his rope, an arm muscle spasmed.

"Don't stop now," Dorje shouted. "Climb up and over to my rope. We've lost time."

A bullet whizzed by, sending a puff of dust into her face, startling her into quick action. Descent proceeded at a pace that broke all the mountaineering rules. She slipped, she slid. Her legs ached. Her breathing came in ragged gasps. An accident up here? She tried not to think about it.

When the way veered behind massive boulders, the bullets ceased, and Alden had disappeared from sight. But that almost made things worse. She couldn't tell if he was catching up or not. What if he were gaining on them? She tamped down the sickening knowledge that he wouldn't give up.

"Into that hole," he urged. "Must have opened up after the last earthquake. It may be a cave or tunnel."

Blood droplets spotted the snow.

"You're bleeding," Cynthia said.

"Bullet. Get going."

"But your wound."

"No time for that."

Cynthia wriggled her way in and waited.

"Go on," he urged. "Entrance's too narrow for me. I won't be long." Then he frantically pulled rocks out of his way to widen it.

"I'll help."

"Not enough room. Go."

Her stomach lurched as she stared into the void. "What if I get stuck in here...or?"

"I'm almost done. Stay, and he'll kill us."

Blindly, Cynthia crawled on her stomach. Loose rocks dug into her knees and elbows. She twisted her body back and forth along the floor, and now and then, when the area narrowed, her gloved fingers gripped the uneven walls as she pulled herself forward. Momentum over the rough, slippery floor was so slow that a geriatric tortoise could have beaten her.

A protruding rock caught her at just the right angle. "Ow!" She yelped and cradled her arm.

Ahead, the dark nothingness.

Get a grip, she told herself. Concentrate on what you're doing. Either cold or fear has frozen my brain, she thought in disgust. I have a helmet light. Why aren't I using it? She blinked as the light chased away darkness then faded back into that nothingness far ahead.

For a minute, she listened to her surroundings with the intensity of a bat searching for prey. But only silence. Where was Dorje?

When she reached a spot where she could turn around, she peered down the tunnel. No one.

While she waited, the adrenaline rush wore off, and exhaustion threatened to overwhelm her. She felt crippled by anxiety. What if Dorje hadn't enlarged the entrance? What if he were stuck? Even dead?

Chapter Forty-Nine

Ama Dablam, Nepal present day

Cynthia stiffened in mid-crawl.

From out of the nothingness came a fuzzy glow of light. Dorje? Or Alden? Go back, her mind screamed, don't wait here. Protect yourself. Alden has a gun. She switched off her helmet lamp and groped the walls. Far too narrow to turn around in. Realizing that she could only move backward, her gut informed her what her mind had just concluded: whoever was coming towards her would soon catch up.

Her fingers searched the ground for a rock and found one. She palmed it. As a weapon, it would have to do.

The light brightened, the fuzzy glow became more focused. She held her breath as a grim-faced figure emerged. She exhaled. Dorje.

"Did Alden see you?" she whispered.

"No. I tried to cover up our trail, but if Alden's a decent tracker, he'll surely read the signs."

For an hour or more, they continued on, sometimes in a crawl, and sometimes, when the ceiling height permitted, walking hunched upright. But how can you really estimate time, Cynthia wondered, in the dark? It could have been ten minutes or two hours when they rounded a corner.

She looked at her surroundings, and a sense of enchantment filled her. An ice cave! A glittering, sparkling, dazzling wonderland, a crystalline environment festooned with frozen ice draperies under an opalescent dome.

"Wow!"

White-gray stalactite icicles, the like of which she'd never seen before, descended from the ceiling to the floor in eerie, contorted shapes. At least thirty feet long, she estimated, and they varied in size and thickness. Some were massive and columnar while others were curved, delicate, and sculpted looking. How many decades, centuries, or even millennia did it take to create this?

Dorje followed her out of the tunnel and quietly studied the cave.

"This one won't last much longer," Dorje stated matter-of-factly.

"How do you know that?"

He pointed. "See all those fractures and fissures?"

Light from their helmets skipped around the cavern, uncovering an area much more extensive than Cynthia had expected.

She nodded.

"Ice is disintegrating, breaking apart. Won't take much to bring the whole damn thing down. So stay away from the pillars."

Cynthia shifted to another topic, "Show me your leg," she insisted.

He rolled up his stained pant leg, and she sucked in her breath. An exit hole. So the bullet went through. She took off her kerchief. If she could bind it, maybe it'd lessen the seeping blood flow. She tied it tight but not tight enough to act as a tourniquet. He had to be able to walk.

"Best I can do." At least it managed to staunch the blood flow.

Dorje blinked back the pain and looked closely at Cynthia. Circles under her eyes were dark as bruises, and her face was taut with exhaustion and fear. Dorje appreciated that she was spunky, but how much more did she have in her reserve tank?

"Going to get some water. Be right back," Cynthia said, picking her way toward the rear of the cavern, careful to avoid the rotting formations. Hard to imagine them collapsing, they seemed stable enough, especially the ones that were several meters thick, but she trusted in Dorje's instincts.

She followed the sound of trickling water and found it pooling in a shallow indentation covered by a skim of ice, just deep enough so that with some finessing, she could dip her helmet in and partially fill it.

Beyond the pool, she discovered a frozen waterfall. Fluted, frost-encrusted waves were encased in a rigid cascade of ice. Seemingly, only a magic wand was needed to make it flow again. Behind the waterfall, another cavern. From what she could determine, composed mostly of rock.

Returning to Dorje, she passed him her helmet. They sat on a boulder drinking in silence. Remembering that she had a Cliff bar, she reached into her pocket. "Chocolate Chip Peanut Crunch," the wrapper read; she divided it in two and slowly chewed. Instead of relieving her hunger, it made her ravenous for more.

Awe of the cavern's beauty soon vanished, and her thoughts reverted to Alden. Maybe they'd lost him. Perhaps he was a poor tracker.

Cynthia leaned into Dorje partly for reassurance and partly because it just felt right. Dorje's arm comforted her, and she snuggled closer.

The sound was so faint she wasn't quite sure of it. Dorje dropped his arm from around her shoulder, and his face tightened with tension, then she knew without a doubt. Alden.

Dorje pulled out his knife. "I'll get him."

"Not without me."

"Go to the back of the cavern. I'll hide by the opening, there's not enough room for both of us. He'd see us."

Working her way back into the shadows, she suppressed a shiver of dread. She squatted behind an outcrop, and they both switched off their helmet lamps.

The scurrying noise from the tunnel became louder, more pronounced, as did the thumping of her heart. It wouldn't be long now. And it wasn't. A few minutes later, Alden stepped out, pausing at the entrance, like a VIP making a grand entry. His helmet light cast a harsh wash of illumination over his face giving it a ghostly look. While his eyes darted around the cavern, he called out, "Come out, come out wherever you are."

Dorje braced himself. Fifteen yards or more over uneven ground to reach Alden. But he'd have the element of surprise, and he was used to functioning at extreme altitude.

"Promise," Alden continued in a voice oozing sincerity and charm, "I won't hurt either of you. Cynthia, just give me the safe deposit key, and we're done. You can go. See, I'm putting the gun in my pocket. Nothing to be afraid of." He took off his backpack, then strode in the direction of the ice formations.

Dorje sprang up.

The knife held chest high, he loped forward. Avoiding rocks, boulders, and ice patches, his feet carved a path in the gravely rock as he closed in. A whisper of movement. Alden whirled, his eyes narrowing in surprise. He leaped back as the curved blade sliced down. Blood trickled from his nicked cheek.

"Clever, clever Gurkha," Alden said, wiping his cheek while maintaining a healthy distance between them. He noted Dorje's bloodied leg. "So it's you I shot. Damn shame about that," he said with a smirk. When he reached into his pocket for the gun, Dorje flew at him.

"Oomff," exploded from the Foreigner as he hit the ground with Dorje on top of him.

Breathing heavily, Dorje staggered to his feet, followed by Alden. While they circled each other, Dorje's eyes rapidly searched the floor for his knife. He feinted to the right then dove for the blade. Standing up again, he went for Alden, who by now had his gun out.

Turning on his helmet light, Dorje came at him, blade ready for a gut stab, Alden chopped down hard with his gun on Dorje's knuckles. Wincing in pain, Dorje involuntarily opened his hand. The knife flew across the floor, skittering to a halt at the base of an ice formation.

"Cynthia, get it!"

Switching on her helmet light, she sprinted, swooped, and grabbed.

Alden's clenched fist snaked towards Dorje, but the Sherpa ducked underneath it and punched Alden twice in the belly. With the desperation of a man whose strength was fading, Dorje gripped Alden's right hand and struggled for the gun.

While they grappled, their helmet lights danced over the walls.

"Got it," Cynthia panted. Both men turned.

Before she could hand over the knife, Alden swung a vicious kick to Dorje's injured leg causing him to collapse, and while Dorje struggled to get up, Alden raised his gun.

"No!" Cynthia leaped over a pile of rocks, and as Alden aimed, her knife arm arced down. He twisted away, but his aim was destroyed. The bullet ricocheted wildly. As it whined around the cave, zinging off rock walls, Cynthia and Alden dove to the ground. When echoes ceased, they scrambled to their feet.

Alden's face scrunched up in rage. He backhanded her with the gun. Her cheek felt like hundreds of bees had stung it. As she crumpled in a dazed heap, she grabbed at his leg. He kicked out. She clung on.

"Get out of here," Dorje roared at her. He was now up again and swinging. Exhaustion etched his face, and his body strained from exertion and blood loss. Bobbing and weaving, the two men fought their way to the ice formations. Alden head-butted Dorje with a violence that sent him staggering into an ice pillar. Fissures raced up the ice. For good measure, Alden threw Dorje against it again. The fissures widened.

"Enough. Dorje, up against the wall," Alden commanded with the gun in his hand. "And you, Cynthia, over here. Now."

"Run, Cynthia," Dorje yelled. "The tunnel."

"If you do, Dorje dies."

While his gun stayed fixed on Dorje, Alden's helmet light hunted for her and saw her crouching behind an ice pillar.

"That's right, Cynthia, stand next to Dorje." Alden took a moment to study her. "Shame, you won't be alive when I publish newly discovered Everest photos from 1924 I found in your backpack. I imagine they're worth a fair bit."

"What?"

"Andrew Irvine's photos. The ones you've been carrying around with you. When I went into your tent looking for the diamond or the key, I found them instead, and your passport. You're making me a wealthy man. Fifteen million for the red diamond, and who knows how much for the photos. "

Her great-grandfather's photos. The ones he so lovingly had sent to Emma! Her mind erupted into a flood of hot lava. She didn't care if he shot her or not. He was going to do it anyway. At least she could pick the time, and the time was right now. With all of her strength, she threw the rock. Alden dodged. It bounced harmlessly off his helmet with a thud.

"You bitch! You're nothing but trouble. Give me your goddamn key, Cynthia."

Dorje spun, grabbed at Alden, who pulled away and fired point-blank. The shot echoed around the cavern. A groan escaped Dorje as he fell facedown clutching at his heart, then lay motionless.

"You bastard," Cynthia screamed. She went after him like a banshee. With fists flying, and tears streaming down her cheeks, she jumped onto Alden's back. He reached behind his back, grabbed her hair, and flung her off. But as he raised his gun, he slipped, and the bullet missed, hitting ice instead.

A shudder, a sharp crack, and the ice pillar split apart, collapsing onto its neighbor. Snapping, popping explosions reverberated around them. Like a row of falling dominos, the pillars crashed into one another, and the cave began disintegrating. Ice of all shapes and sizes rained down.

Alden raced towards the protection of the tunnel's entrance.

A fraction of a second was all it took for Cynthia to decide to take her chances elsewhere. No way was she going in Alden's direction, so, with more strength than Cynthia realized she still had in her, she picked up the knife, stuck it into her waistband, hooked her hands under Dorje's armpits and dragged him into the second chamber. Dodging a boulder and an icicle sharp as a spear, she reached the safety of an overhang and crouched underneath. Tears streaked her face as she cradled Dorje's lifeless body.

Within minutes an eerie quiet settled in. Not a whisper of sound to be heard, no movement whatsoever. Just complete, total silence. The Zen-like peace belied the sheer magnitude of the devastation. The passage between the two chambers was blocked with debris, and only a thin beam of light filtered through from a hole from the other side. She crept to the fist-sized opening and peeked through. Never before had she wished someone dead. But she wanted Alden squished to a pulp under tons of rock.

Alden spotted her. "Looks like I can save a bullet on you, Cynthia, you're not going anywhere. Ever."

"And you're not getting my diamond. Ever."

"Oh, I'll be back with gear. By then, you'll be dead. But I'll dig my way to your body. And…"

A loud rumble tore Cynthia's gaze away from Alden, and she watched as the roof above the tunnel's entrance cave in, pouring down yet more debris.

Chapter Fifty

Ama Dablam, Nepal present day

Cynthia's tears dripped onto Dorje's gray, swollen face. She crooned a wordless lullaby as she held his body, crying not just for him, but for herself too, for the senselessness of his death, and for the unfairness of it all. Gently laying him down, she mulled over her situation. Bleak, that was the word for it. A bleak future. No happy ending in store for her, not here without food at the edge of the Death Zone. Realistically, and she forced herself to be realistic, she had a couple of days left. Was there a silver lining? One. Alden was stuck on the other side.

Might as well explore my tomb, she thought, standing up and turning on her headlamp. A slight stirring shocked her to gasp in disbelief. Dorje's hand moved, then groggily he propped himself up on an elbow.

"You're alive!"

"Day's not over yet," he replied.

The gallows humor brought a feeble smile to her face and a jolt of optimism to her spirits.

"But Alden shot you in the heart. I saw it."

Dorje unzipped his jacket, took out his amulet, and ran his finger over the goddess; part of her was flattened by the bullet.

"Tara protected me."

"Thank you, Tara." She hugged him tight before letting go.

Dorje's eyes searched the cavern. "Alden?"

"Trapped on the other side."

"Good."

He picked up his knife where she had laid it down. "Thanks for this," he said, struggling to get up.

"Stay here," Cynthia ordered. "I'm about to look around."

She stepped over rubble and weaved her way around the cavern's perimeter. As she had surmised earlier, this second cavern consisted mostly of rock with very little ice, and that was good news, for it meant the destruction on this side would be minimal.

She had half circled the perimeter when her helmet lamp flickered. Batteries going, she thought in disgust. She dimmed the light to low to extend its life. To her astonishment, she discovered a tunnel, further on a second, and finally a third.

Returning to the overhang, she plopped down next to Dorje. "Tunnels lead out of here but no idea where to, if anywhere. We'll try and hope for the best. Now show me your leg."

He rolled up his pant leg, and she packed the wound with ice and retied the blood-soaked scarf. It's bad, Cynthia thought, but at least the bleeding's stopped. She looked hard at Dorje's ashen pallor and realized he didn't have the strength to investigate all the tunnels. Hope battled with uncertainty. Unspoken, but hanging heavy between them, was the real possibility that those underground passages meandered for miles and miles under the mountains then just petered out. She stood. Only one way to find out if there was an exit.

Tara, Cynthia implored silently, give us a bit of luck.

When Dorje's helmet light dimmed and died, they stared at each other with expressions tight with concern. Caves have no natural light. If her bulb gave out too, it was going to be very dark and deadly very soon.

"What's going on in there, Cynthia," Alden demanded, peering through the hole, his helmet light shone through like a ray of sunshine. "Dorje! Alive! Next time I'll drive a stake through your heart. You're harder to kill than a vampire. But I'm coming for you."

"Did you hear me, Dorje?" Alden threatened. "I'm coming for you."

"I'll be waiting," Dorje answered. Then he whispered, "Come on, Cynthia."

Dorje limped to the tunnels, sniffed the air, examined the ground, and listened intently. Some odor from the left tunnel was strong.

"We go left." Dorje crawled in first. Behind them, they heard Alden chipping away at the opening. Enlarging it so he could crawl through.

Swallowed up by the darkness, disorientation caused her to lose track of time, and in the confined space, she fought back a growing sense of claustrophobia. Proceeding blindly on, they regularly touched the walls to gauge width and height, and when she could no longer stand it, she'd turn on her lamp for a second or two. Mostly they walked upright, but when they needed to crawl, even wearing her padded jacket and high tech pants, the rough rocks gouged.

After forty-five minutes or so of non-stop effort, they paused for a break. Cynthia slumped to the ground, leaned into a wall, closed her eyes, and fantasized about being warm and safe in her down sleeping bag.

The biting cold and the rough ground made the fantasy a short-lived one.

A chill overwhelmed her. There it was again, the muffled sound of a faraway voice. Without further words, they forced themselves to continue.

***

Not long afterward, the passageway climbed and twisted to the left, and as she touched the wall, it gave way into nothingness. She slipped, fell hard, and let out a startled yelp.

"What's wrong?" Dorje asked, his voice full of concern.

She switched her headlamp on, and in the light, they saw a new passageway which forked into an additional two.

"It's a maze. This mountain is honeycombed with passages. Now what?" Cynthia asked.

Dorje rubbed his forehead and admitted, "I don't know."

Then Dorje heard a faint cawing, and stopped in his tracks. 'Trust to the ravens, the lama had foretold.' Instinctively, he touched the amulet under his parka. "Ravens. Hurry," Dorje urged. "We're near the surface."

She turned around. A faint light like an evil eye glowed behind in the darkness. With a rush of panic, she realized the distance between them and Alden had shrunk significantly. She tugged on Dorje's jacket. He turned and nodded his understanding.

Minutes later, as they squeezed past a boulder, both glanced back. The eye was now enormous.

"Cynthia, help me push the boulder."

They pushed and shoved, rocking it slightly. They struggled until it gave, rolled down, and wedged in the narrow neck of the passage.

Behind, they heard Alden's muffled yells. Dorje saw defused light. "Ice," he said, wrapping his parka around his arm. He repeatedly punched until his fist shattered the ice sheet.

Chapter Fifty-One
Nameless Mountain, Nepal present day

Cynthia kicked out the remaining shards of ice. Fog poured through in a billowy mass, bringing a frigid dampness that further chilled their battered bodies.

Cynthia willed herself not to shiver, but her mind refused the command. Before exiting the tunnel, she rubbed her arms for warmth, stamped her feet, then trudged out into the whiteness. On the mountain, she was met with a void of nothingness, a solid wall of clouds, and the Himalayan peaks lay hidden from view.

Despite the whiteout, Cynthia felt weak with relief. We're going to make it, she thought, Alden's stuck in that maze of tunnels. He can't hurt us now.

A stiff wind blew long and hard, momentarily breaking up the fog, and a flock of ravens dipped, as if in salute before winging their way towards Gorak Shep, the kingdom of the ravens.

The fog lifted. In the far distance, the last rays of the sun touched the peaks. As she stared at Mount Everest, her sense of relief turned into complete disorientation. Mount Everest shouldn't be there! Where were they? Certainly not on Ama Dablam. And sunset! How could it be so late? No wonder she felt spent and shaky. Since dawn, they had been running for their lives.

"Where are we?" she asked in wonder.

"On Nameless Mountain."

Dorje leaned against the tunnel entrance, favoring his blood-soaked leg.

They had to get down fast, she thought with concern. Dorje was visibly weakening by the minute.

"The monastery. We'll go there," she said with hope in her voice.

Dorje nodded. "Turn on your headlamp. We could use it."

She switched it on. Nothing. The battery had finally died. They'd have to find their way down in the approaching darkness without killing themselves in the process.

One bright spot, though, she thought, voicing it aloud, "At least Alden's trapped."

"Is he?" Dorje answered, his tone registering doubt.

"Sure, he is. We blocked the way with the boulder. It's wedged. He can't move it."

Alden's no fool. He'll hunt for another way out."

"Shit!"

Dorje then limped downhill. "Wind's shifting. It'll completely blow away the fog."

***

Funny what comes to mind when you're bone-weary, weak from hunger and cold, and slipping over the edge into exhaustion. Cynthia's thoughts floated to the full moon overhead. It wasn't like back home. No soft light flowed. Here the moon rose in the twilight, as milky and opaque as a blind man's eye. It cast a wintery light over the terrain of snow, rock, and ice and brought into relief an inhospitable shadow world. She played a mental game with herself. One step forward, then another. After ten steps, she promised herself a rest, but instead of doing so, she'd count down from ten back to one before resting.

Cynthia focused on the ground ahead, where moonlight bathed the mountain in a strange radiance. The landscape ahead was unbearably bleak. High mounds of rock massed on the east side dark and threatening. Cynthia prayed that wasn't their route. In front of her, Dorje swayed like a punch-drunk fighter. His limp had noticeably worsened, and he had said nothing since leaving the tunnel.

"Lean on me," Cynthia insisted, her heart full of sick uncertainty about whether he'd make it.

"I am a Gurkha," he answered. "Just follow me!"

"No! Gurkha, lean on me." With reluctance, for a short while, he did. As they struggled on, the wind blew hard and frigid, and the milky eye, opaque as a cataract, rose higher and higher in the night sky. When Cynthia felt she could take no more when all she wanted was a protected place to huddle away from the constant wind that sucked all warmth from her body, the sound of chanting, distant and muted was carried to them on a current of air. Tears of relief froze on her cheeks. They pushed on. She stumbled, fell, and almost didn't get up.

The monastery came upon her unawares. Looming and forbidding, it had walls thick as the length of a man's forearm and windows like slits, the type in medieval days archers used for defense.

They pounded on the double wooden doors studded with rusted knuckles of iron bolts with the little strength they had left and shouted while the wind still blew forceful as ever. Minutes dragged by until a monk, the very one who had opened up for them before stood staring in surprised bewilderment. A dusting of snow swirled in the entry and quickly melted into a patch of water. Dorje and Cynthia staggered inside.

"Please," Cynthia said, her blue lips chattering with cold. "Help him." She indicated Dorje's bloodstained pants.

Bewilderment turned to concern, and the monk spoke rapidly in the Sherpa language questioning Dorje as he led them to the lama's chamber then left, returning soon afterward with the lama and a young monk bringing with him pallets and blankets. Around the room, candles dripped wax into fantastical shapes, which mimicked in miniature the stalactites in the ice cave.

Under the lama's worried instructions, there was a flurry of activity. Dorje was carried to a pallet, where one of the monks cut off the pant leg to expose an angry looking wound. Oh God, Cynthia thought, it's so much worse.

A monk returned with a poultice for the wound, along with a brew in a large bowl.

"He has to see a doctor. He could die!"

"Too dangerous now," the lama replied. "We wait until dawn."

Dorje nodded his agreement then touched her arm to quiet her.

After drinking the bowl dry, Dorje slowly fell into sleep.

While Dorje was gently covered with a blanket, the lama said to Cynthia, "We have some healing skills. We can make him comfortable. Tomorrow we take him to the Pheriche clinic."

The lama's face became unreadable when he asked her, "How did this happen to Dorje? Why were you on Nameless Mountain? No one saw you on the trail or climbing the mountain, and from our monastery, we can see for miles."

A bowl of stew steaming and full of root vegetables was brought to her. She ate greedily, unmindful of the hot liquid burning her tongue. When she had finished, her head began to nod, and her eyes close. After the monks left, she crawled under one of the blankets and promptly fell into a deep sleep.

***

In the middle of the night, Dorje woke up burning with fever. Tossing and turning, he was momentarily disoriented. Where was he? By the light of flickering candles, he saw a room rich in decoration. Memories of arriving at the monastery and speaking to the lama rushed back.

"Cynthia!" Dorje struggled to his knees. Where was she? He spotted her sleeping in a corner and gave a sigh of relief. Then his eyes were drawn upwards to an ancient tangka painting hanging on the wall behind her. It had captured his imagination during their previous visit, and piqued his curiosity, for tangkas are religious. This one wasn't. Why? It depicted three European men, or so they appeared, wearing clothing of centuries past. Who were they? Why were they in the Himalayas leading yaks? And why, underneath the mountains, why was there a maze of lines?

The candles finally guttered out, but even so, Dorje could visualize the painting, and then, a moment of insight almost overwhelmed him. *I know now who they are!* He thought before falling into a troubled sleep.

Chapter Fifty-Two

Nameless Mountain, Nepal present day

Cynthia woke to an earthy aroma, not unlike rain-washed bracken or decomposing compost dark with organic matter. So dense and rich were the undertones and hints of vegetation that fused her sense of smell and taste, and it seemed to her as if she could chew the air. While her subconscious worked to identify the scent, her consciousness suddenly filled with dread. Dorje! Rolling off of her pallet, she found a young monk, the one who spoke some English, propping Dorje up and helping him drink a cup of the earthy brew.

"What's that?" she demanded, motioning to the drink.

"Medicine to help him heal and take away the pain."

After coaxing Dorje to drink, the monk offered him a vegetable stew.

As Cynthia had slept with her clothes on, it took only a moment to lace up her boots and go to Dorje. She ran her hand lightly over his forehead. He was burning up.

She had fought the urge to pee for as long as she could knowing what awaited her in that fetid, dank room housing the toilet. A deep hole covered by planks with a bucket of water positioned next to it. At the toilet, she held her nose while she squatted and would have given anything for an air freshener. Slushing the water down, she went to find the lama.

She found him conferring with the English speaking monk.

"Dorje has to go to the clinic now," she said, her voice heavy with stress.

The young monk translated.

"We wait for Yak Herder to bring his white yak for Dorje to ride. Then we take him to Pheriche," the lama said.

"It'll take too long. He's either at Ama Dablam base camp or Namche Bazaar. There's not enough time to contact him. We'll have to carry Dorje out ourselves."

"I've already contacted him. He'll be here soon."

A look of disbelief crossed her face. She had read stories of the power of Buddhist monks. They could walk on air, lower their heartbeat at will, transmogrify into animals, and use telepathy.

"Are you saying," she said hesitantly to the lama, "that you spoke to Yak Herder by thought?"

The abbot's eyes twinkled as the young monk translated her words. "We spoke by cell phone. It's much easier."

Cynthia reddened with embarrassment. Just as the lama had predicted, Yak Herder arrived.

After a hurried breakfast of fried potatoes and onions, they put Dorje, still groggy, onto the White Ghost. Monks positioned themselves on each side to prevent him from falling, Cynthia and the lama walked behind. As they kept pace with the yak, rocks and boulders gave way to gorse-like scrub brush, and snow clad-peaks shimmered in the distance.

The trail seemed little used, just a dusty feeder path leading from Nameless Mountain. It followed a ravine that, after several hours connected to the path near Dingboche, then split upwards and traversed over a foothill. By the time they had reached the foothill, the yak grunted from exertion. The White Ghost was larger and stronger than most yaks, but Dorje's weight pushed the limit of the animal's endurance. Twice they stopped to rest the animal, and when they did so, lay Dorje down on a blanket where he drifted in and out of consciousness.

Worry sapped Cynthia's desire to talk, and she was relieved that the others seemed of the same mood. Silence, that's what she wanted, just silence, caught up as she was in her worried thoughts. She tried to quash her fear, but it resurfaced anyway. She could still hear the Foreigner's threats and feel his red-hot anger. No longer did she think of him as Alden, that charming and happy-go-lucky persona was an act, to her he would always be the Foreigner. Had he escaped the tunnel? Was he still coming after them?

They trekked on, and by early afternoon when they'd reached the clinic, Cynthia burst inside, followed by monks carrying Dorje.

Dr. Steve Kaiser, along with a western woman no more than five feet tall, was giving, she assumed, the daily lecture on mountain sickness to a group of trekkers and climbers. Understandably all eyes swiveled to Cynthia and the monks carrying Dorje.

In a rush of words, Cynthia said, "Steve, Dorje's been shot."

In no time, they had Dorje on an operating table.

Cynthia, the monks, and trekkers turned to go, but the western woman who Cynthia assumed was either a doctor or nurse stood in front of the door, blocking the exit. And announced, "Don't leave yet. I'm Doctor Florence McDonald. This man needs a blood transfusion. Those willing to take a test to be a donor stand here."

She put a box of surgical gloves on the table next to the medical supplies.

The room filled with the shuffling sound of boots as people positioned themselves around the small space.

In the back, Steve attended to Dorje, examining him and putting him on an antibiotic IV drip.

There was a snapping of latex as Florence slipped on her first pair of gloves. Ripping open a packet, she pulled out a mini lancet and pricked a trekker's finger. She was fast and efficient, and it wasn't long before it was Cynthia's turn. The lancet sliced into Cynthia's finger with a sting. Droplets of red blood balled up and were quickly transferred to a specially treated paper chart.

"Florence, we need to operate. How's the testing coming along?"

"No matches, Steve," she replied, examining the paper cards.

While Florence tested, Cynthia poured out Alden's story, including how he tried to frame Steve for smuggling.

Steve stopped what he was doing. "That Bastard! I'd like to tie him on top of a red ant hill covered in honey and leave him there."

"Get in line behind Dorje and me," she replied.

***

After the trekkers had been shooed out, Florence turned to the monks.

"The villagers. Ask for volunteers. We'll try them next." Cynthia looked at the number of packets and counted four left.

"What happens if there isn't a match?" she asked the doctor, trying to keep the panic out of her voice.

"Plan B. We're a clinic in the high Himalayas with just the basics. We're not sophisticated enough to do anything but the most rudimentary testing. If there isn't a match, he'll be helicoptered to Kathmandu. But Kathmandu is fogged in, no planes are going in or out. Each hour that we wait, his infection worsens. He could lose his leg or worse."

An hour later, the monks returned, bringing with them a handful of villagers.

The first, a young woman with a baby on her back, opened her clenched hand, and timidly presented her finger to the doctor.

Four, three, two, one. Florence was down to the very last packet. She held it in her hand like a bar of gold and assessed the remaining two people, a boy of about fourteen and an old man who seemed oddly familiar to Cynthia.

"I don't know," Florence said aloud, looking from one to another.

The old man stepped forward, "My blood is good, and I know Dorje."

"Okay," she said, snapping on a new pair of surgical gloves.

"Florence!"

"Not yet, Steve. I'm testing this last one."

Tension ratcheted up as the doctor stared at the multiple dots on the test card. Four minutes later, the coloration changed into a pattern only the doctor could interpret.

"Got a match!" she yelled out with gusto. "Universal donor."

"Get me the blood fast," Steve answered.

Florence sat the old man down, and as she applied a tourniquet on his arm, announced to the others, "Everyone clear out. We'll let you know when the operation is finished."

Drained, Cynthia walked outside, found a lodge, and sat down to a meal of lentils and cabbage.

***

Dorje's eyes refused to focus, then little by little, he stopped squinting and let the light come in. The pounding headache, the nausea, it was as if he had the worst hangover of his life. Although he just wanted to lie there, he forced himself to sit up. With a sense of startled disorientation, his eyes swept the cinderblock room that he knew all too well. The Traveler's Aid Station in Pheriche. What in the hell was he doing here?

"You're going to be all right," Steve said, coming over to him with a tired smile.

"What's happened?"

"Cynthia and the monks brought you here on that white yak. That animal is better than an ambulance. Florence said you're the second person he's carried here."

"How long have I been out?"

"A day. With that gunshot wound, you were in a bad way."

Cynthia, Florence, and the lama who had been keeping vigil nearby joined them.

"Alden?" Dorje asked Cynthia.

"No idea. I hope he's dead."

Dorje attempted a smile.

Steve listened to Dorje's heart.

"You're healing quickly. To be honest, I haven't seen anything quite like it before. What should take a week is taking a day."

Steve patted Dorje on his arm. "If you keep on healing like this, you'll force me to write a paper for the *Lancet*. You can thank the Old Trader for your blood transfusion. He was the only one compatible."

Florence added, "I was concerned he might be too old to give blood, but he assured me that he was only seventy."

Seventy, Dorje thought to himself. The man was more like ninety plus.

"That was the Old Trader?" Cynthia asked, her face scrunched up in disappointment. "For weeks, we've searched for him, and here I was in the same room and didn't even know it."

"Oh," Steve added, "said he's leaving for good, taking his yaks over Nangpa-La pass on Friday. Going back to the land of his ancestors."

"Friday? What's today?"

"Thursday."

Dorje nodded to Cynthia. "We'll see him today."

"Holy One, I must speak to you in private," Dorje said, addressing the lama.

"Since no one else here needs our services, we'll leave you by yourself for a bit," Steve said. "Come on, Florence, I'll pick up the lunch tab."

"That's a first," Florence replied. "Maybe your blood should be tested."

"Not fair. What about that packet of gum I bought you the other day?" The banter continued as they strolled out.

Dorje motioned for Cynthia to stay behind too.

He took the amulet from around his neck and handed it to the lama.

"Tara protected me from a bullet."

"Your path was a just one."

As the lama turned to leave, Dorje stayed him with his hand and whispered. "That ancient painting in your chamber," Dorje said.

The lama's eyes widened. "What of it?"

"That painting made no sense to me. The more I thought about it, the stranger it seemed. Europeans dressed in the clothing of centuries ago. Who were they? As I lay in your chamber, the answer came."

The room stilled, with only the laughter of children playing nearby filtering in.

"What was the answer?" the lama asked.

"Marco Polo, his father, and his uncle. Marco Polo's red diamond came from here, didn't it? So did Kubla Khan's."

"What makes you think that?" the lama asked.

"Because of a professor on our climb. He said that Polo had traveled in the Himalayas and possibly had traveled up here. Polo was also in the Khan's court. The professor said of the red diamonds: 'They came from where the highest mountains inhabit the clouds.' I made the connection."

"Marco Polo," the lama repeated the name slowly as savoring it. "Deeds were done and a great service provided. His reward was the diamond. He swore to keep the source secret, and he kept his word."

"And the lines in the mountains?"

"A map of all entrances, exits, and caverns, a means to pass our information down."

"Are there more diamonds?" Dorje asked.

"Very few, but yes."

"Sell them. Just don't tell anyone where they came from. Our people could benefit."

The lama straightened out his robe. "Too risky, Dorje. Think about it. If miners knew stones of great value were here, they'd rip up every nook and cranny in the valley. We can't allow that. Only in times of great need have we ever sold a diamond, and in the past half-millennium, we've found only a handful. Nameless Mountain is a Beyul, a hidden holy place."

"What about my gem and the other one?" Cynthia asked. "Sandy Irvine wrote he had bought them off a porter in 1924. But why would a porter have those priceless gems?"

"The monk carrying them to Lhasa was found with his throat slit. All his valuables were taken, including the diamonds."

"I'll return it then," Cynthia said. "It belongs to you, not me."

The lama raised his hand to stop her. "It's yours now."

She teared up. "Thanks isn't adequate, but it's the best I can do."

He nodded.

She was the first Westerner since Marco Polo, eight hundred years ago, to know where the mother lode of red diamonds was. While Cynthia sat quietly, trying to absorb it all, she had idea. She knew what to do with her red diamond. She'd have Uncle Saul cut it and then sell it. Most of the money she'd give to worthy causes in Nepal, but keep some for herself to live on. A series of tunnels under the mountains. What must the extent of the maze of interconnecting caverns and tunnels be like? Hundreds of miles? More?

The lama's face turned from reflective to grim. "Swear on Tara. Never speak of this to anyone."

They promised.

Florence opened the door and entered chuckling. Steve followed her in.

Florence handed Cynthia her day pack. "A porter just brought it for you, from Ama Dablam."

The lama picked up his walking stick. "Keep your promise," he said with an intensely serious look, then left.

Chapter Fifty-Three

Pheriche, Nepal present day

Steve held out a pill and glass of water to Dorje. "How's my patient?"

Dorje sat up abruptly. "What's that?"

"Something to make you sleep."

"I'm not sleeping, I'm going to the Old Trader's."

"You're too sick."

"You said I was healing at an amazing rate; you can't have it both ways, Steve."

Steve threw up his hands in frustration. "Stubborn Gurkha!"

***

It was a thirty-minute walk to the Old Traders. He greeted them at the door and looked at Cynthia with keen interest. His home was nearly bare; two chairs, bedding, and a kettle remained. All the rest of his belongings were packed and made ready for the next day's journey.

"You look better than the last time I saw you, Dorje," the Old Trader said.

"I have you to thank for it."

"The pretty doctor held my hand, so it was no sacrifice."

The old man motioned for them to sit. Cynthia took a good look at the Old Trader's face, and that sense of recognition she'd experienced earlier at the clinic strengthened. She'd seen him before, but where?

He said to Cynthia, "So you want stories about the old days." Exactly about what?"

"Tales of the 1924 expedition. It was before your time, but I hoped for new information. To get a better sense of my great-grandfather, Andrew Irvine, who died along with Mallory. " Cynthia hesitated. How could she explain to this old man the deep longing to know about her mother's side of the family? How could she describe feeling the same way as adopted kids do who search for their biological parents? Just like those adoptees, Cynthia had a deep, gut-wrenching, visceral need to know. Until that hole was filled, something would always be missing.

"My mother died when I was young. I know next to nothing about her family."

The Old Trader's face filled with warmth and understanding.

"You have English's eyes, the palest blue I've ever seen."

"English?"

"My name for Irvine."

A sense of disconnect settled over her. She couldn't have heard him correctly, because how in the world could he know Sandy's eye color? From a photo, of course, that's how. But then she recalled all pictures of Sandy were in black and white. When had colored film come into commercial use? The 1930s or 1940s?

"What do you know about him?"

As he had done with the lama, Dorje jumped in when there was a need to translate.

"He introduced me to my Mixture 965 tobacco. I still smoke it."

She did the math and exchanged looks with Dorje. Her mind refused to wrap itself around the implications. The expedition had been in 1924, so even if he were a teen at the time, that would make him well over a hundred. Was it possible? Or was Sandy's eye color a lucky guess?

Dorje sat silent, assessing the old man, and from his expression, was having as much trouble grasping his assertion as Cynthia.

Then, with a shiver of insight, she realized why he'd looked familiar. Rifling through her day pack, she found what she wanted; photos from the 1924 climb.

The picture was grainy and faded, yet detailed enough to be recognizable. A middle-aged man surrounded by yaks stared back at her. On the back was scribbled, "Bataar."

She sucked in her breath and whispered, "You're Bataar, aren't you?"

She passed the photo to Dorje, who scrutinized it.

"I have questions," she said.

His eyes twinkled. "I suppose you do. I suspect the first question is my age. I've had 180 winters."

"No one lives that long!"

"I'm not even the longest of my kind. One ancestor reached 330 winters."

"What! How?" she stuttered out.

"My ancestor came from Northeastern Tibet, from a small village whose livelihood depended on a good harvest of Yartsa gunbu, which they sold to the Chinese."

"Yartsa gunbu?" Cynthia said. "What's that?"

"Caterpillar fungus. A rare parasite used for medicinal purposes. It cannot be farm grown and is only found in grass and scrublands. Many hundreds of years ago, while my ancestor searched for the caterpillars, he came across a fungus species completely new to him, reddish-purple in color and fluted. So being curious, he took a chance and ate part of it."

The Old Trader lit his pipe, and momentarily became lost in thought. After a few puffs, he resumed his tale.

"When he returned to the village, he described the fungus to an elder, who immediately knew what he had eaten. It was the fungus of immortal life. Many considered it a legend, a tale for children, but not the elder of the village, the keeper of old wisdom. An emergency meeting was called, and as you can imagine, excitement raced through the village. If they could find this plant, every man would become wealthy. An emperor would pay anything for the fungus of eternal life."

"What happened next?" Cynthia asked.

"My ancestor couldn't remember where he had found it. Perhaps the fungus caused him to forget. For months the villagers searched, but the plant was never located. Before long, anger mounted against him. Threats became increasingly hostile. The villagers thought he'd lied and was merely waiting for the right opportunity to sell it and become wealthy as a prince."

"It became increasingly perilous for my ancestor, so one night after he overheard men plotting his death, he fled eastward and became a trader."

Cynthia said, "It's given you long life, but not immortality."

"No, not immortality, and it's been both blessing and curse. I've outlived five wives and have had no children."

She thought back to the conversation she had with Jon about penicillin, and how, because it cured disease and extended life, our ancestors would have thought it magic, like the fungus of long life.

"Are there others like you?" Dorje asked.

"No. It must be some peculiarity of the fungus, but each generation has produced just one child. I'm the last of my line, and long life dies with me."

While Dorje leaned back trying to assimilate it all, the Old Trader puffed on his pipe then smiled at Cynthia.

"So, you want your story."

She nodded.

"It began in the town of Phari Dzong when I first met up with the 1924 expedition. I was friends with a local bandit, one of the headmen there. He recommended my yaks and me to Karma Paul, the expedition's translator. I was hired to carry supplies and mail. On one trip, I remember bringing in crates of champagne. When the champagne arrived, they partied long that night.

"The journey was lengthy and treacherous. We struggled through desolate lands, lands where few lived, or would want to. Back then, expeditions were fortified like military campaigns, hundreds of pack animals along with a huge support team. It seemed an endless ribbon of men and animals. Irvine was by far the youngest, and I saw him grow in confidence and bravery."

Over the following hours, the Old Trader spun stories of the expedition. The events and people sprang to life. Their personalities became real, and Cynthia could almost feel the pervasive cold and hardships of their journey.

Sandy's photos triggered the Old Trader's memory, and she was introduced to a cast of characters. Karma Paul, the translator who improved the Old Trader's English; the lama of Rongbuk Monastery who offered blessings and friendship yet hinted of probable tragedy on Mount Everest; the brave porters called tigers, and the British climbers.

"Who was this one?" she asked.

Perhaps it was the jagged scar under his eye or the cold, hard stare, but evil seemed to emanate from the photo.

"Vulture. Other porters avoided him whenever possible, especially after he boasted of murdering a monk and taking his money and gems. In fact, those gems he sold to English."

The red diamonds. Cynthia realized.

"I'd warned English of Vulture's reputation, but he bought the gems anyway."

"And Vulture, what happened to him?"

"A bad ending. He snuck into English's tent to steal the gems back, but English returned early from dinner. Vulture attacked him with a knife, but English was too strong. Vulture escaped and fled the camp, but was caught in a storm. Later his body was discovered in a crevasse with strange, giant footprints around it. That had us all talking and wondering."

Cynthia pointed to the final photograph of Sandy and George Mallory looking carefree.

The Old Trader gave a deep sigh.

"Yes, they were happy that day before the summit attempt. Then everything changed. When they failed to return on time, our uneasiness swiftly turned into fear. Three chaps climbed in a desperate search, but there was no sign. Mount Everest took them. Such sadness swept through the camp."

When the Old Trader's recollections wound down, Cynthia asked, "Do you think they made it to the top?"

"I saw the look of determination in English's eyes. He'd make it no matter what."

Tears welled up in Cynthia's eyes, and as she wiped them away, she asked, "Aren't you worried I'll tell others about you?"

"They would laugh at you for believing a crazy old man. Other than your photo, there is no proof of my age."

He then turned to Dorje and cautioned, "Don't translate this. It is for your ears only. My blood saved your life, but it may have done more than that. It may have altered your life force."

The silence was complete and utter. Little ever rattled Dorje, neither gunshot wounds, knife fights, and the dangers of mountain climbing; he'd survived them all, but this shook him to his core.

"Are you saying," Dorje asked slowly, his mouth tinder dry, "that I am to be like you? My life extended?"

"Only time will tell. Perhaps that's why I had no children. You are the 'special one' who now has my blood."

Before the Old Trader could add more, there came a pounding at the door, and Steve rushed in.

"Alden's stolen a helicopter."

"What! He's out of the cave?" Cynthia exclaimed.

"Damn," Dorje said, "So he made it off the mountain after all."

***

Down the valley, the Foreigner grappled with the pilot in charge of the helicopter at Syangboche airstrip. The pilot had definitely been in fights before. The Foreigner wiped his bloodied nose and shoved him to the ground. Flipping on the switches, The Foreigner was preparing for takeoff when the thud of bullets pierced the helicopter's body. Shit, the Foreigner thought, the pilot has my gun, but then he heard the click of an empty gun chamber. He was safe.

As the helicopter rose, he thought, now to China and freedom.

The Ecureuil helicopter raced up the valley towards the high peaks, towards Nangpa-La pass, and as he neared, he remembered Ang's words. It's a pass of bad karma.

***

The thunderous clatter of a helicopter at full throttle stopped all conversation at the Old Traders. Rushing outside, they saw it weave and bob its way higher and higher, then turn eastward.

"Alden! Where's he going?" Cynthia yelled.

"China," Dorje replied.

Nearing the pass, the helicopter pitched and rolled and struggled for loft. A powerful wind whipsawed it back and forth.

"He's not going to make it," Cynthia screamed. The helicopter shuddered. The engine died. The helicopter dropped into a death spiral, hit the side of a mountain and exploded into flames.

Dorje turned to the others. "Evil has left the valley."

Epilogue

Dorje shot Basu an affectionate glance as he honed his knife. For a while, it'd been touch and go.

"Uncle, you've got an e-mail."

Dorje continued to hone his knife. "Who would e-mail me at your trekking company?" In the sunlight, the blade gleamed cold and bright.

"Cynthia."

Dorje was careful not to show his emotions. What had it been? Six or seven months since she'd left Nepal? A couple of e-mail messages checking on his recovery, then nothing. He cast a glance at his nephew. The last thing he wanted was for Basu to think that he cared. He'd never hear the end of it. So he finished honing his knife to his satisfaction and under his nephew's watchful gaze, sauntered nonchalantly over to the computer.

"What does she say?" Basu asked.

"Give me a minute to read it all. Don't you have something to do besides pestering me?"

Basu gave him a cheeky grin and waited.

"Her computer crashed, and she lost her address book, along with my personal e-mail, that's why she's writing to me here. Says she will publish the Sandy Irvine book. Paul Bellame has stayed away and didn't bring felony charges against her father. She believes her father's learned his lesson this time. Fooling herself if she thinks that."

"What else?"

"She's writing a book about the Niah Caves in Borneo and is going there soon. Now go away."

He read the rest to himself, then sat back and thought about Cynthia. Sure he cared, but just how much? She had left Nepal a couple of days after their visit to the Old Trader. There had been no time to explore the possibility of a future between them. Only one way to find out, he decided. He'd see her again. See if the chemistry was still there. She was going to Borneo next month. He'd been stationed there as a Gurkha soldier and still had contacts. He smiled to himself. He could easily arrange to stay with one of them.

He typed his reply with his two index fingers.

What a coincidence, I'll be in Borneo next month too. Did you know there's a new expedition hunting for Mallory's camera? Using satellite photos. Maybe this time they'll find it. Something I forgot to tell you, my name in Tibetan means diamond. Strange karma, isn't it?

The End

CPSIA information can be obtained
at www.ICGtesting.com
Printed in the USA
BVHW081512291020
592032BV00002B/95

9 781647 184506